FIELD OF THE WHITE SNOW

FRANCES COWIE

BLUE BUTTERFLY PRESS

COPYRIGHT

FIELD OF THE WHITE SNOW

To Jane

Thank you for your enthusiasm and time.
I agree, the sentence is stronger without the 'and'.

CONTENTS

FIELD OF THE WHITE SNOW

PART I

1972 - 1977

1

SNOW BEAMS

1972

Vanessa lay perfectly still, listening to the sound of angry voices that filtered through the family room wall. First her father. Then her mother. Her father again. Then a moments silence, before the back-and-forth bout resumed.

"Why? Just tell me why, Ruth?"

"I don't know. Please, Jim."

She stood, moved to the dressing table, and lifted the lid of her jewelry box. 'Swan Lake' played on a loop as the dancing ballerina twirled on pointed toes. It made no difference. She could still hear them. Their irate voices volleying in varying tones of disquiet.

Usually, waiting for trips to the beach or the big city took ages. But this time, it felt like there had been no waiting. When her mother first mentioned it, Monday seemed weeks away. But now, the last day had been marked off the calendar, her boots polished, and even though the house looked the same, small things were missing from almost every room.

She sat back on the bed and looked around, her tummy as tight as her hands. Apart from pinpricks and faded shadows on the wallpaper, the walls were bare—her favorite pictures now crumpled in the wastepaper basket under her desk. But she still loved this room, this house, with its shag pile carpet and big windows overlooking the farm. She loved the spacious garden and the luxury of having a pool. But most of all, she loved her parents the same, equally in every respect.

Which one should she love now?

Vanessa looked up as her father entered the room.

"You all set, sweetheart?"

She nodded. Sniffed. Her dad was a big man, with large hands and a happy smile, and she always felt safe with him. People said he could talk to horses, and in her mind, this made him special. He glanced at the bare walls and frowned. "What happened to all your pictures?"

"I took them down."

"But this will always be your room, Ness. Still, I guess you'll want to take them with you."

She didn't reply.

"Here." He handed her a parcel wrapped in brown paper and tied with a length of thin kitchen twine. "Put this in your case and then get into bed. You have a big day ahead of you tomorrow."

"I don't want to go to a new school," she whispered. "I won't have any friends."

He looked tired as he sat on the bed beside her. Worn out. "Be a good girl for your mother. And don't worry. You can come home for Christmas." He cleared his throat. "I'll collect you from the bus or drive over to pick you up if I can get away. How does that sound?"

"But Christmas isn't for ages."

"The rest of the year will fly by, you'll see." Her dad reached over and patted her hand, then pulled her in for a hug. He'd been doing that a lot lately—hugging—longer and tighter than he ever had before. "Off to bed now. I'll see you at breakfast." He stood, picked up her doll from the floor and handed it to her. "Don't forget Lucy."

As he left the room, Vanessa pulled the string on the parcel and released the bow with a half-hearted tug. She loved receiving presents for Christmas and birthdays, but this parcel didn't have the same appeal. She knew what was inside—stuff she needed, not stuff she wanted.

A kilted dress caught her eye first. Made from red and green tartan and fashioned with a white cotton bodice, it was like the one she already had, but bigger and brighter. A cardigan she'd wanted for ages was there too—pretty in primary red, with buttons like tiny flat pearls —and a pair of pink flannel pajamas that smelled all brand new.

Underneath the clothes, sat a cardboard shoebox. Vanessa lifted the lid and pulled back layers of white tissue paper to reveal a pair of baby pink slippers. She ran her hands over the leather-like material and inhaled. The top of each toe was adorned with a pom-pom, balanced like a ball of cotton, and the sight almost made her smile. Opening her suitcase, she carefully packed her parcel of necessities next to the rest of her clothes and the patchwork quilt Grandma Bidi had sewn for her. She looked at her handiwork, then unfolded and refolded everything neatly, so it all sat precisely in place, ready for the journey.

When Vanessa woke the next morning, snow covered the landscape in a silent cloak. It wasn't unusual for snow to fall in winter, but this year it had come early, and she couldn't wait to finish breakfast so she could make snow angels like her mother had taught her the winter before last.

With everything inside packed up and ready, and the breakfast dishes drying in the dish rack, she ran out the front door, across the driveway and climbed the wire fence separating her mother's flower garden from the fields. Sheep huddled together to stay warm, and dairy cows, milked and on their way to pasture, billowed puffs of hot vapor into the cold air. She scooped up a handful of powder, pressed it into a snowball and threw it against the fence. Somehow that one gesture made life seem okay. The snow hushed not only the land, but also her disquiet. And as she lay on the ground, and fluttered her arms and legs, the sky above was so blue, she almost forgot about the eastbound bus traveling toward them.

She jumped up and twirled on her toes, around and around until she collapsed back down in the snow. In the distance, she could hear her dad's voice, stern and impatient. "What on earth is that girl doing?"

Then her mother's response. "You know how she loves it when it snows."

"You don't want to miss your bus." Her father cupped his hands to his lips as she turned to look at him. "Vanessa, come back here," he yelled. "Vanessa."

"But, Dad, I'm dancing. Dancing in the field of the white snow."

"Well, you can dance right on back. The bus will be here soon."

"Vanessa, be a good girl and come and say goodbye to your father." Her mother's voice sounded flat, as if the energy to muster a shout was beyond her. "Vanessa. Do as you're told."

Vanessa climbed the fence and ran into her father's arms. "Thank you for the parcel, Daddy."

He didn't acknowledge the thanks. She stared at him, trying to understand why he looked so uncomfortable, even sad. Vanessa said nothing more. She held her mother's hand, then clung to the woolen coat draped around the woman's legs. Her father reached for her other hand and gave it a faint squeeze.

"Look after your mum and do what she says. Okay?"

"Okay."

"Come on, get in the truck and I'll drop you at the turnoff."

They stopped at a gate half a mile down the road on the opposite side to their house. During the summer, Vanessa had gone with her father most days to move the cows into the bottom pasture for afternoon milking, and as she stood in the frigid air and watched down the highway for the bus, she let this thought of better days weave through her mind.

The highway had been cleared earlier, grit replacing snow. To call it a highway was an exaggeration. It was more a road with two narrow lanes. One leading east and the other west. She frowned as the bus pulled onto the gravel verge and came to an abrupt stop. The doors opened with a whoosh. With her school bag in hand, she followed her mother up the three steep steps to where the driver sat, irritated and impatient as he waited for them to pay before he stowed their luggage. They took a seat toward the back. The smell of worn leather, stale cigarette smoke, and spicy perfume made her feel queasy and slightly off balance.

She looked up to see her mother staring out the window, into the face of the man sending them away. Her parents held each other's gaze, but neither of them smiled, and when she looked at her mother, she noticed a lone teardrop balancing at the corner of her eye. Vanessa's emotions moved from dread to numb as a lump formed in her throat. Her dad turned and walked toward the truck, his head down until he sat in the driver's seat and watched the bus pull away.

He hadn't even said a proper goodbye.

The sun sat high and bright in the sky as the bus pulled into the depot of Clifton Falls, a bustling port city, where Norfolk pines lined the arterial route along the waterfront. Vanessa skipped down the steps and stood next to her mother, who reached for her hand and gave it a gentle squeeze as they waited for their bags.

Fumes filled her nostrils as cars hurried across the intersection of King Street and Seaview Road. Beyond the pines, the Pacific stretched before her. Vanessa had only seen the ocean twice and had always thought of it as an angry beast, but today it was as flat as a millpond on a still winter's day.

They sat in the depot to wait. Despite the warmth radiating from the bulky bar heater on the wall above the ticket office, icy drafts swept around Vanessa's bare legs. She kicked at the concrete, the toes of her leather boots still damp from her frolic in the snow. Inside the boots, her feet ached with cold. "Where's the farmer?"

"Not here, sweetie. We have to catch another bus to the O'Leary's farm."

"I'm hungry. I thought you said they lived near Clifton Falls."

Vanessa's head dropped, and she bulged her bottom lip in an unimpressed pout. "I don't feel like an apple. I'm freezing. Can't you buy me a meat pie?"

"I don't have any money," her mother mumbled. "It's the apple or nothing."

Although her mother had never seen the homestead, she'd woven such tales into Vanessa's imagination that she had visions of a grand old lady, holding court at the top of a knoll, surrounded by green pastures dotted with white sheep. However, when the bus pulled to a stop outside a mailbox marked M & C O'Leary, the only sign of the house was a chimney pot visible above the shrub line, and a large TV antenna reaching up as if to touch the sky.

As they made their way up the long driveway, Vanessa's gaze moved to a large section of pasture cordoned off on one side by a post and rail fence. There, a black horse stood, his proud stance betraying his haughty nature. Vanessa stared as they walked toward the house. The horse stared back.

He stomped back and forth in a display of superiority. Vanessa stopped mid-step. She longed to straddle the fence, grab a handful of lush grass and feel him nuzzle it from her palm.

"Vanessa." Her mother glanced back. "Hurry up, sweetie. We haven't got all day."

Vanessa let her suitcase drop to the gravel. "I can't go any faster. My feet hurt."

Her mother sighed, put her case down and waited. "Come on. We're nearly there."

"I want to see the horse."

"Not now, Vanessa. We don't want to be late."

Her mother led the way as Vanessa followed a few steps behind. Even though they were expected, no one came to meet them. Vanessa wanted to sit on the side of the driveway and wait for the farmer to realize his ill-mannered mistake, but her mother just kept walking.

As they rounded the bend and Vanessa viewed the homestead for the first time, she halted and dropped the case once more. A lump formed in her throat as she pulled a lace handkerchief from her pocket, desperately wanting the outcome of her mother's choice to differ from the reality. Vanessa had seen houses like this back home—with small windows, long verandas and derelict sheds to the side—but she'd never lived in one. They lived in a new house with a rumpus room, a swimming pool, and an outdoor dining area covered with a pergola. At least, they did.

They crossed the lawn to the back door without uttering a word. Her mother knocked as Vanessa stood to the side, her hands clasped together. Her mum hated her hanging off her coat, and she knew not to speak unless spoken to.

A teenage boy appeared at the door, a half-eaten apple clenched between his teeth. He took one look at the pair and called inside. "Dad, the new housekeeper's here." He turned back to them. "Go in. Dad's in the kitchen."

His gaze traveled down Vanessa's frame, focused on her boots for a moment, then moved back up again. He gave no welcoming smile. She stared back without blinking, straight into his tanned face and stormy blue eyes. Her expression settled into defiance.

His apple core hit the dirt. She watched him walk toward the barn without another word.

2

ACCEPTING TRUTHS

They waited on the porch in silence. Vanessa looked around, taking everything in. Paint flaked off the concrete doorstep, and dirty boots stuffed with socks littered the doorway to an untidy mudroom. She peeked into the kitchen's dark interior. Old-fashioned floral wallpaper hung loosely over scrim-covered walls, adding to her feeling of unease. There were no floor coverings, and the wooden floorboards were dirty and covered in nicks and scratches. The place stunk like they'd fried up potatoes for lunch and forgotten to wash the pan.

"You must be Ruth." A man with a sun-weathered face extended his hand.

Her mother accepted the greeting with a hearty shake and a warm smile. "Mick, isn't it? It's nice to finally put a face to the name."

He bent down to Vanessa's level. "And who's this little cutie?"

"This is Vanessa. Vanessa, say hello to Mr. O'Leary."

"Hello." She clung to her mother's coat now and barely mustered a whisper.

"Hello, Vanessa. It's nice to meet you. I think you'll like it here."

Vanessa didn't reply. That was a lie. She wouldn't like it here. Not one bit. But then, grown-ups always told lies to little kids—as if they didn't matter, didn't understand, didn't have a heart to tear open. She wanted to go home. Back to the farm on the other side of the main divide—where she woke to the sound of cows strolling to the milking shed every morning, swam in the pool all summer, and did cartwheels on the neatly mowed green lawn. But her mother had said they had to leave, and she'd meant every word. Leaving her daddy had not been a lie. It was a horrible truth.

"I'll show you the bedroom." Mr. O'Leary said. "I haven't done anything about putting tea on, sorry. It's been a busy day."

Vanessa didn't like the evening meal being referred to as 'tea.' Tea was something you drank out of a china cup and served with cake and scones. Dinner was the meal you ate with your family in the evening. At dinner, everyone talked about their day, and if you ate all your vegetables, a dessert of apple pie or chocolate pudding would follow. At least, that's what Grandma Bidi had taught her, anyway.

"I'm not much of a cook, so it's good you're here," Mr. O'Leary told her mother. "There's a rack of mutton chops in the meat safe out back. I'll fetch them in. You'll find plenty of spuds and carrots in the garden behind the garage, and I bought some green beans. They're in the fridge."

"Thank you," was her mother's only reply.

Their bedroom matched the rest of the house. Dark velvet curtains hung from a rusty wire cord, and the chest of drawers, covered in carved-out declarations of love and sundry initials, had only two handles to its name. A thin pillow sat at the head of each bed. They hadn't bothered with pillowcases, and Vanessa scrunched her nose in disgust at the stained cotton.

"We have a spare room for the girl, but it needs a tidy up. We'll see how things go. I'll leave you to settle in before you make a start on the meal. There's only me, the boy, and one of the workers tonight. You'll find sheets and blankets in the linen cupboard."

"Thank you," her mother said again.

Vanessa sat on the bed, holding on to Lucy for dear life. She regarded the compact room, threadbare carpet, and soiled comforters, and shivered. Her mother had promised her a room of her own, just like at home. But this house was nothing like home. Another lie.

"I don't want to stay here," she whispered. "It's cold and smells."

"It's only for a little while." Her mother drew her finger through the thick layer of dust on the bedside table. "Just until I get some money together."

"I want to go home."

Vanessa watched her mother remove her coat and change out of her good dress into jeans and a neatly pressed cardigan. She reapplied her lipstick and dabbed her nose and cheeks with a powder compact from her handbag. "Come on, let's go into the kitchen and see what's what."

"No. I hate it here. It's like the house from *The Munsters*, but without the stairs."

"Don't be silly." Her mother crouched to meet her gaze and smiled. Cold hands smoothed the hair from Vanessa's face. "As long as we're together, we'll be fine. Just you and me. What else do we need?"

3

THOU SHALT NOT

Vanessa watched her mother as she stood at the sink and gazed out the window. She'd been there for ages, just looking. "Mum? I asked if I could have a honey sandwich."

Her mother turned and looked around the kitchen. She wiped her eyes with her hands and pressed her lips together. Vanessa wondered if her tears had anything to do with the Ten Commandments. She'd heard her dad shout, 'thou shalt not something, something,' one day when her parents were fighting, but she couldn't remember which commandment her mother had broken. The only one she remembered was not to steal. She wondered if her mother had stolen something.

"Not now, Vanessa. It'll spoil your dinner."

"It won't. I promise."

"I'll make a start on these lunch dishes." Her mother turned back to the sink. "How they can live in this mess, I have no idea. Go to the bedroom and get your school bag. You can read, or draw in your notebook."

Vanessa looked up. She frowned and blew wisps of stray hair out of her eyes. "I don't want to. There's something yucky in there."

"Don't be silly." She pulled Vanessa close. "I told you before. It's just your imagination." She smiled and ruffled her hair. "And don't let

Mr. O'Leary hear you talk in riddles about your imaginary friends the way you do. He'll think you're away with the fairies."

"You said fairies weren't real."

"It's a figure of speech. You're a big girl now, and big girls aren't scared to go into their bedroom in broad daylight." Her mother cocked her head toward the hallway. "Go on."

Vanessa stopped at the bedroom door and peeked inside. She scrunched up her nose, then stepped forward, grabbing her school bag off the bed. The curtains fluttered in the breeze, and through the window, she could see the boy kicking a rugby ball across the lawn. She leaned on the dresser, watching him drop and kick, drop and kick. The sound reminded her of rugby matches at her old school. As if he sensed her stare, he turned and looked at her, the ball under his arm and a questioning expression on his face. She froze for a moment, then quickly dropped to the floor out of his view and tugged on her slippers. By the time she was back in the kitchen, the soles were already soiled from the grubby floorboards.

Ruth smiled again, but it wasn't her usual loving look. It was more like her face hurt and she was trying to ease the pain. "Now, that wasn't so bad, was it?"

"I don't like it here." She lifted her foot. "And look at my new slippers."

Her mother didn't bother to look. "Give it a chance. We're here now, so let's make the most of it, shall we?"

"But Dad said he'd come and get me."

"Not until school's finished for the year. You know how busy he is. Now, come on. We're lucky to have a roof over our heads, so big smiles."

Her mother placed the meat in the oven, then went out to the vegetable patch. All the time she was gone, Vanessa sat on the doorstep and waited for her.

As was the custom at home, by the time five thirty rolled around, her mother had changed for dinner into a floaty floral dress, matched with peach colored lipstick. With her blonde hair left long and loose, Vanessa thought she must be the prettiest mother on earth.

Vanessa set the table. There were no placemats, just knives and forks straight onto the plastic tablecloth, salt and pepper, and a plate stacked high with buttered bread. The boy with the pimples was the first to arrive in from the farm. He grabbed a slice of bread and held it between his teeth as he took a jug of cordial from the fridge. He glanced at Vanessa.

"You want a drink?"

She shook her head.

Mr. O'Leary strolled in next, and after him, another man. The farmer introduced the boy as Liam and the man as Jake. They sat at the table. Vanessa looked around, wondering where she should sit. Her mother pulled out a chair opposite the boy, and Vanessa sat with her head down. When she looked up, he grinned at her like he knew a secret.

She watched the men empty their plates, then mop up the leftover gravy with the crusty bread. The boy ate two more slices, and Vanessa wondered how he could fit everything in his tummy.

Her mother didn't eat her dinner, just moved it around her plate, and when she cleared the table, her food went straight into the pig bucket.

"Any ice-cream?" Jake asked as he was handed his dessert.

"I'll get it," Liam offered.

"We keep the ice-cream in the freezer out in the shed," Mick said as Vanessa watched the boy go out the back door. "One scoop each. No more."

They had the same rule at home, but her mother sometimes gave her an extra scoop. But not tonight. When they'd finished the apple cobbler, the boy thanked her mother for the meal and rinsed his plate before leaving the room.

The men sat and drank tea while her mum washed and Vanessa dried. Every time she turned to put a plate away, she noticed Jake staring at her mother. And when he set his mug on the counter, Vanessa saw him wink at her before he walked away.

MILD DISINTEREST

Vanessa stood in the living room doorway. The room had a strange feeling about it, intensified by a dim light bulb hanging from the ceiling on a black cord. She chewed on a ragged piece of thumbnail as she waited for Liam to engage her in conversation. He glanced her way but said nothing. With his attention back on the TV, she crept into the room and sat on the arm of a large wing-backed chair.

She didn't speak, her focus on the carpet as her foot rubbed back and forth across the floor in front of her. She'd watched Liam a lot since that first day, wondering how old he was, and whether she could trust him. Some days he was kind to her. He'd even driven her to school once when she missed the school bus—but he didn't take her to the gate like her dad had, so she had to walk in alone. He sometimes helped with the dishes as well, but they didn't have a roster.

"You want to watch TV?"

She shook her head. He ignored her for several minutes, his attention flicking from the TV to a sketch pad on his lap as he scribbled on the page. She wondered what he was drawing. She wanted to draw too.

"How old are you anyway?" he finally asked.

"Ten."

"Ten? You're tiny for ten."

Vanessa chewed her lip before she replied. She looked at the black-and-white TV set, its bulk taking up an entire corner of the small room, then back at Liam. "I'm not. You're just big. How old are you?"

"Is that so?" He chuckled. "I'm nearly sixteen."

"Can I ride the black horse?"

"What black horse?"

Vanessa waited a moment to see if Liam would stop playing dumb. As far as she knew, there was only one black horse on the farm. "The one over by the shelter break. The gelding."

"Who, Whisper? How do you know he's a gelding?"

She looked down, then shot him a sideways glance. "I'm not stupid."

He laughed, and she felt the heat creep up her neck and into her face. They sat for several minutes, Liam's gaze firmly on the TV as Vanessa tried not to look at him.

"Whisper." She breathed the word into the still air of the room. "I like that name. So, can I?"

Liam glanced her way without replying.

"I can ride. I went to pony club at home. But I didn't have my own horse."

"Well, we don't have ponies here. And no one rides Whisper anymore. He's too easily spooked."

"So who used to ride him?"

"I did sometimes. But the last time I tried, he dumped me in the dirt."

"But he's beautiful."

Liam chuckled. "Only on the outside. Inside he's as mean as the devil and twice as smart."

"My dad taught me to ride." A long pause followed. "But then he sent us away."

"Why's that?"

Vanessa worried at her lip again. "He just did."

17

SHADOW OF FEAR

Vanessa and Liam hadn't spoken much since she'd arrived at the farm, mainly because he spent weekdays at boarding school in Clifton Falls. When he was home on the weekends, she'd retreat to her room to read. Those hours of solitude became her way of blocking out the lonely reality of living in the Rata River Valley—with a man who wasn't her father, a boy who wasn't her brother, and a mother who didn't seem like her mother anymore. The more time she spent alone, the more she learned to accept it.

Even though she found him difficult to talk to, she had asked him several times if she could ride Whisper, and her gut clenched tighter every time he said no. Vanessa had experienced that clench before, usually when her parents yelled at each other after she'd gone to bed. But there had been other times, too—when she'd first laid eyes on the O'Leary homestead, when she'd seen the look on her father's face as he watched the bus pull away, and on the many nights her mother forgot to tuck her in.

On a particular dull and dreary Saturday, she hung around after breakfast, trying to muster the courage to ask again. Liam had made it into the school's First XV rugby team, and his weekends over winter were focused on the game, so he wasn't home much. She had to convince him while she had the chance.

Her father had taught her to ask for what she wanted rather than beat around the bush. If something needed to be said, stand tall and make your case, he'd advised. But she had never made a case for anything as important as riding Whisper. The last case she'd made was asking Santa for a Little Tuppence doll for Christmas, and Santa hadn't heard her. There was too much noise in the house already that week.

Liam ignored her as he walked through the kitchen. He grabbed an apple from a crate at the back door, before bounding down the porch steps and across the lawn toward the driveway. She was just about to run after him when her mother called her back.

"Where are you off to?"

"Liam said he might take me for a ride," she lied, her stomach dancing with butterflies.

Her mother looked at her and smiled. "Have you made your bed?"

"Yes."

"Off you go then, but be back in time for lunch, and don't be annoying."

By the time she caught up with Liam, he was halfway to the stables. She watched him take several large bites of his apple, then toss the core onto the dirt.

"What's up?"

"I want to go riding. I told you before."

He kept walking. "And what did I say last time?"

"You said no. You always say no. You're such a shit head."

He turned in his tracks and looked down at her with a scowl. "What did you call me?"

She stopped and shuffled her feet in the gravel, her eyes focused on their movement. "I didn't call you nothing."

"Look at me when I speak to you." He waited. "I said, look at me."

She raised her head.

"I heard what you called me, and you don't say, 'nothing.' You say, 'I didn't call you anything.'" He turned and walked away. She stood in the middle of the driveway. Her bottom lip quivered. It felt like her pride had been thrashed with his leather belt. Hot, angry tears fell as she stomped back to the house.

Her mother frowned when she entered the kitchen. "Hey, what's the matter? I thought you were going for a ride with Liam."

"He said not today."

"I'll tell you what, why don't we bake some cupcakes? Then we can pick daisies and make chains, okay?"

The workday usually ended around five thirty, but by the time Liam entered the kitchen that evening, dinner was already on the table. Shifting in her seat, Vanessa ignored his attempts to catch her gaze, her sight fixed firmly on the stew, spinach, and mashed potatoes floating on a greasy film on her plate. She knew the rules—clean plate before dessert, but the smell of the beef made her queasy.

When she finally looked his way, he winked, his grin wide. She dropped her head, shoveled the spinach into her mouth and took a gulp of water from her glass. When her mother left the table to fetch dessert, Liam quickly swapped his plate for Vanessa's.

When she returned, her mother looked at Vanessa's empty plate and smiled. "Good girl. Would you like some dessert?"

Vanessa frowned at Liam and whispered, "yes please," then watched his chest puff out as if he'd done her a huge favor. It seemed he was a smart ass, just like every other boy she'd met.

The next day, Vanessa had better things to do than think about Liam. Mick had agreed she could have the junk room, after her mother claimed she didn't sleep well sharing a bedroom. She spent all morning with her mother, moving tea chests of broken toys and musty books into the shed attached to the garage.

By mid-afternoon, the room stood bare. Her mother, dressed for the occasion in jeans and a t-shirt, but still with a full face of makeup, set to work with a bucket of hot soapy water, and then with Vanessa's help, moved the bed into her new room. A battered nightstand sat to one side, but apart from that, the only other furniture was an old wardrobe—the mirror mottled with rust and broken by a semi-circular crack. Vanessa hung her kilt on the only hanger, then helped her mother make the bed. When they'd finished, her Bidi quilt took pride of place on top of the bed, her flannel pajamas were under the pillow, and her slippers stood in front of the nightstand.

She looked at the curtains—sheets of yellow cotton twill with a large rip halfway up the left one and most of the color bleached from the right. They were neither functional nor decorative, but would have to do. After all, she would be going home soon.

Mick had suggested hanging pictures over the rips in the wallpaper, but she had none. So instead, she stuck a set of Old Maid playing cards in a neat row along the length of her bed. She didn't have anyone to play cards with anyway, and the sight made her smile. Larger-than-life characters, happy in their imaginary lives.

That night, Vanessa woke with a bad dream and a racing heart. She was back at her father's farm, lying in a snow-covered field as angels, formed from ice, danced around her. She looked under the bed, certain she wasn't alone, but a quick sweep of the room assured her otherwise. Outside, a bright moon illuminated the sky, and the temperature had dropped dramatically. She reached into the drawer of her nightstand for socks, then tiptoed down the hallway in search of another blanket from the linen cupboard. She found nothing.

Vanessa went to knock on her mother's bedroom door, but as she took a step closer, she heard hushed voices, followed by a rhythmic thudding against the wall. She stood and listened for a few seconds before Jake's unmistakable voice joined her mother's in what sounded like a command.

She ran back to her room and grabbed her winter coat, draping it over the bed. Next, she put on her special red cardigan over her pajamas, and another pair of thick socks. She hugged Lucy and waited for sleep as a shadow of fear floated down from the ceiling.

She tried not to cry, as she'd tried every night since they'd arrived, but some nights she couldn't help it. She wanted her mum *and* her dad.

Both. Together. Silent tears dripped onto her pillow as she pulled her quilt around her neck and her knees to her chest.

When Vanessa entered the kitchen for breakfast the next morning, she watched Jake and her mother with interest. Her mum wore a red dress, with lipstick to match, and earrings like tiny teardrops dangled from each ear. She'd pulled her hair back into a perfect chignon and bracelets jangled on one wrist. Her mother had looked tired since they'd left the farm, but today she seemed different. Fresh. New.

She pulled Vanessa into a hug. "Good morning, sweetheart."

Jake sat at the table and rocked back in his chair while he ordered her mum to refill his cup and bring him more toast and jam. Vanessa looked up from her bowl of corn flakes into Jake's smug expression, and at that moment, she hated him with a passion she had never experienced before. She didn't understand the reason, just that he was no good.

She looked at Liam. He'd stopped eating and was watching Jake, too. He frowned, shot Vanessa a sideways glance, then continued with his meal. All throughout breakfast, she kept her head down and her jaw tight, but relaxed when Jake and Mick left the table first. Liam sat a while longer, studying a ledger full of columns and numbers. She knew he was good with numbers and wanted to work for a bank when he finished his studies. When Mick couldn't get the totals to tally, he would give the ledger to Liam to sort out.

Her mother stepped forward and peered over his shoulder. "How's it going? Find anything?"

He tore a long strip of tape off the calculator. "Would you mind reading these out to me? Dad's always transposing figures, but I can't seem to find it."

Vanessa watched as her mother sat beside him, calling out numbers in quick succession. Once the mistake was found, they chatted about the farm. Liam had lots of ideas, and she listened with interest and a warm, lipstick smile. Her mother used to do all the books at home. Vanessa wondered who did the books now.

She left the kitchen and sat on her bed to watch and wait. As soon as Liam left the house, she bounded out the door and down the steps after him. Liam kept walking without even a glance her way.

"I want to go for a ride."

"Thought you might."

"Please. Take me with you."

He turned to look at her. She held her breath, expecting him to reconsider after he'd saved her from eating the stew. "No." He spoke the word with such authority, she stepped back. "You can stomp your feet as much as you like. I won't change my mind."

"I hate you, Liam O'Leary."

He chuckled. "Hate me all you want, Vanessa Blinkly."

As Vanessa wandered back to the house, she recalled his expression —his amusement at her request. He'd never spoken her name before. It sounded strange, the resonance of the words rolling off his tongue like he'd said them many times before—like they were now friends.

Back in her room, Vanessa ran her fingers over the four books stacked on her nightstand. They had arrived in a brown paper package covered in postage stamps, courtesy of Grandma Bidi. *Black Beauty*, *Anne of Green Gables*, *Island of the Blue Dolphins*, and *Fantastic Mr. Fox* sat piled on top of one another, largest to smallest. She slumped on the bed and leaned back on her elbows, not interested in reading those same books over again. Her dangling feet bounced gently back and forth along with her thoughts.

She stood up, reached into the wardrobe for her suitcase, and pulled out a pair of jodhpurs and a white riding shirt. She hadn't worn them since arriving at the O'Leary's, but she'd decided to visit Whisper and would dress accordingly. She loved how the stretchy beige material fit so snugly. Jodhpurs made her feel like she belonged to a group of like-minded people who loved riding. However, there was no like-minded group—just her and Whisper.

After a quick change, she cut across the drive to the poplars at the back of Whisper's field. Liam said Whisper was easily spooked, but Vanessa didn't care. Sometimes, she was spooked too. In her mind, she and Whisper were equals. Friends who identified with each other. He had no other friends, and neither did she.

Whisper lifted his head as soon as Vanessa climbed the fence. At least a hundred yards divided them, but he watched her every move as she strolled toward him, softly calling his name on the breeze. The air remained fresh, and an early morning frost meant her fingers ached with the cold. As she inched closer, his nostrils flared and puffed, the vapor white against the rough black of his coat. It reminded Vanessa of dragons in picture books she'd read as a little girl.

She wondered if he was just as fierce.

She wondered if she was still a little girl.

With careful steps, Vanessa offered the apple from her pocket, balancing it on her flat palm. She cooed and purred his name and showered him with endearments. "Hey, beautiful, come on. There's a good boy. What a handsome boy you are."

He reared up to show his reluctance, then stamped his feet in a display of equine supremacy. She didn't let up. She called him, soothed him, and looked him straight in the eye without a single blink. Not once did she feel fear, but the apple stayed untouched.

As she climbed over the gate, Whisper took off around the perimeter of his enclosure, vocalizing his resentment at her intrusion. She sat in the damp grass, softly singing his name, and telling him stories of her life on the farm over the great mountains that separated the west and east of the island.

"Do you want to be friends, Whisper? I don't have any friends here. Our school only has fifty-two students. Did you know that, boy? There's only three other girls my age. The rest are boys, like you, but they have stinky feet."

The next day, Vanessa waited until the men were gone before making her way to the stables. To call them stables was an exaggeration. Half-broken sheets of iron and rusty nails seemed to be the only thing holding the place together, and all four stalls reeked of putrid hay and horse manure. If her father were here, he'd throw a fit. He'd been in the navy, and he liked a tidy ship.

In the soft interior light, she noticed several old saddles covered in dust and grit. Touching them one by one, she made her choice. The opportunity to ride Whisper would come soon enough, and she wanted to be prepared.

Over the next few hours, Vanessa polished the old leather with saddle soap, elbow grease, and spit until it gleamed. The smell reminded her of home, and she thought of those early mornings at pony club when she could hardly contain her excitement.

That night in bed, she dreamed of how it would feel to go riding again—to hold the reins in her hands, sit in the saddle with the warmth of Whisper's body under her, and to inhale his smell. She didn't care what Liam said. She would ride Whisper, and it would be none of his business.

Over the next few days, Vanessa visited the gelding every chance she could get. Just when she thought they were starting to understand each other, Whisper would rear up and pull away. But she never gave up, practicing everything she'd learned from her father. The verbal cues, how to use the lead rope, the way to make him back up, and the importance of eye contact. And every day, she introduced something new, until it was Whisper who approached her, not the other way around.

Later that week, with the men away for a full day, she led Whisper to the stables, placed the saddle on his back, and walked him up and down the drive, stopping and starting to let him get the feel of it, and to build his trust and respect. By the end of the day, she knew he was ready.

On the way back to the house, Vanessa picked daisies and made a chain. As she passed Liam's bedroom, she let herself in through the French doors and left it on his pillow.

6

WHISPER

Liam left the kitchen straight after lunch, determined to make the most of his last full weekend at home by meeting up with his friends —including Anna Cook, her boyfriend, Rob, and the attractive Ava Rigby. He was due back at school on Sunday of the following week, and the thought of it filled him with dread. The staff at Saint Francis of Assisi Collegiate ran the institution like an army barracks. Because of this, Saint Franks—as the school was affectionately called—wasn't his favorite place to be; especially in the winter, when frost clung to the inside of the dormitory windows, and hot showers were the luck of the draw. The dorm's housemaster, a weasel of a man named Grove, said the cold bred men, not pansy girls. Liam loathed that kind of talk. He also loathed the housemaster.

Dancing footsteps on the gravel interrupted his thoughts. "Liam?" Her soft call made him smile. He didn't mind the kid. In fact, most of the time, he felt sorry for her.

"Take me riding?"

"Not today. Maybe when you're a bit older."

"I won't be here when I'm older. I won't be here much longer at all actually—"

"Why's that?" he interrupted. "Where are you going to be, *actually?*"

"Home. Dad's coming to get me."

Her determination amused him, and he smiled to himself again. He seemed to do that a lot when she was around. Smile. "Well, if your father lets you ride, you can do it at his place."

She followed him into the stables. "But I want to ride Whisper."

He reached for his saddle and heaved it onto Gracie, an old girl the color of chestnut and one of his mother's favorites. "You will never ride Whisper, is that clear?"

"I hate you. You smell and have pimples."

He laughed loudly. "And you're a brat, whose eyelashes are too long for her face."

Dusk fell between six and six thirty in late winter. So when Liam entered the kitchen just before six, his thoughts on Ava Rigby and her knowing smile, it was almost dark. With a mitt over his hand, he opened the oven and grabbed his plate.

"Where's Vanessa?" Ruth asked.

"No idea." He set the plate on the stovetop and lifted the aluminum foil. "I haven't seen her since lunchtime."

"But she's been gone all afternoon. I thought she was with you."

Mick looked up from his meal. "She won't be far away."

Liam stabbed a roast potato with a fork and returned his plate to the oven. "You guys finish dinner. I'll go find her. She's probably with Whisper." He took a bite. Chewed. He was starving, and the last thing he needed was to babysit a ten-year-old kid.

"I thought you told her to keep away from that damn horse," Mick said.

"I did, but she's got a mind of her own."

"She gets that from her father," Ruth said. "I should have taken her riding. She rode all the time at … the farm. It's getting dark. What if she's lost?"

"Don't worry," Liam said as he put on his jacket and finished the potato. "I'll find her."

Once outside, Liam looked toward the poplar shelter belt, his eyes straining against the shadow of the tree line. "That shitty little brat." He picked up a long switch of willow from the side of the driveway, bringing it down on the gravel with a swift crack. A string of swear words left his mouth as he stormed toward the stables. When he noticed one of his mother's old saddles missing, he cursed some more.

He was about to mount Gracie when he noticed Vanessa roughly three hundred yards away.

Her tiny frame bobbed up and down with a steady rhythm, and strands of white-blonde hair escaped from a small black helmet as she crooned her commands. Vanessa had told him she could ride, but he was surprised by how naturally she moved with her mount for a ten year old. Like most farm kids, she'd probably been in the saddle before she could even walk. But riding Whisper? What the hell?

He stood with his mouth half open as he watched Vanessa walk Whisper the last few yards. Whisper showed his displeasure at Liam's presence by rearing up. Vanessa held on tightly with her knees and whispered in his ear to calm him before her dismount.

Keeping his distance, Liam leaned on the yard railing as she led Whisper toward the stable to remove his saddle. After a quick rub down, she walked him back to his solitary confinement, took off the bridle and strolled toward Liam as if she had all day.

With the switch still in his hand and his arms crossed over his chest, he waited for an explanation. Vanessa's eyes narrowed when she noticed the switch, but she didn't say a word.

Liam couldn't hold his anger in any longer. "What the bloody hell do you think you were doing? Get back to the house."

She stepped back, hands flying to her hips. "You shouldn't say rude words to me."

He stepped forward. "And you shouldn't disobey me. You could've been hurt if you came off that darn horse."

"Don't shout at me. I hate it when people shout."

"I'll shout at you all I want. I said you couldn't ride Whisper. But here you are, the minute my back's turned."

"Well, you wouldn't take me. You didn't even believe I could ride." She started to sniffle. "I hate you, and I hate it here."

Liam sighed. He had no idea how to treat little girls, especially ones who cried. He stood and watched her bite her lips as she fought to compose herself.

"Come on." He grabbed the bridle and hung it on a nail inside the stable door. "Your mum's worried about you."

"I'm not going back to that house. She doesn't even care about me. She only cares about that horrible Jake."

"What?" Jake made no attempt to hide his interest in Ruth, but Liam hadn't realized the feeling was mutual. "Don't be silly. Of course she cares about you. And you can't stay out here all night. You'll freeze."

"I don't care." She kept her gaze on the switch. "And I'm not gonna let you hit me. Daddy said never let a man hit you."

Liam dropped the switch onto the dirt. "I'm not going to hit you." He moved closer, so close he could see her jaw tighten and her eyes darting between his. "As if I would. Now get over to the house."

Vanessa stamped her foot. "No."

"I said, get over to the damn house."

"And I said no."

Tall for his age and youthfully strong, Liam had no hesitation in using his strength against her. He picked her up, threw her over his shoulder and carried her kicking and screaming all the way back to the kitchen. Just before he reached the back door, he put her down and pushed her over the threshold.

"Vanessa, where were you?" her mother asked. "I've been worried sick."

"Riding."

"Excuse me? You can't just go off on your own whenever you feel like it. What if something happened to you?"

"I don't care what you all think. You know I can ride, and I'm going to keep doing it."

Vanessa opened the oven and pulled out their plates, practically throwing one on the table in front of Liam. He suppressed a smile as he thought about how people came to resemble the animals they loved. At that moment, Vanessa's face had taken on the same look as Whisper's, with flared nostrils and chin held high in defiance.

"Vanessa Marie Blinkly, that's enough," Ruth said. "Go to your room. I won't have you speaking to us in that tone."

Muffled sounds of early evening filtered through the bedroom wall. Utensils scraping over plates as her mother cleaned up, chairs sliding in and out, and the deep voices of Mick and Liam as they discussed their day. Vanessa didn't care about missing dinner, but she did care that she'd miss her favorite TV show, *The Waltons*. She wanted to sneak into the living room and cuddle up on Mick's favorite chair, but instead, sat on her bed with Lucy, plaiting the doll's hair. She reached for her copy of *Black Beauty* and opened it. Now and then, she glanced toward the door, expecting her mum to appear with a glass of creamy milk and a jam drop cookie.

Her mother never came.

The house had quietened into sleep when she heard a soft knock on the bedroom door. When she didn't respond, Liam pushed the door open.

"Go away," she whispered. "I hate you."

He stepped into the room, leaving the door ajar. "I made you a sandwich. Thought you might be hungry."

She lowered her head, her lips pouting as tears trickled down her cheeks and emotion welled up in her throat. She swallowed hard. "I don't want a stupid sandwich."

"Suit yourself." Liam placed the plate and a glass of milk on the nightstand, then sat on the bed. He picked up Lucy. "Is this your doll?"

Vanessa huffed. She hated it when people asked stupid questions.

"I didn't think you would be a doll kind of girl."

"All girls have a dolly." Vanessa reached out, snatched Lucy back and tucked her into the bed. "Sometimes you're so dumb, and you think I'm the same."

She expected Liam to leave, but he stayed on the bed and said nothing.

"What do you want to be when you grow up?" he eventually asked.

"A nurse … and I want to talk to horses."

"Horses don't talk."

"They do so. You just need to know how to listen. That's what my dad says."

"You sure you're not hungry?" He leaned forward and offered her the sandwich. "Here."

Vanessa shrugged. Frowned. Pouted. She wiped her nose with the back of her hand. The smell of yeast and peanut butter stirred up her hunger. She took the sandwich without making eye contact, sunk her teeth into the soft white bread, and moved the smooth peanut butter around her tongue. The sweetness calmed her gut as she swallowed.

"Tell you what," he said. "I'll meet you at the stables after work tomorrow and take you for a quick ride. Okay? Would you like that?"

"Why would I?"

"I thought that's what you wanted. But what do I know? I'm stupid, apparently. Do you want to come or not?"

Vanessa fiddled with Lucy's bonnet. "Okay, thank you."

"Right. I'm going back to school next Sunday, but if I have time, I'll take you on a few rides before I go. Now eat your sandwich."

He moved to the door, but she called him back with a whisper. "Liam?" Vanessa looked up at him with a frown. "I'm cold, and I can't find another blanket."

He smiled. It wasn't the first smile he'd given her, but it warmed her insides all the same. "I'll get you one from my room. Make sure you drink your milk."

The first day Liam took Vanessa riding, he insisted she ride Tiger, a calm old horse who couldn't trot to save himself. She picked the same saddle she'd used on Whisper, the one with no fancy stitching or embellishment.

"Why that saddle?"

"Whisper likes it." She touched his mother's favorite. "I like this one, but it's the lady's."

Liam looked at her and frowned, a rush of emotion gripping his gut. "What lady?"

She shrugged. "I saw her on Friday. Under the tree in front of the house. She goes there to pray."

"What?" He was almost too nervous to ask the next question. "What does she look like?"

"Pretty, with long black hair pulled back in one of those pearly combs."

Liam inhaled deeply and rested his head on the side of Gracie's neck. An image of his mother flashed into his mind. He couldn't ever remember seeing her without her hair secured with a pearl comb. For the first few months after her death, his dreams of her were so vivid, he'd swear she was standing beside him. But he'd never told anyone about them, and as time passed, he dreamed of her less and less.

He'd been drawn to that tree the day after she'd died. It was the only place he'd ever shed a tear for her. Even as they lowered her casket into the grave, he'd never cried—not because he didn't want to, but because he couldn't. "We don't have any women here, apart from your mum. You must be seeing things."

As he led Gracie out of the gate, Liam searched for a rational explanation as to who the woman could be. Maybe one of the fertilizer reps, or even a friend of Ruth's, although he'd never seen anyone visit Ruth in the past. And why would they be sitting under the elm tree in the front yard? The alternative didn't bear thinking about.

"Mum says ghosts and fairies aren't real, but I don't believe her."

"Your mother's right." He sighed. "Come on. Let's go."

7

TIPTOED VISITS

SUMMER 1974

In December 1974, when school finished for the summer, Vanessa boarded the bus to visit her old home, west of the great divide. During the month she was there, she spent Christmas Day with her father and his new wife, watched the fireworks on New Year's Eve from the town square, and celebrated her birthday with a thickly frosted chocolate cake. Her father always remembered gifts—small knickknacks and sometimes, sweets and books. Usually, her mother did too, but there had been no parcel in the post that year.

On her arrival back in the valley, Vanessa stood on the side of the highway and watched the bus pull away. She waited for several cars to pass before making her way to the mailbox and up the driveway, her small suitcase in hand and flip-flops on her feet. She hadn't yet spent a Christmas or birthday at O'Leary's, and secretly hoped she'd find a gift waiting for her on her bed. Vanessa pushed the expectation down as she entered the kitchen. She'd hardly ever seen her mother go shopping lately.

Ruth welcomed her with a stiff hug. "How's my girl?"

"I'm good."

"And your father?"

Vanessa didn't know if she should tell or not. But then, her mother probably already knew. Her parents talked on the phone sometimes—short conversations. Her mum attentive as she followed his instructions. *Yes. No. Okay.*

"He got married."

Vanessa watched as her mother tensed and inhaled sharply. "What? When?"

She shrugged. "I don't know. But he has a new wife. Her name's Karen. They have a baby coming."

Ruth went to the sink and poured herself a glass of sherry. Her dress still looked pretty and bright on her now thinner frame, but in place of the usual lipstick and full makeup, her lips were dry and bare, and her face pale. "You'd better go unpack. Then I need a hand with dinner."

Vanessa looked around her tiny bedroom, the air muggy and stale. After all this time, it still didn't feel like home. She felt more at home out in the fields than she did inside her room—with its musty-smelling floral sheets covering the mattress and threadbare blankets that reeked of mothballs. She sat on the chair Mick had rescued from the shed and gave Lucy a tight hug. Lucy came courtesy of her old world, and while many girls of twelve had by now relegated their dolls to boxes in the attic, Vanessa couldn't bear the thought of being without her.

Her mother appeared in the doorway. She offered an envelope. "Here. Happy Birthday for yesterday." The words sounded flat, almost slurred. Vanessa hardly had time to say thanks before she was gone again. She opened the card and looked inside. *Happy Birthday, love Mum.* A blue handkerchief sat folded neatly in place, and underneath was a small bar of chocolate. She brought the card to her nose and inhaled. It smelled of rose talc. There was no other message. No words of love or praise as there had been in the past, just those four words scribbled with an unsteady hand.

She put the card under her pillow and returned to the kitchen. Her mother sat at the table with the same glass of sherry, but now, the open bottle sat next to it. Vanessa looked at the lunch dishes still piled up in the sink. "What can I do to help?"

Her mother didn't look up. "Make a start on those dishes, would you."

"Are you all right, Mum?"

"I've got a headache."

That night, Vanessa sat alone in the living room and watched TV before going to bed at eight thirty as per her mother's strict instructions. Once in her pajamas, she spread Bidi's quilt across the bed and snuggled between the sheets. She stared at the ceiling, wondering why her mother hadn't come to say goodnight.

Vanessa peeked over the side of the wooden bed frame, checking the space beneath. Her mother usually stored all kinds of junk under the bed, but tonight it was clear. She pulled the quilt secure against her neck, hugged Lucy tight and waited for sleep to find her.

She woke three hours later, her heart pounding and her mouth dry. As she lowered her feet to the floor, she snuck a peek upward to the corner of her room where the wall and ceiling merged. She shuddered as she grabbed her quilt from the bed. Tiptoeing over to the door, she peered into the hallway. Mick snored loudly as she crept toward her mother's room.

Voices filtered through the closed door. It reminded Vanessa of home two years earlier.

Her mother, *Why?*

Jake, *I'm sorry, Ruth, please.*

She stood still for a moment, trying to make out other muted words, but as she walked away, the only sound was a rhythm she'd heard before. Thud, thud, thud on the bedroom wall.

On the other side of the house, Liam's door was also closed. Sometimes, like her mother, he locked it. She didn't know why. But tonight, the doorknob turned with a click. She let herself in and stood beside his bed. With the moonlight shining through his open curtains, she could see him clearly. He slept on his back, with one hand draped over the edge of the bed, palm-side up. It reminded her of how ballet dancers held their hands—with the index finger almost straight and the other fingers curling inwards in graceful succession. She touched the inside of his wrist.

Liam started. "What?"

Vanessa shivered as she stood next to his bed. Her nightdress barely reached her thighs, and she was freezing. She wrapped her quilt around her shoulders.

"What the hell are you doing in my room?"

"I'm scared."

He turned away, punching his pillow into comfortable submission. "Go see your mum."

"I can't," she whispered as she watched him drift back into semi-sleep. "Her door's locked."

Liam sat up and pulled a pillow behind his head. "Just go knock."

"I've upset her."

He reached for his watch, frowning at the glow of the numerals in the dark. "Why? What have you done now?"

"My dad, he has a new wife. She's real pretty. They're having a baby. I told Mum, and now she's mad."

Liam nodded as if he understood. "You'd better get back to bed."

Keeping her head down, Vanessa fidgeted with the bow on the front of her nightdress. "Please, don't make me."

"What will your mum say if she finds you in here? Go on. You're being silly."

She stayed for a moment longer, hoping he would change his mind and let her sleep next to him, but as he turned his back, Vanessa knew he didn't care if she was scared or not. She left his room without a sound, making it as far as her bedroom doorway, where she stayed until Mick found her the next morning.

"What are you doing on the floor?" Mick asked as he nearly tripped over her.

She sat up and rubbed her face. "Waiting for the bathroom."

Mick narrowed his eyes and offered her a hand up. He gave her hair a friendly ruffle. "It's free now. Then go back to bed. It's not even six yet."

8

MOKO WOMAN

SUMMER 1975

Liam watched as Ruth carried a small cardboard box from the living room and sat it on the kitchen table. "That's the Christmas decorations taken care of."

"Sorry, I said I'd take the tree down days ago."

"I'll let you do the rest." Ruth smiled. She looked better today than she had recently. The lipstick was back and she had a spring in her step. "It's too big for me."

"Some years I wonder why we bother when there's just the three of us here," Liam said.

"You miss your mother a lot, don't you?"

Despite the open sherry bottle on the kitchen counter, Ruth spoke clearly and her step was steady. He'd never discussed the loss of his mother with anyone before. Being a male, he was expected to just get on with it. Ruth did this every now and again. Made some out of the blue comment, showing a side of her that few people saw—compassionate and caring—the Ruth they knew before the booze started speaking for her.

"I thought it would get easier," he said.

"Yes, me too." She fiddled with the top of the box, folding the flaps in on one another. "Although mine wasn't from someone passing away like yours, I still feel the loss. I wrote to him"—she stopped to gather her thoughts—"every week for those first few months, asking if we could go home. He never bothered to reply. When an envelope finally came, it was our divorce papers. He has a baby now, did Vanessa tell you?"

"She mentioned it."

"Nothing says finality like a new wife and a baby. Still, Vanessa will be back this afternoon, so life's good."

Liam hesitated. "She's not happy here."

Ruth said nothing for several moments as she tied the box shut. Liam worried that he'd spoken out of turn. After all, Vanessa wasn't any of his business.

"I know," Ruth said finally, "but she'll be away to nursing school soon enough. Or maybe she'll end up working with horses. Did you know that her father imagines he's a horse whisperer?" She didn't wait for Liam to reply. "It's all a load of rubbish if you ask me."

The soft light of early morning usually acted as nature's alarm clock, but it was still hours before dawn when Liam woke to the sound of his door opening. He knew it was her. With the moon fuller that night, he could see her clearly. "What's the matter tonight?"

Vanessa stood perfectly still and gazed down at him, her eyes wide. "I saw something," she whispered.

"Shit," he cursed under his breath as he pulled a pillow behind his head. "What do you mean, you saw something?"

"A lady, with one of those Māori drawings on her chin."

"A *moko*? Where?"

"In my room. She floats on the ceiling."

"This is getting ridiculous. You must have been dreaming."

"I'm scared. She comes a lot and just stares at me. It's creepy."

He flicked on the bedside lamp and looked at her. She stood pigeon-toed—white ankle socks on her feet, her hands clasped—and even though it was a warm night, the soft blonde hairs on her arms stood erect.

"It's okay." He softened his response. He'd expected the pout and she didn't disappoint, but he couldn't encourage her. "It was a nightmare. Go back to bed and get some sleep."

She didn't move.

"You can't stay here."

Lowering her head, she step backward and let herself out of his room with a soft click of the doorknob. He tossed and turned for a while, thinking about Vanessa and her wild imagination, before drifting off.

When he woke about an hour later, the sound of rustling on the floor beside the bed, startled him. There, bundled up in a quilt, with her head on the floorboards, lay Vanessa. He climbed out of bed and, without saying a word, went down the hall to the bathroom. When he returned, he could tell she was pretending to be asleep, so he got into bed and did the same.

By dawn, she was gone.

Vanessa didn't come every night, but he often found her either at the side or foot of his bed—wrapped tightly in her quilt—the cotton casing protecting her from both the hard floorboards and her demons. How she could stand being bundled up in the middle of summer, he had no idea. Sometimes, she'd climb in beside him, and he'd feel her small frame snuggled up to his, but when he woke at daybreak, he was always alone.

During the day, she would appear for lunch dressed in jodhpurs and a white shirt, discolored from age and constant laundering. She rarely spoke unless spoken to, but apart from the odd command from her mother and a bit of cheek from Mick, no one talked to her much.

The evening before the start of the new school year, Liam noticed Vanessa leaning on the fence by Whisper's field. After she'd been grounded that first time, she'd always asked Liam's permission before riding the gelding. Mick didn't approve, but Liam knew how much she loved Whisper, and he couldn't bring himself to say no. He pulled a blade of grass, sucking the sweetness into his mouth while he walked over to join her. "What are you up to?"

She sat cross-legged on the grass. "Just talking to Whisper. He's going to miss me during the day."

"Are you looking forward to school?"

"What kind of stupid question is that? I hate school."

"It can't be that bad." He sat next to her. "Tell me five things you love about school."

She thought for a moment. Her expressive face held the usual frown. "There's nothing I love about school, but I love other things."

"Like what?"

"Whisper, my dad, Karen, chocolate pudding."

"That's only four."

"Mum, I guess. Even though she doesn't love me back anymore, I still kind of love her. In the mornings anyway." She whispered the next words, as if saying them aloud was a betrayal. "When we lived with Dad, she'd tuck me in and say she loved me to the sky and back. She doesn't do that here."

"Maybe she has a lot on her mind."

Vanessa watched Whisper's every move with sad eyes. Liam understood. Ruth's day usually started with promise but deteriorated as soon as she unscrewed the top of the sherry bottle. There was no doubt in his mind that Ruth loved her daughter, but some days she couldn't get out of her own way to express that love. Lately, he'd scarcely seen them speak to one another. "I still love my mum, too."

"Is that why you wear her charm?"

Liam touched the charm hanging from a silver box chain around his neck. "How do you know it's hers?"

She shrugged. "I love charms."

He looked away. "I'm sure your mother loves you. Sometimes we think our parents are heroes, but they struggle too, just like the rest of us." Liam reached over and ruffled her hair, then stood to leave. "Don't mess around. It's almost dark."

"Liam?" She called him back. "What do you miss the most about your mum?"

He paused, looking into the distance. He'd never really thought about what he missed the most. *Hugs, laughter, teasing, cheesecake.* "Holiday dinners in the dining room. Mum was a great cook, and we always had heaps of friends and family visiting at Christmas and New Year. I never felt like an only child then. We don't use that room now. Dad can't handle it. I sit in there occasionally, just to feel close to her spirit."

"She knows you're there."

He huffed, but stayed a moment longer, thoughts of his mother forming the usual lump in his throat. Maybe he needed a Whisper in his life. Vanessa treated that horse like he was her best, and only, friend.

He probably was.

9

IMMACULATE HEART

SUMMER 1976

On January tenth, 1976, a northbound bus stopped at the verge of O'Leary's driveway, just as it had in previous years. From his position near the shearing shed, Liam watched Vanessa drop her bag on the gravel as she ran to greet Whisper. He stood spellbound as horse and rider poured affection over one another. He'd seen her charm Whisper many times, but their bond never ceased to amaze him.

Liam shot Mick a sideways glance as his father squinted against the sun. "What have you decided?" he asked.

"Nothing yet."

"I used to have a lot of respect for Ruth, but you can't keep her on. She's wasted every night, and the house is always a mess. And this thing with her and Jake. That guy's a prick."

"And what would happen to Vanessa? She's like a daughter to me. I can't see them out on the street. I thought you, of all people, would understand."

"I guess, but Ruth's not fit for the job. You know that. But you let it slide, just like everything else."

"You're way out of line. You think just because you're top of your class, you know how to run a farm? You have no idea what I've been through since your mother died."

"Of course I do, but this isn't about Mum or the farm. It's about Ruth."

"I'll handle it."

"You do that." Liam walked away. He knew when to shut up where his father was concerned. The one positive to come out of the conversation was Mick's obvious compassion for Vanessa. Liam knew his father cared, but until that moment, he hadn't realized how much.

"I don't want to go to boarding school," Vanessa said to her mother the following day.

"Your father has other ideas. And if you didn't want to go, you should have discussed it with him and that wife of his. He's paying for it after all, and it's an excellent school. Immaculate Heart girls go places."

"I don't want to be an Immaculate Heart girl. I know girls from that school, snooty bitches going nowhere but to bimbo land with a rich husband and two snotty-nosed kids."

"Vanessa Blinkly, stop that right now. I won't hear another word about it. Now go and make Liam's bed."

Vanessa stormed out of the kitchen and down the hallway to the linen cupboard. She hated changing the beds. Her mother insisted on hospital corners and would often turn up unannounced to inspect the job. Her arms ached as she flipped the heavy cotton sheets across the mattress.

"Hey, sis. What are you doing in here? Snooping?"

She hadn't heard Liam as he entered the room, and she turned with fright when he spoke. "I'm not your sister, and if you don't want me in your room, change your own damn sheets."

"What's got up your nose? I see your attitude hasn't improved any."

"Yeah, well, I have to go away to school soon, that should make you happy." Vanessa picked up his brand-new pillow and held it under her chin as she pulled the pillowcase on with several strong tugs. She liked Liam well enough but did the teenage girl thing and pretended not to. "They're sending me to Immaculate Heart."

Liam reached for the other pillow to give her a hand. "So I heard. Are you okay with that?"

"Too bad if I'm not."

"You'll be fine. It's a good school."

"Will I? You think you know everything, but you don't know jack shit."

He sat on the bed. Vanessa felt like his eyes were drilling into the side of her head. "I know you," he said gently. "You'll do okay."

"I'm not a boarding school or rules kind of girl. Those nuns will smother me. They'll make me wear stockings and a ridiculous kilt that reaches my ankles, and a tie around my neck, choking me half to death as they tighten the knot."

Liam chuckled. "Look, if you play the game for four more years, you can have all the freedom you want. You'll go off to nursing school, then travel all over the world."

She stood at the window and looked out to the west farm, her sight on the hills in the distance. "I'm scared," she whispered.

"You know there's nothing to be scared of."

How do you describe fear, she mused. What makes one person fretful and someone else breeze through life without a care or concern. Had Liam ever experienced that feeling—where your lungs beg for air, your palms sweat, and you can almost feel the color draining from your face. Where you open your mouth to scream and nothing comes out, not even your breath. "That's easy for you to say."

"Come on, let's go for a ride. You need to blow those cobwebs out of your pretty little head."

Vanessa turned away, a prickling heat creeping up her neck and face. It was the first time he'd called her pretty.

And the first time she'd felt it.

44

As the days of January flew by, Vanessa snuck into Liam's room most nights. And each time, she'd rock herself to sleep while he lay in his bed, listening to her soft breath and the occasional whimper from the floor beside him.

It was the last night of the summer break. The next day, Vanessa would leave for boarding school, and he possibly wouldn't see her for months. For some reason, the thought troubled him. She'd been in his room earlier to make the bed, and as usual, had left a daisy chain on the pillow to indicate the clean sheets. The sight of those tiny linked flowers always made him smile. He leaned over the side of the bed. "Hey," he whispered. "Come up here. Come on."

"No. You'll make me go back to my room."

"I won't, I promise. Come on." He held back the covers. She slipped in beside him. They didn't look at each other once. "What's going on?"

"I told you. The *moko* lady. But, I know you don't believe me."

"Is she there every night?"

"Not to see. But she's there. I know she is."

Silence stretched before them. They didn't generally talk much, and most of the time, Liam had no idea what to say to her. After all, what did they have in common, besides sharing a house? He lay still, listening to her breathe. He couldn't imagine what it would be like to sense things beyond reality, like the woman with the *moko*, and wondered if Ruth had ever taken her to see someone—a counselor or doctor—or if Vanessa had ever voiced her fears to anyone else.

"I have a big room at Dad's." The words brought him back to the present. "And we have a color TV and a swimming pool. And in the office, there's a huge bookcase full of books. We even have a rumpus room with a pool table."

Although Vanessa never spoke much of her home, none of this surprised Liam. When they'd first arrived, he would have described Ruth as glamorous—cultured and well educated. It made sense they were used to living with the finer things of life. "You can read some of my books when you're home next."

"Why would you let me?"
"Because we're friends. Now go to sleep."

THE INTERVIEW

There were four clocks on the wall: Auckland, London, Paris, New York. Vanessa stared as each one ticked through the minutes. It seemed strange to have London, Paris, and New York. Apart from five Japanese girls, there were no other international students at the school. So where was Tokyo? Maybe away for repairs. She checked Auckland. One fifteen. Her mother should have been here by now. Footsteps broke her train of thought as Mick walked into view. Vanessa expected to see her mother two steps behind, but he was alone. She stood to greet him.

"Where's Mum?"

There was no need for Mick to reply. His frown spoke for him.

"She's not coming, is she?"

"I tried, I really did," he said. "She's been in bed all morning. Couldn't even make it to the car let alone down the driveway. I thought about calling your father, but in the end, there wasn't time. She's worried herself sick."

She flopped back down in the seat. "I knew she wouldn't come."

Mick sat beside her. She'd never seen him look so neatly presented. In his corduroy pants, polished boots, and a button-down shirt, he looked out of place. Awkward.

The door to Sister Mary Monica's office opened. "Mr. O'Leary, Vanessa, please come in."

Vanessa followed Mick into the wood-paneled office and took a seat. She'd been in here before, many times, but walking through that door never got any easier. Mick sat upright as Sister Monica offered him tea and banana bread. He declined. Vanessa knew he was uncomfortable around women in authority, especially nuns. They'd talked about it once when Mick was driving her back to school. He said nuns made him feel inadequate. They were holy, and he was flawed and battered and had sinned—like all men.

"I called Mrs. Blinkly in to discuss Vanessa's behavior," the Sister said eventually. "I understand she's appointed you as an intermediary in her absence."

"She has, yes."

"May I speak frankly, Mr. O'Leary?"

"Of course."

"It's important I make myself perfectly clear."

Vanessa shifted in her seat. It made her impatient when people in authority rephrased the same thing to make a point. She wished the headmistress would get on with it instead of treating Mick like one of her pupils.

"I'm all ears," Mick said.

"Good. Because I need to be frank here."

"So you said."

Vanessa caught the slight amusement in Mick's reply.

"Vanessa. Would you like to tell us why we're here?"

"I don't know why we're here, Sister."

"Is that so? Well, it's been brought to my attention that you've been saying some rather unfortunate things around school." The Sister sighed heavily as she linked her hands under her scapular. She looked directly at Mick as if Vanessa wasn't there. "It would seem that Vanessa is growing up too fast, way too fast." She didn't need to add, 'tut-tut,' her expression said it for her. "Do you understand what I'm saying, Mr. O'Leary?"

"Not exactly, no."

"Well, I don't know how to put this without causing embarrassment to the three of us, but it seems Vanessa has informed her peers that she sleeps in the same bed as a much older boyfriend. According to Vanessa, this is a regular occurrence over summer break. She has also discussed subjects of a sexual nature with her dorm mates, including male arousal."

Hundreds of thoughts raced through Vanessa's head, all trying to reach the finish line first. She wanted to see Mick's reaction, but she couldn't bear to look. Her stomach dropped, along with her pride. She pressed her lips together and shoved her hands into her blazer pockets.

"I see," was all Mick managed to say.

"Is this the truth, Vanessa?" Sister Monica asked.

Vanessa swallowed hard, the saliva suddenly absent from her mouth. What should she say? She was in trouble. She'd take the punishment, but she couldn't betray Liam. She repeated Mick's words. "Not exactly."

"So what exactly *is* the situation at home?"

Vanessa didn't reply.

Mick cleared his throat and ran his thumb and forefinger down his lips and chin as if smoothing a beard. "As you know, Mrs. Blinkly is my housekeeper. Vanessa has her own room in my home and has been like a daughter to me since she was ten."

Vanessa noticed Mick didn't mention Liam either.

"That may be so, but Vanessa is definitely displaying the kind of behavior that suggests something is going on. She's withdrawn and has no friends. Also, she's not comfortable in social situations and has been at the center of altercations in the dormitories more than once."

"You mean she fights with the other girls?"

"Oh yes, and quite viciously."

He addressed Vanessa, his expression that of a parent who believed their child could do no wrong. "Why would you do that? Are you bullied?"

She looked away. "Sometimes."

"We do not condone bullies at our school, but we are not immune to the practice." The headmistress sighed. "Our pupils represent a cross-section of society, the same as any other institution, and Vanessa often stands out."

"But surely," Mick said, "if Vanessa's being bullied, something should be done about it."

"Well, unfortunately, if Vanessa refuses to talk, our hands are tied. I'm aware that many of our students have boyfriends. It seems it's the norm these days." She looked at Vanessa. "But if this bedmate story is a fabrication, then please, don't mention it again. If it's not a fabrication ... well, that's an entirely different matter. You're underage, and your parents need to be notified and steps taken to ensure your safety. We are suspending you for the next three days."

"You mean I have to take her home?" Mick asked.

"Precisely, and I would expect a frank and honest discussion between Vanessa and her parents—*both* of her parents—to take place over that time. I understand Vanessa has an active imagination. She's an unusual child, but she has potential, which is why we want to see her continue at the school. She's also a good all-rounder, who excels at swimming and athletics, but her team skills are sadly lacking. Being part of a team is not her forte, and as you may be aware, Mr. O'Leary, 'there's no I in team.'"

Vanessa watched Mick inhale sharply. How she hated that saying. She didn't want to be part of a stupid team. Never had and never would.

"Here at Immaculate Heart," the sister continued, "we pride ourselves on making something of the young women in our care. However, I'm not sure how long we can accommodate this destructive behavior, Vanessa."

"Yes, Sister."

"That brings me to the second reason why we're here." She handed Mick a sheet of paper. "Please give this to Mrs. Blinkly and make sure that on her return, Vanessa has everything on this list. We have asked her repeatedly to bring more clothes from home, but to no avail. How is Vanessa expected to socialize if she has nothing to wear? Even her pajama's and underwear are too small."

Vanessa kept her head down. She'd asked her mother more than once to buy her new clothes, but the promises to do so were never kept.

"I'm sorry, I had no idea," Mick said. "I'll see to it." He went to stand, but sat again, as if the weight of the conversation had pushed him back into the seat.

"I'm fond of you, Vanessa," Sister Monica said. "We have our moments, but you're full of spunk, and I like that. I wouldn't want to see you leave us because you refuse to implement our code of conduct. Is that what you want?"

"No, Sister."

She turned to Mick. "Please have her back here on Monday afternoon at five thirty."

The scene reminded Vanessa of a court of law—as though the headmistress had just banged a gavel down on her desk and she'd have to live with the shame of her sentence for years to come.

They drove home in silence. Whenever Vanessa tried to speak, Mick raised his palm.

When they parked outside the homestead an hour later, they both sat for a few moments. Mick mumbled under his breath, "Fighting with the other girls," and then louder, "What the hell's got into you? Go to your room and don't come out until I say you can."

"But I want to see Whisper."

"You'll do as you're told. You're not on holiday. You've been suspended. And while you're there, think about what you've done, and whether there's any reason why I shouldn't call your father and tell him to come collect you."

"Please, don't tell Dad."

"And what's this business about the clothes? Don't you know how to follow a list and pack a bag?"

Vanessa choked back tears. "I don't have anything to pack."

She jumped from the truck, slamming the door behind her.

INTERNAL CONJECTURE

Liam had no sooner walked through the door than Mick pounced. It had been a long day, and his jeans and t-shirt were covered in grease from the tractor. He'd been looking forward to a hot shower, but it appeared that would have to wait.

"What the hell's been going on with you two?"

Liam strolled to the fridge and grabbed two beers, offering one to Mick, who was making no sense as usual. His father refused the beer. "Who are you talking about?"

"You and Vanessa."

"What do you mean?" Liam frowned and stared at his father. "I've hardly seen the kid lately. I've only been home a week."

"Yeah, well, you'll see her at dinner. She's been suspended."

"Suspended? For what?"

"According to that nun, the school's head, she's been acting up. Telling her dorm mates she has a boyfriend at home who she sleeps with at night. I swear to God, if you've laid a hand on her, I'll wring your bloody neck and you'll be out on your ear."

"Shit." Liam pulled his bottom lip between his teeth and chewed while he formed his reply. He'd worried about this all along. Mick or

Ruth finding out and jumping to conclusions. "I haven't touched her, I swear. But—"

"But?" Mick interrupted. "There's a 'but.' I damn-well knew it."

"It's not what you think, but she sleeps in my room sometimes."

"You can't be serious."

"She's scared of the dark and Ruth couldn't give a damn. She locks her bedroom door and won't let Vanessa in. And she's so hammered, she has no idea whether or not Vanessa needs her. But I've never laid a finger on her, I swear on my mother's grave."

His father hadn't moved from the spot all the time they spoke, and Liam welcomed the physical distance.

"What the hell are you talking about, Liam? Are you sure you haven't interfered with her?"

"Don't be ridiculous, Dad. What do you take me for? I told you I haven't."

"And what do you mean she's scared of the dark? She's a teenager for heaven's sake."

Liam relaxed his shoulders. He understood his father's reaction, but he'd done nothing wrong, so didn't need to feel guilty about anything. "Yes, but you know what Vanessa's like. She's different. You've seen how she is with Whisper. She says she sees a Māori woman with a *moko* in her room sometimes. It scares the life out of her."

"Why haven't you told me this before?"

"I don't know. It seemed easier to let her sneak into my room when she was scared."

Mick studied his son. "But you're a man. You can't have a young girl in your bed, even if she's afraid of the dark. What the hell were you thinking?"

"She's not in my bed." Liam had no intention of telling his father the whole story. Mick didn't need to know Vanessa sometimes slept under the covers. "She sleeps on the floor. Look, I try to keep my distance. Most of the time I pretend I haven't noticed."

"You'd better be telling me the truth, Liam O'Leary."

"What the hell do you think I'd do to her? She's like a sister to me."

"Yes, but she's not your sister, is she? And now she thinks you're her boyfriend."

"That's bullshit."

"Is it? Girls think all sorts of crazy nonsense when they're that age."

Liam sat in the chair at the head of the table. He closed his eyes and massaged his forehead with the fingertips of both hands as he realized how stupid he'd been. "Shit. I'll talk to her. Hopefully, the whole thing will blow over in a few weeks."

"It damn-well better. And there's something else. According to that nun, Vanessa's short on clothes."

"Figures. I never see her out of those jodhpurs."

"So what can we do about that? Ruth won't leave the house to go shopping with her."

Liam thought for a moment. "Leave it to me. I'll have a word with Anna."

When Vanessa came in for dinner that evening, Liam approached her as she left the bathroom. He blocked her way. "We need to talk. Meet me at the stables after dinner."

"Why?"

He lowered his voice and leaned closer. His hand gripped her forearm with a gentle yet firm hold. "It doesn't matter why. Just be there."

All through dinner, Vanessa kept her head down and didn't make eye contact with anyone, not even her mother. If her suspension angered Ruth, she didn't mention it. In fact, Ruth said very little of anything that evening.

It was after seven thirty when Vanessa finally arrived at the stables. Liam was sitting on a small wooden stool at the end of the stalls, legs outstretched, ankles and arms crossed. He could tell by the look on her face she expected an ear bashing.

He grabbed another stool. "Sit." She did as she was told. "So you've been suspended?"

She responded with defiance, her usual reaction to his authority. "So what? It's no big deal."

"It's a huge deal. What will you do if you're expelled?"

"I don't care. There are plenty of other schools."

"Well, you should care. Tell me what's going on? What have you told your friends at school, about us?"

"I don't have any friends at school."

"Why not?"

"Because they tease me. Say I'm weird, and that I'm not pretty, and no boys will ever like me because I don't have … boobs, and what boys want." She sniffed and wiped her nose with the back of her hand. "It doesn't matter anyway. I hate that school. 'Immaculate Heart girls go places.' What a load of crap. I'm an Immaculate Heart girl, and I'm not going anywhere."

He removed a handkerchief from his jean's pocket and handed it to her. "Here." A resigned sadness washed over him. Now he thought about it, he'd never seen her with friends, apart from Anna's younger brother, Billy. "What have you been saying about me?"

The question went unanswered.

"I can't be your boyfriend. You know that don't you?"

She sat still, her shoulders hunched and her fingers busy with the hem of her shirt. "Of course I do. That would be yuck."

"So why did you tell the girls at school you had a boyfriend you sleep with?"

"I never did."

"What exactly did you say?"

"I can't remember."

"So, do you have a boyfriend? What about Billy Cook?"

"As if. I don't even like him that way."

"What way?"

"Stop asking me. I can't explain it."

"You can't talk about me like I'm your boyfriend, because I'm not and never will be."

"But you like me like I'm your girlfriend."

Vanessa's words were barely a whisper, and while she didn't look directly at him, his eyes were fixed squarely on hers. He shook his head, again realizing what a huge mistake he'd made by allowing her nightly visits. "Why do you say that?"

"Because in the morning … your thingy gets hard. The girls at school said when a guy likes you, his thingy gets hard."

Liam muttered a few 'shits' under his breath. "Look, you're too young to be talking about this. Besides, you're like my kid sister, and brothers and sisters shouldn't sleep in the same bed."

"I'm not your kid sister. I already have half-brothers, and I don't need another one."

"I know that, but you have to stay in your room from now on, and you need to go back to school on Monday and knuckle down. Once you've finished school, the world's your oyster."

"Really? Where in the world am I going? Off to some posh university? Away to London, New York, or Paris, like it says on the back of those fancy shampoo bottles? As if."

"Get a good education, and you can go wherever you like." He waited for her to reply, but she said nothing. "Have you been saving your pocket money?"

"I don't get pocket money."

"How do you buy what you need?"

She shrugged.

Liam leaned back against a vertical support post, his gaze fixed on hers. She looked away. He'd often wondered how her life must be, but tonight was the first time he'd fully grasped her predicament.

"Can I go now?" The question came soft and unsure. Her arms formed a shield across her front as her feet kicked at blades of straw covering the stable floor.

"Go on." She turned to leave. Liam reached out and grabbed her hand—it sat cold and limp in his. He pulled her back without force. It wasn't up to him to parent the kid, but he knew she received little or no guidance from her mother. "You understand?"

Tears tracked down her cheeks and dripped off the tiny cleft in her chin. He pulled her closer as the need to protect her rushed at him. She nodded and pulled away.

He let go.

Later, as the house stilled, and Ruth and Vanessa were in bed, father and son resumed their conversation.

"Did you talk to her?" Mick asked.

"Yep."

"And she understands?"

"How the hell would I know? But I do know she's not getting that pocket money."

Mick sighed. "I'm not surprised. I should have given it to her myself instead of to Ruth. It'll be gone—tipped down Ruth's throat. She hasn't even asked me what Sister Monica said. Still, I expect she'll ask in the morning. She's not so good at night."

"Or any time."

"Did you talk to Anna?"

"Yep. She's going to Clifton Falls on Monday. She'll drop Vanessa back at school after they've been shopping."

"Right. I'll get some cash out of the safe."

"Good luck convincing Vanessa."

THE SUEDE WAISTCOAT

SPRING, 1976

Through the smudged window of the northbound bus, Vanessa noticed Liam leaning on the hood of his pickup at the end of the driveway. She glanced at the other passengers, wondering who he could be waiting for. As she disembarked onto the road verge, Liam stepped forward to grab her bag. He flung it onto the tray.

"Who are you waiting for?" Vanessa asked.

"You. I saw the bus. Thought you might be on it."

He looked different, his skin clear and tanned, and he'd grown another inch or so over the past year. His hair was longer too, the loose waves touching his shoulders, but the most significant difference was in his physique—he'd filled out, especially around his upper body. Vanessa frowned when she noticed him staring back at her, his smoky eyes still.

"Is everything okay?" she asked. "With Mum, I mean?"

"What? Yes, fine."

"Can I go see Whisper?"

"Course you can, I'll put your bag in your room."

"Thanks." She walked toward the poplars without looking back.

"And, Vanessa?"

She turned. She'd never been shy around him, but since her school suspension, there had been a subtle shift in their relationship—an awkwardness had crept in.

"I left a bag on your bed."

"What do you mean?"

"One of my friends had a clear out. I thought you might like her cast-offs."

"Why?" She didn't mean to sound ungrateful, but her tone took on a mind of its own. "Mick bought me some things, so I'm good."

"Take a look anyway. If you're not interested, I'll pass them on to someone else. See you soon."

She trudged up the hill with a heavy step. Whisper approached with reluctance as she leaned on the fence and called his name—shy of her after the time they'd been apart. She thought about how many of life's relationships were like that. Full of uncertainty, almost as though absence made the heart grow shyer.

After a quick hello to her mother, she went to her room, curiosity getting the better of her. Sitting on her bed next to the bag, she slowly unzipped the top opening. She reached inside, pulled out two pairs of jeans and draped them over the chair. She looked back in the bag, wondering why his friend would want to give all those clothes away.

When she'd finished the inspection, shorts, t-shirts, and a muslin top joined the jeans. There was even a pair of leather sandals with ankle straps, and a colorful, flounced peasant skirt. But the jewel in the crown was a brown suede waistcoat with tassels that fell from under the bust line. Vanessa had wanted a suede waistcoat ever since she'd seen one of the girls from school wearing one. But now, as she rubbed the soft suede between her fingertips, she struggled with the concept of pride versus want and need.

She had never let herself love clothes like her peers. There was no point. Now, she had a choice. A choice she didn't know how to make.

"I can't take those clothes."

Liam glanced up from his sketchpad as she entered his room. She hadn't bothered to knock. He closed it and placed it on the nightstand. "Come in, why don't you?" He waited for her to continue, but she didn't. "Why not?"

"Because, what would Mum say?"

"Probably nothing. It's no big deal."

"But why doesn't your friend want them?"

"Honest truth?"

"Is there any other type, of truth I mean?"

Liam huffed a chuckle. "They don't fit. She's bought new stuff."

"I don't need hand-me-downs."

Liam looked her up and down. She sensed his penchant for reverse psychology was about to make its presence felt.

"Suit yourself. I'll give them to Anna to pass on. Christie doesn't want them back."

She smiled to herself. No matter how desperate her situation was, she often found Liam amusing and could read him like a book. "I'll pack them up for her."

"Sit. Tell me about school. Are you behaving?"

"Like an angel on a cloud."

He laughed. "You're not breaking too many hearts with those Saint Frank's boys?"

"As if. We only see them at school sports and drama club." She turned to leave.

"Don't treat me as the enemy," Liam said. "I'm on your side. Keep the clothes."

"I don't have a side." Vanessa spoke her truth. The truth she'd believed since her tenth birthday. "I'm stuck in the middle. All by myself."

As soon as she'd helped with the dinner dishes, Vanessa rushed back to her bedroom and tried everything on, not only once, but two or three times. Between fittings, she lay each piece on the bed and imagined where she would wear her new wardrobe, as if it belonged to her. But by bedtime, she'd promised herself she would return the clothes to Liam's room first thing in the morning.

The trouble was, when she opened her wardrobe the next day to find something to wear, her clothes seemed old and small and threadbare.

She unzipped the bag, pulled out a baby blue t-shirt and a pair of white cotton shorts, and held them up for size. When she slipped the t-shirt over her head, she felt different. Alive and excited and all brand new.

Over breakfast, she sensed Liam's stare as she served the men toast and scrambled eggs. As she handed him his coffee, he thanked her with a smile. She'd never felt so special, or so undeserving.

The blossoming of Vanessa Blinkly had begun.

NEW FRIENDS

Late in the morning of the same day, after the beds were changed, and the bathroom cleaned, her mother sent Vanessa to the general store with a scribbled list and instructions to charge the groceries to Mick's account. Mick handed her a dollar as she left the house—just enough for a Coke—and as she walked along the highway in her new suede waistcoat, she felt happier than she had in a long time.

On the way back, she sat on a bench at the playground, drinking her Coke and watching the world go by, wishing she could go some-where too. Vanessa didn't pay much attention to Billy Cook as he hurried past on his farm bike, until he did a U-turn and stopped in front of her.

"Vanessa. Hi." Billy removed his aviators and grinned, displaying perfectly straightened teeth. She hadn't seen him without braces before, and he looked different—handsome. "I'm off home. Do you want a ride up the hill?"

"No, I'm fine."

Billy flicked down the stand of his bike and joined her on the bench. He reached for her Coke and took a cheeky sip. "How's it going at Immaculate Heart? I heard you were suspended for fighting."

"Who told you that?"

"Word gets around."

"I guess it does." Silence stretched before them. Vanessa was never one to fill a void with meaningless words, but she enjoyed talking to Billy. "I'd leave school as soon as I turn fifteen, but I want to go nursing, so ..."

"Yeah, I feel the same way about Saint Frank's, but I want to be an architect. So I guess we're both stuck for a few more years yet." Billy stood and offered his hand. "Come on. I'll give you a ride. That backpack must weigh a ton."

She hesitated. "I don't know."

"I'm not supposed to ride on the highway until I get my license, so we'll have to go cross country." He grinned again and shot her a sly wink. "Takes a bit longer, but it's heaps more fun."

Vanessa slung her backpack over her shoulders and straddled the bike, and as he followed a farm track that ran beside the highway toward O'Leary's, she couldn't remember a time when she'd felt so alive.

She tapped him on the shoulder when they reached the mailbox, knowing if her mother saw her with Billy, she would jump to conclusions. "I'd better walk the rest of the way. Thanks for the ride."

Billy lifted his chin toward Whisper. "So that's the gelding? Looks like a mean bastard. People say you tamed him."

"People say a lot of things. We understand each other, that's all."

"You know Nikau Hughes, right? His parents have a farm down Tuckers Road. His sister wants you to look at her horse, Tosca. We could ride over this afternoon if you want?"

Vanessa didn't know what to make of Billy's request. She'd met him at an inter-school's drama club, and sometimes they were on the same bus from Clifton Falls, but they weren't close friends. "I don't usually look at horses unless I'm with Dad. Anyway, I have to help Mum with the dinner prep straight after lunch."

"I'll wait under the bridge around two thirty. If you're not there by quarter to three, I'll know you're not coming."

Vanessa hesitated for a moment. Apart from Whisper, she'd never worked with a horse on her own before. "I don't know."

"She said she'd pay you."

"So you're not worried about what people say about me?"

He laughed. "What? That you're a witch?"

She frowned her response, allowing a little of her hurt to show. She knew the girls at school gossiped about her and called her weird, but she hadn't realized they called her a witch.

"Doesn't bother me," he said. "See you later."

The universe had blessed Billy Cook with heart-melting good looks, long black hair, and eyes so blue they could pierce the darkest of night. Even at fourteen, he exuded maturity. She sensed theirs would never be a boyfriend-girlfriend bond, but as she watched him ride away, she relaxed. Billy was a nice guy. Kind and accepting, and she wanted to be his friend.

But when Vanessa arrived at the designated spot just after two thirty, Billy wasn't alone. She pulled her mount, Kingi, to a stop several yards from the bridge as she eyed the two boys with interest. They moved forward.

"You two know each other, right?" Billy asked.

The other boy looked Vanessa up and down and greeted her with a lift of his chin. "Nikau." He offered a warm dimple-filled smile. "You go to Immaculate Heart, right?"

Vanessa nodded as Kingi stepped back under her command.

"Thanks for agreeing to help out," Nikau said. "My sister loves Tosca, but she's hard work. Roxanne's nervous around her."

"Don't thank me yet. I haven't done anything."

"Come on," he continued. "We'll take a shortcut across Rata River Road. The farm's not far from there."

They rode along the river track until they reached the old pump house. Carefully guiding his mount up the steep bank, Nikau led the way past the lavender farm and across the back of his parents' property. The early afternoon sun warmed Vanessa's back, and for a moment, she relaxed. But, as the stables came into view, she started having second thoughts. The girls at school already thought she was weird—and called her a witch, apparently. She didn't want Nikau and Billy thinking the same, then talking about her behind her back.

Vanessa sensed Tosca straightaway and could feel the horse's fear as she moved closer. Dismounting, she watched the boys do the same. A striking older girl strolled across the lawn from the house, her eyes a similar tone to Tosca's mid brown coat. "Hi, I'm Roxanne. Thanks for coming."

"No problem." The words flowed from Vanessa out of habit, not because she truly meant them. She disliked meeting new people, especially older girls. "How old is she?"

"Nearly five," Roxanne said.

"It's a good age to work with." Vanessa looked at Billy and Nikau. "It's okay if you watch, but can you stand back?" Roxanne and Vanessa stepped closer to Tosca, and Nikau and Billy moved to the opposite fence. "You're scared of her? What happened?"

"Her last owner did a crap job of looking after her. The first time I went near her, she got me good with a swift kick. I'm nervous around her now. But, she's hard to resist, if you know what I mean."

"Sure." Vanessa's voice never raised above a murmur, and all the time she spoke to Roxanne, her eyes focused on Tosca. She'd always been a deep thinker, even as a little girl—wondering about the world and the people in it, but when it came to her bond with horses, there was no 'why.'

"Remember the difference between fear and respect," she said to Roxanne. "Stay alert, but still treat her like she's your best friend. Use your breath to calm her and make a connection. Horses greet each other by touch, so first, I'll slowly run my hand from her neck to her withers." Vanessa stepped forward, offered her hand, and whispered to Tosca. She held her ground, and the horse stepped back first.

"Keep your touch firm, and when you walk away, leave her wanting more. You're in control, but she's your partner. And remember, don't expect miracles. Like any other relationship, you need to work at it."

The fear of disapproval vanished as Vanessa shifted her concentration to Tosca. When she finally signaled for Roxanne to join her, forty minutes had passed.

"How do you do that?" Roxanne asked.

"My father works with horses. I've watched him all my life." Vanessa looked at Tosca. "I'll come back to check on her if that's okay?"

"Thanks. I'd like that. So, how much do I owe you?"

"Oh, I don't want anything, but thank you." She turned to Billy. "I'd better get going."

"Sure." He jumped off the fence. "I'll ride back with you."

They didn't speak until they stopped under Rata River bridge to say goodbye. Vanessa caught Billy's stare and frowned. "What?"

"You. That's what. You're amazing."

Vanessa felt the heat sweep up her face and neck. She'd never been praised by one of her peers before. "Not really. I just love horses more than people."

Billy laughed. "You know Nikau has a huge crush on you?"

"As if." She shrugged and cantered off.

1 4

UNFAIR ADVANCES

When Liam arrived at the stables later that afternoon, Kingi and Vanessa were gone. He'd told her repeatedly not to ride alone, but his words fell on deaf teenage ears. It was five thirty when she finally rode up the driveway. Liam waited for her to dismount before he let rip.

"Where have you been?"

She led Kingi through the stable gate, her back ramrod straight and her chin held high. "With Billy."

He followed, watching her fill the trough from the hose attached to the fence. "You could've left a note."

"Sorry, I must have forgotten." Vanessa walked back through the gate. She still hadn't looked him in the eye.

"What's with the attitude?"

"I hardly ever see you, and when I do, suddenly you're all over me with the whole 'where have you been' routine. I'm not a kid. Stop trying to tell me what to do."

He had no idea why she was in such a shitty mood. Sure, she didn't like to be told off, but he didn't have to put up with her brattish behavior. "Firstly, you are still a kid. Second, Kingi is my horse, so if you want to ride him, leave a note. Understand?"

"Yes, sir."

"And stop the crap, or you can forget about riding, period." Liam picked up a twenty-four pack of beer from the stable floor. "And if you want to know where *I'm* going, I'll be in the shearing shed with the guys."

"Can I come?"

"Seriously?" Liam couldn't believe how her mood could change in an instant when she wanted something. "No. You're too young."

"You never let me have any fun. And if I try, you want to know all the details."

Vanessa's attitude amused him. She was a real contradiction. Feisty as hell during the day and as scared as a little mouse at night. "Yeah, so? I care about you, sis."

"Well don't. I don't need anyone caring about me. And I'm not your sis. You're just trying to wind me up."

Liam usually enjoyed hanging out with the shearing gang over a few beers. But that evening, he had other things on his mind. Things like Ava Rigby.

Ava worked at the village bakery during university breaks, and Liam had eaten more donuts and meat pies that year than ever before. They'd spent the odd night together throughout the year, but she wasn't interested in a serious relationship, which suited Liam just fine. He'd never met a girl who played the field and made no bones about it. She used him, and he didn't mind one little bit. He'd called her earlier, asking if she wanted to meet up and with some reluctance, she'd eventually agreed.

Liam looked over and saw Vanessa standing at the shed's entrance, a small basket in her hands. He shook his head and put his beer down, then pushed off the bench seat and made his way over to her. "What are you doing here?"

"Mum sent me with chips and dip."

He took the basket. "Thanks. Now go back to the house."

A young fencer named Steve Brown looked Vanessa up and down

and spoke. "Don't be such a mean bastard. She's not doing any harm. Let her stay." He held out a hand to Vanessa. "Come over here, sweetheart."

Liam glared at Vanessa, ignoring Steve's comments. "Vanessa, what did I say? Go back to the house."

Tears welled up in her eyes, and she sucked in her bottom lip to compose herself. "I hate you," she whispered, but she still didn't leave.

"You've upset her now. Let her stay." Steve smirked, then glanced at his mates for approval he didn't receive. "I'll look after her."

"I bet you would," Liam said.

"What the fuck does that mean?"

Liam shot Vanessa a pointed look and cocked his head toward the homestead. She turned on her heel and stormed out of the shed.

"She's only fourteen," he said to Steve. "You're what, early twenties? I'd keep my dirty thoughts to myself if I were you."

"Fourteen's fair game where I come from. If there's grass on her little mound, she's ready to play ball."

"What the hell?" Liam shoved Steve with both hands. "Piss off."

Steve spat at Liam's feet. "You're a gutless white boy, just like your stuck-up friends. University posers who think they're better than the rest of us."

"Don't play the race card with me. This has nothing to do with a trickle of Māori blood, which we *both* have in our veins. Where the hell do you think I get my olive skin from?"

"Don't you dare call yourself a Māori around me, you pansy-faced asshole."

"Assholes come in all colors," he murmured. "It just so happens, yours is more tainted than most. Why the hell Dad ever hires you I don't know."

"Because you're not up to it, boy. Lazy prick."

"Hey, you two." The foreman of the gang walked over to them and gave Steve a shove. "Cut it out, Steve. You're way out of line. I think you'd better leave, don't you? And show some goddamn respect next time."

When Liam came in from the shed around ten, Vanessa's light was still on. He moved quietly down the hallway and into her bedroom. He sat on her bed, but her gaze stayed firmly on the novel in her hands. "You okay?"

She slammed the book shut and placed it on her nightstand. When he reached out to touch her, she shrugged away, moving as far over on the bed as possible, and covered her head with the sheet.

"Don't be mad. I'm just trying to protect you." He rubbed his hand over her back and shoulders. "Come on. Talk to me." She remained silent. "The reason I didn't want you in the shed tonight is because you're too young to be around guys who are drinking."

Her muffled voice came from under the sheet. "I only wanted to see what you were doing."

"Yeah, well … it's inappropriate at your age."

"I'm fourteen."

"And some guys see you as fair game."

She turned over now, her face wet with tears. "What do you mean?"

"Let's leave it at that." He stood and looked down at her while he chose his next words, then decided to say nothing more.

"I just want to belong."

"But you don't belong. Not in that situation."

Liam shut the door without another word. When he reached his bedroom, the daisy chain she'd left on his pillow that morning had been torn into pieces and strewn all over his freshly made bed.

15

NEW MOON

Vanessa lay in the dark and mulled over Liam's words. She knew about sex and what he was referring to. Sometimes she wished she had a boyfriend. Someone who loved and cared about her—who made her the center of his world. Liam said she didn't belong, and she wondered if she would ever belong, anywhere. She had liked it when he rubbed her back. She didn't want to, but her mother never touched her anymore, neither did her father for that matter. No one ever touched her now.

Hours later—when all that could be heard was Mick's loud snore and the soft hoot of a barn owl outside—Vanessa snuck along the hallway to the opposite side of the house. She carefully turned the doorknob and pushed open Liam's bedroom door.

With the new moon, the night sky was as black as a mineshaft. Even though a lamp on the veranda post glowed dimly across the lawn outside, she couldn't see him in the darkness.

"Liam?" She shook his shoulder. "Liam?" she repeated as she reached for the switch on the bedside lamp. A firm hand gripped her wrist.

"Ouch."

"Don't." He barely spoke above a whisper but kept his grip tight. "Get out of here and go back to bed."

"But—"

He released her arm. "I said, go back to bed."

She couldn't see his face, but the grit of his teeth was evident in his tone.

Then, another voice in the dark. "Liam, what's going on? Who are you talking to?"

Vanessa froze. The voice wasn't familiar, but it was definitely female.

"No one," he soothed. "Go back to sleep, babe."

In the seconds that followed, Vanessa—with her sight now adjusted to the darkness—watched as Liam turned away from her and pulled his half-naked bedmate closer. She heard the girl murmur and Liam say, "shush"—the tone soothing and soft, his attention solely on her as their bodies wrapped around each other.

Vanessa tiptoed from Liam's room, making it as far as the living room, where she grabbed a blanket from Mick's favorite chair and snuggled down on the couch. She understood betrayal, but this new sensation had an added intensity. Now, she was no one at all. Just a girl who slept down the hall in a house full of people who didn't want her around.

A girl who never belonged.

At dinner the following day, Vanessa couldn't bear to look at Liam. He didn't seem to notice; his attention focused instead on talk of crop rotation, subsidies, and wool prices. He and Mick sat at the table long after dinner was over. The discussion progressed to diversification, biodynamics, and other words she didn't understand, with Liam talking like an adult and Mick shaking his head in disagreement. Vanessa made them cups of tea and offered fruitcake, then reset the table for breakfast.

Occasionally Liam would shoot her a sideways glance, but his expression conveyed preoccupation. He and Mick were talking business, and Vanessa toiling away in the kitchen was a regular occurrence. So much so that no one even noticed her.

Mick left the table first. Liam sat in silence until she reached for the cups and plate in front of him.

"You all right?"

"Why wouldn't I be?"

"About last night. I'm sorry I was short with you."

She said nothing as she rinsed the dishes before filling the sink with scalding hot water and detergent.

"Here"—he reached for the tea towel hanging over her shoulder and grabbed a plate from the dish rack—"let me dry."

They did the dishes in silence. Once finished, Vanessa plunged a dishrag into the soapy water and wiped the counter and stovetop, still without a word.

"You're full of banter tonight," Liam said.

"What's there to say?"

"You could ask me how my day was."

"And you could kid yourself I give a shit."

Vanessa stormed out the back door, heading for the stables. Once there, she sat on the bench just inside the door and muttered under her breath about the state of the stalls and why she had to do all the work around the place herself. She picked up her saddle and the saddle soap from the shelf and buffed the leather like her life depended on it.

Liam left in his pickup soon after. She had no idea where he went in the evenings. Probably to the pub in the village to meet up with the half-naked girl from the night before. *Babe.* She kept telling herself it wasn't her business, but that didn't stop her thinking about it.

When she returned to the house around ten, she once again lay on the couch in the living room, struggling for warmth under the thin blanket. She stayed awake for what seemed like hours, and tossed and turned, not only her body, but her thoughts as well.

.   .   .

"Vanessa?" She woke with a start, her eyes straining to focus as Liam shook her gently. That sweet smell of hops and yeast wafted on his breath. She hated the stench of alcohol on her mother, but for some reason, on Liam, it smelled different. "It's after three. Come on, time for bed."

"I want to stay here."

"You're freezing." He picked her up, still covered in the blanket. Vanessa's arms instinctively wrapped around his neck, and she closed her eyes and inhaled deeply as he carried her down the hall. He lay her on the bed and helped pull back the covers. He was so tall now, over six feet, and he loomed over her. "Do you want a drink of water?"

She shook her head. She was still mad at him, but she couldn't deny that she liked the security of being in his arms, liked his smell, and the way his hair brushed against his shoulders. Liked the way he looked at her right at that very moment. Liked—

"Sleep well, Ness."

16

THE LAST SUMMER

1977

The bus from Clifton Falls usually went past just after two, and sure enough, at six minutes past, the hydraulic brakes hissed as the driver pulled onto the road verge. Mick had recently trimmed the shrubs surrounding the yard, and as Liam peered out the kitchen window, he now had a clear view from the house to the highway.

Vanessa stepped into view, the usual small suitcase held tightly across her front, and her slight frame overshadowed by the spruce plantation on the neighboring farm. She waited while the bus pulled away, then looked up, her gaze on the homestead.

He grabbed his keys, and as he drove down the drive, smiled. She was home. Vanessa always said she had no home, but that wasn't true. As far as he was concerned, she would always be welcome at the farm, and he knew Mick felt the same. Any respect he'd initially held for Ruth had long gone, but Vanessa belonged in his world.

Cutting the engine, he jumped out of the cab. "Do you want a lift?"

Vanessa didn't often make eye contact for more than a moment, and today was no exception. Some days, he wanted to grab her face, hold her still, and make her look at him.

"I'll walk."

"How have you been?"

She shuffled her tennis shoes in the dirt as he flung her case on the tray of his pickup. "Not bad."

"I'm just going to the store. Do you want to come?" Liam stared. From her face along the curve of her neck and beyond. They had only seen each other twice over the past year, the last time a few months before, but in some ways, it seemed like a lifetime ago. "Hop in."

She hesitated. "I'd better go see Mum. She's expecting me."

"She's not here. The old man went to town, so she tagged along. They won't be back until later tonight."

Vanessa looked straight ahead. He sensed her disappointment. After all, it was her fifteenth birthday and her mother wasn't even at home to celebrate with her.

"She went to town?" The wind picked up her muslin skirt, and she held it down with her hands. "What for?"

"She's visiting a sick cousin or something. Maybe it's a step in the right direction." He smiled, but she wouldn't meet his gaze. "You coming?"

"No, I'll get settled in."

"Do you want anything from the store?" He knew what the answer would be, but he asked anyway.

"No thanks, I'm good."

As Vanessa walked up the hill toward the house, she noticed Whisper wasn't in his usual spot. Although right now, the hurt of her mother's rejection meant she didn't want to face him anyway. Self-indulgence was a trait she had recently vowed to curb. Karen was always prattling on about positive thinking, telling her to choose her thoughts wisely, but today she needed time to wallow—just for a while.

She opened the door to the kitchen and placed her bag on the sideboard. The familiar smell of fried fat and chopped onions filled her nostrils. Any happiness of the day faded as she moved through the house to her bedroom.

She stood on the threshold of the tiny room for a moment. *Goose-*

bumps. Soft light washed the walls a pale lemon—a reflection of the summer's daylight muted through the closed curtains. *Goosebumps.* The stale air hung like a thick fog, and she quickly opened the window. She sat on the bed, the hair on her neck lifting as she glanced up at the corner of the room. *Goosebumps.*

Her return to the valley always brought with it a measure of dread. She preferred to stay at her father's. At least there, she could relax into their family routine almost as if she belonged, even if it no longer felt like home. But then, there was Liam. She had missed him, but their interaction earlier seemed different. Awkward like before, but somehow intensified.

Physically, he was different as well—now a grown man. He'd always had strong features, as if everything on his face was a little too large. The heavy brows over stormy blue eyes, the strong nose, and the pronounced chin—now covered with a patchy beard—seemed to fit better now. His broad mouth—courtesy of his Māori heritage—and full lips, were vibrant with color, and his hair was longer, too. To Vanessa, he looked like a movie star.

She couldn't sleep in his bed anymore. He'd made that clear last summer. She'd talked to her stepmother about boys and Karen had explained sex without embarrassment. However, Karen was pregnant again, and Vanessa struggled with the thought of her father and Karen being intimate. Every time she looked at them, she felt embarrassed, offended.

She didn't know how long she'd been lying down, but by the time Liam returned, soft tears misted her vision and fell in tiny droplets down her cheeks. He knocked softly on her bedroom door, entered without waiting and placed her suitcase on the old chair in the corner of the room, and a Coke and Sante bar on her nightstand. She stilled—feeling nervous—and kept her eyes averted from his.

"Hey." He sat on the bed next to her and reached for her hand. "You okay?" Gentle thumbs smoothed a trail over the back of her left knuckles. "Don't be upset. I bought you a Coke and some chocolate."

She whispered her thanks as she looked at the treats on the nightstand. "I don't want to be here."

"I guessed as much."

"Mum doesn't care whether I'm here or not."

"Yes, she does. She just didn't know you were coming home today, that's all." His index finger lifted her chin slightly. "And look at you. You're all grown up, with your ears pierced."

She retreated from his touch. "I told her I'd be home today."

"Don't be mad. She does her best."

"You think being wasted most days is doing her best?" There was no malice in her tone; she was merely stating a fact. One she couldn't alter, no matter how much she wished she could.

Liam didn't address the 'wasted' comment, and she wondered if she'd spoken out of turn.

"Happy Birthday, by the way."

She wiped her eyes with the back of her hand and blew her nose with a handkerchief plucked from the hem of her cardigan sleeve. "Thanks. I came back early to spend it with Mum, and she's not even here."

He rose from the bed. Vanessa fiddled with the handkerchief, her eyes cast downward. She'd thought the hurt would get easier to deal with as she got older, but the opposite seemed true. When she was younger, she'd sometimes wondered, if she willed it hard enough, would her mother come back to her? But as Vanessa slipped into her sixteenth year, she realized that wishing could never change her mother's path. The only path Vanessa could change was her own.

"Come to my room when you're ready, I have a present for you."

She glanced up. "What kind of present?"

"A birthday present."

17

NIGHT THUNDER

Liam closed Vanessa's door and stood staring at the doorknob for a moment, then stepped away, returning to his room at the other end of the house. He quickly made the bed and picked up a pair of dirty jeans off the floor, throwing them into the hamper. Sitting at the small desk, he held the gift he'd wrapped earlier, unable to get the sight of Vanessa's disappointment in Ruth out of his mind.

He smiled when she knocked on his door twenty minutes later. "Come in. You don't have to knock"

She stayed in the doorway. "I've been thinking … about what you said last time. I understand why I can't sleep in here. It would look bad if Mum or Mick found out. People believe what they want to, don't they? No matter how innocent things are." She moved to the bed and sat on the edge at the foot, her gaze cast downward as she fidgeted with the hem of her blouse, her usual response to discomfort.

"I guess. How have you been sleeping, anyway?"

"Good." The faint dark circles under her eyes told him otherwise.

"I wondered if you understood when we talked last year."

"Not so much then. But I do now. You're a man, and I'm a girl. It's not appropriate."

A long pause followed as he let her words sink in. "Here." He handed her the package wrapped in navy blue paper and tied with a baby-blue ribbon.

"Thank you." She managed a small smile. "I love blue." She carefully untied the ribbon and pulled back the paper. *"Blue Sky – Night Thunder."* She turned the sleeve over and read the list of tracks. "I've never had an LP of my own before."

"Every time I hear the first track, I think of you and Whisper."

"Why's that?"

"It's about a girl on a horse, and freedom, maybe." He took the record and placed it on the turntable, then sat back on the bed as the first track began. She lowered herself to the floor and crossed her legs, her head resting on the side of the bed, and eyes closed until the last note of 'Wildfire' played.

"Play it again. I love that song."

He realigned the stylus, then sat on the floor next to her and reached into the pocket of his jeans. "Here." He handed her a small square of pink tissue paper.

"For me too?"

"Just a little something extra."

With unsteady fingers, Vanessa pulled the Scotch tape away from the tissue. Inside, a tiny horseshoe attached to a gold chain caught a ray of sunlight streaming through the window. She held it in her hands, her eyes wide, and swallowed hard before she spoke. "It's beautiful."

"Here, let me put it on."

Vanessa held her hair off her neck as Liam reached around her. His fingers fumbled as he secured the tiny clasp, his breath warm on her skin. She closed her eyes for a second—sensing his touch, his closeness. The horseshoe sat neatly in the small hollow at the base of her throat. She lowered her head and touched the charm.

"According to superstition, horseshoes bring good luck if they're hung upright." He leaned back against the edge of the bed as the LP played through the song.

"Why did you buy me presents?"

"Because, you're like the kid sister I never had."

Her hand touched the horseshoe again, small fingers smoothing over the shape. "I don't know what to say. Thank you."

He lifted himself back onto the bed. "It looks good on you. Get your butt up here." She stiffened when Liam reached over and pulled her up beside him.

They sat on his large bed, a bed she'd once shared with him without hesitation, but now, her reluctance showed. She moved to get comfortable—sensing the familiarity of their friendship, yet also noticing a subtle difference. Liam moved closer. Their arms touched as he rubbed the pads of his fingers gently back and forth over the knuckles of his other hand.

"I should unpack," she said finally.

"Stay a bit longer."

They stayed that way for some time, her eyes drifting in and out of focus as she relaxed. Neither one spoke until the stylus swept across the center of the record and stopped.

"I brought some of my LPs home, for you to play while I'm away."

"Can I? Really?"

"Sure." He looked at her, smiled and pushed himself off the bed. "I better go feed the dogs. What are you doing tonight?"

"Oh, um. I might phone Billy and Nikau. See if they want to hang out."

"Okay. Otherwise, I'll shout you a burger. We can eat at the beach."

"But it's Saturday night. Don't you usually go out with your friends on Saturday?"

"I'm meeting them later," he said quietly. "I'll be back in half an hour. That'll give you time to go talk to that crazy bastard of a horse. He needs a good ride, but he has a gash on his hock, so you'll have to wait a few days. He's over by the barn."

"How did you manage that?"

"With great difficulty. He'll be pleased you're home."

As Liam left the room, Vanessa flopped back on the bed, stared at the ceiling and sighed. She rolled over, buried her face in his pillow and inhaled. The bedding in the house usually smelled musty, the result of years of use and laundering, but Liam's had a distinct aroma—one that swamped her in feelings of calmness, and another sensation she didn't want to think about.

Vanessa was waiting in the kitchen when Liam returned from the kennels. She glanced up as he walked in, and he smiled to himself, still trying to get his head around the change in her. "Did you get hold of the boys?"

"No, they're not home."

"Okay, I'll jump in the shower. Be ready in ten minutes."

As they drove into the village, Vanessa gazed out the window as Liam hummed to a song on the radio. He glanced her way. She was no longer all teeth and white-blonde pigtails with wispy strands of hair that moved to the side of her forehead. Vanessa had matured into a beautiful girl, with a golden summer tan and tiny freckles sprinkled over the bridge of her nose.

As he drove, he lost himself in the music and his thoughts. He'd met a girl, Christie, the first year of University, and they'd recently started dating. They hadn't been intimate, not yet anyway, and he was still unsure of his feelings for her. He liked her a lot, but wondered if their friendship would turn into something more.

"What kind of burger do you want?" he asked as they pulled into a parking space outside the valley's only burger bar.

"A cheeseburger. And fries."

"Okay, stay put. It's a bit rough down here at this time of day."

As Liam placed their order, he gave a casual hello to the other regulars. Having grown up in the valley, he knew most of the locals, but he had little in common with guys of his age who worked in the district. He moved outside and sat at one of the tables provided. Steve Brown wandered over and sat opposite him. "What are you up to tonight, O'Leary?"

"Not much." Liam preferred to avoid the company of men like

Steve. Men ready for easy women, easy money, and hard fights. With a long mullet and arms full of tattoos, he was the kind of bad boy girls went for. Liam had seen him in action many times. Charming as hell until he got what he wanted, then he'd revert to slimy-bastard mode before moving on to his next victim.

"A few of the guys are off to a party down Rata River Road. You keen?"

"I'm busy."

Steve turned his head toward Vanessa sitting in the pickup. "Well look at that. I see your little sister's back." He raised his eyebrows and smirked. "She legal yet?"

"Piss off. I warned you last time. Don't talk about her like that."

"Lucky bastard. She's a cute package with that tight little ass. I saw her on that crazy horse a few months back when I was fencing up the gully. If she rides you like she rides that gelding, you'll be in heaven."

The heat rose in Liam's blood as he shot Vanessa a sideways glance. When he turned his attention back to Steve, all self-control vanished. "Say any more, and I'll fucking deck you."

"There's nothing like a bit of tight young pussy, eh?"

Liam's hands tightened into fists. "What did I just say? Shut the fuck up."

"I'm just having you on, you stupid prick," Steve said, his smirk still in place. "That's the trouble with you stuck-up university boys, you lose your sense of humor." He spat in the dirt.

Liam stood and stared Steve down. He wanted to wipe the smirk off his stupid face but knew it wouldn't solve anything. "You need to learn to shut your damn mouth." An angry finger pointed in Steve's direction as Liam took a step closer. "And keep away from her, understand?"

A guy in a white apron approached with Liam's order.

"Have a good night," Steve said, the smirk back on his pockmarked face.

"Screw you." Liam strode to the truck and jumped into the cab, slamming the door before driving off.

Vanessa looked out the window at Steve staring back. "What was that all about?"

Liam glanced her way, knowing his expression held no warmth. "Stay away from that bastard, understand? He's trouble."

"What do you mean?"

"Let's just say he has his eye on you."

"But I don't even know him."

"Make sure you keep it that way."

They sat in silence as he followed the dusty gravel road toward the beach. He pulled up beside a rocky outcrop that sheltered the small bay from a persistent southerly drifting up the coast. Even with its strong undertows and angry waves, Liam loved this stretch of the Pacific. The view from the shore never ceased to invigorate him.

They walked side by side down a sandy track toward the surf, a rug tucked under his arm and their takeout in a brown paper bag in his other hand. An orange sun sat low on the horizon as he shook the rug and let it float down onto the sand. Vanessa kicked off her flip-flops and sat cross-legged. Her peasant skirt draped between tanned legs as she reached for her burger. Liam loved to watch her eat. She did so with dainty bites as she held her food in equally dainty fingers.

She groaned with pleasure as she took a bite. "This is delicious. I haven't had a decent burger all year." She questioned his stare. "What?"

"Nothing." He took a bite and chewed slowly. "There's a guy on campus in the Student Union building," he said, his gaze now focused on the small roll of surf zipping along the shore. "He makes the best burgers. It's the homemade relish."

"What are you going to do when you finish your degree?"

"Not sure." He paused. Looked her way. "I may have the chance to go to the UK on an economics scholarship. I'd like to do my Master's in Edinburgh. My grandfather on mum's side was born in Scotland. He left me a small inheritance, just enough for a plane ticket. I've always wanted to go there."

Moments passed before she spoke, and he'd noticed it too—the hesitation, the finality in his words.

"I'll have left high school by the time you get back." Vanessa took another bite of her burger. "Dad wants me to move home for my final year."

"Are you keen? You've always wanted to go back to your father's farm."

"I can't leave Mum."

He wasn't surprised at her reply. The roles between mother and daughter were slowly turning, and Vanessa obviously felt responsible for Ruth. "You're so grown up for your age."

She paused again, then tossed the last of her hamburger bun into the air, watching as hungry seagulls staked their claim. "Do you think? Inside I still feel like that scared little girl."

He cleared his throat. While her admission didn't surprise him, the fact that she confided in him did. "What will happen when you go nursing? To your mum I mean?"

"I'll study at Clifton Falls General, so I won't be far away."

"Ever thought of doing med?"

"Is that a joke? I'm not smart enough."

"You're smarter than you think. I know you want to be a nurse, but you could definitely do med if you put your mind to it."

"Maybe, but that's not what life's about, is it? I don't want to be a doctor, and …"

The breeze stirred, and Liam licked the salt from his lips as he inhaled the ocean air and waited for her to continue. He knew what she was going to say, so finished her sentence. "And, you can't leave your mum. But Dad will look after her."

She unwrapped the parcel of fries and ate them one at a time. "He's so kind to her."

"Yeah." Liam finished his burger, then paused, wondering whether he should make his next comment. Ruth had been a liability for a long time, which made him angry when he thought about it. "But her drinking's a problem."

She sighed. "Yep. Still, she won't change now, will she?"

SURROGATE SISTER

The moon gently bathed the night sky as Liam drove northeast toward the river mouth. Vanessa knew where they were going but hadn't been to this part of the coast before. With no car and little enthusiasm, her mother never took her swimming, or anywhere.

"My friends are having a bonfire party down here." He sent her a sideways glance as she sat cross-legged on the bench seat.

"What will they say when you turn up with me?"

"Nothing. Most of them know who you are."

"Don't tell anyone it's my birthday. I hate being the center of attention, especially around people I don't know."

"I won't say a word."

As they parked on the grass beside the riverbank, Vanessa eyed the small crowd gathered around the smoldering bonfire and immediately wished she hadn't come. She followed him across the stony sand. The dozen or so guys all looked around Liam's age—clean-cut sons of local farming families who probably hadn't worked a low-paid day in their lives. She would never be a part of this scene and never wanted to be. Being the daughter of a housekeeper meant she was several rungs down the social ladder, no matter how nicely Liam's friends treated her in front of him.

"Everyone, this is Vanessa," Liam announced to the group.

She kept her head down for a moment, then glanced up. She could feel the gaze of the men in the group as an unwelcome physical presence down her spine.

"Ah, the surrogate kid sister," one replied with a broad smile. He looked her up and down. "You're cute, and not a kid anymore."

Liam laughed off his friend's comment. "Yeah something like that, so keep your eyes off." He pulled her to his side and handed her a Coke.

The word '*surrogate*' was new to Vanessa. She muttered it under her breath, committing it to memory for later. At least ten girls sat around the fire, each as pretty as the next. The 'in crowd' had never interested her when she was younger, but as she watched marshmallows and fat sausages hovering over the embers on long sticks, Vanessa wished she had girlfriends too.

Liam called out to one of the girls. "Sophie, keep an eye on Vanessa, will you?"

"Sure." Sophie patted next to her on the log. "Come sit."

"Don't let her smoke though," he warned. "She's too young."

As the girls passed around a joint, Vanessa sat quietly and watched the way they inhaled, in case they gave her a turn, but they followed Liam's orders. She noticed Sophie didn't smoke either.

Every so often, Vanessa would look Liam's way. She'd never seen him with his friends before, and the way they interacted with ease and teasing banter, intrigued her. He caught her gaze and smiled. She quickly turned away.

"Vanessa?"

"Sorry. What?"

"You were miles away," Sophie said. "So are you and Liam related?"

She hesitated as she searched for an explanation of their relationship. "My mother's their housekeeper, but I don't live at the O'Leary's most of the time. I go to Immaculate Heart in Clifton Falls."

"Is Sister Mary Big Tits still there?" one of the other girls asked. "When I was there, she ruled that school with an iron fist."

Vanessa relaxed slightly. She'd never heard Sister Monica referred to like that, and she couldn't help but smile.

"Do you have a boyfriend?" Sophie asked softly. "You're so pretty."

Vanessa shrugged. "Kind of."

"What's his name? Anyone we know?"

Unsure of how to reply, Vanessa focused on the fire, watching as the night air obliterated its tiny sparks. Her inner voice told her to keep quiet, but Sophie's attention warmed her almost as much as the fire. "Nikau."

"Nikau Hughes? I know his sister. He's cute," Sophie teased. "Has he kissed you?"

Several of the girls stared at her as they waited for an answer. She picked up a stone, felt the smoothness, then let it drop. "No. We haven't even been out together yet."

"How old are you?" one of the other girls asked as she handed Vanessa a freshly toasted marshmallow.

"Fifteen."

"Well, be careful. You know what boys are like," Sophie said. "And what about Liam? Do you have a little crush on him?"

"As if. He's like a big brother to me."

"If you say so." Sophie laughed now, and even though they were teasing her, Vanessa didn't take offense. "He's handsome though, eh? Half the girls at university fancy him."

Vanessa felt the heat flush her face and neck.

"Wait. You're the Vanessa who tamed Tosca. Roxanne talks about you all the time."

"I didn't tame Tosca. We just talked."

"Actually," Sophie continued, "we have a horse you could look at. Would you mind?"

Vanessa shifted uncomfortably. She'd worked with two more horses since Tosca, but didn't want Liam or his friends to know. "I'm not sure."

They sat for some time before Liam joined them. The air had cooled, and a light breeze rumbled through the pine trees bordering

Tuckers Road. He squatted next to Sophie and leaned in close. "Are you off home soon?"

"Yes." Sophie checked her watch. "I better get going. I said I'd be back by eleven."

"Could you drop Vanessa off?" He looked Vanessa's way, then continued, "Is that okay with you?" It occurred to her that Liam had never looked at her like that in public before. Usually, he kept those looks for when they were alone. "Your mum will be back soon."

"Okay."

"I'll see you tomorrow, yeah?"

The girls listened to Crosby, Stills, and Nash most of the way home, Sophie singing along softly to the familiar words of 'Suite: Judy Blue Eyes.' When they reached the turnoff to the homestead, Vanessa's curiosity got the better of her.

"Do you know a girl called Christie?" she asked.

Sophie reached over and turned the stereo down. "Christie? Liam's girlfriend?"

"Christie's his girlfriend?"

"Off and on." Sophie kept her eyes on the road. "She's such a sweetie, thinks he's the one. She's liked him for years, but he's a bit slow on the uptake is our Liam."

Vanessa adjusted her pride. "She gave me some clothes. It was ages ago, but I wanted to thank her. If I wrote her a note, would you pass it on?"

"Sure. But she'll be here on Friday. We're going to a wedding. I guess you'll meet her then, so you can thank her in person."

For some reason, the thought of meeting Christie filled Vanessa with dread. She knew Liam had girlfriends, she'd even caught him with one that night in his room, but she didn't want to meet any of them.

There were no lights on when Sophie pulled up outside the homestead, but as Vanessa opened the car door, Mick's new security lamp flooded the lawn and driveway in dim light. She stopped with her hand on the door handle and one foot on the ground, then leaned back in the seat.

"Are you okay?" Sophie asked. "I'll come in with you if you want. I hate going into an empty house at night. Freaks me out."

Vanessa smiled. She could tell Sophie was a kind soul by the faint color of light that surrounded her. She'd seen similar colors around people before—not all the time, but occasionally, when she viewed them slightly out of focus. Liam was usually green and her mother used to be all yellows and oranges. "I'll be okay. Thanks for the ride."

"Lock the door when you get inside, and I'll call you tomorrow, about Folly."

The light switch was just inside the kitchen door, but she still struggled to find it in the dark. And even with the light on, the room didn't come to life. Mick had a thing about the cost of electricity, so every light bulb in the house was low wattage. She moved to the sink, her hands clammy and mouth dry, and filled a glass of water.

The air in her room was close—too muggy for sleep—and her mother had stored yet another cardboard box of junk under the bed. She thought about her ability—as her father called it. Why could she talk to horses when others couldn't? Usually, she would have refused Sophie's request, not wanting to expose herself as different. But she'd warmed to Sophie straight away and wanted to help.

Unable to stand the stale air any longer, she tiptoed down the hallway to the other side of the house and peeked into Liam's large room. He always left it in a mess. Piles of jeans and work shirts littered the floor, and on the nightstand, an open bottle of Coke sat untouched. She opened the French doors wide, then turned on his stereo and put her record on to play.

Liam's room reflected his personality, and it had a distinctive aroma—aftershave mixed with spruce gum and wool from the shearing shed. He'd bought a new black-and-white checked cotton comforter, or a duvet as he called it, since last summer. He had new sheets too—red. Not what her art teacher would call fire engine red, but darker, like deep rust. She sat on the bed and cuddled his pillow as 'Wildfire' played on.

Vanessa noticed his sketch pad on the desk. It was the first time she'd seen it left out. She picked it up and flicked through its pages. Inside, divided rectangles covered the paper—like strips in a comic book—and in each section, tiny drawings of everyday life filled the spaces. Insects, acorns, and flowers. Rams and roosters—even tractors and cars and motor bikes—all drawn in minute detail, down to the last petal, feather, or wheel spoke. Each page looked similar, but when she got to the end, a life-size daisy chain—infused with small touches of watercolor—filled the back inside cover. She looked at it for a long time, then smiled, shut the pad and lay on the bed.

Vanessa recalled the night she'd caught Liam with a naked girl snuggled up beside him and shuddered at the thought. Even so, she found herself wanting to be that girl and wondered—hoped even—if he wanted her, too. Every time he came close, she sensed the energy between them. The girls at school would say it was all in her head, but she understood more than they did. She could read people as well as horses, and Liam *had* called her pretty.

Each time 'Wildfire' finished, she would jump up and play it again, until the lights of a car alerted her to Mick and Ruth's return. She switched off the stereo, ran down the hall and jumped into bed. When her mother peeked into her bedroom several minutes later, she feigned sleep.

"That's funny. Vanessa's here," she heard her tell Mick in a tone thick with booze. "She came home a day early."

Her mother said nothing more. She obviously didn't remember their telephone conversation from the previous day, or if she did, she chose to ignore it.

Vanessa stayed awake until she heard Liam's pickup come to a stop outside the front door. Fifteen minutes later, she snuck down the hallway to his room.

He rolled onto his side as she entered, his head resting on his arm. "You okay?"

"I feel kind of anxious."

He looked at her for several moments before he spoke. His face showed no trace of the intimacy of their earlier shared glances. "Go back to bed. You can't be here, you know that."

"But—"

"Vanessa, don't. Go back to bed."

The next morning, Vanessa grabbed the large dictionary off the bookshelf in the living room. She flicked through the paper-thin pages until she found the memorized word:

Surrogate: one that serves as a substitute…

For the rest of the day, she kept her distance from her *surrogate* brother and her vacant mother, who never once mentioned Vanessa's birthday. There was no hug, no cake, and no gift.

She mulled over the word *surrogate* throughout the day. Did he, and everyone else, think of her as his substitute sister? She didn't want to be anyone's substitute anything.

19

TOO INNOCENT

Despite her best intentions, Vanessa hardly ever made it up in time to eat breakfast with the men and her mother, which suited her just fine. She liked eating alone. But at dinnertime, everyone, often farm workers included, congregated around the large kitchen table for a daily debrief.

Liam and Mick came in through the back door and went to wash up before dinner. On their return a few minutes later, Liam took the chair opposite Vanessa as always. He caught her eye and opened his mouth as if to speak, then obviously thought better of it.

Even when he'd worked all day on the farm, Liam always looked tidy, in well-fitting jeans and t-shirts. When the midday heat became too much, she'd sometimes seen him remove his shirt and work naked from the waist up, his skin glowing with sun and sweat, and his hair tied into a short ponytail. However, today his t-shirt clung to his torso, and his loose waves touched his shoulders. She'd never seen such a handsome man.

As usual, Vanessa kept her gaze lowered while her mother served the meal. She gagged at the sight of Brussels sprouts joined by dry, fatty meat and thick, pale gravy. Her mother used to be an excellent cook. Not anymore.

When she eventually looked Liam's way, he winked at her and grinned. It was the first time she'd felt like smiling since he'd told her to leave his room hours before.

Vanessa knew she couldn't share Liam's bed, but that didn't stop her wanting to return to his room when fear overwhelmed reason. She slept better when next to him, and longed to inhale his scent and nuzzle into his back as she had in summers past, when life had seemed much less complicated.

But times had changed. She was fifteen and understood the concept of actions and consequences. She'd never asked him how he felt about her—never questioned what he was thinking. They once comforted each other. Now they didn't. Now they couldn't.

Liam watched Vanessa play with her food. He needed to talk to her about the night before, but the dinner table wasn't the place. They ate in silence until Mick addressed Vanessa.

"I'll need your help next Saturday, so make sure you keep some space in your busy social calendar." He winked and shot her a cheeky grin. "We have a load of sheep going to the meat works, and Liam has a fancy wedding to go to. We could do with an extra pair of hands."

"Okay. I might have to cancel a few dates, but work is work."

"And Stuart Young from next door wants you to look at one of his horses on Sunday. He said he'd pay you."

Liam stared at her across the table. He turned to his father. "What do you mean, 'look at one of his horses'?"

Mick smiled at Vanessa. "This one's getting quite a name for herself around the valley with her horse work. What's it been now? Three? Four?"

Vanessa lowered her gaze. "I'm not sure," she mumbled.

Swallowing a forkful of food, Liam glanced at Vanessa and frowned. If she'd been working with horses around the district, this was the first he'd heard of it.

"So when do we get to meet this girl of yours, son?"

Shit. Why did his father have to bring up his private life at the dinner table, in front of everyone? "We're just friends. You know how it is."

"So it's not serious?" Mick asked with a grin.

Liam stared at his father for a moment until he sensed he'd made his point. "Maybe I'll ask her to come for lunch before the wedding. Would that be okay, Ruth?"

Ruth looked up as if surprised by Liam's request. "Of course. I'll make some scones."

"May I leave the table?" Vanessa asked Mick. "I might go for a quick ride."

"Go on then," he said. "Make sure you give that damn horse of yours a good workout. He's long overdue for a run."

Vanessa went to collect the men's plates. "Leave that," Ruth slurred. "Have time with Whisper. I'll take care of the dishes."

Liam waited ten minutes before he followed her to the stables.

"What's your problem?" he asked when he caught up with her. "You've hardly spoken to me all day."

Vanessa heaved her saddle off the rail and stepped past him.

"Talk to me," he said.

"What's there to say?" She slung the saddle over Whisper's back and slid it into place behind the withers as Liam kept his distance.

"So you're pissed off because I won't let you sleep in my room?"

Vanessa reached over to fasten the girth.

"You're fifteen," he continued. "It's time you acted like it."

"I am acting like it."

"Yeah right," he mumbled as he grabbed his saddle off the rail and dumped it on the bench outside. "Wait for me to saddle Gracie. I'll come with you."

"I'd rather go alone."

He narrowed his gaze, realizing he was seeking answers she obviously didn't want to give. "Suit yourself, but it'll be dark soon, so stay around the house. It's too late to go up the hill."

"I *can* tell the time."

20

CHRISTIE

Dawn appeared, silent and serene; but by noon, the southeast wind puffed through the poplars along the driveway, making their leaves dance and rustle, like a taffeta dress around the legs of a beautiful woman on her way to the ball. Christie had arrived.

Vanessa watched from her bedroom window as Liam strolled across the lawn to greet her, his smile wide and full of warmth. He kissed ready lips—not with unbridled passion, but he kissed her all the same—then interlaced their fingers in a clear display of affection. He led her into his bedroom through the French doors, where they stayed shut away until lunchtime.

Vanessa fiddled with the cord around her braid and held Lucy tight. Her bedroom bordered the kitchen wall. It didn't usually bother her being so close to the table, but today, it did. She didn't want to be privy to the lunchtime conversation. Didn't want to hear everyone fuss over their guest. She pulled her pillow over her head. It made no difference. The muffled sounds of their cozy chitchat remained.

"Where's Vanessa?" she heard Liam ask, then the sound of a chair scraping across the floorboards. She knew Liam's manners would be on show for Christie, as he pulled out her chair and played the doting boyfriend.

"You know what she's like," her mother said. "I expect she'll get something later."

"I'll go call her," Liam replied.

She heard his footsteps in the hallway, then a soft knock. She quickly grabbed a book off her nightstand and positioned the pillow behind her head.

"Vanessa?" He opened the door slightly. She stayed on the bed. Cold fingers worked through the strands of wool on Lucy's head as her lips mumbled the words of the novel on her lap.

"Lunch is ready."

Her focus remained on the page. "I'm not hungry, and I hate sitting at the table with that horrible Jake."

"Jake's not here." Liam hesitated for a moment. "Come on. Christie's been looking forward to meeting you."

He stepped into her room and shut the door. She looked up and met his gaze. There were so many words running through Vanessa's head at that moment, she wasn't sure how to form them, so she said nothing. She continued to stare at him as he sat on the bed. His hand reached out to smooth the stray hair from her face. She shrugged away from his touch.

"I thought you'd want to meet Christie."

"Why? She's your friend, not mine."

"What the hell's got into you?" As he rose from the bed and looked down at her, his expression showed an immediate change. "We have a lunch guest, so get your ass out to the kitchen. Don't be so damn rude, or I'll pick you up and dump you in the middle of the table." He hissed the words through gritted teeth, and yet, they boomed in her ears.

She stared him down. "Fine."

"And put a smile on that pouty face."

Vanessa followed Liam into the kitchen where the others chatted around the table.

"Here she is," Mick said. "Our resident horse tamer."

Vanessa went straight to Christie and extended her hand. "Hi, I'm Vanessa. It's nice to finally meet you." She heard Liam cough.

A pretty girl, in a city kind of way, Christie's flawless skin struggled to shine through liberally applied pancake makeup. Her eyelids were a touch too blue, her hair too blonde, her eyeliner too black, and her lips too pale.

"It's lovely to meet you too, Vanessa. Liam's always talking about you and Whisper."

Vanessa sat at the table opposite Liam, and her mother handed her a plate of food. "Do you ride?" she asked Christie.

"Yes, I've been riding for about ten years—dressage mainly. I'd love to meet Whisper after lunch. Maybe you and Liam can introduce us. Boys like him fascinate me."

"Whisper doesn't get on with Liam, but then horses are a good judge of character, don't you agree?" She glanced at her *surrogate* brother. "They can sense fear and indifference."

Christie shot Liam an amused look, and she and Mick both burst out laughing. Ruth stared into space, then took a small forkful of food —not even enough to feed a sparrow—and placed it in her mouth as their banter went straight over her head.

"I told you she has a smart mouth," Liam said.

"Gosh, by the way Liam talks about you, I thought you were a lot younger. But you're all grown up."

"Not quite," Mick said. "You turned fifteen just the other day, didn't you, lass?"

Vanessa glanced at her mother. "Yes. I did."

Later, while Liam showered and dressed for the wedding, the girls strolled down the driveway to meet Whisper. Vanessa stepped forward, offering an apple in her outstretched hand. "Here he is. Hey," she cooed. "Who's my beautiful boy? Come here, my gorgeous."

Vanessa sensed Christie's attention as she soothed the gelding. She moved closer as Whisper stepped back—nostrils flared, and ears pinned—his hooves beating a rhythm on a bald patch of dirt. He whinnied loudly.

"I don't think he likes me," Christie said.

"He's like all males. You can't expect anything when you first meet him. Just feed his ego, soothe him and give him treats and kisses, and he'll soon come around."

Christie laughed. "How old are you again?"

"Fifteen."

"You could have fooled me."

"We understand each other, that's all, don't we, darlin'?" Vanessa patted Whisper's mane, then turned to Christie. "Um … I wanted to say thank you for the clothes. I grew a couple of inches when I turned fourteen, so they came in handy."

"My pleasure. I miss that suede waistcoat. But it wouldn't fit me now. I put on weight when I went on the pill." She laughed. "But at least my acne has cleared up."

Christie's candid remark surprised Vanessa. She had no close girl-friends so had never talked to anyone about the pill. But she'd read *The Little Red School Book* when one of the older girls smuggled a dog-eared copy past the nuns and circulated it around the dorm. If Christie was on the pill, it meant she and Liam were probably 'doing it,' acne or no acne.

An image of Liam and Christie together as they kissed and laughed at each other's jokes stuck in her mind, and she balked at the feelings this imagery aroused. In some ways, Christie was now her competition for Liam's affection. Competition she could never compete with. A gust of wind rustled through the shelter break, and Vanessa shivered. "We should get back to the house. Liam will be wondering where you are."

As the two girls ambled up the hill, Christie chatted about dressage and horses, Vanessa only replying when necessary. As much as she'd told herself she wanted nothing to do with Liam's girlfriend, she'd warmed to Christie more than she'd expected to. They shared a love of horses and had a good rapport. Even so, she didn't want to deal with this complication. As they reached the parched front lawn of the home-stead, Liam sauntered out to greet them, with a cheeky grin on his face.

"Well, don't you look handsome." Christie walked toward him, linked her hand in his and pecked him on the lips. Vanessa stared. She'd always considered Liam a good-looking guy, but Liam in a suit—wow!

He tugged at the collar of his shirt. "How the hell do men wear these damn things all day? I feel like a trussed turkey."

"Well, I think you look amazing," Christie cooed. "Don't you agree, Vanessa?"

"Um … sure, I guess."

Liam shot Vanessa a smile. "Okay let's get this show on the road."

Christie turned to Vanessa. "Hey, it's been nice meeting you. I'd better say goodbye to your mum and thank her for lunch." She looked at Liam. "I'll be back in a sec, handsome."

Liam moved to Vanessa's side and fiddled with his collar. "Can you make sure my tie's straight, Ness?"

She looked him straight in the eye. "Piss off, *handsome*," she muttered and stormed off toward the stock truck coming up the driveway.

Vanessa arrived home around four to find the house deserted. When Nikau phoned not long after, she was surprised. They had spent a bit of time together at Billy's recently, sharing small flirtations, but he'd never phoned her before. She wasn't sure if he was shy or just not that interested. He told her *Jaws* was on at six o'clock, which she took as an invitation.

Scary movies made her uncomfortable, but she went anyway, telling her mother she was going with a group of school friends. They sat in the back row of the packed church hall—a makeshift theater on Friday and Saturday nights. Nikau held her hand, rubbing the pad of his thumb along the tips of her fingernails. At intermission, he shouted her an ice-cream dipped in chocolate, and a large tub of popcorn. When Jaws jumped out of the water, Vanessa buried her face in Nikau's chest.

Later, when he kissed her and sucked the skin on her neck and shoulder, she let him.

✳

The next morning, Vanessa found her mother in the mudroom, her hands in the concrete tub as she washed Mick's woolen work jumpers. A few unsteady notes of a pop song escaped her lips, and she gazed out the window as she worked.

A familiar smell hit her—eucalyptus oil, Castile soap, and male sweat mingled with the sweet sherry on her mother's breath. It wasn't even half past ten. She looked at her mother and frowned. "What happened to your eye? It was swollen yesterday, but it's worse today."

"I fell over."

"Did you ice it?"

Her mother didn't reply as she plunged her hands into the tub and rubbed a jumper back and forth over the silvered washboard with exaggerated force. Vanessa hated this room, with its spider-web-covered corners and dirty floors, so she stayed in the doorway. "I'm going for a ride with friends if that's okay."

"What time will you be back? I'll need help with dinner."

"No problem." Vanessa tugged the hair tie from around her wrist and pulled her thick mane into a high ponytail, exposing her nape. "I'll be home around four. I promise."

Ruth picked up the stick leaning against the old washtub—smooth and bleached from years in the water. It reminded Vanessa of a crooked walking stick from a book of nursery rhymes at home.

"What's that mark on your neck?"

"What?" Vanessa turned to look at her but stayed out of reach as she realized her mistake. A shiver raced up her spine as she recalled Nikau's lips on her skin.

"You have a mark on the back of your neck." Her mother grabbed her upper arm and pulled her closer. "It's a love bite. You let some boy mark you like a common slut. Is this what that Billy boy does to you when you're out riding?"

Vanessa raised her other arm in defense. "Mum, stop! Let me go."

Ruth held on tight as she brought the stick down on Vanessa's legs. "What sort of girl are you? You let boys touch you? Let them suck your skin? Is that the type of girl I've raised?"

"Mum, don't. It wasn't Billy. I got snagged on a branch."

"Liar."

21

BLINKLY'S FARM

Liam sprinted across the lawn toward the commotion. He could hear Ruth yelling and Vanessa crying as he bounded up the porch steps and into the mudroom.

"Ruth!" He pulled Ruth away. "That's enough."

She lunged forward, determined to have another go. "Stay out of this."

He crouched in front of Vanessa, her tiny frame drawn into a ball in the corner of the filthy room. He soothed her with his left hand and held his right out toward Ruth in an obvious display of authority. "Don't you fucking touch her. Don't you dare touch her again."

"Stand aside. I've had enough of you poking your nose in my business."

He rose to full height, using his bulk as a shield, and took a step toward Ruth as Vanessa ducked out of the room. Liam stared her down. "Get the hell out of here and cool off."

"I won't have you talk to me like that," Ruth yelled. "What would your father say?"

Liam's rage showed itself in the heat of his cheeks and the clench of his jaw. "I don't give a shit what Dad says. You're out of line. If you have something to say, damn well talk to her. Now, get out of my sight." His breath heaved in his chest. He'd never been so angry in all his life. "And stay away from her."

He picked up the stick and stormed from the room, swearing under his breath. When he reached the bank, he hurled it into the gully. He knew Vanessa's physical bruises would soon heal. Ruth was a shell of her former self, so had little strength to administer the discipline. But he also knew the mental scars would remain in her subconscious, to appear in times of sorrow, loss, or regret.

Back at the house, he knocked on Vanessa's door and let himself in. She lay on the bed with her arms wrapped around a pillow, convulsing as silent sobs overcame her. When he reached out to console her, she flinched at his touch.

He sat next to her and rubbed her back. She said nothing, but removed the hair tie, covering the mark. Touching his hand to her nape, he gently moved her hair aside. He hadn't even known she had a boyfriend, but the love bite was more than a tiny bruise, and there was another one on her right shoulder.

"Is it bad?" she whispered. "I can't tell."

"No. It just looks like a bruise, but your mother knew what it was. Maybe you should wear your hair down for a few days."

She nodded.

"I have to go. We have the after-match function for the wedding in half an hour, but stay out of your mother's way, okay?"

"She's never hit me before." Her sobs slowed but she struggled to control the hitching in her breath. "Never. I know she doesn't love me … but she's never hit me."

"Hey, it's over now." He stayed close, his words soft and his touch gentle and caring. He wondered if Ruth's rage was an isolated incident, or if she was turning into a mean drunk like some men he knew. "I'm sure she'll be hurting too."

"I doubt it," she whispered. "She'll just drink it away. But I can't do that, can I?"

"We all have pain in our lives we have to deal with."

Vanessa nodded as if she understood. She checked her watch.

"Nikau's waiting for me down at the bridge … to go riding. I can't go now."

Liam stopped himself from making a snap judgement about Nikau. He liked the kid okay, but he wanted to tell him to keep his hands to himself. "Okay. I'll drive past and let him know you're not feeling well."

"Thank you."

"I'll see you tonight, yeah?"

The men had already left when Vanessa entered the kitchen the next morning, stiff and sore from her mother's punishment. The bruises weren't bad. Sure they hurt, but not as much as her mother's rage. She nibbled on toast and cherry jam, drank tea, and studied the job list Ruth had left for her on the table.

With all her chores done, she was just about to put the vacuum cleaner away when her mother walked in with a basket of eggs. Ruth never said a word, and as she went about her day, didn't seem to register Vanessa's presence.

After setting the table for lunch, she hurried to Whisper's field with an apple from the orchard for her favorite boy. Anxiety at the thought of seeing Liam tightened her gut. He had come to her aid, but he'd also witnessed the beating and seen the love bite on her neck. She wondered if he knew about her and Nikau. What he would think about her having a boyfriend? She didn't want to upset him.

Rather than returning to the house for lunch, she stayed with Whisper until she heard her mother's call.

"Vanessa! Vanessa!" Ruth stood on the bank waving her arms, her voice a feeble screech rather than a shout.

"Coming." Vanessa took a shortcut across the driveway, scrambled up the bank and sprinted across the lawn. She followed her mother into the kitchen. "Is everything all right?"

"Go pack your bag," Ruth said without an ounce of emotion.

"Why, where are we going?"

"*We* are not going anywhere. *You* are going to your father's."

Her stomach twisted into knots. "Is something wrong? Is Karen sick?"

"Go pack, or you'll miss the bus."

"I don't understand. Is Dad expecting me?"

"I'll call him."

"But I promised to help with the Young's horse. They said they'd pay me."

"You should have thought about that before you let some boy put his dirty mitts all over you. Now do as you're told. I won't have you running around town like a common tramp. Your father can deal with you."

"I don't want to go to Dad's. I need that job. And I haven't had lunch yet."

Her mother never once turned from the sink as she peeled potatoes and carrots, popping them into a bowl of cold water. "You made your bed, young lady. Now go. You'll have to flag the bus down. There's money on the table for your ticket. Grab yourself an apple. Lunch was over half an hour ago."

With her suitcase in one hand and too-small cardigan in the other, Vanessa trudged down the driveway, her anger increasing with every step. Her mother had annoyed her before—many times—but she had never despised her as much as she did at that moment.

As Vanessa waited on the roadside in the oppressive afternoon heat, her gaze flicked to the homestead on the knoll. Her mother stood at the living room window, but there was no wave of goodbye. She squinted against the sun and moved into the shade of the neighboring spruce trees. When the bus came into view ten minutes later, she stepped forward to the edge of the road, waving to attract the driver's attention.

The door whooshed open as the wheels came to a halt. "Going all the way, miss?" The driver looked her up and down. A look of concern accompanied the question and Vanessa felt like the word 'slut' was branded on her forehead.

"To Blinkly's farm. It's by Wong's Market Garden."

"I know it. We have to make a change at Clifton Falls, but I'll be your driver all the way. That'll be seven dollars, miss."

Vanessa looked at the crumpled note in her hand. "But I only have five," she whispered.

The bus driver jumped out of his seat. "Put it back in your pocket and hop on," he said with a wink. "Here, give me your luggage, I'll put it in the hold."

"Thank you."

Once, Vanessa had enjoyed a bus ride, but that pleasure had vanished the day she and her mother left her father and traveled to Rata River Valley via Clifton Falls. Just like that day five years before, the bus was three-quarters full as she pushed her way down the aisle to an empty window seat toward the back. As she glanced at Whisper, movement in her peripheral vision caught her attention. Liam, riding Gracie, galloped across from the shearing shed. He pulled his mount to a dramatic halt, his gaze fixed firmly on Vanessa's.

As the bus hissed away from the road verge, his eyes expressed a soundless question. Vanessa placed her palm on the dirty window and watched until he became nothing but a dot on the horizon of regret.

By the time Vanessa reached her father's farm, the sun had set over the western hills, and on the wind, rain clouds gathered in the distance with a disapproving air. Dropping her suitcase in the gravel, she stood on the road verge and looked left and right for any sign of him. Deep down, she knew her mother wouldn't have made the call, meaning another long driveway and another trudge up a hill.

As she made her way to the back door, she could see Karen through the window of the lit up kitchen as she washed the dishes, and her father—all smiles and sunshine—leaning on the counter talking to her. They seemed so in love. Did he ever love her mother like that? And if he did, what went wrong?

She knocked and waited. It seemed the right thing to do. After all, the house was no longer her home. It was her father's home, and Karen and the boys' home now.

"What are you doing here?" Her father didn't offer a hug but opened the door wide in invitation.

"Mum threw a hissy fit and told me to get on the bus. Didn't she call you?"

Her father frowned his answer. "Well, come on in." He turned and called down the hallway, "Karen, look who's here."

"Vanessa. Are you all right, love?" Karen asked as she walked toward them.

"Kind of."

Her stepmother patted her on the hand. "Let's have a cup of tea, and you tell me all about it. Jim, grab the banana cake, would you?"

They sat at the table for over an hour. Vanessa drank tea and picked the chocolate icing off the cake. She spoke many words yet explained nothing, then played cards with the boys. Later, when everyone readied themselves for bed, she did the same.

A copy of *The Black Stallion* kept her company until just after three in the morning. She didn't care it was a kids' book; she still felt like a kid. Like she'd missed out on an important part of her life, and that part would never slot into place.

In the morning, when her alarm clock chimed, she couldn't rouse herself. Daylight sleep had distinct advantages—nothing seemed as scary in the light of day, even sleep.

The boys left her alone for once. She suspected Karen had warned them to back off for a few hours and was thankful her stepmother had correctly read the situation.

When the family went to the river that afternoon for a swim, Vanessa used her period as an excuse to stay home. The heat over-whelmed her, but she kept herself covered in jeans and a long-sleeved t-shirt. She couldn't imagine what her dad would say if he saw the bruises.

When they returned home several hours later, Karen hovered over her like a mother hen as they cooked real spaghetti and served it tossed with fresh tomato sauce rather than the canned stuff they ate at Mick's.

All through the week, Karen asked pointed questions about Vanessa's life in the Rata River Valley. Questions Vanessa couldn't answer.

She thought about Liam every day. How he made her feel safe and secure—even loved in a way. Nikau never made her feel that way. She knew he liked her—liked to kiss her and leave his mark, but somehow, they didn't click. She couldn't explain why, not even to herself.

22

PARTY FAVORS

When Vanessa returned two weeks later, O'Leary's looked deserted. Hardly a surprise. After all, the men would be out mustering sheep, and her mother was probably passed out on her bed.

Vanessa repeated her now familiar routine. She trudged up the steep hill, her suitcase heavy in her hands, and along the way, stopped to pet Whisper. Just the smell of him helped soothe the tension from the bus ride.

When she finally entered the house through the back door, dirty dishes lined the kitchen counter, and the floor looked like it hadn't seen a broom or mop in days. The radio was on high volume, drowning out all other sounds. She reached over and turned it off, then missed the racket as the refrigerator hummed and vibrated through its cycle. A tear escaped as she surveyed the mess.

She wandered down the hallway to her bedroom door, dropped her case and made her way to her mother's room. She knocked and turned the knob. *Locked.* Vanessa hadn't heard from her mother all the time she'd been away. Did Ruth ever think of her? Ever wonder what she was doing? Or did a mind steeped in sherry, think about anything much at all.

By the time her mother surfaced later that afternoon, the place had been transformed. "You're back, I see. Got that father of yours wrapped around your little finger, haven't you?" Ruth ran a glance around the room as she reached for the sherry bottle. If she noticed a difference, she never said a word.

Vanessa couldn't move the words stuck in a lump in her throat. Couldn't swallow them down or offer them up.

"You'd better phone your boyfriend, that Billy boy. He's called half a dozen times since you've been gone."

"Billy's not my boyfriend," she mumbled. "He likes Rose Churchill, not me."

Ruth listened in as Vanessa called Billy and ignored her when the call ended.

"There's a party in Smith's barn tonight. Can I go?"

"Please yourself. You'd probably sneak out anyway."

Vanessa knew the game must be played, the waters smoothed. "Thanks, Mum. Is Liam here?"

"He took Christie back to her friends. She's been in the valley all week. What a lovely girl—so polite and helpful. And Liam can hardly keep his hands off her. It's so sweet to see them together—like a pair of lovebirds joined at the hip. They're just so in love, it's like they were made for each other."

Vanessa didn't outwardly respond to her mother's remarks, but inside, the reaction was swift and painful. The word 'lovebirds' stuck in her head and her jaw clenched. *So in love.*

Her mother pulled a cabbage out of the pantry. "Here, get started on the coleslaw, then go down to the cornfield and pick me four ears of corn. Make sure the silks have turned brown." She stared impatiently at Vanessa. "Come on. We haven't got all day. And you can wipe that look off your face, or you won't be going to any party."

With the coleslaw made and corn picked, Vanessa sat in her bedroom and flicked through the *Seventeen* magazine Karen had given her for the trip. She studied the cute girls on the glossy pages. How would it feel to be that perfect girl—with flawless skin, impossibly white teeth, and girlfriends who helped you with your hair and makeup? To wear Pot o'Gloss lip gloss and have a 'mom' and dad with membership to a country club. To be 'so in love' and 'made for some-one' and have a boyfriend who 'couldn't keep his hands off you.'

Vanessa wondered if, in her insignificant life of school and chores and picking corn, she would ever have the chance to find out. She grabbed her diary and scrawled across the page.

What if I was made for someone?
What if my mother loved me instead of the bottle of sherry
hidden behind the jars of preserves in the pantry?
What if my father knew how much I loved him?
What if I was one of a pair of lovebirds?
What if I was a girl called Christie?

When Liam arrived at the party, he was shocked to see Vanessa there too, surrounded by young guys including Billy Cook, Nikau Hughes, and a few others from Saint Franks. With her pretty face, long blonde hair, and expressive eyes, Vanessa never had any difficulty attracting male attention. She was the type of girl guys gravitated toward, radiating raw sexuality without even realizing it. But she was too young to be at parties, and he didn't understand why Ruth had let her come.

He pushed his way through the crowd, stopping to talk to friends as he went. The barn was hot and stuffy, the music way too loud, and when he finally reached her, she pretended not to notice. He leaned forward, his mouth close to her ear. "You made it back, then?"

Vanessa regarded him with an expression that could have frozen the sea. She folded her arms and looked away. "Looks like it."

"Does your mum know you're here?"

"She said I could come."

He picked up her cup and took a sip. "Right. Well, make sure you stick to Coke, nothing else. Understand?"

"What's got up your nose?"

"You." He walked away.

All evening, Liam watched her flirt with every guy who looked her way. It pissed him off, seeing her work the room at her age. By ten thirty, he'd had enough and decided to head home and take Vanessa with him. He'd told Christie he'd be back by midnight, and hoped she'd visit him after her girl's night out.

"Where's Vanessa?" he asked Nikau.

"Not sure. Why?" Nikau looked around the room.

"She went up to the house to use the bathroom," Billy said. "We'll make sure she gets home before eleven. Mum can drop her off."

"No need. I'll find her."

As Liam walked around the back of the barn, he stopped abruptly, struggling to focus on the sight before him. Steve Brown had Vanessa up against a tree, holding her upright as he shoved his tongue down her throat.

Liam raced forward and grabbed the back of Steve's shirt. "What the hell are you doing? Get off her, you prick."

"Piss off. We're busy, aren't we, sweetheart?" Steve drunkenly shoved Liam, falling backward into the dirt in the process.

"Me piss off! Screw you. She's so drunk she can hardly stand. Vanessa, get in my truck," Liam shouted. "Now!"

"I'm not going anywhere with you." Her words slurred, and she wiped her lips with the back of her hand. "You don't own me. Nikau's taking me home."

Steve pulled himself upright and shot Liam a wide smirk. "Prick. What would your father say if he knew you were interfering with your little sister?" He spat at Liam's feet.

"What the fuck?" Liam yelled. "I said piss off. Now!"

Steve turned to Vanessa. "Catch you later, sweetheart. We have unfinished business." He leaned in close and whispered loud enough for Liam to hear, "I only let a girl tease my cock once. Next time, I'll collect."

Grabbing Steve by the scruff of his neck, Liam slammed him against the wall of the barn. "Stay away from her, understand?" He let go. "And as for you"—he gripped Vanessa by the arm and dragged her across the grass—"I told you to get in my truck."

She dug her heels in, fighting against his grip. "I'm not going home with you."

Nikau ran down the steps toward the commotion. "What's going on?"

Liam cocked his head toward Steve. "Ask him. But next time you take her to a party, look after her. She's wasted."

"Vanessa. What the hell?" Nikau yelled. "Tell me you didn't let that asshole kiss you?"

Drunken tears welled in her eyes. "I didn't mean to. He thinks I'm pretty."

"And you think I don't?"

At least a dozen partygoers had crowded around the ruckus, the guys keen to fight, the girls keen to judge. "Okay guys. Show's over," Liam said as he struggled to keep hold of Vanessa. He turned to Nikau. "Have it out with her when she's sober."

"Why are you blaming me?" Nikau said. "I didn't even know she was drinking."

"She shouldn't even be here." Liam tightened his hold as he tried to steady her. "She's only fifteen for fuck's sake."

"We'll take her home," Nikau said.

"No you won't."

Vanessa pulled away and staggered toward the truck with Liam right behind her. She stopped at the passenger door, her arms folded and her expression defiant.

"I said get in the truck"—he whispered through gritted teeth—"before I pick you up, dump you on the back and tie you up like one of the dogs."

"I hate you," Vanessa hissed as she climbed in and collapsed on the front seat.

Liam reached into the cab and clicked her seat belt in place. He could sense his blood pressure rising, and his jaw clenched like a vice. "Yeah, well, that's too bad. Because right now, the feeling's mutual."

"I'm going to be sick."

Liam pulled over. "Don't you dare throw up in my truck. Open the door and lean out." Apart from undoing her seat belt, she didn't move. He reached over, opened the passenger door and gave her a light nudge. She stumbled out onto the gravel road, skinning her knees in the process.

"Ouch," she screamed. "You attacked me."

"As if." He jumped out of the truck and bent down to help her up.

"Don't touch me. You're a two-timing bastard. I hate you."

"Tough, because at this point, I'm all you have." He helped her to her feet and grabbed her hair into a knot, holding it in place while she leaned over to rid herself of everything she'd consumed over the last few hours. He moved her sideways and sat her in the damp grass. "Better?"

"No."

"Good. Maybe you'll think twice before you get yourself into this state again. I told you to stay away from Steve, and not to drink."

"I had it under control."

What the hell? He didn't need this, but what choice did he have? He couldn't just walk away. Cursing under his breath, he said, "That guy wanted to bone you against a tree. And you think you had it under control. You're just a kid. You have no idea what control is."

"You're just jealous. Jealous other guys think I'm pretty."

He moved closer, his breath hot on her neck as the meaning of her words started to sink in. "This isn't about me. Every guy at that party would think you're pretty, no surprises there. But some of them, like Steve Brown, would screw you senseless if they had the chance, then they'd go to the pub and brag about it to anyone who'd listen. Is that what you want? Learn some self-respect. You're better than that."

"That's not true. He likes me."

"Is that right." Liam shook his head, his gaze fixed squarely on hers. Sure, she was young and drunk, but he couldn't work out what she saw in Steve. "You have no idea, do you? Not a goddamn clue. I'm trying to protect you here."

"You're the one who has no goddamn clue."

"I won't listen to this bullshit while you're drunk. And keep your voice down—the whole valley can probably hear you." He held the passenger door open. "Get in. And pull your lips in. You look like a spoiled brat with that pout."

They drove down Rata River Road in silence, the sound of the tires on the metal drowning out the radio. Liam had plenty to say but needed to calm down before he said it. Apart from that day in the mudroom, he couldn't remember the last time he'd felt so angry.

"I can't make you out," he finally said as he turned onto the high-way. "You swan off to your father's without a word, and when you get back, I'm suddenly the biggest asshole on the planet."

"I didn't swan off. Mum made me go because she thinks I'm a tramp."

Liam shifted in his seat and shot her a sideways glance. He reached over and turned off the radio. "Is that what she said?"

"Actually, she called me a slut."

The words *mean drunk* flashed through his mind. "Shit. I'm sorry."

"Don't be," she mumbled. "I don't need you feeling sorry for me. That's one job I can do all by myself."

A single bulb glowed dimly over the kitchen table when they entered the back door. Liam had half-expected to see Mick sitting deep in thought as he read the *Reader's Digest*. Sometimes when his father was feeling lonely, or worried about the farm, he stayed up well past midnight to read. But the room was empty and still. Vanessa slumped into a chair and rested her head in her hands.

Liam opened the fridge and grabbed a jug of water, setting it down in front of her, then handed her a glass and an aspirin. "Here, take this. It might help how you feel in the morning."

She sipped the water, her hands shaking as she held the glass. "Don't tell Mum. Please."

"I won't say anything, but we have to be up in a few hours for drenching, so you'd better get some sleep. Mick's relying on you."

"I'm not going drenching. Why are you being so mean?"

Liam mumbled 'shit' under his breath as he watched her swallow the aspirin. Now might not be the right time to talk, but he had to set a few things straight. Whatever he said, or how he said it, it was going to hurt, so he wanted to get it over with. She stared into space, her mascara—perfectly in place earlier in the evening—now smudged all over her cheekbones, and her lips still swollen from Steve's assault. Even though Vanessa usually shunned makeup, she was particular about her grooming, with neatly plucked eyebrows and manicured fingernails. He wondered how she would feel if she saw herself in the mirror now. He took a deep breath. "What's going on?"

She met his gaze. He closed his eyes as he rubbed the bridge of his nose with his thumb and forefinger, wondering for a moment if he'd misread the situation. When he opened them again and looked at her, her brows had joined in a tight knit, and she was looking at him with sad, puppy-dog eyes.

"I don't know what you mean."

Liam held her gaze. He shouldn't have encouraged her with the birthday presents. It had been a mistake. He realized that now. "Listen carefully," he said gently but with conviction. "I'm not mean or jealous, and I'm certainly not a two-timing bastard. You think I don't have a clue. Well, I do, and whatever this … this crush is that you have for me, it's all in your head, understand? You're a kid. A kid who happens to live in my home. I've told you before, I am not, and can never be, your boyfriend. Now please, go to bed. I don't want to discuss this ever again."

She reached for the glass in front of her and drained it, then stood and left the room without a word.

Liam sat with his head in his hands and his gut tied in knots. He'd expected an angry retort and more tears, but she didn't even slam her bedroom door.

Despite the aspirin and several gulps of water during the night, Vanessa woke the next day with a throbbing headache. She'd dreamed again of snow-covered fields where ice angels danced to life—like a message to her soul she didn't know how to decipher. Nikau phoned just after ten. He sounded distant—hurt. When Vanessa asked if he wanted to hang out after lunch, he said he was going to Clifton Falls with his father and wouldn't be back until Monday. Vanessa found herself wondering if she should finish with him before they had even started, but that was more to do with her feelings of guilt over Steve and Liam than how she felt about Nikau.

Feeling bored and out of sorts, she walked to the village, spending over an hour at the library, before making her way to the general store where Rose Churchill worked over the summer. Billy liked Rose and had been asking her out for weeks. But Rose had seen Billy and Vanessa together, and according to Billy, impressions had been made. Vanessa wanted to set the record straight.

Her talk with Rose went better than expected. Vanessa explained how she and Billy were just friends, and Rose seemed to accept the information with grace. But as she walked back home along the highway, Vanessa questioned her need to interfere.

Around four, she ambled over to see Whisper. As if sensing her disquiet, the gelding fussed around her as she filled his trough and offered him an apple. He nuzzled the fruit from her hand, then ran back and forth in front of her.

She stood, gazing at a flock of swallows as they darted across to the stables, then checked her watch. Four thirty-one. The heat of the day suddenly seemed oppressive, and she couldn't shake that feeling of dread. She sat in the grass, leaned back against a fence post and stayed there for some time.

Later, she wandered back to the house to help with the dinner prep, and later still, she phoned Billy. The line was engaged.

The air remained still until around six o'clock when the wind churned up from the south. Along with it came Christie. She stayed for dinner, and even helped with the dishes. She joked with Liam and Mick and tried to engage Vanessa in idle chat before she and Liam left for the movies at seven forty-five. All through the meal, Liam hadn't looked at Vanessa once.

By eight thirty, Vanessa was already in bed, staring out the window at the twilight sky. The complexities and misunderstandings of life filled her thoughts. Tears slipped down her cheeks and across her jaw, and her face felt so flushed she was sure she must be coming down with a cold.

Out of the corner of her eye, she thought she caught a glimpse of *moko* woman, then convinced herself otherwise. *Moko* woman was merely a figment of her vivid imagination.

Vanessa awoke with a start. Switching on the bedside lamp, she peeked under the bed as fearful thoughts crowded her mind, then lay awake, watching for shadows on the ceiling. When the loneliness became unbearable, she snuck down the hallway to Liam's room and opened the door. She knew what he'd said, but surely he hadn't meant they couldn't talk.

As she tiptoed over to his bed, her eyes adjusted to the soft light coming through the window. He lay on his back, one bare leg on top of the covers and his hand dangling over the edge as it always did.

But this time it was different, as next to him lay Christie.

23

ACCIDENTAL ENDINGS

The phone in the living room rang several times before Liam picked up. He listened to the caller, giving them one-syllable replies, then hung up and sat for a moment to let the information sink in. His thoughts drifted back to his friend Roger's funeral, and to Rose Churchill, the timid girl standing beside her parents on the steps of the cathedral.

"Where's Vanessa?" he asked as he entered the kitchen.

"Out riding," Ruth said. "She's been away all morning. I worry about her on that flighty horse."

"That was Anna. Billy was in an accident yesterday afternoon."

"Is he all right?" Mick asked.

"They're hoping to move him out of intensive care tomorrow. He's beat up pretty bad. And the sad part is, Rose Churchill was with him. She went to Immaculate Heart with Vanessa. Sounds like they hit a sheep not far from the Rata River Road turnoff. Rose was thrown from the bike and died at the scene."

"No!" For once Ruth showed her long-neglected compassionate side, her expression one of disbelief. She sat at the table, shaking her head. "That poor girl's family." She took a swig from the mug beside her.

"She's Annie Churchill's granddaughter," Mick said. "Annie loved her like crazy. Young guys on farm bikes, it should be illegal until they're at least eighteen."

"Anna thinks the funeral will be in the Immaculate Heart chapel on Wednesday," Liam said. "I'll take Vanessa. She can visit Billy then."

"Is that a good idea?" Mick asked. Since the interview with Sister Monica, his father didn't want him anywhere near Vanessa's school.

"Someone has to take her, and I guess you won't want to, Ruth?" Liam looked at Ruth, waiting for a reply.

"Liam's right, Mick. Vanessa should go to say goodbye to her school friend," Ruth said, ignoring Liam's question. "Liam will look after her."

He found Vanessa in the east hay barn, her usual place of solitude. She looked up, her eyes red and her expression raw. "What do you want?"

"I need to tell you something."

She grabbed the novel sitting face down on a hay bale, and the remains of her lunch and stuffed them into her bag.

"Stand still for a moment and listen. It's about Billy. He's in hospital."

She frowned, her attention now focused on Liam.

"Billy and Rose Churchill were in an accident yesterday afternoon. They came off his farm bike down by the river. They didn't find them until last night."

Vanessa's gaze darted toward the river, barely visible as it snaked through the valley miles below. "Four thirty-one," she muttered under her breath as she stepped away from him. She sank down onto a hay bale and stared into space. "Rose is dead, isn't she?"

Liam crouched beside her and nodded. "She died at the scene." He waited for his words to sink in. As far as he knew, Vanessa and Rose hadn't been close, but the news would still be a shock.

"This is all my fault. I saw Rose yesterday morning. She thought I had a thing for Billy. I wanted to put her straight. He's liked her for months and I wanted him to be happy. I asked Rose to give him a chance."

"It's nobody's fault. It was an accident."

"But it wasn't her time. That's why I saw the snow." Vanessa stood and paced as Liam's gaze followed her.

"What snow? It's the middle of summer."

"The field of the white snow … in my dream."

He looked at her and frowned. She was speaking in riddles, and he had no idea what she meant. "Come on. I'll take you home."

She looked at him and shook her head, her eyes brimming with tears. "Why did this have to happen to Rose?"

"Sometimes life makes no sense." Liam stood and reached for her, his arms wide. "Come here." He scooped her into a hug and whispered into her hair, "Who knows when our time's up? For any of us."

She pushed away from him. "I need to see Billy."

"I told your mum I'd take you to the funeral. You can visit him then."

"Why are you doing this? Pretending to care?"

"I do care."

"No, you don't!" Her rising voice startled him, and he reached for her again, but this time, only her hand. "You don't care about anyone but yourself."

"That's bullshit."

Vanessa sat back on the hay bale, her head in her hands. Liam wanted to sit beside her, but instead, he gave her some space.

"I've been on Billy's bike so many times. Why couldn't it have been me?"

"Because it wasn't. There are no what-ifs, so don't even go there."

"It would have been so simple. No one would miss me. But *no*. God takes a girl who's gentle, clever, and kind. A girl Billy's liked for ages. And he leaves *me* behind." She thumped her chest with a fist. "Me."

"You're in shock. Come on. I'll send Whisper back. You can ride on Gracie with me."

"No!" A stomp of her foot accompanied her declaration as she stood. "I'll ride."

"No, you won't."

Liam grabbed Whisper's bridle, secured it to the horn of the saddle on the second attempt, and whacked him on the rump. "Home, boy. Get off home."

He heaved himself into Gracie's saddle and extended his hand. Even at fifteen, Vanessa hardly weighed more than a hundred pounds, and as he pulled her into position behind him, he sensed her resistance lessen.

24

WHITE ROSES

On the day of Rose Churchill's funeral, hundreds of mourners gathered inside Immaculate Heart's chapel. Those that didn't fit spilled out of the doorway into the garden, many taking refuge from the sweltering heat under trees along the path. Teenage girls clung to each other while lanky boys stood with stoic expressions as their parents looked on.

Liam and Vanessa had arrived in Clifton Falls over an hour earlier, heading straight to the hospital where Vanessa sat at Billy's bedside not knowing how to form the words she wanted to say.

During the service, Vanessa stayed close to Liam's side, her hand only half an inch from his as she drew strength from his presence. She hadn't known Rose Churchill well, but she had been everything Vanessa aspired to be. Smart, poised, and musically gifted, Rose had conducted her shy outward persona with elegant, cello playing hands. Hands that Billy had loved. Vanessa wondered how he would cope.

As the soft-pink coffin crowned with white roses left the church in the hands of her family, Rose's string quartet, with a guest cellist from Saint Franks, played the John Denver classic, 'Sunshine on My Shoulders.'

Vanessa watched through tear-filled eyes as the hearse pulled away from the curb. She wanted to reach for Liam's hand but knew those who looked on would judge, so her hands held each other instead.

Neither spoke as they joined the steady procession of vehicles crawling toward the cemetery. And while they stood at the graveside in the harsh afternoon sunlight, watching the coffin disappear into the warm body of the earth, Vanessa thought of Billy, his expression vacant as he lay in traction at Clifton Falls General, not two miles away.

"I don't want to go back yet," Vanessa said as she climbed into the cab of Liam's pickup after the burial. "Can we go to Petrie Bay? Billy loves surfing at Petrie Bay."

"I guess. Do you want something to eat?"

"No, just a Coke." She reached into her pocket and pulled out a crumpled dollar bill. "Here."

He looked at her with kindness. "Keep it. I'll get you a burger too, just in case."

The drive from Clifton Falls to Petrie Bay took around fifteen minutes. Once parked, they sat with the windows down, the late afternoon still hot, dry, and windy. Vanessa stared into the distance, searching for answers in the roar of the surf.

"What happens when we die?"

"Who knows," Liam paused for a moment. "Maybe our souls are finally at peace. In a place where our egos and fears can't spoil our happiness."

Vanessa had thought about death many times but had never had anyone to share those thoughts with. Now, her questions spilled from her in a desperate rush.

"But what if our souls get stuck and can't move on? What if Earth is heaven for some and hell for others? Or purgatory is just down the road where some poor kid's being abused? And how do we know what happens until we're gone? Is there a better life waiting for us if we play the game, or is that just religious nonsense?"

She inhaled an unsteady breath. "And … when your time's up, is it really up? Or can one simple action change your fate? What if Rose and Billy had left earlier, or later? Would she still be alive?"

Liam shifted in his seat and leaned his arm on the open window before he responded. "Maybe. But I try not to think about it."

"And if you die young, like Rose, do you get the chance to come back? That's what I really want to know."

Her tears flowed, and within minutes, soft sobs turned into uncontrollable grief. Vanessa rocked, lost in her thoughts. It was as if Liam wasn't there. He reached over and took her hand. "Don't cry, Ness. I know it's sad, but life goes on, and it's up to us to make the most of it."

Liam waited for her to still.

"Come on," he said gently. "You need some fresh air."

He opened the passenger door and helped her down. Vanessa removed her shoes, and he did the same, rolling his pants up to mid-calf. She wanted him to hold her hand like he did when he walked with Christie, but he kept them in his pockets. They strolled along the beach in silence, the ebb and flow of the waves washing over her feet calming her until her thoughts subsided into numbness.

Vanessa was sound asleep when they arrived home just after ten p.m., the events of the day left behind—floating on the waves along the eastern shoreline. She stirred as Liam carried her into her room and lay her on the bed. As he went to close the door, she called him back with a whisper.

"I don't want to go back to Immaculate Heart."

"We all have to do things we don't want to." He went to walk away. Funerals unsettled him—no matter whose they were—and he knew the sight of Rose's sister, Louisa, lost in her grief outside the chapel would stay with him for a long time.

"Liam?" She smiled when he looked at her, and it made him sad. "Thank you."

"You're welcome," he said, then closed his eyes for a moment, sighed, and left. The door swung shut behind him.

Back in his bedroom, Liam lay on top of the bed, his dress shirt and pants in a crumpled heap on the floor, and the air muggy and close. He thought back to Vanessa's questions about death, and it dawned on him that there was much about her he didn't know. She'd never expressed the depth of her feelings to him before, and at that moment, he realized what an extraordinary person she was. There was no doubt about it, she'd always been an unusual girl; but as she matured, there was something almost ethereal about her.

Liam had a basic understanding of the human condition, but Vanessa was barely fifteen. So much of this made no sense. Her dream of 'the field of the white snow', as she called it—in her mind, a sign that something was amiss. The woman with the *moko* who appeared in her room, and the sighting of a woman praying under the elm, who matched the description of his mother—something she'd done every fine day until her death. He turned over, punched his pillow into semi-comfortable submission and waited for sleep.

Just after three, he heard her enter his room. She stood at the side of his bed. "Please don't send me away ... not tonight."

He shifted to the left, and she slipped in beside him, but they didn't touch. He waited several minutes, then spoke. "You okay?"

"For now."

THE FANCY BALL

NINE MONTHS LATER

The Deer Stalkers' Ball, a major event on the Rata River Valley's social calendar, took place every year on the first weekend of November. Vanessa, after her imprisonment at Immaculate Heart for most of the year, had five days study leave and pleaded with her mother to let her come home on the bus, instead of staying at school with the younger girls. Not that Vanessa would go to the ball. No, the ball was for the pleasure of debutantes and ruddy-faced farm boys, stuffed into ill-fitting tuxedos, and looking for action.

She'd had little contact with Liam during the year. He hadn't visited her as he usually did when in town. There had been no care packages delivered. It was as if she didn't exist—to him, or to anyone else.

Vanessa was almost at the stables when Christie pulled into the main farm gate. She recognized the car—a Volkswagen Beetle—so stayed away late into the afternoon. By the time she got home around six, the happy couple had left. Off in their fancy clothes, in Christie's bright red car, to their fancy ball as they played at being so fancy in love.

Her mother had retired to bed early, wasted out of her tree as usual and barely able to brush her teeth, let alone inquire after her daughter's well-being. Vanessa ate dinner alone, then snuck two slices of pound cake from the tin in the pantry, devouring them without thought or pleasure.

On her way to bed, she slipped into Liam's room—one of the few places in the house where she could relax—and played her record. With 'Wildfire' streaming from the speakers of the stereo, she felt at ease. Content.

"Hey, what are you doing here?"

"What? What time is it?"

"Two thirty. Why are you home? Don't tell me they've suspended you again."

Vanessa sat up and rubbed her eyes. Through the open window, the lawn glistened with a late spring frost, and the skin on her neck bumped with the chill. "I'm on study leave. Go away."

Liam chuckled. "You're in my bed."

She looked around the room at the bookcase, his stereo, and the checked duvet, all in shades of gray. He was right. She had fallen asleep in his room. "Where's Christie?"

"What do you mean?"

"Didn't you go to the ball together?"

"Yes, but she's not staying here. We're just friends these days."

Vanessa took this information and stored it away. Liam had never said he didn't care about Christie. Not once. He'd never made excuses. Never explained their relationship or complained she didn't appreciate him. When it came to Christie, Liam kept his opinions to himself, so this admission surprised her.

"I need to use the bathroom," he whispered. "I'll be back in a minute. Wait there."

She flopped back on the bed and stared at the ceiling as his foot-steps triggered creaks in the timber flooring along the hallway. She went to leave but then changed her mind, longing for his touch, his breath.

Liam crashed back into the room and sat on the bed. In the dark, she could hardly make out the contours of his face, but as her eyes adjusted, she could tell he was smiling.

"You're drunk."

Liam chuckled. "A little."

She rose from the bed. It was bad enough dealing with a drunk mother, she didn't have the energy to deal with a drunk Liam too.

"Stay and talk to me," he said. "We haven't seen each other in months."

"It's the middle of the night."

"That's never stopped us before."

"You're breaking your own rules."

Less than a foot separated them. Her gaze dipped to his throat as he yanked his bow tie free and undid the top buttons of his shirt. He scrunched his face into an annoyed frown as he ran his fingers through his hair and down the back of his neck. And no matter how many times she'd tried to convince herself otherwise, her fascination with him hadn't waned.

"Aren't we past all that?" he said as he removed his cufflinks and placed them on the nightstand.

"You tell me."

"Shit, Vanessa. It's been almost a year. Let it goddamn go."

When Liam woke a few hours later, in a haze of sleep and hangover, he thought for a moment that Vanessa was lying beside him. But as the earth spun its way to dawn, he realized he was alone. He stayed awake for a while, his arms wrapped around a pillow—her pillow—as he inhaled her scent. He resisted the temptation to go to her. What was there to say that hadn't already been said?

He thought about Christie. Liam had broken up with her months ago. He'd loved her in his own way, and if he was honest, wanted her sexually, but Christie didn't believe in sex before marriage, and without that physical connection, Liam's feelings for her had drifted back into a platonic friendship before he'd even realized what was happening. Still, they'd remained close, and he'd enjoyed taking her to the ball. They'd danced and partied with their friends, and at the end of the night, she'd told him she'd met someone else.

Liam drifted back to sleep just before six, and when he woke later, his head throbbed with a headache and dehydration, and his room felt like a sauna. With his mouth as dry as a slice of stale bread, he swallowed hard, then grabbed the glass of water from his nightstand and gulped it down. The sudden assault of liquid made him feel sick, and he flopped back on the pillow. *Shit. It was going to be a long day.*

Once up, he expected to see Vanessa helping her mother with lunch, but no one was home, not even Ruth. When she appeared a while later, cold toast sat on the plate in front of him, and he was on his third cup of coffee.

"Rough night?" Ruth asked.

"Something like that. Where's Vanessa?"

"Off with Mick. They've gone up to the Crawford's to look at a horse. She's a good kid. She'd do anything for anyone."

Liam looked at Ruth, wondering if she'd finally kicked the booze. He hadn't heard her praise Vanessa in years. He and Ruth hardly spoke these days, apart from casual greetings and domestic conversations concerning meals and laundry, and he missed the old Ruth. Mick sometimes talked about Ruth and AA like they belonged together, but Liam didn't know if Ruth had actually taken that step. "Isn't she meant to be studying?"

"You know her. She can't stay inside for long. Still, she's an excellent student. Never has any trouble passing exams."

Grabbing an apple from the fruit bowl, he left the kitchen without saying anything else. He spent the afternoon bent over the engine of the tractor. He'd tried to persuade Mick to replace it years ago, but now the farm couldn't afford the expense. By late afternoon he was covered in grease and sweat, so headed back to the house just before five thirty to shower and change.

When he entered the kitchen half an hour later, Vanessa was standing with her back to him, spooning rice into a large serving dish.

He hadn't seen her clearly the night before, and when she turned to face him, he stopped short. Everything about her screamed beautiful. Her hair—the color of half-ripened corn silk and streaked from the sun, glistened in the light streaming through the kitchen window; her eyes seemed larger and more intense, and she'd grown at least two inches since January. He stepped closer as she turned away. She hadn't smiled, and he wasn't sure if she'd even said 'Hi.'

"What's for dinner?"

"Chicken curry," she said, without turning around.

He surveyed the table, already set with a large bowl of steaming curry, several side dishes, and a basket of flatbread sitting in the middle. The kitchen smelled delicious, and for a few moments, he just stood and stared.

Ruth looked up and smiled as he sat in his usual place. He could tell by her bloodshot eyes that she was wasted. *No AA then.* When Vanessa put the dish of rice on the table, Liam couldn't help but stare again. Her skin was clear and kissed with a light tan, her plump lips slicked with gloss, and her lashes long and dark. She looked more mature, so much more mature, like one of his peers rather than a teenage kid. *Shit.*

Moments went by. Liam said nothing until Mick interrupted his unsteady thoughts. "You gonna sit there all day?" He held his plate across the table. "Can you drop a spoonful of that yogurt stuff on my plate, please?" Liam looked at Mick, wondering if he'd walked into a parallel universe. Ruth smiling, his father eating curry and the kitchen clean and tidy. *What the hell?* "Sorry, of course."

During the meal, Liam tried to catch Vanessa's gaze, but she ignored him as she centered her conversation on Mick and their visit to the Crawford's. He'd never seen her like this—she seemed so animated as they discussed their afternoon, and so damn pretty he could hardly look away.

He left the table as soon as everyone had finished and went to his room to read, then realized some time later that the change in Vanessa had left him so unsettled, he'd forgotten to thank her for dinner or help clean up.

26

SMALL TALK

At dusk the following day, Liam knocked softly on Vanessa's bedroom door, then waited for her to say "come in." She'd said only a few words to him at dinner earlier, and he wondered if she was mad at him for some reason.

Vanessa dropped her novel on the bed and glanced up. "Hey."

"What are you reading?"

"*My Cousin Rachel*."

"Is it any good?"

Vanessa narrowed her gaze and frowned. "I've only read the first chapter."

He still couldn't get over the change in her appearance and tried not to stare. "I overheard you talking to Billy earlier. Do you need a ride somewhere?"

"I wanted him to take me to the beach for a swim, but he's busy."

"The beach? What tonight?"

"The surf helps clear my head."

"I'll take you if you want. I could do with some fresh air."

Vanessa glanced back down at the page. "It's okay. I can go tomorrow."

He continued staring at her for longer than necessary. "Come on. I'll get my keys and meet you at the truck."

It took over fifteen minutes for Vanessa to emerge from the house. She secured her seat belt without a word, and sat upright, holding a small bag in her lap. As they left the driveway, she reached over and fiddled with the radio dial, and sang along quietly to Elton John in perfect tune. He'd never heard her sing before. She had a seductive, husky quality to her voice—something else that shocked him.

They pulled into a makeshift parking area at one of the popular swimming spots where Liam often surfed with his friends. He'd expected to see people walking their dogs and surfers riding the last waves of twilight, but apart from a few seagulls, the place was deserted.

"Wait here," she said. "And don't watch me."

"Don't go out too far and make it quick. It'll be dark soon."

Vanessa ran from the truck to the beach, her feet leaving delicate imprints in the wet sand. He looked away as she undressed, and by the time he looked back, she'd wrapped herself in a flimsy sarong—one he'd never seen before. He expected to see her in the same black swim-suit she'd always wore, but as he followed her movements, he wondered if she was naked underneath the colorful fabric. He stayed in the truck with the windows down, tuned the car stereo into Classic Rock FM and, despite her instructions, stared across the sand at the sight before him, smiling at the irony as 10cc's 'I'm Not in Love' played through the speakers.

She stopped for a second at the shoreline before paddling into the breakers. The trees lining the dunes to the northeast rustled with a sudden puff of air, distracting his attention. When he looked back, Vanessa had removed the sarong and stood naked in the water, a perfect representation of female beauty. With her arms outstretched toward the dusky sky and the sarong billowing kite-like from her hands in the breeze, she looked like a goddess of the sea.

In less than a heartbeat, she disappeared under the waves.

He opened the truck door. "Vanessa," he yelled. "Vanessa." He ran toward the water. Panic overwhelmed him as his breath caught and his heart pounded in his chest. When she bobbed up out of the swell, he relaxed, watching her drift on the light current. He stood motionless for a while, spellbound by the sight of her, then cupped his hands to his mouth. "Vanessa. It's getting dark. Time to get out."

"Coming." Her response was barely audible against the roar of the surf as she covered herself with the sarong, but he heard her say, "Turn around."

"Hurry up." He watched her struggle against the pull as she dragged her legs through the roll of the waves. Hesitant fingers dangled below the surface of the dark water as the sarong clung to her curves. She stopped and looked back, her skin glistening in the sunset as the steady breeze wafting off the coast made her shiver. He knew he shouldn't stare, but his mind wasn't comprehending rational thought. He'd never seen anything more beautiful.

Once out, she secured the sarong in a knot above her left breast, grabbed her things and strolled up the beach.

"What the hell was that all about?" His question concealed his fascination with the sight before him. Wet skin kissed by the sunset. Goosebumps. Tight, erect nipples.

Vanessa shivered. Strands of blonde hair clung to her shoulders as small droplets of salt water dripped from her skin. "Nothing. It's not important."

He hesitated, struggling to take his eyes off her body draped in wet cotton. He couldn't see her naked breasts or the color of her nipples, but the cling of the fabric left nothing to the imagination, and that imagination manifested in an uncomfortable tension within him. "Hurry up and get dressed."

"Don't watch."

"As if."

But that's precisely what he wanted to do. Watch.

The homestead was unusually quiet when they returned. They sat at the table, eating leftover scones slathered in butter and jam, and drinking hot chocolate topped with marshmallows. Their stop-start conversation said little, but her gentle actions, plenty. And as they sat there, he couldn't get the image of her standing naked in the surf out of his mind. Now, in the dull light of the kitchen, her face held such an allure, he struggled to look away from her.

"I'd better go to my room," she said. "I'll probably be up cramming most of the night. Thanks for taking me to the beach."

Vanessa wasn't usually shy around him, but here she was, more reserved than he'd ever seen her. "You still having trouble sleeping?"

"Depends. Sometimes."

Ruth's appearance at the kitchen door startled them both. Apart from a skimpy pair of white panties and an unbuttoned cardigan, she was naked, without shame or realization. She stumbled over the threshold. Liam went to grab her but stepped back when she regained her balance.

Vanessa jumped up and buttoned her cardigan. "Mum, what the hell were you doing outside dressed like this?"

"I went to find Jake. I'm so thirsty."

Liam filled a glass of water and sat it on the table. He looked away as Vanessa stood in front of her mother.

"Go to your room," Vanessa scolded. "You're practically naked, and you know Jake's not here anymore."

"Jake left?" Ruth slurred. "Where's he gone?"

"Mum, come on. You're drunk."

"Don't talk to me like that, sweetheart. I've been trying my best." She slumped forward, and Vanessa caught her.

"Well, your best isn't good enough. Come on. Let's get you back to bed."

Liam stepped forward to lend a hand. "I've got this," Vanessa said as she heaved Ruth's arm around her shoulder. "You shouldn't have to see her this way."

He'd seen Ruth that way several times before, but he didn't let on. In fact, he'd put her to bed himself occasionally, and Mick had done the same. But Mick seldom talked about Ruth; he didn't want to think about the problem, or even consider there might be a solution.

It was like everything else in his father's life. The farm was losing money year after year, but once again, Mick wouldn't be told there was a problem, or how to deal with it—especially not by a twenty-one-year-old economics graduate. Liam had talked about possible solutions and had suggested diversifying many times, but his father had never embraced the concept that views could, and should, be adjusted.

27

SHIFTING SAND

When Vanessa entered the kitchen the following morning, she was surprised to see Liam still sitting at the table, leisurely reading the paper and eating toast. It was after eight, and normally, he'd be out feeding the dogs or up the hill helping Mick move a mob of sheep.

Her mother smiled as Vanessa poured herself a bowl of cornflakes. Breakfast was one of the few times she still felt connected to Ruth. Every morning Ruth would ask her how she slept, and Vanessa would reply with one of three affirmative words. *Good. Well. Okay.*

She sat at the opposite end of the table from Liam, ignoring his stare as she sliced a banana on top of her cereal. He shot Ruth a sideways glance as she left the kitchen, then spoke. "What was last night all about?"

"What do you mean?"

"Down at the beach. It looked more like a cleansing ritual than a swim. What's going on?"

She widened her eyes and looked at him as she chewed, then paused to give her words more impact. "I wasn't going to tell you. I didn't want you to worry."

"Tell me what?"

"I saw something."

Liam frowned. "What? Like before?"

Vanessa struggled to keep a straight face. "A flying saucer. It landed on the front lawn yesterday morning."

He looked at her for several seconds before a slow grin lit up his face. "You're making a joke. Who would have thought."

She returned the grin and raised her eyebrows. "Too easy."

"So what was the swim really about? Some pagan ritual?"

"What? You think I'm a witch too? Just because I understand horses. Thanks a lot." She thought for a moment, wondering if she should discuss her business with Liam. "If you must know, I had a run in with a guy at the Crawford's. He came from the 'spare the rod and spoil the horse' school of idiots. I told him what I thought of him and his approach, and he didn't like it. So he refused to pay, which made me angry, and anger restricts energy flow. Saltwater and sand always calm me."

Silence stretched before them while Liam sipped his coffee. He leaned back in his chair, and as she watched him, she knew what he was about to ask.

"So people pay you?"

"I give them my time, why wouldn't they?" She stood and began clearing the table. Just how much people paid was between her and her clients, and she was glad he didn't push her further.

"I'm thinking of going for a ride later. You keen?"

Vanessa wondered why he was being so nice to her. After all, he'd practically told her to piss off that night of the party. "I have a job on."

"Do you want me to drop you off?"

"No thanks. Billy's taking me. He's my agent."

Agent? "Is he back at school?"

"No, he's not going back. His leg took ages to heal, so he's been working for his dad."

Liam stayed at the table and watched Vanessa leave the room, still struggling to reconcile this Vanessa with the Vanessa of a year ago. He chuckled to himself. Now she had an agent and had made a joke at his expense; and all the time they'd talked, he'd desperately wanted to kiss her, until his knees weakened just thinking about it.

He'd long admired the way she lived her complicated life, with a steady determination to succeed. But now, his admiration of her had turned to desire, and no matter how much his conscience screamed at him with moral arguments, he couldn't shake the attraction. When he thought about it, how did he differ from Steve Brown or any other guy that wanted to claim her?

That night, Liam tossed and turned until well after midnight, his inner voice barely overriding his physical need. He longed to go to her but he knew if he did, there'd be no turning back. He didn't fully understand Vanessa's ways, but right now that didn't seem so important. What did seem important was the recollection of her taut and perfectly formed body, struggling through the surf as she reached out to Earth Mother or the Universe.

It seemed the more time they spent together, the more his moral fiber tangled into an irreparable mess of knots and frays.

PHYSICAL STRENGTH

Vanessa sat at Mick's office desk in the living room for most of Monday, textbooks and study notes spread before her. When Liam entered the room through the French doors just after three, she stretched her arms above her head while she waited for him to speak.

"Want to take a break? We could go for a swim in the river."

Vanessa's mind drifted to the waterhole down by the old bridge, where she'd swum with Billy and Nikau, before Billy's accident. Rose Churchill had died not far from there, and Vanessa hadn't been back since. The thought made her uneasy.

"We'll go up past the old pump house," he said as if sensing her reluctance.

"I don't know."

"Come on. You can't study all day."

Even though she needed a break, spending time alone with Liam wasn't ideal. She chewed her lip while she considered the invitation. Surely an hour wouldn't hurt. "Okay. I'll just get my stuff."

Vanessa flipped down the sun visor and looked out the side window as they passed the old pump house and adjacent lavender farm. She'd never been on this part of the road before. It seemed to lead to nowhere

—and the thought of going to nowhere made her nervous. "How much farther?"

He shot her a sideways glance. "There's another swimming hole at the end of this ridge."

"It says, *Private Road.*"

He pulled to a stop but kept the engine running. "I know the owners. They don't mind. Can you get the gate?"

Vanessa jumped out and opened the half-broken gate, then closed it behind them as he waited on the other side of the cattle stop. Gravel dust clung to her nostrils as it swirled in the light breeze. The heat of the late afternoon and the lack of sleep the night before had her dragging her feet, and despite an aspirin, a dull headache tugged at her temples.

Liam continued down the track to a secluded area, flanked on one side by a towering cliff face. Along the bank, willows dipped their spring green branches into the clear water, and swayed in the current. He cut the engine and looked her way.

"Coming?"

"I'll just get changed."

She watched Liam strip to his board shorts and climb down the steep bank. He waded into the water and took a deep breath before diving through the slow-flowing current, emerging further downstream. He stood in the shallows, flicking his hair off his face as he turned to look at her. His head cocked to one side in an invitation. His chest hairs glistened and his brown nipples puckered tight with the cold water. She struggled to look away.

Life had seemed so simple before she'd arrived back in the valley three days ago. He'd told her straight that night of the party that her crush was all in her head, and she'd worked hard to move on. But with Liam in front of her now, practically naked, his long hair loose and his chest heaving from the exertion, she felt like she had nowhere to hide.

She removed her jeans and t-shirt and stood on the bank, adjusting the school-issued Speedo swimsuit over her butt. She'd always been a skinny kid growing up, but lately, thin had turned to willowy, and she sensed the difference—that sexual energy of adolescence when heads turn, and boys try to hold your gaze. And plenty of boys looked Vanessa's way, but Liam wasn't a boy.

She was preparing herself to dive when he called out.

"Hold on. Let me check first." He dipped underwater for several seconds before bouncing to the surface in front of her. "Okay, it's deep enough. Dive into the middle."

"Get out of the way."

He kept staring, his stormy blue eyes sparkling in the sunlight and his straight, white teeth a stark contrast against his olive skin. He moved to the side. "Come on. The water's beautiful."

Liam watched Vanessa's body form the perfect arc as she cut through the water. She'd always been a strong swimmer. In fact, her strength was evident in everything she did. Even in the way she'd carried Ruth to bed the night before.

She emerged less than two feet in front of him. Her long hair fell from a perfect part to well below her shoulder blades and clung in seamless strands around her face. When she blinked, droplets from her eyelashes dripped onto her cheeks. As he watched her tread water, her nipples, tight with cold, peaked through the black nylon of her swimsuit. He swallowed hard.

"It's freezing."

"Harden up." Liam grabbed her around her waist and threw her high into the air, then dipped below the water to watch her fall.

Vanessa came up spluttering. "You're gonna pay for that."

He looked at her and laughed as she swam toward him and jumped onto his shoulders, trying to dunk him. He waded to the riverbank, his piggyback cargo holding on tight, and dumped her on a flat boulder. With their faces parallel and eyes locked, he struggled to hold his arousal in check. Seconds ticked by before he spoke. "Are we okay?"

She continued to look him straight in the eye without a single blink, her lips paused on their way to a smile, and she nodded. "Why wouldn't we be?"

"You gonna set that smile free?"

"Not for you." She looked away.

Liam's head dipped to catch her gaze. "Come on. Just a little?"

"But then you might think I actually like you."

"I don't have to think it. I know it." His face was so close to hers he could feel her breath on his wet lips. She stayed on the boulder, and despite the hot day, shivered with the cold. He put his arms around her in a bear hug and threw her back into the water, simply to create distance between them.

She bobbed to the surface, laughing. "I hate you."

He swam in after her. "No, you don't. Just remember that over the next few years." She looked at him, scraping her teeth over her lips as if forming a retort, but nothing came. Liam wondered if she understood how he felt—confused and more unsure of himself than he'd ever been in his life, but for now, he pushed those feelings down deep.

He waded toward her until they were so close he could see the bronze flecks in her irises. "I'm not the enemy, Ness." She dropped her focus to the water, but small worry lines tracked across her forehead. He lifted her chin until she met his gaze. "Don't shut me out. I'll always be there for you."

"Will you?"

Liam wanted to say more, but the timing wasn't right. He had to break the mood before he said something he shouldn't. "Come on. I'll show you the cave across the river."

They walked further downstream to the shallows. His hand reached for hers as they navigated the slippery river stones and gradually increasing current that pulled strongly toward the coast.

The cave—a small indentation of about thirty feet in the rock face —smelled of damp, brine, and muddy water. With the ocean less than half a mile away, the sand under their feet felt more beach-like, instead of the coarse river stones upstream.

Vanessa visibly relaxed. "What an incredible space." She placed an outstretched hand on the wall. "Look at the colors of the schist."

Liam loved watching her fascination with nature. Her enthusiasm for the small, but significant, wonders of the natural world had always intrigued him. He cleared his throat. He'd practiced what he wanted to say to her hours before, but the timing hadn't seemed right until now. "About the night of the party, I wanted to explain—"

"I get it," she interrupted. "No explanation necessary." She turned and walked away. "We'd better get back."

As he stood and watched her scurry across the shallows and clamber up the bank, he mused over the shift in their balance of power. From the moment he first saw her, looking scared to death on the doorstep five years ago, he'd felt an odd connection with her—a need to protect. And even when they didn't see each other for months on end, her presence filled the house, and quelled the sense of solitude.

Now, she had a job, Whisper, and Billy—her agent. She didn't need his explanation. She didn't need him at all.

29

WATCHING ME, WATCHING YOU

Vanessa's eyes burned with irritation as she studied her notes. She leaned back in her chair, realizing her ability to retain information had reached its limits, and gazed out the window to the eastern hill line where the moon washed the sky with a soft, tranquil light. When she turned back to the desk, Liam, dressed in boxer briefs and an open bathrobe, stood in the doorway watching her.

"Why do you always do that?"

He stared for a moment. "What?"

"Sneak up on people?"

Among the clutter of Mick's writing desk, a dull banker's lamp illuminated the shadowed planes of Liam's chest and abs. She didn't dare look any lower. She'd seen him in underwear before and couldn't go there—especially now he'd insisted that any attraction she sensed between them was supposedly all in her head.

"You should get some sleep," he said. "It's almost one." The words came out husky and low—a 'come back to bed' kind of tone. The kind guys in movies use.

She returned to the work in front of her, her pencil skittering across the lines on the page. "You should do up that robe."

Liam moved closer. "Why, am I distracting you?"

Vanessa caught the amusement in his tone. She looked at him and frowned. He'd been casually flirting with her all weekend, but this was his first shot at blatancy.

He pulled the robe together and tied the cord. "Sorry, that was—"

"All in my head," she muttered, "or inappropriate?"

"Probably the latter."

He perched on the arm of the other chair. Vanessa could tell he wanted to talk, so left the space free of her own words. In her experience, men only spoke when they wanted, and rarely when pushed.

"When are you going back to school?"

"Wednesday, on the bus. I have to be there by seven."

"I'll drive you. Then you can have an extra couple of hours at home."

"Nah, I'm good."

"I'll be in the UK by the time you're back in January," he said with a touch of reluctance.

"Yes, I know." She closed the book in front of her and packed up her things. "I'm off to bed. Goodnight."

She sensed his stare as she walked away, and as she turned into the hall, "Goodnight, Ness," followed her.

Back in her room, Vanessa couldn't sleep—the air was too close and clammy, and her mind raced with pointless thoughts and fears. She went to the kitchen for a glass of water, then sat on the steps of the veranda, grateful for the cooler air and the silence. As she looked at the night sky, the enormity of Liam leaving began to sink in. In a few weeks he'd be gone—completely faded from view.

Hot tears trickled into the corners of her mouth, and she sniffed and licked them away. When she looked skyward again, the stars were a blur of liquid light.

She heard Liam's footsteps on the decking and looked away when he sat beside her.

"What are you doing out here?"

Vanessa closed her eyes tight, forcing tears to overflow around the rims. "I was just thinking." She stopped to compose herself. "By Christmas, your life will be so different. Are you excited?"

"In some ways, but it's a big step." He stayed silent for a few moments. "Is that why you've been so distant? Because I'm leaving?"

"What did you expect? Smiles and daisy chains?"

Liam reached out and took her hand in his. "Come to my room. Just for a while?"

She shook her head. "Don't ask me to do something we both know I shouldn't do."

"Please. This might be the last night we spend together. I don't want to leave knowing you're sad because of something I've said or done." Liam let go of her hand. He stood and walked to the door, turning to look back at her before he disappeared inside.

Vanessa stayed on the veranda. His bedroom light came on, then went off. She wanted a reason to go to him, but there was none. She went anyway.

Liam sat up in bed and flicked on the lamp, his naked torso—with rounded pecs and well-defined shoulders—once again on full display. She often wondered why men flaunted their upper body without thought. If he only knew how the sight made her flush.

She sat on the chair in front of him. Vanessa was familiar with that trait of human nature where one speaks of the mundane while the real issues are ignored. Liam excelled at such conversations, and sure enough ...

"Are you looking forward to going back to school?"

Stupid question. Vanessa hated boarding at Immaculate Heart and couldn't wait to leave. "Not really."

"Do you have many friends there?"

All girls her age wanted to be popular with their peers, and Vanessa was no exception. She didn't want Liam to know she couldn't relate to the other girls and had made no close friends. "A few."

"Have you had any more ... visits?"

"No, but then they were probably all in my head, too."

Looking around, Vanessa recalled the hours she'd spent in this room—playing LPs, reading books, and lying in his bed, sometimes too close to him for comfort. Masculine energy filled the space—the jeans on the floor, the oversized stereo speakers, the dark desk with a large print of the moon on the wall above and his sketchpad open on it. This room had always been familiar to her, and yet, with the curtains drawn, it seemed foreign. Isolated.

They stared at each other across the space. Liam offered his hand. "Come here."

She shook her head. "You don't even like me." She barely spoke above a whisper, as if verbalizing her inner thoughts would somehow make them tangible. "You like pretty girls, with makeup, and flashy clothes, and tortoiseshell clips in their hair."

His gaze narrowed. "I like you …" he whispered, "more than I should."

He pulled her onto the bed beside him. She swallowed hard, her reply faltering as she struggled to exhale. His hand stroked her hair, which was tied, as usual, in a single braid finished with a length of black corded leather.

"You're a beautiful girl, Vanessa, inside and out," he said, smoothing his thumbs over her knuckles. "And that's more than makeup and tortoiseshell hair clips. There's a connection between us. You understand that, right?"

Short, shallow breaths escaped her lungs. His words skipped across her heart, leaving delicate footprints in their wake. "Don't say things like that."

"Why? It's true."

"But is it honest?" She sat perfectly still, eyes locked on his. "Tell me it's not all in my head."

Liam looked away and sighed. "It's complicated."

It was a soundless night. No wind or rain. No freight trains bound for northern and southern markets, or cars traveling the highway, but her heartbeat drummed in her ears. She crept in beside him, her small frame molding into his large one, like a frightened bird in the palm of a man's hand, not knowing if it was a place of safety or a place of danger.

They slept for several hours, but as the pearly light of dawn crept across the sky, she awoke to the strength of his erection firmly in place against the base of her spine. He stirred and pulled her closer. Sleep-warm lips caressed her nape. "I'm going to miss you." He moved his lips to the side of her neck as he gently kissed her soft skin.

She heard him sigh, felt the heave of his chest and could almost taste his reluctance as she stilled, his hands flat on her stomach. She wanted to move them to her breasts, for him to feel the firmness of her need but …

"What's going on?" she whispered.

"I have no idea." He turned her to face him and touched her lips with his—soft and slow—as unsteady thumbs stroked her jawline. "Not a damn clue."

Liam pulled back for a moment, his eyes locked on hers and a smile softening his features, then moved a little closer toward forbidden territory. He held her gently, trailing his fingertips over her skin. He kissed her again, his hand wrapped around her braid as his tongue told her secrets.

Vanessa had imagined this moment many times, as she lay on her narrow bed in the school dormitory. How would it feel to be wrapped in his arms, to have his lips caress her neck—her hands and face? Now, the urgency of their situation meant she wouldn't back away.

With her braid still twisted around his hand, Liam caressed the hollow at the base of her throat where her horseshoe always sat. "I'm sorry." His forehead came to rest on hers. "So sorry." He let the braid go, rolled onto his back and stared at the ceiling. "I shouldn't have started this. I'm a selfish bastard."

"You didn't start anything."

"Have you noticed," he whispered, "me watching you over the past few days?"

He already knew her answer. *Yes.* She watched him. He watched her. It had always been that way, those secretive looks between them—sometimes feigning disinterest, sometimes not. She nodded.

"And how does that make you feel? Knowing you have that effect on me when you're off-limits? Taboo?"

"I'm nobody's surrogate sister."

He turned to look at her. "No, but other people don't see it that way."

He nuzzled against her skin. She smelled of Pears soap mingled with a hint of perspiration, and he loved that smell—the raw scent of a woman. Pure and clean. But complicated.

Unsteady hands smoothed another lock of hair away from her face. He kissed her again, tenderly. He sighed and inhaled—the breath heavy in his lungs. She reached up, her lips not even an inch from his, and this time, *her* hands cupped his face. *Her* lips found his. *Her* tongue pushed through his barrier.

Liam responded gently, letting their shared passion build in a sensual dance as sleep left them both. He pulled Vanessa closer, his legs tangled around hers, his erection solid and ready to burst as he rubbed against the light cotton of her pajama pants.

He dismissed the narrative screaming in his head in favor of the poetry, wondering what it would be like to lead her through each stanza —the arousal, the intensity, the plateau, the release.

30

WINDSWEPT WHISPERS

"What the hell's going on? Get off her." Mick switched on the light. Vanessa buried her head in the pillow while Liam reached for the crumpled sheet at the side of the bed. "Dad, get out."

"Vanessa," Mick shouted. "Go to your room. Now!"

Liam held her firmly around her waist. "Stay where you are," he whispered as he pulled the sheet over her.

"I'll not have this … this *fornication* going on under my roof. You promised me you wouldn't touch her. She's only fifteen for God's sake." Mick's eyes stayed firmly focused on Liam's. "Vanessa, I said go to your room."

"Get the hell out," Liam said through gritted teeth. "Show some respect. It's not what you think."

"Respect? Respect?" Mick yelled. "Don't you dare talk to me about respect. What you're doing with that girl means you get no respect, not from me nor anyone else. I thought you were better than this, Liam. She's been like a sister to you. I promised her father she'd always be safe in this house."

Mick looked at Vanessa, whose eyes were wide with fear. "And you," he pointed a stern finger. "When I close this door, get out of that bed and get to your room. And don't come out until I say so. Understand?"

She said nothing.

Mick narrowed his eyes. "I said, do you understand?"

"Yes."

"Right. You have five minutes. If you're not out by then, I'll come back and drag you out by the ear." Mick left the room, slamming the door behind him.

Vanessa pressed her lips together, as she struggled to control her emotions. "What's going to happen now? He'll tell Mum."

"Don't worry." Liam bent down and kissed her lightly on the cheek. "I'll sort it out."

"But she'll send me to live with Dad, and we'll never get to see each other."

"No, she won't. We haven't done anything wrong." Vanessa moved toward the door. "Come here." Liam pulled her back into his arms. "You okay?"

She kept her focus downward. Liam dipped his head to make eye contact. "Ness?"

She nodded.

"Go back to bed for a while. We'll talk later."

Liam stared at the door long after she'd left the room. He'd crossed the line, that line that dawn often blurs. *We haven't done anything wrong.* He reached for his alarm clock—two minutes past six—then flopped back down on the bed, regretting how he dragged her into his complication and wondering just how he would 'sort it out.'

As she stood at the sink and filled the kettle, Vanessa watched puffs of spring cloud cover the gray morning sky—swirling together and apart like a time-lapse documentary she'd seen recently. She glanced up at the sound of footsteps, her face flushed with heat as she blinked away persistent tears.

"I thought I told you to stay in your room," Mick said.

She'd stayed in her room as long as she could, trying to study while her stomach growled with hunger and humiliation. Mick had always been so kind to her and her mother, and she'd repaid him with betrayal. "I'm hungry. I'm just getting a drink and a banana."

"Right. Well when you're finished, go pack your bag for school."

"But I don't have to be back until tomorrow. Liam's driving me."

"No, he's not. I've found you another ride." Mick moved into her personal space. "How could you be so stupid? How could you both betray Christie like that? How could you, Vanessa?" He reached over and took the kettle out of her hands. "Now, do as you're told. The Smiths won't want to wait around all day."

Her lip quivered. Every 'how could you?' had felt like a punch in the gut. "I'm not going today," she muttered. "I don't want to go back. I hate school, and Liam and Christie aren't—"

"Don't you dare answer me back. I'm in charge in this house. Now, if you know what's good for you, you'll do as you're told."

She stayed put. Not out of defiance, but rather, to mend this aggravation between them. She hated the thought of going back to school when Mick was upset with her.

Mick stared her down. "Fine have it your way. I'll phone your father and tell him to come and pick you up. Is that what you want? To leave here under a cloud?"

Vanessa tried to clear the lump in her throat. Mick had never threatened her in the past, and she knew he was serious. "Please, don't do that. I'm sorry."

He softened his stance and cocked his head toward the hallway. "Go on," he said softly. "I'll bring your tea down when the kettle's boiled."

He looked sad and tired—disappointed. She felt the same. Sad that Liam was leaving, tired of having a mother who didn't give a damn, and disappointed in herself.

"I've told your mum you have the chance of a ride today. You need to play along. If she or your father finds out what's been going on, there'll be hell to pay."

When Liam returned from feeding the dogs later that morning, his father was waiting for him at the garage door. He said nothing as he walked past Mick and dumped a broken leash on the work bench, then headed toward the house.

"You're not seeing her before she goes,"

Liam kept walking. "It's not what you think. We just kissed."

"Sure looked like foreplay from where I was standing."

He winced at his father's use of the word 'foreplay.' They'd never discussed anything of a sexual nature before. His mother had taught him about 'the birds and the bees' as she called it. "Dad, don't."

"What if I hadn't come in when I did? How far would you have gone, eh?" Mick's voice quietened as he fell into step beside his son. "Ruth would be furious if she knew you were in bed together … and rightly so. I can't even begin to imagine what the hell Jim Blinkly would say."

Liam stopped and turned toward his father. "So what do you expect me to do? Pretend I don't give a shit?"

"What about Christie, your girlfriend?"

"Christie and I broke up. We haven't been together for months."

"What? But you went to the ball with her the other night."

"As friends."

"I thought you two made a great pair. But what the hell do I know?"

They stood on the lawn for a moment, then made their way to the back door. Liam didn't want to discuss Christie. He'd meant to tell his father about the breakup when it happened, but the timing never seemed right. "We didn't have that connection. There wasn't a spark."

"So what are you saying? That you have that spark with Vanessa? She's just a kid," Mick reminded him. "There shouldn't be any damn spark. Not to mention, you're moving to the UK in a few weeks. You can't lead her on, then just up and leave."

"I'm not some randy schoolboy with a crush. I'd never intentionally hurt her, but what do you expect me to do? Pretend I don't have feelings for her?"

"But you have hurt her. No matter what happens now, you'll always be the boy she grew up with who crossed the line. The one who sent mixed messages then left before she could sort them out. You know she's had a crush on you for years."

"What makes you say that?"

"Well, she didn't leave daisy chains on my pillow. What the hell were you thinking? She's only fifteen."

Liam sank onto the steps of the back porch, his head in his hands. "I know. It's just ... She's different. Mature, confident. It's like I've suddenly seen her in a whole new light."

"And you want her to shine some of that light on you, is that the story?"

"I don't know. I guess. I don't expect you to understand. I hardly understand it myself."

"Well, let me tell you something. That light isn't as bright as you might think. She makes out she's doing fine when someone's looking, but don't forget to look behind the mask."

Liam frowned. Maybe his dad was right. Maybe he'd been blinded by that light for a moment—the light she switched on for those who glanced her way.

"Look, I know the score." Mick's voice softened. "I remember falling in love with your mother when she was seventeen. Our age difference was much the same as yours and Vanessa's. Her father wouldn't let me near her for the first few months. We were married within the year and moving to the farm was hard on her at first. I sometimes wonder if she ever thought about other men, ever wondered what life with someone else would have been like."

"Don't say that, Dad. Mum loved you. She worshiped the ground you walked on. You know she did."

Mick twisted the wedding band still in place on his left hand. "And I her."

"So what do I do now?" Liam asked. "Ignore her?"

"Give her time and space. You have an opportunity that a lot of guys your age can only dream about, and if you're so hell-bent on a career in finance, you need to take that scholarship."

"I thought you didn't want me to leave the farm for a city job?"

"It doesn't matter what I want. I'd never hold you back—you know that. As for Vanessa, if you still have feelings for each other in a couple of years, well okay. But there's no way in hell you can pursue her now. So make yourself scarce until she's gone. I'll tell her you said goodbye."

"I need to see her."

"Well, that's too bad."

Vanessa walked back and forth from the wardrobe to her bed, packing bits and pieces into her school bag. She could hear Mick and Liam talking but couldn't quite make out their words. She moved closer to the window, catching drifts of their conversation as it floated on the breeze.

Sitting on her bed, she wiped salty tears from her cheeks and frowned. She'd heard Liam's words carried as windswept whispers, and those whispers told her everything he didn't have the guts to say to her face.

It's not what you think. There wasn't a spark. I don't have feelings for her.

Grabbing her bag, she made her way through the living room French doors and down the driveway. She'd barely had a chance to pat Whisper when she noticed the Smith's car coming along the highway. She ran to the mailbox to meet them, and as they drove away, she noticed her mother standing on the bank waving goodbye.

FLUSHED HEART BRACELET

Liam and Mick worked through Tuesday morning without a break, any conversation between them curt and peppered with 'yes' or 'no' answers. At two o'clock, Liam left the farm without a word, and arrived in Clifton Falls an hour later. He headed straight to Immaculate Heart and parked outside the gates. He checked his watch and slouched down in his seat to wait.

Just after three thirty, he walked into the park-like grounds and made his way through a long avenue of plane trees to the office. He'd been here many times before. When he was still at school, Immaculate Heart was Saint Frank's sister school, and because of the facilities, inter-school athletic sports, concerts, and tennis matches had all taken place on this campus. The nuns had creeped him out when he was younger—they still wore full Dominican habits then—but with age came tolerance, and as he entered the hallway leading to the office, he smiled at every nun he met.

"How can I help you, young man?" The nun on duty shuffled toward the sliding glass window of the office. She looked to be at least eighty, and Liam didn't think he'd easily charm her. "Are you the brother of one of our boarders?"

"Liam O'Leary. I'm here to see Vanessa Blinkly. I'm on her list."

"Wait right there." The nun picked up a file from behind her and scanned the page through smudged round glasses perched on the end of her nose. "Liam O'Leary, you say?" She ran an arthritic finger down the paper. "Oh, here we are." Her lips settled into a disapproving line. "I'm sorry, Mr. O'Leary, but our headmistress has removed you from Vanessa's list of approved visitors."

"But I've been on Vanessa's visitor's list since she started at this school. There must be some mistake."

An imposing figure, in full habit, entered the office. "What's going on here, Sister Paul?"

"This is Mr. Liam O'Leary, Sister Monica. He's here to see—"

"I'm well aware why Mr. O'Leary is here, and I'm sorry, but you are no longer on Vanessa's list."

"That's bullshit. I need to see her."

The headmistress flashed a frown as she slipped her hands under her scapular, resting them on her ample stomach. "We don't use that kind of language here, Mr. O'Leary. Now, I'm afraid I'll have to ask you to leave. I'm well aware of the reason, and so are you."

"I have no idea what you're talking about."

She leaned in closer and lowered her voice. "It seems our little Vanessa has taken quite a shine to you and is calling you her boyfriend. I'm sure I don't need to remind you that you're treading a fine line here. Leave her be and give her a chance. She's already been in serious trouble at this school. Don't make it any harder for her than it needs to be."

"I only want five minutes, please."

"I'm sorry, but that's not possible. Sister Paul, please show Mr. O'Leary out."

As he walked back to the gate, pupils watched—whispering and grinning as they tried to catch his eye. In contrast to his entrance, Liam looked straight ahead, unable to muster a smile.

He sat outside in his pickup for another five minutes, then turned it around and parked down a side street. Like all streets in the area, an avenue of trees lined the roadside, and on every lot, small swimming pools and full-sized tennis courts adorned large mansions, which were surrounded by immaculate lawns and gardens. He'd always liked this area, not for the snob value, but more for the peaceful tranquility and its proximity to one of the city's largest green belts. In addition, the view across Carter Bay and the northern shoreline, was the best in the city. But right now, he couldn't care less about the view, or the gardens, or the green belt.

A small group of girls, all dressed in Immaculate Heart's senior uniform, walked into view. He opened the door and strolled toward them. "Do any of you know Vanessa Blinkly?"

One stopped and looked his way. The other girls kept walking. "Yeah, I do. The kid with a stiff-bristle brush for a backbone." Liam smiled at the accurate description. The girl looked older than Vanessa, and the various pins on her blazer indicated a leadership role. "I'm head girl. She's in my house."

"That's her. Can you ask her to come out for a minute?"

"She's on detention, kitchen duty. She's not allowed out of the dorm for the rest of the week, except for meals, class, and vespers."

Not again. "Why, what did she do?"

The girl leaned forward, ready to impart a secret. "She called Sister Monica a controlling fat cow in front of a group of girls and their parents."

Liam suppressed a laugh. "Shit. She didn't."

The girl giggled and raised a knowing brow. "I'm surprised she didn't get suspended. What do you want her for anyway? You look too old to be her boyfriend."

"I'm just a friend."

"Yeah? Lucky girl." She looked Liam up and down, twisting a lock of hair around her finger as she removed her Panama hat with the other hand. Her eyes narrowed. "I know you. You led the *haka* at Roger Walker's funeral."

"How do you remember that?"

She smiled. "I just do. There's something about a man leading a *haka*."

Liam felt his face flush. The girl was a blatant flirt, but he wasn't in the mood. "Look, sorry I didn't catch your name ..."

"Amber."

"Well, Amber, can you give Vanessa this?" He handed her a small brown paper bag. "Make sure she gets it, please. Tell her it's from Liam."

"Will do." She went to walk away but hesitated. "Hey, Liam? I have a pass for next Friday night if you want to thank me properly." She looked up at him through her lashes. "It's my eighteenth birthday, *and* my last day of high school."

If Liam wanted Amber to play ball, he'd have to flash his charm. "I'd love to, but I'll be back at university by then for graduation. Maybe some other time?"

"Pity."

Vanessa didn't make vespers that evening. She'd worked in the kitchen from three thirty on, and by the time the clock struck seven, she couldn't shake her mood, so sent a message to the dean saying she had a sick stomach, then lay on her bed to read. She hadn't meant to be rude to the headmistress, but sometimes her resolve vanished when she felt threatened, and she lashed out without thinking. She'd spent many days in detention at this school and that had to change. Because, although Immaculate Heart wasn't her favorite place to be, enrolling in a new school this late in the year would bring all kinds of other problems.

Soft footsteps broke into her thoughts. She looked up from her unread page and stood to attention when she saw the head girl walking toward her.

"I'm allowed to be here," she said quickly. "I'm sick. Sister Paul said I didn't have to go to vespers."

"I'm not here about vespers, but if you treat me like the enemy, I won't give you this." Amber dangled a paper bag in front of Vanessa.

"From where I sit, everyone's the enemy."

"Well, I'm trying to help, so shut your face, or I won't tell you what Liam said."

Vanessa looked at Amber with suspicion. "You've been talking to Liam? When? What did he say?"

"Not much." She held the parcel just out of Vanessa's reach. "How do you guys know each other?"

"My mum is his dad's housekeeper." She reached out to grab the bag. "Give it."

Amber gestured for Vanessa to sit and she did the same. "Only if you let me watch you open it."

Trust wasn't something she gave easily, but Amber had always treated her kindly in the past, and what other option did she have. "Fine."

As Vanessa opened the bag, Amber watched over her. Inside was a white card with a black horse sketched on the front, and a small package. She read the card then handed it to Amber, her fingers trembling and her throat dry.

"*Linked by Whisper's pulse.*" Amber ran her hands over the sketch. "Mean anything?"

"Kind of." Vanessa removed the ribbon from the tiny blue box and pulled out the gift—a silver charm bracelet—then rubbed her thumb and forefinger over the heart linking the chain.

"Cute, is it your birthday?"

Vanessa swallowed the lump in her throat, barely able to shake her head.

"So why the gift?" Vanessa didn't respond. "Wait. Have you two been"—Amber let out a two-tone whistle—"you know?"

Heat crept up Vanessa's neck and face. She wasn't one for sharing, and didn't want to confide in Amber in case she went straight to Sister Monica. Silence was her best option.

"Look," Amber continued, "if there's something going on with Liam that's upsetting you, I'm here to listen."

"Nothing's going on."

"Good, because he's taking me out next Friday."

Vanessa's response was swift and her words echoed around the dormitory. "You're a liar."

"Sometimes we have to lie to get the truth. If this guy is pestering you, someone needs to know about it."

"He isn't pestering me. I love him." Vanessa immediately regretted opening her mouth.

"But you grew up together? That's a bit incestuous isn't it?"

Vanessa didn't expect Amber to understand. "Everyone says he's like my brother, but he's not."

"Maybe, but the truth is, you're underage and he should know better." She rose from the bed and went to walk away. "You'd better hide that bracelet before one of the nuns finds it. And don't worry—I'm not your competition. Your competition is circumstance."

32

SET THEM FREE

On the drive back to the valley, Liam recalled Vanessa telling him about Friday afternoon swimming lessons at the Municipal Pool. She'd said it was her favorite day of the week, and while trying to see her was a bad idea, sometimes bad ideas were disguised as good ones when you were desperate.

He waited until Thursday evening to tell Mick. Ruth had been in bed all day with a cold, so the men cooked steak, onions, and creamy mash. He knew his father would be suspicious, but Liam's thoughts had been all over the place this week, and there was still no clarity to them.

"I have to go to town tomorrow, to see the travel agent about my trip."

Liam watched Mick cut through his steak and take a bite. He chewed for several seconds, his gaze on Liam. "Oh yeah? Well, stay away from that school."

"What do you think I'm going to do? Kidnap her? You've already had me removed from the visitor's list."

"Yeah, well, I don't want another phone call from that nun telling me you've been in her office throwing your weight around."

"You've made your point."

"When do you have to be in Scotland?"

"The second week of December."

"Right." Mick sighed. "So it's just me and Ruth then. For Christmas, I mean."

Consumed with self-doubt, Liam turned his pickup onto the southbound highway and made his way toward Clifton Falls. The heat of the afternoon sun intensified the further south he drove, and his sweat-soaked shirt stuck to the vinyl of the seat.

The sax intro of 'Baker Street' seemed to blast from every available radio station, and when Gerry Rafferty and the endless stream of jingles for new tires and TV sets became too much, Liam slotted a Bob Seger tape into the stereo. He pumped up the volume and wound down his window, hoping the wind and 'We've Got Tonight' would clear his head.

As he pulled into a parking space opposite the pool, Liam saw Vanessa standing alone at the back of the group while they waited for the doors to open. She was dressed in Immaculate Heart's summer uniform—a light blue cotton pinafore and a white blouse. Instead of the usual braid, she wore pigtails secured with navy blue ribbons that matched the band of her Panama hat. He couldn't get over how young she looked. Like a little girl, lost in thought as she fiddled with the cord of her PE bag.

Liam rested his head on the headrest and let out a heavy sigh, then pinched the bridge of his nose under the base of his sunglasses. He'd thought he had grasped the situation, but now, as she stood across the road, her school uniform baggy around her chest, the enormity of her feelings—their feelings—punched him in the gut.

He looked back, mentally urging Vanessa to do the same. When she eventually noticed him, she went to bolt across the street. Before she reached the curb, Amber stepped in front of her, blocking her way. Vanessa's head dropped as Amber spoke to her. She nodded several times, and when the pool opened a few moments later, she walked through the front door, without glancing back.

As the consequences of his actions overwhelmed him, he once again leaned back and closed his eyes. He let out yet another heavy sigh and sat lost in his thoughts, until a sharp rap on the driver's side window drew his attention. He wound down the window.

"What the hell are you doing here?" Amber stood, hands on hips, waiting for a reply.

"I need to talk to Vanessa."

"Look, I don't know what's going on, but I can guess. You need to leave. Vanessa can't afford another suspension. She's inside crying as it is." Amber went to walk away.

Liam called her back. "Amber?"

She turned and waited.

"Thanks for looking out for her."

"Someone has to. She's a likable brat. But she's also underage, Liam. Remember that."

On the drive back to the farm, Liam thought of nothing but Vanessa, his concentration so deep, he almost didn't register he was back in the valley. He hadn't eaten lunch, and now his stomach churned with nerves and regret.

Mick glanced up when he entered the kitchen. "How did it go? Get everything sorted?"

"Not yet."

"Ruth left your dinner in the oven."

Ignoring the dinner comment, Liam sat at the table opposite his father. He rarely confided in Mick about his personal life, but he felt the need to talk. "I saw Vanessa today, outside the pool."

"I told you to stay away from her."

Liam knew his expression reflected his pensive mood. "She looked so lost. I've acted like a complete asshole."

"Go to the UK, give her time. Let her have a chance to be a normal teenager."

"And what if we never see each other again?"

"Then she was never yours to have."

"Is that your best advice, Dad? That 'if you love someone, set them free' bullshit? People stay apart for all kinds of reasons. It doesn't always mean they weren't meant to be together. It just means life, or circumstances, or the damn universe got in the way."

PART II

1978 - 1980

PART I

A PAPER PLANE

Liam sat on the bed in a small hotel not far from Edinburgh Castle. He'd slept better than expected, given the hotel's location and the overly heated room, and had woken late, reluctant to start the day. He sat for some time, mentally listing the regrets eating him up inside. He'd thought about contacting Vanessa at her father's before he left, but in the end, he'd decided against it. Instead, he'd slipped out of the country without a word—like the coward he thought himself to be.

He glanced at his watch. Eight forty-five, January the eighth—Vanessa's birthday. It had been barely four weeks since he'd left the valley, but it seemed like months. The day before, he'd trekked up the cobbled streets in the freezing cold to Castle Rock and looked out over the city, like any other tourist. When he'd arrived back at the hotel around six, he hadn't taken a single photograph.

Heading out in search of breakfast, Liam pulled his jacket tight around his chest. The air was frigid, and his socks and gloves weren't nearly thick enough for the Scottish winter. He crossed the busy street toward a row of specialty stores, making a mental note to buy warmer clothes.

Through the barred window of a small jewelry store, a paper airplane charm displayed on a black velvet stand caught his eye. It reminded him of the time he and Vanessa had thrown paper planes around the living room, trying their hardest to hit one another.

"How may I help?" The assistant beamed as she fiddled with the hair around her face.

"That airplane charm in the window, may I see it?"

"I'll fetch it. Is it for your sweetheart?" The girl had a broad Scottish accent, so strong Liam had to listen carefully to understand her.

He smiled but said nothing as he held the tiny charm with thick fingers, turning it over several times. "I'll take it."

"Would you like it wrapped in pretty paper? What's her favorite color?"

"Blue. Thank you."

As she wrapped the charm, the assistant fired endless questions across the counter. His nationality, why he was visiting Edinburgh, and as she handed him the package, whether he would like to take her out for a drink. He declined with grace, saying he wasn't sure if he would be around later.

Liam entered a bookstore, two doors down, and picked out a plain white card, an envelope, and a black ink pen. Later, as he waited for his breakfast in a crowded pub across the road, he thought of Vanessa again. Her richly colored perception of horses and people, so different to his black-and-white view of the world; and the difference in their ages, which would begin to mean less as the years passed. Fifteen to twenty-one may seem inappropriate, but twenty-five to thirty-one—an inconsequential gap.

The card sat open in front of him as he held the pen. Conversations laced with a thick Scottish burr hummed around him as his own words stopped and started. Only a few words, but he hoped they were enough to convey his message. His drunken New Year's resolution had been to get on with his life and let her do the same. And in the lonely days since, he'd decided the only way forward was to draw a line under what had happened—to give her closure. He owed her that much.

He sat back in his chair, trying to recall the lines of the charm in his pocket. He closed the card and began sketching, stopping only when the server placed his cooked breakfast in front of him. People came and went, and young women glanced his way, but his attention stayed on the pen in his hand. His breakfast remained virtually untouched.

Standing outside the Post Office later, he placed a row of stamps on the envelope and turned it over, ready to write his return address on the back flap. He stopped. He didn't want a reply, so he left the space blank.

His stomach flipped over once, twice—like an engine struggling to fire. He kissed the back flap, and before his thoughts could hold him back, pushed the envelope through the slot labeled *First Class and Airmail*.

Liam stood beside the red mailbox for several minutes, wondering if he'd done the right thing by not including a letter. But what would he have said? In his opinion, physical action always trumped the written word, but at that moment, he had no action to give.

It was late morning when he arrived back at the hotel. Tomorrow, he would move into a small flat in Marchmont, and the following day would start his lectures.

THE INTERNATIONAL STUDENT

"You wanted to see me?" Liam cleared his throat as he studied the dean's expression. He knew why he was here.

"Mr. O'Leary. Please, come in."

Liam entered the office and closed the door behind him. It was a stereotypical space, with bookshelves lining the walls and a large Persian rug on the floor. The dean indicated a chair in front of her desk and tossed Liam's assignment across the polished hardwood. Her expression gave nothing away. As Liam picked up the stapled pages and stared at the red circled 'C' on the top left-hand corner, she sat back in her chair and folded her arms.

It was worse than he thought. "A 'C'? I got a 'C' on my first assignment?"

She leaned forward, her left hand cradling her chin. "You think you deserve more?"

"I've never had a 'C' in my life."

"We can't all be straight 'A' students, Liam. But I must admit, I expected more from you given your previous university's academic transcript. Is there something else going on? You're a long way from home. Have you made any friends here?"

"I'm not homesick, if that's what you mean. I've just been a bit unfocused and sick with a head cold."

The woman nodded and offered a thin smile. It wasn't the first time Liam had called a hangover a head cold and it wouldn't be the last.

"Okay. But try not to miss any more lectures, or we will lock horns, do you understand? 'C's might get degrees, Liam, but prove to me you're better than that. If past cycles are anything to go by, world financial markets will shift significantly over the next ten years. And it is my observation that mediocre financiers struggle to survive instability in the marketplace."

"I understand."

"Good. You may leave."

As he left the dean's office, Liam greeted his roommate, Hamish, sitting outside waiting for him. Hamish cracked a grin. "What did she say?"

Liam showed him his paper. "Just the 'I expected more' speech before she pointed out the perils of mediocrity."

"So she likes you. Deans don't usually mollycoddle students. This calls for a celebration."

"Piss off, it was one of your celebrations that got me into this mess. I've worked my butt off since I was thirteen to save for this opportunity, and I'm not about to walk away with a fistful of 'C's for my efforts."

"Nice speech, but the occasional beer never hurt anyone."

"I'm laying off the booze for a while. I need to focus." Liam shoved his assignment in his backpack. He'd go over it when he had time to study his mistakes. "She also asked if I was homesick."

"And are you?"

Liam hadn't really thought about this until the dean prompted him. Maybe she was right. He was restless and not sleeping well, and Vanessa flitted in and out of his thoughts most days. "Maybe. It's certainly an adjustment."

"Come on, mate," Hamish stood and zipped up his jacket. "It's time you drowned your sorrows over Vanessa the schoolgirl once and for all."

Liam looked at Hamish and frowned. He remembered telling Hamish about Vanessa, but not exactly what he'd said. "Vanessa, 'the schoolgirl'? What else did I tell you that night?"

"To be honest, it was mainly your inflated ego talking, and I was pretty wasted myself. But from what I remember, you played for the varsity First XV rugby team, graduated with honors and earned a scholarship to study in this fine city. Your father wanted you to stay home and run the family farm, which he's slowly destroying because he doesn't see the value of diversification, but you want to see the world first. And you may have mentioned, more than once, that you're in love with a beautiful blonde who rides a black horse."

Liam stood, speechless for a moment. "Shit. That's the last time I spill my guts when I'm wasted. In fact, I'm never getting wasted again."

"Famous last words." Hamish slapped Liam on the back. "Right, let's go to the pub. You can introduce me to that American chick that works the bar. What's her name again? Cassie? Kassandra?"

BLACK INK, WHITE CARD

1978

"You have mail, lass." Mick took the envelope from the mantelpiece above the coal range and handed it to Vanessa. "It's from Scotland."

Vanessa searched Mick's bronze, weathered face—suddenly seeing him in a whole new light. His tone conveyed a warmth, and she could tell by his expression that he was genuinely pleased for her. She accepted the letter with thanks, hurried to her room and sat on the bed. Once settled, she flipped the envelope from front to back, searching for a return address, but there was none. The stamps, with their profile of Queen Elizabeth II, and a January the eighth postmark were the only indication of the envelope's origin.

She opened the flap carefully, expecting to find a long newsy letter, but there was no folded note. Running her fingers over the sketch of a paper plane on the front of the card, she wondered what it meant. When she flicked the card open, the inscription inside explained its significance in less than two dozen words:

> *I left you on a paper plane.*
> *Creased and fragile.*
> *There's no way back.*
> *The wind isn't blowing south.*

Take care.
Liam xx

There had been no finality in Liam's departure before, but now she had a message from the man himself. Life had been difficult since that November dawn, and yet, as the hours slipped into days and days into weeks, Vanessa had made an uneasy peace with Liam's decision to leave. He had his future to consider, and she didn't play a part in that future.

Even so, she still half-expected him to walk through the kitchen door before every meal. To sit at the table and wink at her as her mother served up plates of greasy mutton and boiled-to-death cabbage. She smiled at the thought.

Then she cried.

The day had dawned with a promising air—warm without the closeness of recent days—and a cloudless, bright blue sky. The card, while not the news she had hoped for, had brought with it a sense of inevitability … of finality. She slipped it under her pillow for safe-keeping while she went to help her mother with dinner. As she reached the kitchen door, a familiar voice lifted the hairs on the back of her neck.

"Vanessa, is that you?" her mother called. "Vanessa, come here this minute."

As Vanessa entered the kitchen, the smell of freshly brewed coffee greeted her. Her mother sat at the table drinking out of a large pottery goblet. And she had company. Steve Brown sipped from his mug as he made eye contact with Vanessa. His lazy stare turned into a smirk as he returned his mug to the table and leaned back in his chair, chest puffed out in self-importance.

"You wanted to see me?" Vanessa asked as she looked away from Steve. He was an obnoxious prick and not worthy of a response to his attempt at intimidation.

"I'd better be off," Steve said. "I'm sure you two have plenty to talk about."

Ruth rose from the table and saw Steve to the door with a spring in her step and a coy smile that Vanessa hadn't seen in a long while. She stood motionless as she listened to the conversation drifting from the back porch. "Thanks, Steve, both for your honesty, and the tipple," her mother said.

"No problem," Steve replied. "Don't be too hard on her. She's still a kid."

Vanessa waited with a mixture of dread and impatience as her mother returned and moved to the sink where she washed a head of lettuce before placing it on an old cotton tea towel to drain.

"Is it true?" Her mother didn't even look at her. "About you and Liam?"

"Pardon?"

Ruth turned side on, the lettuce-filled tea towel in her hand dripping above the sink. "According to Steve, you let Liam touch you before he went away."

"He's a liar."

"You're the liar. Does Mick know about this? Does he know you're responsible for Liam and Christie breaking up? That it's your fault Liam left?"

"It's not what you think. That's not true. I didn't break—"

"And how do you know what I think? Steve said everyone's talking about you. Everyone. All over town. How do *you* think it makes me feel, knowing my daughter spread her legs for a man who's like a brother to her? That's like incest Vanessa … incest. Not to mention you were underage."

"I never did. And even if I had, Liam's not my brother," Vanessa yelled, her face tense with frustration. "He was never my brother, and he will never be my brother. Why does everyone keep saying he is? I hate it here without him. I can't breathe … can't stand being here when you're drunk all the time. I can't stand it."

The sting of her mother's palm registered before Vanessa even realized she'd been slapped. "That's enough," Ruth yelled. "Don't you ever talk to me like that again. In fact, don't ever talk to me again, period."

Vanessa hurried to her room and slammed the door. She didn't have to look in the mirror to see the imprint of her mother's hand. The sensation was enough. The heat, the bite, the shame.

She stayed shut away. There was no dinner. No music. No Liam to creep to when she needed him. And worst of all, in the corner of the ceiling, at the junction between light and dark, she swore *moko* woman had returned to stand in judgment over her.

3 6

KEEP AWAY

The next morning, Vanessa hurried to Whisper's field, eager to spend time with her flighty friend. She liked to think they understood each other's ways. They were both headstrong, and in her mind, misunderstood, so that made them equals. Her mother didn't speak to her at breakfast, and as she watched Ruth move around the kitchen, she realized how much of a shell of a woman her mother had become. She looked similar, but inside there was nothing left.

She rode for at least an hour, worrying the small cut on her lip—courtesy of her mother's hand—with an insistent tongue. Vanessa didn't realize how far from home she'd ventured until the sight of Steve Brown reminded her. She pulled Whisper to a halt.

His gaze rested on her chest. "What are you doing way out here on your own?"

Vanessa had once thought him a handsome man but now saw him for the creep he was. "Mind your own business and keep away from me."

Steve removed his work gloves, pulling at the fingers one by one. He fiddled with the wire cutter in his right hand and used his bandana to wipe the sweat from under his hat with his left. "Don't be like that, sweetheart. Tell you what, why don't I take half an hour off? Let's go to the creek for a quick dip, then you can show me some tricks. I've heard you can do talented things with that pretty little mouth, and from what I remember, you're a decent kisser."

Vanessa struggled to hold Whisper in check as he reared back, away from Steve's outstretched hand. "Piss off," she shouted. "I'm not that kind of girl, no matter what you told my mother."

Steve took a step back and leaned on the fence post, a cocky smirk on his face, and a knowing glint in his cold eyes. "That's not what your brother said. In fact, he said plenty about what type of girl you were before he left—"

"Shut your face. You're a dirty-minded bastard. As if I'd want to spend time with you. You creep."

"Come on, Vanessa. It's okay. I won't get run out of town like your brother. Not now you're legal. I just want a bit of fun. No harm in us rubbing each other's backs."

"Liam is not my brother. He wasn't run out of town, and the only back I'll be rubbing is Whisper's."

"I heard his father told him to piss the hell off. That's the gossip around the district anyway. They say he dirtied his own nest."

"That's not true."

Steve stepped forward. "Come on, sweetheart."

"Didn't you hear me? I'm not that kind of girl."

"So you still have your cherry? I sure as hell would love it if that's the case. I like a little bit of cherry myself. But that bastard Liam took the first bite, didn't he? Here"—he stepped closer and grabbed Whisper's reins—"let me help you down, darlin'." Steve gripped Vanessa's boot as Whisper reared back, struggling against Steve's hold.

Vanessa kicked her foot free. "Let go, you asshole."

"Come on, Vanessa. Don't be like that. The harder you fight and the more dirty words you say, the harder I get. I bet you love a bit of hard cock."

"Whisper, up. Whisper, up." Reacting to her command, Whisper reared up and lashed out with his front hooves, sending Steve stumbling backward into the fence, breaking the wire he'd been repairing.

"What the fuck," he yelled as he struggled to his feet. "Get that goddamn horse away from me before he kills me, you cock-teasing bitch."

"You'll come to a fiery end one day, Steve Brown. Mark my words," Vanessa said through gritted teeth. "Stay away from me, or next time he'll grind you into the ground."

"Next time you won't be on that fucking horse, and the only person doing the grinding will be me. I'll find you, sweetheart, and when I do, you won't be in the position to refuse. Predictions or no predictions."

"Whisper, giddy up. Giddy up, boy."

Her mother glanced up as Vanessa walked into the kitchen. It seemed every time Ruth looked at her now, she did so with annoyance. "What's the matter with you?"

"What do you care?"

"Don't you dare talk to me like that."

"How *should* I talk to you? You never believe anything I say. You didn't even ask me what happened with Liam. How do you know what went on?"

"I know enough."

"You believe that asshole Steve over me?" Vanessa couldn't contain her anger, and her words bounced off the kitchen walls. "Well, guess what? He just tried to drag me off Whisper, so we could have a bit of 'fun.' Would that make you happy, Mum? Me and Steve Brown having some fun?"

"Don't be ridiculous." Her mother moved between the fridge and the sink, not once making eye contact with Vanessa. "Steve's a grown man. What would he want with a young girl like you? You're letting that imagination of yours run wild again. Are you sure you haven't been leading him on like you did Liam?"

"As if. He's a pig. And I never led Liam on. Ever."

"Stop that talk." Her mother slammed the fridge door. "Steve's a good worker, and Mick would be furious if he knew you were trying to stir up trouble. You just want to punish him because he told me your dirty little secret."

"There is no dirty secret. I love Liam."

"You love him?" Her mother scoffed. "Well, he obviously doesn't love you, does he?"

Vanessa swallowed hard and blinked several times, hands clenched at her sides. "You don't know how he feels. You don't know a damn thing."

"He'd come back and face the music if he did, you silly girl. Now go to your room."

Vanessa went to her room, but there was no way in hell she was staying there. Not this time. She lifted the casement window, climbed out onto the veranda, and ran to the stables, her lips pressed together in an attempt to hold the fall of tears. They fell anyway.

She hated the stables. Hated how everything on the farm was broken, old and smelly. She grabbed a shovel and started mucking out the stalls, greeting everything she touched with an angry curse. Vanessa worked until she was so tired, she could hardly stand. When she finally returned to the house, her mother hadn't left her dinner, so she went to bed hungry.

CRACKS IN THE GLASS

1979

Vanessa stood at her wardrobe door and flicked through the few items hanging from wire coat hangers. Mick had promised four years ago to replace the mirror, but like most things around the O'Leary homestead, the job had been added to a very long list. So the crack in the glass remained, distorting her image every time she looked at it.

She grabbed a floaty skirt, and the white muslin top Christie had given her three years before. After what had happened between her and Liam, the clothes felt tainted—stained with regret. Christie had been so kind to her, and Vanessa had repaid that kindness with jealousy. She hadn't comprehended this as she kissed Liam that November dawn, but whenever she'd thought of him over the following months, she'd also thought of Christie, and the part she'd played in their breakup. Liam may have said he and Christie were already over, but that didn't stop the sense of responsibility she sometimes felt.

On warm sunny days, she didn't feel so bad, but on stormy nights, when she lay in her room listening to distant thunder, and crossed another day off the calendar, she understood what it felt like for a man to discard you. To cast you aside as if your feelings meant nothing to him.

Her mother's appearance at her bedroom door broke into her thoughts. "What are you all dolled up for?"

"I'm going to Nikau's birthday party with Billy. I told you last night."

"Yes, well, stop the attitude, or you can stay home."

Vanessa peeked out the window as Billy arrived in his father's car. She wanted to tell her mother to butt out of her life, but she knew if she did, there would be no party. "I have to go. I won't be late home."

Ruth stood aside. "Go on, then. And, Ness?" She called her back. "You look very pretty in that top."

A solid lump formed in her throat. "Thanks, Mum."

"What's going on with you and Steve Brown?" Billy's tone conveyed his concern as they pulled up outside Nikau's.

"Nothing, why? You know I can't stand the guy."

"He's told everyone he's sleeping with you, and not only that, he's described the act, or rather acts, in graphic detail. You need to be careful. He's a filthy bastard."

Vanessa wasn't surprised by Billy's words, but they still hurt. Small town judgement was alive and well in the valley, and she'd been judged enough already. "You think I don't know that? He's in my face every chance he gets. Keeps telling me he doesn't like a tease."

"What? Why didn't you say something sooner?"

Vanessa stared straight ahead. Liam had warned her about Steve and his caustic mouth, but she'd underestimated how far Steve would take his revenge. She'd thought of telling Mick, but her mother was right. Steve was one of Mick's best contractors. What right did she have to interfere with their working relationship? "I can handle it."

"Have you told Mick?"

"I don't want to cause any trouble. You know how it's been since Liam left. Mum hardly speaks to me as it is."

Billy sighed and reached for the door handle. "Come on, let's go inside. You can forget about Steve Brown and his filthy mouth, and I'll forget about the Churchills and how I screwed up their lives."

Vanessa wanted to ask Billy how he was coping but now wasn't the right time. She knew he felt uncomfortable being around Rose's friends. He said they looked at him with pity instead of compassion. Sure enough, conversation stopped as they walked inside until Nikau came over and slapped Billy on the back. He looked at Vanessa and smiled. Even though they'd disconnected, he still called occasionally just to talk. But she couldn't go back. And anyway, his parents wanted him to join the priesthood, so what was the point? She leaned over and kissed him on the cheek. "Happy Birthday."

"Thanks. What are you guys drinking?"

Billy held up a bottle of Summer Wine and a six-pack of beer. "It's the only thing I could find at home that Mum wouldn't miss."

Vanessa followed Nikau and Billy into the kitchen. Three of Rose's friends whispered to one another as she walked past. That feeling of inadequacy slammed into her gut. She hated parties. To her they were the loneliest places in the world. She leaned on the kitchen counter and sipped from a paper cup as Nikau and Billy talked about surfing and rugby, and drank beer. At seventeen, they were underage but living out in the country, with hardly a cop in sight, they drank anyway.

No one spoke to her, but plenty stared. She moved closer to Billy. He glanced at her and smiled, that special 'I've got you' smile he always had for her.

It wasn't that she didn't want girlfriends, her life was just simpler without them. That way she didn't have to explain about her mother, or why her parents had split, or the stupid crush she had on a man who now lived on the other side of the world. Her bubble was the better place to be.

She hadn't even noticed Nikau moving away to talk to someone else until Billy's words interrupted her thoughts. "Let's go outside."

Vanessa followed Billy out the back door and across the lawn to a huge fire pit surrounded by hay bales, picnic rugs, and wooden bench seats. They sat in the shadows and drank the alcohol, lost in their thoughts and oblivious to those around them. "Any word from Liam?" Billy asked.

"I don't expect to hear from him again."

"Why not?"

"We're from different worlds. We just happened to share a space for a while, that's all."

"You're not the first girl to have a crush on an older man. Don't put yourself down for that."

Vanessa watched the flames dance, and across the fire, she noticed Nikau with his arm around a girl she'd never seen before. She looked away. "Some days, after he left for the UK, all I managed to do was breathe. Coming from a broken home, and with Mum the way she is, I just wanted to be like other girls. Maybe I was simply looking for a father figure."

Billy chuckled. "The guy's only six years older than you … hardly a father figure." A long silence followed. "Did you two ever …?"

"He kissed me once—before he left. You know, really kissed me. I feel stupid when I think about it." Vanessa bit her bottom lip as she recalled laying with Liam in his large bed, his hands on her face and the heat of his body close to hers. "Mick found us in bed together. I've never been so embarrassed in my life."

More silence. "I've never had sex," Billy confessed.

Vanessa's gaze moved from the flames to Billy. It had never occurred to her that he'd still be a virgin. "You're a virgin? No way."

"Yep. I always thought I'd lose it before any of my friends. Now I can't even think about other girls. I feel like Rose is looking down on me. Judging me."

She offered him the bottle. He shook his head. "I've already had too many beers. Shit, I hate parties. I want to go to the beach, lie on the sand and let the tide carry me away."

Vanessa downed the remainder of the wine straight from the bottle and sat it on the ground. She stood and offered her hand. "Come on. We have a beach waiting."

"I can't drive. I'm wasted."

"It's not far. We can walk."

It was just after ten. The sun had set over two hours ago, but a luminous moon peeked above the forest of tall pines to the east. Tuckers Road was quiet and deserted at this time of night, but they could hear the roar of the surf as they climbed the gate to the beach track. Vanessa remembered the last time she'd been here—the night of her fifteenth birthday. So much had changed since then, she could hardly keep up.

The beach was deserted. It reminded her of a book Billy had given her for her last birthday, 'Jonathan Livingston Seagull.' She and Jonathan were of the same cut—outcasts, determined to succeed for no one other than themselves.

Driftwood scattered the shore, the result of a recent storm. It made the beach seem more fascinating—an abstract work of art. They sat— Vanessa with her legs crossed in lotus position, Billy with his elbows resting on his knees as his eyes skimmed the horizon. The sand felt cool and slightly damp under her skirt, but the air was warm and still, the waves full.

"Do you ever wonder what would've happened … if she'd lived?"

Billy looked at her but didn't reply. He lay back and gazed at the sky. "I talk to her sometimes … when I'm alone. But I never feel like she hears me."

"Sorry, that was a dumb question. I'm tipsy. Sorry for being so stupid."

He turned his head to look at her. "You're not stupid. Far from it. And I think of nothing else. All the what-ifs. They screw with my head."

Minutes crept by before they spoke again. She lay beside him and traced the stars with a fingertip. The only constellation she knew was Orion—the 'iron pot' as her mother called it, so that had always been her favorite. "Billy, do you think I'm plain looking?"

"Now you really are being stupid." Billy staggered to his feet. He reached out and pulled her up, then ran into the water, his jeans becoming soaked to the knees. He called back over his shoulder, "You're very pretty, Ness. Never think you're not."

She ran after him, prancing like a filly into the surf, the waves lapping around her legs as she held her skirt above the water. Billy slid an arm around her and pulled her close. They stood, molded together for a few moments until he let go and took her hand. "You okay?" he asked.

"I'm getting there."

He turned toward her, his face barely an inch from hers and whispered, "You're amazing, Ness. Inside and out."

Vanessa stepped back. She frowned. "We should go."

He stepped closer. "Not yet."

"Billy?"

"I haven't kissed anyone since that day … the day she died." Billy let out a soft sigh. "I want to remember what it's like."

"I haven't kissed anyone either, since Liam." She stood on tiptoe and kissed him gently on the lips as the sea-foam crept around them. "There."

Billy looked at her, eyes wide. She kissed him again, and again until he slipped one hand under her top while the other fumbled with the button of her skirt. Vanessa continued responding to his touch as they stumbled up the beach, and let the energy of the moment carry her away to a place where, from that point on, their friendship would never be the same.

Afterward, as they lay on the sand—the muggy February air and the booze suffocating her thoughts—Billy's hand slipped into hers. He held on tight. "I'm sorry."

A tear mingled with the sand on her cheek. She hadn't imagined her first time would be with Billy. "Don't be. I wanted it too." She sat up and stared across the water, physically uncomfortable and emotionally spent. "I wanted to feel alive, cared for. Needed."

"I care about you, Ness."

"I know. But we're each other's second best. You know that, too, right? We can't be lovers ever again, Billy. I need you for other things. And besides, your soul mate is coming for you."

Billy scoffed. "Really? I doubt it."

3 8

FIRST YEAR RULES

Jim and Karen had given Vanessa a used Mazda five-door wagon for her seventeenth birthday, and as she drove into Clifton Falls and along Seacliff Road, the sense of independence was so intense, she grinned from ear to ear.

Clifton Falls General Hospital had been a major presence on the city's skyline since the 1930s and she had always thought it impressive. But as she entered the nurses dorm parking lot, her hands gripped the steering wheel as she surveyed the building up close.

Vanessa stepped out of the car, grabbed her bag, and after taking a deep breath, walked to the main entrance. Once inside, her room—sporting a narrow bed, a tiny locker, and one small nightstand—looked more like a cell than a bedroom. Still, as she stood at the window and looked out over Carter Bay glistening in the sunshine, she smiled. Anything would be better than her room at the O'Leary's.

Startled back to reality by a knock at the door, Vanessa turned and waited, wondering if she was hearing things. No one knew she was here. She opened the door a fraction.

"Well, haven't you changed over the last two years? You actually look like a teenager instead of a little kid."

"Amber, what are you doing here?"

"Same as you, but I've got two years under my belt, so it's Nurse Amber to you." Amber laughed and jumped on the bed. "I saw your name on the list. Welcome to the antiseptic grindstone."

"Thanks. I'm so excited. I've been counting down the days."

"Yeah, well don't get too excited. You're at the bottom of the food chain, remember. None of the resident doctors will even look at you in the first year, but we do have some handsome male nurses on the team."

"That's fine by me. I'm not here to find a boyfriend."

"Don't tell me you're still pining over that O'Leary guy? What's his name again?"

Vanessa thought for a moment. She'd asked herself that question only a few days before. *Was she still pining over him?* "Liam, and no, I haven't seen him in ages."

"How come?"

"He's in Scotland, doing his master's."

Amber frowned. "Really? That's a million miles away. Still, the world is full of eager men." She checked her watch. "Come on. I'll show you around before dinner. It starts at five thirty so we can't be late. They have a new dessert bar. It's the only thing I look forward to."

Vanessa followed Amber down four flights of stairs to the ground floor. Amber pointed out the dining hall before entering a long internal corridor leading to the main wing of the hospital.

"My rules for your first year," Amber said as she showed Vanessa around. "Number one. Take the stairs, always. I put on ten pounds in as many months when I first started. Two, don't gossip. Three, don't flirt with the patients, especially the young guys in Male Orthopedic. Some of them are in traction for weeks and have nothing better to do than mentally strip the modesty panels off a nurse's bodice." She leaned in closer. "They found a third-year nurse naked in the shower with a patient the other night. It's been hushed up because her father's a bigwig on the board, but if you get caught doing something like that, you're usually out. Mind you, he was hot, and apparently, his cock was enormous. Sorry, penis, I mean. We're nurses, so we should use the correct anatomical term."

Vanessa felt her cheeks flush. She wanted to giggle but stopped herself. "You're joking."

"It gives the term 'sponge bath' a whole new meaning. I'll point her out to you one day, but remember"—Amber put her index finger to her lips in a shush gesture—"loose lips sink ships."

"What's a modesty panel?"

Amber ran her hands over the double strip of material running down her chest. "This right here. I like to think of it as a nipple warmer."

Vanessa's eyes were as wide as her grin. She'd never heard of such a thing.

"Next, rule number four, stay away from the registrars. Most of them are married anyway, and if you think they're keen, it's all in your head. If it's in their head, then they're trouble. And finally, rule number five, you must always remember—Matron's word is law, same for the ward sister and the nurse educators. It's like being in the army. You say, 'Yes, Matron,' and then 'yes' some more. Get it?"

Vanessa grinned. "Yes, Nurse Amber."

"Good."

They were back at the dining hall right on five thirty. Vanessa paused for a moment. The scene reminded her of Immaculate Heart, but strangely, she no longer felt like she was in the lion's den. As they entered, several other nurses joined them, introducing themselves to Amber's younger friend, and by the time they'd finished dessert, Vanessa couldn't stop smiling.

39

SILVER SNOWFLAKE

1980

Vanessa turned left and followed the familiar driveway to the O'Leary homestead. The sky was overcast, and the late February day couldn't decide whether or not to rain. She'd volunteered to work through the festive season, and in the weeks that followed, she'd been too busy to visit her mother, until today.

Whisper looked up with mild interest and, when he realized it was her, danced along the fence line calling her name on the wind. Vanessa pulled over onto a narrow passing verge and ran to greet him, her hands smoothing love into his mane as she whispered secrets into his ear.

She stayed there for some time before making her way to the house. The thought of sleeping in her old room, even for a night or two, filled her with anxiety, something that had all but left her over the past twelve months. Life at O'Leary's was no longer part of her world, and she wanted to keep it that way. Sure, Vanessa loved the farm, but the house held years of ghosts and memories she couldn't process. Staying away seemed the best defense.

When Vanessa entered the kitchen, her mother was sitting at the table, looking frail and vacant and wearing a dress that had seen better days. "Hi, Mum." She bent down to kiss her on the cheek.

"How are you, sweetie?" She spoke her words with great care, and Vanessa wondered if she could possibly be sober. "It seems ages since you were home."

Vanessa sat opposite. The change in her mother's appearance shocked her. Her nails bitten to the quick, her complexion pallid and her hair unkempt. "Yes. It's been a while."

"How's your father?" Ruth asked. "He was always such a good-looking man. I suppose he's still with that woman?"

"You mean Karen, his wife."

Vanessa's terse reply didn't seem to register.

"So. You're near the top of the class at that nursing school, are you? It seems I must have done something right if I raised you into the woman you've become."

"Yes, I'm doing okay, and I love it there." Vanessa ran a critical eye around the dirty kitchen. "Shall I give you a hand with dinner?"

"What should we have?"

"Aren't you cooking for the men?"

"Only Mick tonight. Maybe we should get something out of the freezer. Some days I just can't be bothered thinking about it."

Vanessa stood and opened the fridge. Bowls of moldy leftovers sat alongside limp vegetables, and in the door shelf, an open bottle of soured milk, which had separated into curds, stunk out the interior. She let it fall shut and cleared her throat, struggling with a dry heave. "When did you last clean out the fridge?"

"The other day maybe."

Vanessa turned and leaned on the kitchen counter. "What are you doing, Mum? Drinking yourself to death? Don't you want more out of life?"

Her mother sighed loudly. "What kind of 'more' should I want?"

"I don't know, but for God's sake, look at the state of you." Her hand swept the room. "Of this kitchen."

"I'm doing okay."

"No. You're not. You need help. Have you thought about AA?"

"Do you think I want this? You're still a child. What would you know?"

"I'm eighteen. You were nearly married at my age."

"Eighteen?" Her mother stared into space. "My little girl, all grown up and making her way in the world. I guess you'll want to catch up with your friends while you're here. How's that Billy boy doing?"

"I'm not sure. I haven't seen him lately."

Ruth stood and moved to the sink for a glass of water. Her meaningful conversation with her mother was over. She had been dismissed, the only way Ruth knew how—by avoidance.

A few minutes later, Ruth excused herself for an afternoon nap and didn't surface for over two hours. By the time Mick arrived in from the farm, Vanessa had cleaned out the fridge, washed and dried the dishes, and in the oven, a lamb roast was just about cooked.

"Well, aren't you a sight for an old man's sore eyes."

Vanessa raced to hug him. Mick had been good to her over the years, and she gave thanks every day that he looked after her mother without complaint. "Hey, less of the old man. You still look like a spring chicken to me. Always will."

"You're a sweet girl. How long are you staying?"

"I'm due back at the hospital on Thursday."

"Whisper will be pleased."

"Did you make up Vanessa's bed, Ruth?" Mick asked as Ruth entered the kitchen and made a beeline for the pantry.

"Not yet. I'll do it after dinner. Plenty of time."

"Let's eat," Vanessa said. "I've made roast potatoes."

"God, how I've missed you," Mick replied.

Vanessa had planned to ride Whisper after dinner, but just as she went to leave the house, the sky opened with a sudden downpour. She moved through the French doors of the living room onto the veranda, and sat in her favorite wicker chair. It felt only like weeks ago that she and Liam sat on the steps in this very spot; when his concern for her seemed genuine, but his emotions as confused as hers. She tried not to think about him when she was working. That conversation with his father, only partly caught, were the last words she'd heard him speak, and they still hurt.

Yet, why had he come to the school that day? To say goodbye, to apologize? To say again that it was all in her head despite the way his large hands gently cupped her face as they kissed. Would she ever know?

It was after nine when she strolled back inside. She'd thought about calling Billy, but because of what had happened between them at the beach, she decided against it. He'd tried several times to reach out, but they'd rarely spoken since that night. She missed him, but in this case, guilt overrode sentiment.

Mick sat at the table reading, his cup of tea half-empty. Her mother had gone to bed early as usual, so it gave her the chance to talk with Mick in private.

Vanessa pulled two mugs off the mug tree. "How about a hot chocolate?"

"I'd love one."

She cocked her head toward the hallway. "Mum's not good, is she? I don't know why you still employ her."

"Where else would she go? She manages to cook most of the time. She left it tonight because you were coming. It gave her a bit of a breather."

Vanessa thought about this. Her mother might need a breather, but so did she—a breather from an alcoholic parent. "Please don't think I'm not grateful, because I am, but how does she get the booze if she can't even leave the house?"

"She walks to the pub three times a week. Takes her small shopping trundler and stocks up. Some days I find her lying on the side of the road, drunk as a skunk and not able to make it any further."

"What? She can't go to the grocery store but makes it to the pub. That's crazy. I don't know what to do, Mick. She can't go on like this."

"Don't worry about it for now, lass. She's safe here with me. We know each other's ways."

"It shouldn't be your responsibility, but apart from me, she has no one. I've been working most of my days off, mainly with showjumping horses. I'm earning good money, and I'll be able to afford a small place of my own in a year or two. But getting Mum off the farm won't be easy."

"Doesn't she have anywhere else to go?"

"My grandparents are both dead. They died in a boating accident when I was a toddler. She's an only child, and neither of her parents had siblings. They had her late in life, and from what I can gather from Dad, they fussed over her and spoiled her rotten."

"That must have been tough for Ruth, losing her parents. But, on a brighter note, how's it going at the hospital?"

"It's going great. I'm loving it. I never thought I'd fit in, but we have lots of fun."

The two of them sat and talked for over an hour. Vanessa never asked after Liam. She wanted to, but she knew he wasn't coming back, so she tried her hardest to shut him away in the farthest corner of her soul until—

"I almost forgot." Mick rose from the table and opened the sideboard drawer. "You have a letter. From France."

He handed her a square white envelope. "What? Is it from him?"

"I guess." Mick winked. "Unless you've met a Frenchman in your travels. Good night. I'm off to bed."

Vanessa tiptoed into her old bedroom and looked around. She didn't know why she expected to see change. The room had been the same for years so why would another year make any difference? It still had that same stale smell, the same tatty mattress, and the same faded yellow curtains—but the rip in the fabric had grown longer. She sat on the chair, staring at the card in her right hand for several moments, then turned it over. As before, there was no return address.

The thick and waxy envelope was similar to the last. She lifted the flap and pulled out the plain, white card. On the front, drawn in his usual black ink style, a single snowflake floated down into the right-hand corner, its symmetrical proportions perfectly formed.

She opened the card with a delicate touch as if the inscription might burn her like a hot iron.

Dearest Vanessa,
I'm sitting in a café with friends,
drinking strong black coffee
and eating the best almond croissant
I've ever tasted ... all without enjoyment.
Looking out the window,
I watch as snowflakes fall softly onto the earth,
landing on umbrellas, mittens, and wet pavements.
As I sketch, a feeling of dread
overshadows my memories.
I'm reminded of the 'field of the white snow,'
and recall times when sorrow consumed you.
When you were sad, fearful, and restless.
Today, I'm sad and restless too.
I hope you're happy and well,
and I mean that sincerely.
Liam xx

The field of the white snow. The last time she'd sensed it was her night of drunken sex with Billy—that night they'd crossed the line between platonic caring and unfortunate indifference. As she held the card, she wondered why Liam was sad and restless. Was it because he was homesick, or had something else happened in his life. A dull ray of hope washed over her. She had no business being sad herself. At least Liam was alive. Billy would never see Rose again.

Vanessa slumped on the bed, resting her head on the lumpy foam chip pillow as she recalled the nights she'd spent in Liam's room. She better understood now, how he'd seen her as a sisterly figure and nothing more—until those last few days in November. Now, he kept his distance for his own reasons. She understood the intention, but it didn't make his absence any more bearable.

Ruth hadn't managed to make up the bed, but Vanessa didn't care. And rather than doing the job herself, she shut the door and snuck down the hallway to Liam's room. For a split second, she imagined she saw *moko* woman out of the corner of her eye but soon recognized it for what it was—a figment of an unforgotten time.

Stepping into his space, Vanessa ran her fingers along the broken spines of the paperbacks loitering on his bookshelf, making a mental note to take a couple with her when she left. She opened the wardrobe and touched the remainder of his clothes—the work shirts and worn-through-the-knee jeans—before flicking through the cassette tapes stacked in a neat pile beside his stereo. One by Bob Seger and the Silver Bullet Band caught her eye.

At the intro of *We've Got Tonight*, Vanessa turned up the volume. She lay on the bed and let thoughts of Liam flood her mind while she gazed at the rain through the window. The memory of his scent stayed with her until well after midnight, and when she woke around nine, she felt like she'd slept for days.

PART III

1985 - 1988

40

THE WHITE ENVELOPE

1985

Torn at one corner and creased with age, a square white envelope sat in a side pocket of Liam's backpack—unopened, unread. He'd had many opportunities to post it, even entered a Post Office more than once, but each time he'd stopped himself. This card required hand delivery.

Despite the business class seat his company had paid for, he'd struggled to sleep on the flight from New York. The lack of oxygen in the cabin added to an already throbbing headache, and the apprehension he felt at the thought of returning home didn't help. He smiled when he thought about Vanessa. She'd always had an expressive face, and she wore the chip on her shoulder for the entire world to see. He liked that about her—the raw honesty, the determination. He'd once been told that she had a stiff-bristle brush for a backbone, and for some reason, that analogy had wedged in his mind. He'd been on the receiving end of that brush more times than he cared to remember.

He looked out the oval window as they made their descent. The day was fine and clear, and he could see across the yellow plains to the peninsula two hundred miles northeast. The district had seen no rain to speak of in months, and Liam had never seen it look so dry.

As he walked across the tarmac toward the terminal, he noticed his father peering through the window, and relaxed with that comfortable feeling of home. The building seemed smaller than he remembered, as did everything about the airport. Even his father seemed smaller as he shook Liam's hand and gave him a self-conscious hug.

The two men talked on and off as they drove back to the Rata River Valley, their conversation superficial and insignificant—the dry season, the drop in lamb prices, and the cost of fertilizer, with the odd awkward silence thrown in. Everything that didn't matter, nothing that did. When they finally reached the homestead, the apprehension he'd felt on the plane returned.

The house seemed the same. The same drab color scheme, same smell of musty mold layered on stale air. Liam didn't know what he'd expected. Maybe a fresh coat of paint or new furniture, but it was like time had stood still. He'd never realized how shabby the interior was when he lived here as a teenager but now saw his childhood home through different eyes.

"I'll grab your other bag."

"Thanks, Dad." Liam dropped his backpack on the bed and surveyed his old bedroom. He'd once enjoyed this room, but now the energy seemed flat. He lay on the bed for a moment, staring at the paint flaking off the ceiling and the single light bulb that hung from the central point of the room. He longed for Vanessa to appear in the doorway and call him for dinner, then meet him at the stables afterward to groom the horses as they used to. He wanted to talk about his day, and later, hear her tiptoe along the hallway.

Mick's soft knock broke into his thoughts. "I told Ruth we'd eat at the pub tonight. We should make tracks."

Liam jumped off the bed and followed his father into the kitchen. He'd forgotten the small things—that smell of roast meat and boiled cabbage mingled with the sweet scent of overripe apples from the fruit bowl, the faded fabric of the window seat, and the pile of mail on the sideboard.

"Where is she?"

"She'll be resting in her room."

Liam said nothing more. He wanted to ask why Ruth was still there, but it wasn't his business. He wondered if his father's stubborn streak had mellowed. By the look of the place, he guessed not. He'd been away eight years—analyzed international financial markets, traded stocks and bonds all over the world, and traveled to places he'd only dreamed about as a kid, but at home, Liam was still very much the boy.

When Liam came into the kitchen for breakfast the following morning, Ruth met his greeting with a smile. Her vacant demeanor remained, but she also seemed friendly, and genuinely so. In between small talk, she served up eggs and buttered toast, poured a half decent coffee into his mug and asked of his plans, as if she were any other housekeeper and he any other son home for the summer.

Plans? Apart from finalizing a property deal, he had no plans except one. The hand delivery of the white envelope he'd carried around for the past two years. Did he need Ruth's help for that—her permission? Maybe he did.

Liam didn't mention Vanessa for the first two weeks. He needed time to relax and take stock, and to recover from the head cold he'd caught on the flight. However, at the beginning of the third week, the opportunity to talk to Ruth came early one morning. Even before breakfast, the humidity was oppressive. Liam hadn't slept well, the mattress he'd always thought of as comfortable, now musty and lacking support.

Ruth turned and greeted him with a cheerful 'good morning' when he entered the kitchen. The first of her many mugs of sherry sat to the right of the stove, ready for the next sip. She looked older than her years and thinner than he remembered. Her skin had a sallow tinge to it, and in the mornings, the sound of her dry cough filled the house. Mick had told him that her memory wasn't the best, but so far, Liam had seen no evidence of this.

As Ruth served his breakfast of coffee and toast, he stared at the plastic tablecloth that had covered the white pine for the past ten years, and marveled at how nothing about the house had changed.

There wasn't much to the toast—white bread, spread with soft butter and licked with tart apricot jam. Liam preferred wholegrain bread these days, but Ruth wouldn't know that. He wondered if Ruth had ever eaten grainy bread, croissants, or waffles for breakfast. Did she even eat breakfast?

"Does Vanessa come home much?" he asked as she refilled his cup, his voice steady as if the question was an afterthought—part of casual conversation.

"You mean to the valley? This isn't her home anymore."

"No, I guess not. But she must visit."

"When she can." Ruth busied herself at the sink as she rinsed a colander of potatoes in preparation for dinner. "I'm not sure where she'll be this Christmas."

Liam stared into his coffee for a moment. He hadn't held a decent conversation with Ruth in years, but now, he needed information. "I've been thinking—"

"If this is about my Vanessa, you can hold your thoughts. She has a career now, and she's happy. I must have done something right. She's a good girl. Loving and kind."

He leaned back in his chair, playing with the crumbs on his plate with the tip of his index finger, and then took a deep breath. "I'd like to see her."

Ruth turned, a peeler in one hand, and potato in the other. Liam wondered why she was peeling potatoes before he'd even finished breakfast, but then remembered how wasted she became as the day progressed. It seemed nothing had changed.

"I thought you would."

"Look, I don't want to cause any trouble." He stood and put his plate on the kitchen counter. "But—"

"She won't want to see you. She has friends, a good job ... her doctor."

"Doctor?"

"The boyfriend, he's one of those ... what do you call them"—Ruth looked to the ceiling, as if to find the word—"obstetricians or suchlike. Course he's a lot older than her, but they seem well suited."

"Is it serious?"

"Oh yes. It's been six months now. Vanessa brought him here for lunch one day. Worships the ground she walks on. And he's made of money. Comes from some important, wealthy family."

"I see." Liam watched Ruth move around the kitchen. From the sink, to the fridge, to the pantry like a dance she'd learned long ago. Back and forth. Open and close. Sip, sip.

"How was she after I left?"

"Fine. She went back to school and really knuckled down. She's always been a happy wee girl."

His response to Ruth's words stayed on the tip of his tongue. Her pride in Vanessa was clear, but he wondered if her grip on reality was secure. Had she ever asked Vanessa how she felt, about anything?

"She's come a long way." Ruth carried on at the sink, the peeler scraping over the potato several times before she rinsed it under the trickle of cold water. "Always knew she would once, you know, she found her feet."

Liam saw no point in questioning Ruth's account of her daughter's life, of confronting it. He'd learned long ago that everyone sees life differently, and Ruth had seen little of life since she'd moved to the valley. She rarely left the house according to Mick. "Where's she living?"

"In Wellington. It was her graduation last month. Some posh affair at the Town Hall. She's a midwife now." Ruth dried her hands on her apron and reached for an envelope stowed behind the clock on the mantel above the coal range. She looked at it and smiled sadly. "I didn't go. Your father needed me here to feed the shearers, but I have pictures."

She handed Liam the envelope, then lifted the pig bucket from under the sink. "I'm going for a walk to feed the pigs." She motioned to the envelope. "Put them back when you're finished. Mick said he'll buy me an album when he's next in town."

Liam waited until Ruth had crossed the drive toward the pigpen before opening the flap of the envelope. He removed the half dozen snapshots and lay them on the table.

The first one stayed in his hands for a long time as he took in every detail. In the photo, Vanessa stood tall and elegant, not in height but stature, and while her face was familiar, her body certainly was not. Her hair had darkened from light blonde to a warmer tone, and soft curls hung to below her shoulders. Under the black gown of academia, she wore a shift covered in large red poppies, with lipstick and strappy heels to match. Gone was the girlish demeanor of her sixteenth year. She exuded a confidence and poise that shocked him to the core. He stared at the photo and then stared some more.

There was no mistaking who the man in the next photo was, with his arm wrapped around her waist. He was older, as Ruth had said, and dressed formally in a dark suit and tie. The peppered strands at his temples made him look older still, and the warmth of her expression as they looked at one another conveyed a radiance Liam had never seen in her before.

He could see where the last eight years had painted their picture across her face, but in his imagination, she was still fifteen, skipping off the bus at the end of the driveway, ready to ride Whisper up to the east hay barn. The thought brought a smile to his face.

When Ruth returned, Liam was still at the table, the pictures fanned out in front of him. He turned as she looked over his shoulder.

"She's a beautiful girl," she said, "isn't she?"

"Very." He gathered the photographs and placed them back in the envelope, then handed it to Ruth. "I'll be in Wellington next week, on business. I'd like to see her."

"I told you last time you were home. I'd rather you didn't."

"Why's that?"

"Because that boat's not yours to rock anymore, and I want you to promise me, here and now, that you'll stay away."

The air was bitterly cold when Liam arrived at Petrie Bay. He loved the beach, but his visit that afternoon was more about clearing his head than enjoying the surf. He walked for a while, the white envelope in the breast pocket of his jacket. His thoughts turned to his mother. What would she have said about Vanessa? She'd always told him to fight for

208

his beliefs and to firmly stand his ground. But at the moment, the sand beneath his feet slipped through his toes as the ground moved back to where it had come from.

A strong wind stirred through the pines, competing with the roar of the waves. Liam reached into his pocket, pulled the thick waxy envelope out and, before he could think about it, tossed it into the water like a frisbee.

It bobbed and floated on the crest, then appeared back at his feet as the ocean returned the card to its rightful owner.

41

BLADES OF GREENER GRASS

1987

Sometimes the years pass with mundane normality. Sometimes they pass with well-lived excitement, and sometimes, they slip by with a blend of both. Life just *is*.

Vanessa was still awake when Julian arrived home just after midnight. She switched on the bedside lamp, her eyes squinting as light intruded into the dark.

He looked at her and smiled. He was a kind man—softly spoken with impeccable manners, and in the time they had been dating, they'd seldom had a cross word. At first, she found his dependability suffocating. After all, she'd struggled to depend on anyone when she was younger. But she'd slowly realized her journey didn't have to be alone, and that her penchant for self-sabotage wasn't necessarily a flaw, but a habit she could break.

He bent down and kissed her on the cheek. "This is a nice surprise. I thought you weren't coming tonight."

Vanessa sat up and leaned against the headboard. "I've been trying to get hold of you." He moved to the window and pulled it shut. Vanessa hated sleeping with the window closed, but the autumn days were drawing in, and the night air held that distinct chill of inevitability. "You were in theater."

"Yeah, it's been one hell of a day. What's up?"

"I have to go home for a bit."

Julian pulled his tie from around his neck and unbuttoned his shirt. "What do you mean home? You are home."

She hadn't cried once since hearing the news. Instead, the energy of grief churned in her stomach until she couldn't eat or concentrate on anything other than practical plans. But now, her eyes stung with burning tears, and as they trickled down her cheeks, she couldn't swallow them back.

He sat on the bed, his eyes darting between hers—pleading, concerned. "I know we haven't had much time together lately, but please, Vanessa, don't do this."

"What? No. It's not what you think. I had a call from Mick earlier. Mum has cancer." The tears turned to a sob. "It may be only a matter of weeks."

"Come here." Julian reached for her. "I'm so sorry. We'll shift her down here. You can fly up and collect her. I'll call her oncologist tomorrow and make the arrangements."

"She wants to go back to the valley. Besides, she'd never agree to come here. Her dignity, or what's left of it, wouldn't allow it, you know that."

"It's not up to her now. I can arrange the best care."

"But it's complicated, isn't it?"

"So you're going back there, to the farm? You hate that house."

"Mick said we can stay in the neighbor's cottage. I have to go, Jules. I'm all she has."

"I know." Julian entered his closet as he undressed. "But that doesn't make it any easier, does it? Take a few days off and go talk to her. Sound her out."

"She hates cities." Vanessa tried to keep her voice even and calm, but the tears had turned to hiccups, and the air in Julian's bedroom suddenly seemed oppressive. "I spoke to her two weeks ago. She sounded fine. Forgetful, but fine."

"Your mother hasn't been fine for a long time."

The following day, with her new Subaru full of the few possessions she loved, Vanessa made the long drive to Clifton Falls. She stopped at the hospital where she had trained, and sat for hours at her mother's bedside, refusing to believe what she knew in her heart to be true.

By the time they brought her mother back to the cottage in the valley, her skin had yellowed dramatically, and she could barely eat. The days became those days of nothing. Groundhog Days where routines followed routines and tears were shed, only to be repeated the next day, and the day after that, as her mother faded away before her eyes.

Occasionally, Ruth became lucid enough for ordinary conversation to flow, but mostly her memory had slipped away along with everything else. Vanessa wondered if they would ever have the chance to open old wounds and talk to one another as equals—adults—and when that chance came one dull winter's day, she was surprised.

"You never told me what happened. With you and Dad, I mean."

Ruth shook her head, but said nothing.

"I never wanted to leave our farm." Vanessa was retrospective rather than resentful. "I don't think you realized how unhappy I was."

"You were a kid. I thought you'd get over it."

"True, but I would have given anything to go home those first few years."

"It's funny how I remember that day we left as clear as a bell, but what happened last week, I have no clue." She closed her eyes for a moment. "I had an affair."

"Mum, no."

"Your father never forgave me. He tried, but the trust was gone. I was barely nineteen when I fell pregnant with you … so young. Your dad was, *is*, a good man—kind, compassionate. But I wanted romance … and excitement. All I seemed to do was clean the house, cook for the men, and look after you. Once we lost that connection, I thought the grass was greener on the neighboring farm."

"And was it?"

"Not even one blade. I made a huge mistake, and we all suffered. But when you're young and foolish, you believe that men hold the secret to your happiness."

Vanessa thought of how true her mother's words were. She'd once thought that of Liam, but how wrong she'd been. "But they don't, do they?"

"Not in my experience. You can be happy with any man if you feel a connection with him. Your dad and I had that in the beginning, but I didn't nurture it. I needed more, but couldn't communicate that to him."

"And you never found that connection with another man?"

"Not really. The guy—he said he wanted to marry me, but it was just pillow talk." Ruth rolled her head to the side and closed her eyes for a moment. Vanessa thought their conversation was over, but her mother had more to say. "After we came here, I worried myself sick about every little thing. When I found out your father had remarried, a part of me died inside. Then, the drink got me. I wanted to start over so many times, but it's too late now. There's no second chance for me. Where did that second chance go?"

"I don't know, Mum."

"But it's not too late for you. When are you going to settle down?"

Vanessa frowned at the thought. She didn't have a clear snapshot in her mind as to how she wanted that part of her life to play out. But the negative was there—even if the film was undeveloped. She reached for her mother's hand. "I'm only twenty-four. Don't sign me up to the Clifton Falls Spinster Club just yet."

"Do you think the Doctor is 'the one'?"

"I honestly don't know. Anyway, he's married to his job right now so we've decided to have a break in the meantime. And I have plenty of horses to whisper sweet nothings to before I settle down."

"I used to think it was a load of rubbish, but according to Mick, you have a real talent."

Vanessa looked at her mother, surprised by her compliment. They had never had an intelligent conversation before, and the words Ruth spoke now seemed out of character—almost like another soul lay in the bed before her. Moments stretched out in silence before she spoke again. "It helps pay the bills."

"You know what Liam told me once?"

The abrupt change of subject surprised Vanessa. Her mother never talked about Liam. "What?"

"That you slept on his bedroom floor because you were afraid of the dark. He called me a bad mother for locking you out of my room. But after a while, it wasn't you I was locking out. I want you to know that. It was Jake."

"Jake?"

"We had a fling. When I tried to end it, he wouldn't take no for an answer. He was controlling and insanely jealous. It got so bad—he hit me. Mick was away, so Liam fired him. I was so confused, I hated Liam at the time. I blamed him for Jake leaving me. I'd convinced myself that Jake would change, but it turned out he had other women all over the district." Her mother took a sip of water to wet her lips, and pointed to a spare blanket on the chair beside the bed. The room was hot and stuffy from the oil column heater, but Ruth had always felt the cold, even when she was well. "I still think about it after all these years and realize how stupid I was."

"We all make mistakes." Vanessa folded the blanket in half and lay it on the bed. She remembered happier times when her mother had tucked her in before she went to sleep. Now, it was time to return the gesture.

Ruth paused as she measured ragged breaths. "I know you must still think about him, even after all these years. Liam, I mean. I'm sorry I said he didn't love you."

"Don't be sorry. It was true."

"Well, I don't know about that, but he wanted to see you last time he was home."

This was news to Vanessa. She didn't even know he'd been in the country. "So why didn't he?"

"Because you were with that nice doctor. What's his name again?"

"Julian."

"Julian, that's him. I told him not to rock the boat. Asked him to stay away."

Vanessa closed her eyes for a moment and sighed. What would she have done if Liam had made contact that year—invite him for coffee and small talk? "It's all murky water under a very tall bridge now. Nothing I do will ever change the course of the flow."

"Don't be too sure about that. And I'm sorry. I didn't understand at the time and I believed Steve's lies. I thought Liam had interfered with you, but he hadn't, had he?"

"No."

"If he comes back, give him a chance."

"He's long gone from my life."

"But you see what it means though, don't you? He must still care for you, even after all these years."

"But I'm not that girl anymore, am I?"

"No, you're not. You're so much more. I know I wasn't the mother I should have been, but I've always loved you, Ness. Loved you to the sky and back. You've made me proud, every day of your life."

Vanessa cleared her throat and blinked back tears. Her mother was trying to rewrite history, but at that moment it didn't matter. She would believe what she wanted to. "It's funny you mentioned him. Mick gave me a card from him today. He'd sent it in January. The ink was all smudged, but it finally made its way to the valley last week."

"From Liam? What did it say?"

"It was just a cryptic few lines. It's in my room. I'll go get it."

Back at her mother's bedside, Vanessa handed her the card. On the front was a sketch of a lighthouse, drawn in black pen and ink on white, like the other two.

Her mother passed it back. "Read it to me."

Vanessa opened the card.

> *"I've seen you together, inside the envelope.*
> *You seem so happy,*
> *but my light still shines for you.*
> *Stay off the rocks and keep safe.*
> *Liam xx"*

"Inside the envelope?" Vanessa repeated. "What does that even mean? And why, after all these years, would he write?"

"I know what it means. I showed him your graduation photos."

Inside the envelope. Vanessa watched her mother struggle with a recollection.

"I wanted to say something, but it's gone." Ruth tapped her temple as though trying to dislodge the elusive thought. "No. I remember now. What did the other cards say?"

"This is the first one in years."

"No, the other cards he sent you. I forwarded them to you. Or did I put them away somewhere safe? I can't think. But I wrote to you … and so did he." Vanessa's heart raced. "My memory's not so good these days. I'm sorry, Ness."

"Mum, it's okay. Get some sleep now. We'll talk again in the morning."

"I need to use the bathroom."

"Okay. Let's get you out of bed." Even though her mother weighed less than a hundred pounds, Vanessa still struggled to lift her, and the trip to the bathroom always took longer than expected.

Later, as she sat holding her mother's hand, she wondered about the other cards she'd mentioned. Were there more that she'd never received?

The next morning, Vanessa tried to engage her mother in a discussion about the cards, but Ruth didn't even remember the lighthouse card from the day before. She ate lunch at her mother's bedside, and when the agency nurse arrived just after, she drove to O'Leary's in search of mail that may or may not have come. The sight of the homestead as she rounded the bend in the drive still provoked a sense of dread. But the day was sunny and bright, and when she opened the car door, she recalled happier times when she hung out with Billy and Nikau, and the many days she spent with Whisper.

Mick's new housekeeper, Molly, greeted her warmly as she

knocked on the kitchen door. Vanessa liked Molly. In her mid-fifties, and a poet of sorts, she wore her black hair long, and flowing skirts around her ankles, like some throwback from the seventies. She never wore shoes or makeup. Vanessa often wondered how and why she had ended up at the O'Leary's.

"Mum said she might have left something here," she said to Molly. "May I take a quick look in the dresser in her old room?"

"Sure. Look all you want. Musty old thing. We put it out in the shed when I arrived. I think it's still there. Unless Mick took it to the Salvation Army store in Clifton Falls. But I can't imagine that, can you?" Molly said with a chuckle.

The doors of the shed were wide open as always. Old woodworking tools, boxes of rusty nails, and anvils littered the interior, and around the walls, stenciled outlines marked the place of tools long gone. Nothing about it had changed in years. Vanessa spotted the chest of drawers in the far corner, its back to her. She turned it around and opened the top drawer. There, under a purple-and-white spotted liner, sat a bundle of envelopes held together with a black rubber band.

She held the bundle with shaking hands, her heart threatening to explode out of her chest. She strolled to the front garden and sat on the love seat under the old elm tree. The prayer tree she always called it.

Molly popped her head out of the kitchen window. "Find what you were looking for?"

"Yes, thanks. I might sit here for a while. Soak up this beautiful winter sun."

"Okay. Let me know if you need anything else."

As Vanessa removed the rubber band, she remembered the woman she'd seen sitting in this very spot years earlier—her long dark hair held back with a pearl encrusted comb and her hands clutching rosary beads. She never did find out her name or where she came from, or indeed, her connection to the farm. Maybe she too had been a figment of her imagination.

She shuffled through the mail. Several envelopes carried her mother's spidery hand. She opened one of these first and read the rambling narrative of everyday farm life. Her mother had written to her at least a dozen times—one small Croxley page at a time—but had never managed to take the next step to the postbox at the general store.

The cards came next, each one a different size, the envelopes thick and sometimes glossy. They had one thing in common—a postmark of January the eighth for the years 1979, 1981, and 1982. 1983, the year she turned twenty-one, was missing, but the years 1984, 1985, and 1986 were there.

Stacked in chronological order, the first held a German postmark. A slight breeze stirred around the tree as she lifted the flap. Drawn on the outside of the plain white card, in the same black ink, was an anchor. She opened the card and read the inscription aloud:

"I feel like you're drifting away.
Don't drag your anchor.
Bury it deep against the shifting sand.
Liam xx"

The 1981 card had traveled from New York. On the front of this card, a tiny Aladdin's lamp sat in the same corner the snowflake had done years before. Inside she read Liam's message:

Three wishes would be wasted on me.
All I need is one.
The other two I would gladly give to you.
Liam xx

As Vanessa read each card, she considered the words, sometimes unable to grasp their meaning. She read 1982's message—again from Paris, the City of Love—several times. It was simple but clear. On the front was a key decorated with hearts, and a four-word inscription inside the card read:

You still hold it.
Liam xx

By 1984, he was back in Scotland. The envelope displayed similar stamps to the first one from years ago. Inside, a single acorn, life-size and in intricate detail, graced the center of the card. The message in this one was longer:

> *Remember the oak tree across from Whisper's field?*
> *Close your eyes and imagine us there.*
> *Lay with me, touch me, kiss me,*
> *let me love you, feel my fire …*
> *Liam xx*

She closed her eyes and shook her head in disbelief. What the hell had been going through his mind when he wrote such intimate words? What gave him the right? Had he thought she still had feelings for him? She was aware that recollections of love lost are often filled with foolishness, but he didn't love her; he'd said so himself. *I don't have feelings for her.* So what if he'd kissed her? So had other guys when she was a teenager. It meant nothing. They hadn't kissed her because they loved her—they'd kissed her because they loved themselves.

There were two envelopes left. She looked at the familiar stamps of the 1985 card and frowned. He'd been in New Zealand that day—in Wellington—and she never even knew. The sketch was of a turtle, and the inscription read:

> *It seems slow and steady doesn't win the race after all.*

Unable to fathom what he meant, she opened the final envelope. The faded postmark told her that the year she'd turned twenty-four, he'd traveled to Argentina. She thought of all the countries he'd visited over the years, and on opening the envelope, smiled when she saw he'd drawn a compass with a smiley face on the dial.

> *I long to move south.*
> *To come home.*
> *L xx*

Vanessa stayed under the tree for over an hour, thinking about how homesickness can weave tales into your heart that have no business being there. Maybe he'd had lonely times, too. Times when he missed her. True love may have eluded him, so it's possible he conjured up a fantasy where she was still a fifteen-year-old virgin under his spell. Perhaps his *mana*—his power and influence—wasn't as she had imagined. Maybe Liam was just an average man, with average dreams, and an average life. No different to the next guy. Who would know?

On her way back to the cottage, she stopped to see Whisper, asking his opinion about the cards. As she spoke, he never took his eyes off hers, and when she'd finished, he simply nuzzled into her palm and, as she moved closer, her neck.

Back at the cottage, she thanked the agency nurse, checked on her sleeping mother, then made a light dinner of soup and toast. After a full day nursing Ruth, eating a balanced meal was the first thing she thought of, but the last thing she could be bothered with. As a result, she had lost weight, and her energy levels were low.

She longed to talk to her mother about the cards and unsent letters. To say what mattered—what Ruth's drinking had never allowed her to voice. To share her doubts and fears, and talk to her about her life in Wellington.

And what about 1983? Had Liam sent a card that year? Had her mother received it? Or had it gone astray somewhere, floating around in the atmosphere of possibilities?

Two nights later, as her neighbors slept, and Liam went about his business on some distant continent, Vanessa first phoned the doctor, and then Mick. Ruth's breathing had deteriorated as she drifted in and out of delirium, and the rattle in her chest told its own story.

Vanessa sat at her mother's side, held her hand and wiped her brow while she listened to the gasps for air and soft sighs, triggered by some primal need for acceptance at the end. The chance to hold that conversation of conversations slipped from Vanessa's grasp just a whisper after four. The darkest hour before the dawn.

42

RUTH RESTS

1987

The snow fell late that year. Most unusual. Some years there was no snow at all. But on that particular day, a white blanket covered the graves and settled on the headstones and monuments to the dead. Liam stood at the edge of the cemetery as they took Ruth's coffin from the hearse, then joined the small crowd standing at the freshly dug gravesite. He hadn't made it to the church. The highway, blocked that morning because of snow and ice, remained closed until after one. By the time he arrived in the valley, the service had all but finished.

Rain clouds danced around the sun, but Liam barely noticed as he surveyed the grave, the plain wooden coffin, the priest flicking holy water onto the casket as he chanted words in Latin—then Vanessa as she stepped into view. The need to go to her hit him like a bolt of current, but his needs surrounding Vanessa had ceased to be important years ago, so he stood still, his hands clasped tightly and his thoughts racing.

She wore a black woolen double-breasted coat and medium-heeled leather boots. A chunky-knit purple scarf half-covered her face as she wrapped it around her neck and across her chin, and in the reflection of her sunglasses, Liam could see a beam of sunlight as it cut through the clouds.

He moved a step to the right, to get a better view. Vanessa's father —still a young-looking man for his age—her stepmother, and three half-brothers stayed close. The middle boy stood in front of Vanessa, and she placed her hand on his shoulder. He leaned back into her as a small frown tracked across his forehead. To Liam, they looked like any other loving family, and he was grateful for that.

Two spaces to her left, the man from the photographs—the doctor Ruth had enthused about—stood with his hands clasped in front of him. Billy Cook was there also, standing at the foot of the grave with Liam's old friends Anna and Rob, and that girl Amber from Immaculate Heart. Vanessa's old flame, Nikau Hughes, mingled with a dozen other young men and women Liam couldn't place, their serious expressions befitting the occasion.

As the pallbearers lowered the coffin to rest, six feet down on the hardened clay, Vanessa reached for a handful of dirt and sprinkled it on top of the casket. In her other hand, she held a single pink tea rose, its petals loose with maturity. She pulled each petal from the stem and let them float one by one into the grave. Each time, repeating the old, 'She loves me, she loves me not' phrase, except this time she said, "I love you, I love you more. I love you, I love you more." It was something he remembered Vanessa and Ruth doing as they picked daisies from the garden outside the kitchen window on warm summer days. Happier times, before Ruth lost her dignity down the neck of a sherry bottle.

As the song from the portable stereo finished its last note, he wondered if Vanessa had recognized him. If she did, she gave no sign. She looked skyward and blew a soft kiss to the invisible spirit of her mother, then turned, accepted her father's arm and walked away without acknowledging the man who'd once held her in his arms as she slept.

When they reached the car, Vanessa lingered. She looked straight ahead toward a bank of silver birch trees bordering the main gates of the cemetery. Her gaze fell on Liam O'Leary as he moved to his father's side and into her view. At first, he was almost unrecognizable, with his short hair and stylish clothes. However, it didn't take her long to view him as she remembered, and although he stood over six feet tall, he seemed less imposing than he had in her youth. As he stood there in a long coat, aviators, and expensive-looking leather boots, he seemed to be looking only at her.

She had rarely seen Liam dressed formally. He had grown into an incredibly handsome man, and Vanessa couldn't help but stare back. He must be thirty-one she thought, but he looked younger.

Other than the odd comment about his studies, Mick hadn't discussed Liam much over the years. And except for the postmarks on the cards, Vanessa didn't know where he'd been, or who he'd been with. She shivered as her thoughts stirred memories she had worked so hard to forget. Memories that didn't deserve consideration on such a somber day. Her thoughts should be all about her mother, but thoughts of her had numbed hours ago.

Vanessa had expected him to come—had sensed that certainty for weeks. And along with that certainty came a tight grip of the gut and an abundance of confusing emotions.

She'd thought she'd feel differently when she saw Julian, too. Their relationship hadn't survived her return to the valley. It wasn't a surprise in the end, because even though they had similar values, they held differing beliefs. When he'd first arrived at the cottage and reached for her, they'd hugged like old friends rather than past lovers, and she realized that's all she could cope with right now—she and Julian being friends.

Back at the church hall, members of the Country Women's Institute gathered to farewell her mother—who'd never once attended a CWI meeting—with club sandwiches, tiny cakes, and freshly baked scones topped with jam and cream. While the women busied themselves in the small kitchen, fussing over cups of tea poured from large galvanized teapots, Vanessa chatted to mourners paying their respects, nodded recognition to her few distant relatives and tried in vain to close her mind to the babble that surrounded the return of Liam O'Leary.

As she looked around the church hall, she wondered, with some relief, why he hadn't shown up at the afternoon tea. Maybe he'd had to head home—wherever that was now—before the mountain roads closed with the forecasted further dumps of snow. Perhaps, he was already on a plane, about to leave Clifton Falls Airport.

Instead of driving to the church hall, Liam strolled back ten years through the door of the local pub. He ordered a beer from the same bartender he'd known in his youth and looked for answers in shades of liquid amber. His thoughts turned to Vanessa—controlled and gracious as she'd farewelled her mother—and the friends and family surrounding her.

He left the pub a couple of hours later, opened the door to a waiting cab, and made the short ride to Anna and Rob's for dinner. They were the type of friends who welcomed you with an open invitation, no matter how long it had been between visits. And as he sat at their table, enjoying good food and warm hospitality, he realized how much he'd missed them.

When he arrived home just after eleven, he was surprised to see Mick still up, reading by that same stupid dim light that hung above the farmhouse table. Ruth's passing would leave a gaping hole in his father's life. Mick had always had a soft spot for Ruth, even when the booze had robbed the function of her liver and her mind. But then, his father always had needed someone to protect. Someone to fuss over.

"You okay, Dad?"

"Don't much feel like sleeping tonight," Mick said. "You didn't come back for the afternoon tea. I thought you wanted to talk to Vanessa."

"I'll leave it a few days. Where have they been living?"

"In the old cottage at the Smith's place."

"That depressing dump."

"I wanted them to stay here, but Ruth wouldn't hear of it. Vanessa's nursed her since she left the hospital, sometimes going for days without a break. She had to quit her job, but I suppose she'll find another one soon enough. There's plenty of work around for midwives."

"Maybe I should go see her. Make sure she's okay."

"What, tonight? You're not going there now, son. Her father's staying for a few days anyway, and she'll have her friends around her. She and Billy Cook are close. He's been a great help to her and her mum. Best you stay away."

"But there's no need for me to stay away now, is there?"

"I noticed her doctor friend at the funeral, I'm not sure what's going on there. I heard they broke up, but he stayed close at the service, and closer at the afternoon tea. There's no point ripping open old wounds unless you have something to calm the fester."

"We're not kids anymore, Dad."

"But that's the whole point. You weren't a kid when you left. You were a man. Vanessa was the kid."

"Nothing happened between us. It was a few fleeting kisses, nothing more."

"Maybe, but the intention was there. And Vanessa certainly struggled afterward."

"Did she?"

"You should have seen her that first summer. She hardly left her room, not even to ride Whisper. Slept during the day, then wandered around the house at night, too scared to sit still. They sent her home from school after the first week of the sixth form, they couldn't cope with her. It took three weeks before I persuaded them to let her return. It was only by the grace of God they let her stay. What happened between you two took its toll on her, surely you realize that?"

"How would I? You never told me anything about her, so how *could* I realize? Shit, Dad, why didn't you tell me?"

"It's not the kind of thing you write in a letter ... other people's business, I mean."

"But it was *my* business. I kept asking how she was. But you ignored me every time."

"We thought it was best. Well, Ruth did. I reluctantly agreed. And you agreed to keep your distance."

"Her mother is dead. As far as I'm concerned, my agreement with Ruth Blinkly to stay away from Vanessa was buried at three o'clock this afternoon."

"That may be so, but leave Vanessa be. She's a city girl, with a life of her own. If you came back to the farm, would you expect her to follow you? It's been nearly ten years. You can't tell me that after all that time you haven't let go."

Back to the farm? "How do I know until we reconnect? But one thing I do know—she's the kind of girl you dream about long after she's gone from your life. Do you have any idea what that's like?"

"You think you're the only person who's lost someone they love? How do you think I felt when your mother died? I still remember her every day of my life."

"I'm sorry. I wasn't thinking." Liam made himself a cup of herbal tea and carried it to the table. He hadn't intended to come home and throw his weight around, to be selfish and stubborn, but seeing Vanessa again brought with it a rush of emotions he hadn't expected.

"We all have to bear the cross of lost loves. It's not only a burden for the young." Mick stood and placed his hand on Liam's shoulder. They seldom expressed their emotions with touch, but Liam appreciated his father's physical support. "Anyway, I think I'll hit the sack. It's been a long day. I miss Ruth. I know the booze ruled her life, but I liked having her around."

"I liked her too, in the beginning. She was so … vivacious and capable. I'm pleased you've met Molly. I know you still feel loyal to Mum, but she wouldn't want you to be alone for the rest of your life."

"Who would have thought? Molly and I dating at our age."

Liam laughed. "Dating? It's a lot more than just dating, isn't it?"

Mick looked at Liam and chuckled. "Speaking of which, I'm off to bed."

It had never occurred to Liam that Vanessa wouldn't have received the cards, but when he woke the next morning, it was the first thing on his mind. What had she thought of his sometimes cryptic words and miniature sketches? Did they make her smile or frown? Did she toss them in the wastepaper basket without opening them, or keep them to read in times of loneliness or reflection?

Breakfast was a different affair with Molly at the helm in the kitchen. She'd made bread—dense and full of whole grains—and granola with nuts and seeds. It was after nine by the time he sat down to eat. Molly dashed in and out, but didn't offer to make his toast or coffee like Ruth used to do. In Molly's kitchen, you fended for yourself, and that's the way he liked it.

All the same, the house seemed strange without Ruth's presence. He was still at the table reading the newspaper when Mick arrived in for morning tea.

"Did Vanessa ever get the cards I sent her?"

Mick flicked on the kettle and leaned on the counter as he waited for it to boil. "As far as I know. I passed on the first couple and then the one for her last birthday."

"But I sent one every year."

"Ruth would have readdressed them." Sitting at the table, Mick spooned sugar into his mug and stirred it slowly. "She usually collected the mail during the week."

Liam nodded. He wouldn't have trusted Ruth to even lick a stamp let alone redirect an envelope. Still, he would find out soon enough.

"Vanessa still comes here, you know, to see Whisper. It's a remarkable sight, her on that bastard of a horse. Your mother would approve. She's a beautiful girl."

"So much more so than I remembered."

"Yeah, well, I've heard she's popular with the lads, so you probably wouldn't get a look in, even if you wanted to."

"We'll see."

Mick took a sip of his tea, then grinned at Liam. "You always were a cocky little shit."

43

ORDERED THOUGHTS

For the next two nights, Vanessa hardly slept as she imagined the spirit of her mother nearby. They had made an uneasy peace during her last weeks, and over that time, Vanessa had gradually come to terms with her mother's impending death, but that didn't make it any easier to accept the loss. It had reminded her that life can be unfair, no matter how well you thought you were doing—and that sometimes, choices weren't yours to make.

Julian had left straight after the afternoon tea. He'd told her he still loved her and asked if they could start over, but it hadn't been the time to revisit their failed union. Her feelings for him had never been passionate, but the more she thought about it, the more she wondered if perhaps friendship and affection could be enough to sustain their relationship, even with his determination not to have children.

Three days after Ruth's service, Vanessa cooked her father an early breakfast before he headed home. Karen and the boys had gone the day before, and that night over a glass of red wine, she and Jim connected like they never had before—telling stories, reliving memories—sometimes with laughter, often with tears.

There had been no sign of Liam since the day of the funeral. Maybe he'd gone back overseas. It was probably just as well if he had.

Grief and anger often held each other for company, and she still wasn't sure how she felt about some of the card inscriptions.

After breakfast, while her father fixed a broken window latch, Vanessa busied herself with chores. In between, she sat at the small kitchen table and sipped cups of tea—warming her hands on the delicate china—and gazing into the liquid as she tried to bring order to her thoughts and gather enthusiasm for the move.

As she sat in contemplation, a knock on the front door startled her. She called out for the visitor to come in, a country custom people in the valley lived by. When no one entered, she went to answer it.

She stepped back when she saw him, willing the lump in her throat to stay put as her fingernails dug into her palms at her sides.

"Vanessa." Liam stood on the front porch, his fingers busy with the car keys in his hand. She'd sometimes wondered if her mind had manipulated her youthful memory of his physique. But contrary to what she'd observed at the cemetery, everything about him was still large and imposing.

"Liam."

He moved to kiss her cheek, but she stepped back. He stared at her for a moment, then frowned. "I'm sorry about your mother. I know the two of you had become closer of late."

"Thank you." She opened the door a little wider but said nothing more, unable to tear her gaze from the stormy blues staring back.

"May I come in?"

"Sorry, of course."

The snow had melted, but on the south side of the house a heavy frost held the net curtains against the windowpanes, and inside the cottage was almost as cold as out. Liam followed her down the dark hallway and into the kitchen—where the old coal range heated the back rooms as it chugged away on a few nuggets. He stood in front of it and stared at her.

"Please, take a seat."

He remained standing but removed his leather gloves and lay them on the table. "How are you coping?"

"Not too bad. I've had some time to prepare and grieve. Still, it's a shock when the end finally comes."

"I agree. I felt the same when Mum died."

She knew Liam of all people would understand, having lost his mother to cancer as well. But, as he stood there, Vanessa found herself unable to concentrate on her loss. For some strange reason, all she could think about was how stylish his gloves were and where they might have come from. *London, Paris, Rome?* "Sorry, may I take your coat?"

"Thanks."

He eased the coat from his shoulders and handed it to her. The lining was warm to the touch, and the woolen fabric felt heavy in her hands. For a split second, she had the urge to slip into it and wrap herself in his warmth.

"Time seems to drag when something like this happens," Liam said.

Her father walked into the room with his bag in one hand and car keys in the other.

Vanessa looked his way. "Dad, Liam, I don't think you've met." She made the introductions as Liam stepped forward. "Nice to meet you, Mr. Blinkly. Vanessa's talked about you a lot over the years."

"Please, call me Jim." Her father offered a warm smile with his handshake. "Likewise. You were like a brother to my little girl, and I'm sure that wouldn't have been easy."

"Dad. You make it sound like I was a brat."

"I'd call it determined, and that determination has stood you in good stead. Look where you are today. I'm proud of you, Ness."

"Stop it. You're gonna make me cry."

"I must admit," Liam said, smiling at Vanessa, "we had our moments. I remember you saying you hated me with alarming regularity."

"What?" She returned the smile. "Surely not."

Jim cleared his throat. "Anyway, I'd better make tracks. No doubt our paths will cross again, Liam. Next time, I hope it's under happier circumstances."

"I hope so too."

As she walked to the car with her father, Vanessa tried to ignore the fact that Liam O'Leary, the man she'd thought about for years—sometimes with romantic folly, and at other times with resentment—was in the kitchen waiting for her.

"He seems like a nice guy." Jim frowned. "Is there something going on between you two? Something I don't know about?"

Vanessa looked down the driveway, away from her father's gaze. "What do you mean?"

"It's just … ah, never mind."

She blew a warming breath into her clenched hands as Jim reached in for a hug. He sat in his car and wound down the window while they carried on talking. "Take care. And remember, you have our support."

"Thanks. I appreciate it, you know that."

"I loved your mum once. Loved her like there was no tomorrow. I've thought about her a lot over the past few days. I guess I let my work stifle our relationship. I wasn't there for her, and I didn't meet her needs the way I should have, but I'll always have a special place for her in my heart."

Vanessa held back the lump forming in her throat as her eyes warmed with tears. "Thanks, Dad. I needed to hear that."

"Hey, come on, don't cry. You'd better get back to Liam. I'm sure you two have a lot to talk about."

"Damn." She sighed. "I forgot about him for a moment. Bye, Dad. Love you to the sky and back."

"Love you too. See you in a few weeks."

Vanessa hurried to the bathroom and checked her face in the mirror. Her eyes looked red and bloodshot, but how else would they be when she'd only just lost her mother? She ran a brush through her hair and took a deep breath.

Liam stood as she walked into the room, more impressive up close than she would have thought possible. The defined jawline, eyes the hue of a winter's storm, and wide, richly colored mouth were the same as she remembered, but everything seemed more intense—even his voice had deepened. But then, what did she expect? People change over time, in every way. She assumed he'd reach out again—in some strange way, she even longed for him to do so—but his arms remained motionless at his side.

"How have you been?"

After all this time ... that was his opening line? *How have you been*? She busied herself filling the kettle and spooning coffee into a plunger as she inhaled and exhaled deeply to calm herself. In and out. Nice and slow. "You know ... it's not an easy time."

He pulled out a chair, the way any other friend would—relaxed and unhurried.

She set down a basket of freshly baked scones Mrs. Smith had dropped off earlier, then moved to the pantry for butter and jam while he sat at the table. "So what brings you back to the valley?"

Liam made eye contact now as he absentmindedly tapped his index finger on the tabletop. He leaned back in his chair, legs wide. "Unfinished business."

"Sounds mysterious."

"There's no mystery. Just something I should have addressed a long time ago."

She continued to keep the conversation light, while inside, her thoughts were volleying back and forth. *Unfinished business. No mystery.*

She watched as he pushed the coffee plunger down, then poured coffee into the two mugs in front of him. A buttered scone sat uneaten on her plate as she struggled with her easygoing act and his formal tone. "What did you end up doing after you finished your degree?"

"I went into finance."

Vanessa took a sip of her coffee and let the warm liquid soothe her. "So what exactly is that?"

"Stocks and bonds, currency trading for financial institutions, that sort of thing."

"Interesting." He'd always spoken with authority and was a natural born leader, but for some reason, she found his businesslike words and tone amusing.

"But what about you? Dad said you studied nursing. You always wanted to be a nurse."

"Yes, I'm a midwife now, but I did general nursing first."

"How long are you planning on staying in the valley?" he asked.

"I'm not sure. I have the cottage for another two weeks. That should give me enough time to get Mum's things in order, but then I need to find a job." She took another sip. "What about you?"

"The markets are hugely volatile right now. I'm trying to get my finances together for an investment. But we'll see."

A knock at the door came as an unwelcome interruption. "I need a *Do Not Disturb* sign. It's been like Grand Central Station around here."

"It's a busy time for you. I'm sorry to intrude. Anyway, thanks for the coffee. I guess I should get going."

"Of course. Thank you for coming."

Liam lifted his coat from the arm of the sofa. She expected him to offer his hand, but he didn't. When he reached the front door, he turned, his gaze soft and deliberate.

"Dad said you still ride Whisper. Maybe we could get together in the next couple of days. Take a ride up the hill."

"Um ... I'm not sure. I have a lot going on."

He held her gaze as her visitor knocked again. "Okay, well, call me, yeah?"

"Of course." She opened the door and pasted on a smile. "Mrs. Winter, so nice to see you. You remember Liam O'Leary?"

The moment Mrs. Winter left, Vanessa cranked up the coal range and snuggled under the quilt on her bed. She tried to recall Liam's features, but the image remained hazy. His face had lost its youthful appearance, but what remained was altogether ... 'more.' More handsome. More chiseled. More charming. Perfectly, wonderfully—more.

Opening the drawer of her nightstand, she removed a large envelope. Inside, the ten cards sat ready for moments such as this. And as she shuffled through them, then read each inscription aloud and smoothed her thumbs over the tiny sketches, her heart ached for the loss of opportunity they may have extended if only her mother had remembered to pass them on.

Whisper's pulse, a northbound paper plane, a steadfast anchor, a cautionary snowflake, a lamp of wishes, the key to his heart, the tiny acorn, a slow and steady turtle, a southbound compass, and finally, a lighthouse for safe passage.

Her thoughts raced as she tried to understand the reason for Liam's return. Had he come back after ten years to shine his damn lighthouse lamp at her—to finish his unfinished business under the oak tree across from Whisper's field? Or did he return for her mother's funeral out of some sort of misplaced loyalty or courtesy.

Vanessa simply had no idea.

PETALS OFF DAISIES

The winter sun was absent for the next few days, and because of this, the cottage held a depressing air. Everywhere Vanessa looked, she imagined her mother, her hands outstretched as she caught snowflakes and pulled petals off daisies. She'd only just finished breakfast when she heard a vehicle stop on the gravel driveway. She peered through the peephole, inhaled sharply, and opened the door. This was only the second time she'd seen Liam up close since he'd returned, but each time she noticed something new. Today, it was a small piercing mark in his left ear. She couldn't imagine him wearing an earring and smiled at the thought. She wondered how that went with his suits and ties, and 'fund transfers in a volatile market.'

He followed her into the open-plan living area at the back of the house, a quaint space with French doors leading out to a north-facing courtyard. The grapevine over the pergola had been bare since she arrived, but now, the small buds of spring were showing. On sunny days, she had sat under it, amazed at how the crumbling structure could ever support the weighty vine.

They exchanged stilted hellos, but after that, she couldn't find her voice. She'd often dreamed of him, as he'd kissed and held her that November dawn, but now, she just wanted him to finish his unfinished business and get back on a plane and out of her life, before those dreams started all over again.

"I was wondering if we could have dinner together tomorrow night?"

"I don't think that's such a good idea."

He paused. His expression indicated he was searching for more than answers. "Why not?"

"Why are you here?" Vanessa's annoyance was preparing to show its unpleasant face. She'd had little sleep over the past few weeks and had entertained far too many people. And to top it off, her period was due, so she felt bloated and on edge. She wanted to crawl into bed and hide. Liam standing in front of her only stirred up emotions she longed to still.

"The valley's my home," he said with a frown.

"I don't mean that. I mean why are you here now, with me ... trying to stir up the past?"

"I'm not trying to stir up anything."

"Good, because if you are, you may as well leave right now. I can't deal with this ... this, 'let's be friends' game. Not when I've just lost my mother."

"I understand. And I'm sorry for your loss, but it's not a game. We were friends once—"

"Were we?"

"Of course we were."

"I was a mixed-up mess. Young, lost, lonely. My mother was a drunk, and my father remarried without even bothering to tell me. I had a crush, a stupid, immature crush that was all in my head, and to be honest, I've moved on."

"It wasn't your imagination—not in those last few days."

Vanessa shook her head. She didn't need him and his desire to rewrite history. "And you're telling me this now? Why?"

"Aren't you and I all about the honest truth?"

"But you're ten years too late, so none of it matters."

"You've always mattered to me."

"I mattered so much that you left without a word and, apart from this bracelet and those scribbles on pieces of card, didn't contact me for ten years. Why?"

"You know why. You were too young. Underage."

"So you couldn't wait for me to turn sixteen? You abandoned me for the sake of forty-eight days? Forty-eight sunsets?"

"So sixteen was the magic number was it? What did you expect me to do? Ask you to wait? I may be a selfish bastard, but I had to let you go. Don't you see that? And I may not have been honest with you that November, but those 'scribbles' as you call them, were my way of telling you I was thinking about you and still cared."

"Maybe. But this isn't some sad movie where I've sat around with my heart broken, waiting for your return. I've moved on, grown up."

"I realize that. But why can't we spend some time together?"

"Why? I buried my mother less than a week ago, and we haven't seen each other in years. And I heard you tell your father that you didn't have feelings for me. That's why."

"What? I never said that. When did I say that?"

"I was packing in my room when you and Mick were talking outside. I didn't hear everything, but I heard that."

"Shit. I asked him if he *expected* me to say that I didn't have feelings for you. That's why I came to Clifton Falls, to say goodbye. But the nuns wouldn't let me see you. Then, when I saw you at the pool, you looked so young—lost—I realized what a selfish prick I'd been."

"So you left without saying goodbye."

"The bracelet was my goodbye. What did you expect me to do? Break into your dorm?"

She stopped for a moment to gather her thoughts. Liam was making perfect sense, but she didn't want to hear it. "I don't know. Not that it matters now anyway."

"Why didn't you write? Respond to the cards?"

"And say what? Beg you to return? 'There's no way back.' That's what you wrote in that first card. And you never left a return address so …"

"But the tone of the cards changed over the years. And Dad knew where to find me. All you had to do was ask."

All she had to do was ask. It sounded so simple, but the reality was a complicated mess. "I only ever received the first two until recently."

"What?"

"Mum put them away in a safe place. If it wasn't for one lucid conversation we had a few days before she died, they'd still be hidden, along with half a dozen letters she'd written. And before you go jumping to conclusions, I'm sure she didn't do it out of spite."

"So you've only just read them?"

Vanessa nodded. "It was quite a shock, knowing you'd written so many times. And thank you. It was a kind thought."

The seconds ticked by. "Even the one about us together under the oak tree?"

Vanessa didn't blush easily, but his words had the desired effect. And as the heat crept onto her cheeks, she looked away.

"Look, I understand you're grieving," Liam said, changing the subject. "I should go. But, have dinner with me tomorrow, please?"

"I'm going to William's parents' for dinner tomorrow night."

"William? You mean Billy Cook?" He frowned. "Are you and Billy in a relationship?"

"Yes, William, as he now likes to be called, is my best friend, and he's never forgotten me, no matter how hard his life has been. But if you're asking if we're dating. No, we're not."

"And what about the doctor?"

Vanessa remembered his words from that November night so many years ago. "We're not together at the moment, but it's complicated."

"Meaning?"

"Simply that."

45

KNOCKING SOFTLY

The Smith's cottage sat on a rise above the river, with a long drive in from the main road. During the day, the peace and quiet calmed Vanessa. The nights were a different story. She hadn't stayed late at William's. His parents were two of the kindest people she knew, but making small talk while grieving was just plain hard work.

She ran a bath and soaked for a while, reading under the dull light until her eyes felt strained. As she readied herself for bed, a soft knock on the back door startled her. If someone was here, she hadn't heard an engine or noticed headlights. Then she remembered she'd locked the gate. Turning on the hall light, she stood in the bedroom doorway, wondering if her imagination was playing tricks.

"Vanessa. It's me. Open the door. It's freezing out here." He knocked again.

She opened the door. "What are you doing here at this time of night? You scared me half to death. How did you get here?"

"I walked up from the road."

Liam followed her to the kitchen. Once there, he stretched his hands toward the warmth of the banked-up coal range.

"How come the gate's locked?" he asked.

"It's just a precaution. Anyway, what can I do for you?"

He looked at her and grinned, the type of 'that's a silly question' grin they'd always shared.

Her only response was a slight shake of her head.

"I thought you might be nervous, being on your own," Liam said.

"How do you know I'm alone?"

Liam looked around the room and down the hallway. "A calculated guess. Yours is the only car outside."

"And you've come to spend the night, have you?" She hated the sound of her voice—the harsh, almost scathing tone—the result of a long held grudge, perhaps.

"I'm heading off in a few days. I want to spend time with you before I go, to be here for you."

"And then what? You fly off to New York, and next birthday I get a card with a sketch of a gun and an inscription that reads, '*Sorry I had to shoot through*'"

"Very funny."

"I'm not trying to be funny." The sound of the phone ringing made her jump. She looked at it for a moment, but didn't move to answer it.

"Do you need to get that?"

Vanessa pulled the cord from the wall. "No." She opened the linen cupboard next to the coal range, pulled out a sleeping bag and a pillow, and threw them on the sofa. "I'm going to bed. Sleep well."

He looked at her and frowned. "You too."

Liam lay in the dark on the smallest sofa he'd ever slept on, the insistent tick of the clock on the mantel even more irritating than the loud trickle of water running through the outside spouting. And as the embers of the coal range died down, his weary body ached with the cold. Drifting off to sleep, he wondered why she didn't answer the phone and why she'd locked the gate.

He woke around midnight, thinking it must be dawn. His feet hit the floor, and he leaned forward—closing his eyes and resting his head in his hands. Turning on the lamp, he studied the framed photographs on the side table—one of Vanessa in her cap and gown and the other of her and the doctor. In it, Vanessa looked at the man with love—the kind that isn't formed from lust alone, but rather, from a deeper understanding of one another. An acceptance of life's difficulties, along with an appreciation of its simplicities.

He checked the time. Spending another six hours with his feet dangling over the edge of the sofa, his limbs heavy with cold, wasn't an option. Especially when the woman he longed to be with and had thought about for years, was within easy reach. With the pillow and sleeping bag under his arm, he took a deep *here goes* breath and crept down the hallway.

Vanessa woke with a start. "What on earth are you doing?"

"I'm freezing, and that sofa's made for a midget. Move over."

He couldn't see her expression but heard the deep sigh of annoyance. She moved toward the wall. "Don't you dare touch me."

"I'll stay zipped up all night, I promise."

She turned her back to him with a humph and pulled the comforter around her neck and shoulders. He rolled onto his side, his hand reaching out to touch her back. She shrugged away.

He waited another few moments before tentatively touching her again. "You okay?" he whispered.

"Why do men ask stupid questions when they already know the answer?" she whispered back. "It seems such a waste of words."

Vanessa hadn't yet shed many tears for her mother, but now, with Liam close, his scent wafting around her pillow, and the touch of his hand on her back—the stress of the past week overwhelmed her. At first, soft tears rolled down her cheeks, followed by small sobs, before finally, her whole body convulsed with pent-up days of raw grief. He pulled her close and held her until the sobs eventually became ragged breaths, and the tears dried on her cheeks.

And they slept. Not comfortably, but they slept. When she woke around eight, Liam had gone.

This pattern continued over the next few nights. Liam arrived at the same time, and sometimes they talked briefly about their day. Nothing too intimate or heavy. The words that mattered remained unspoken, just like they did years ago. However, as much as she protested his presence, she was also lonely and craved the company.

On the fourth night, Vanessa waited until after eleven before going to bed. Liam hadn't come, and the house seemed eerily still without him. There had been a storm forecast, but as she opened the front door and looked out into the night, there was no sign of it.

As she lay in her bed, she thought about how isolating her life had been at times—not only recently, but during the years at the O'Leary's, and at Immaculate Heart; and in her relationship with Julian, where she'd sat alone night after night as he worked eighty-hour weeks. Now, with her mother gone, the chance to rekindle her relationship with her was buried in the grounds of the Rata River Valley Cemetery.

She read for a short time before turning out the light. Just as she was drifting off to sleep, headlights flashed across the side of the house, briefly lighting her room. She sat up and grabbed the throw from the end of the bed, wrapping it around her. His footsteps on the gravel, the clunk of the flowerpot, and the sound of the key in the lock, told her it was him.

Liam appeared in the doorway of her room, his face bathed in the moonlight that filtered through the bedroom window. "Sorry, did I wake you?"

"I didn't think you were coming tonight, so I locked up."

"I went into town to see some friends. I should have called you, but I didn't realize how late it was."

"You don't have to call. It makes no difference to me."

Liam smiled. "You really shouldn't leave that key hidden outside. Anyone could find it." He stripped down to his briefs and t-shirt, used the bathroom, and lay next to her on the bed. She shifted to the side by the window and turned to face him. The coolness of the cotton sheets as she moved over made her shiver.

"You okay?" he asked.

Stupid question. "I don't sleep well when there's a full moon."

"So I remember." Liam rolled onto his back and clasped his arms behind his head. "You want to talk about Ruth?"

"What's there to say? She's gone. It's over."

"Ruth loved you, Ness. More than you probably realized. But addiction has its own agenda. One that's cruel and unkind."

"And deceitful," she said sadly. "Sometimes, I felt as though I was being swept out to sea by a strong current. I had my hand up, begging for rescue, but no one ever noticed me. I had to fight for my life on my own. Even though I pretended otherwise, you became my lifeline."

"I never really understood your ways," he said softly, "but I always sensed your sadness."

"You gave me the touch, the connection, I needed."

"I also stepped over the line. I still regret that, but when I saw you that spring, something in me shifted. And that day we kissed, I regretted it straight away. Not the kiss, but that I ignored our situation and your age, and just acted on some self-indulgent whim. I can't explain the attraction."

"You think I didn't feel the same attraction? I was too young though, I realize that now."

"Yeah. But that didn't stop me, did it?" He turned to face her. "I know I hurt you when I left. I never meant to. When I came home after seeing you at the pool that day, I wanted to call the university and cancel my scholarship."

"What!"

"Please don't think I just up and left. I thought I had to go, to give you space. But looking back, I can't help but wonder if I did the right thing."

"I'm pleased you didn't stay."

He chuckled. "Thanks."

"I don't mean it unkindly. You're right, I needed space. We all need to learn how to make our own way in the world. I spent years feeling sorry for myself, but that doesn't get you anywhere."

He touched her face, his fingers soft as they traced across her cheekbone. "You had plenty to feel sorry about, so don't be too hard on yourself."

Vanessa didn't respond for several minutes as she listened to the rhythm of his breath. "You're a complication I don't need in my life at the moment," she said finally.

"Life is as simple or as complicated as you make it."

"Maybe, but I've never mastered the art of simplifying my emotions." He reached for her hand and laced his fingers through hers. She thought back to when he'd held her that November—the arousal she couldn't resist as his lips caressed her neck, and the strength of his arms as they held her close. "You shouldn't be here." She whispered the words, but there was no conviction in her tone.

"Yes. I should."

Initially, Vanessa had dismissed the thought of being intimate with Liam as inappropriate. But now, numbed by grief and desperate for human touch, her reasoning no longer seemed relevant. And no matter how many times she told herself it was foolish to revisit the past when they had no chance of a future, she couldn't help wondering how it would feel to make love with Liam O'Leary. To have him desire her, to build her arousal until uncertainty became pleasure, and pleasure an all-engulfing release from feelings and thought.

Liam reached over and turned off the bedside lamp. Vanessa waited for him to slide an arm around her, to kiss her neck and run his hand over the breasts that ached for him. But he did none of these things. And as they lay together between cotton sheets warmed by their body heat and quilted feathers, Vanessa felt hot tears trickle down her face while Liam fell asleep beside her.

THE INVITATION

Although their talk the previous night had brought some small sense of closure, the unresolved feelings and tension had left Vanessa feeling drained and raw. So when Liam strolled in the next afternoon with a coffee invitation, her emotions got the better of her.

"What can I do for you?"

"I thought we could grab a coffee," he said.

"So you think you can just waltz back into my life and expect to pick up from where we left off?"

"Old friends reconnect all the time."

"But I'm not just an *old friend*, am I? And I'm not that girl anymore. You don't know the first thing about me."

"Of course I do." He sat at the table and took a deep breath, his hands steepled in front of him and a wry smile on his face. "Your lucky number is six. Your favorite color is blue, and you talk to crazy horses like they're your best friends. *Romeo and Juliet* was your favorite movie when you were younger. Do you remember that? But you weren't interested in Shakespeare, just the guy who played Romeo."

Vanessa relaxed as she recalled the film. "Oh my goodness. I'd almost forgotten that. He was so handsome. I used to dream about him at night."

He grinned and then continued. "And you love reading, desserts, and music."

"What's my second favorite song, after 'Wildfire'?"

"I have no idea. Give me a clue."

"Elton."

"'Tiny Dancer.' And," he said, a grin forming a dimple in his left cheek, "I still think you're one of the most beautiful women I've ever seen, and believe me, I've seen my fair share of beautiful women."

Uncomfortable with the compliment, Vanessa felt her face flush. Julian had often told her she was cute and kind, but Liam was still the only man who had ever called her beautiful. She recalled his words from the morning they'd kissed—*you're a beautiful girl*—and while flattery wasn't something she ever craved, having Liam repeat that word still left an impression.

"I don't understand what you want from me," she said, her mood now serious.

"When I first went to Scotland, someone asked me if I was home-sick. I didn't think I was at first, but do you know what I missed the most?"

"I have no idea. Your truck?"

Liam frowned. It was now his turn to be serious. "You. The warmth of you, your smile, our first kiss, and the daisy chains on my pillow. It took me a long time to get over leaving you ... to let you go."

"But let me go you did." Her words were soft but deliberate, and she kept her expression kind, rather than confrontational. "Now you're back, and for what? So I can change your sheets and warm your bed at night?"

"I'm quite capable of changing my own bed, but we have a strong connection. Always have and always will."

"Maybe, but I have an interrupted life to sort out. I don't mean to sound insensitive. Despite our differences, I loved my mother, and I would have nursed her no matter what, but I need to focus on getting my life back on track."

"I understand. I'm not here to interfere."

"So why *are* you here? So we can have a quick fling for old times' sake? Is that it?"

"Let's start by taking that first step and see where it leads."

"You mean that first step into bed."

He stared at her, a slow smile lighting up his face, and even though Vanessa pretended otherwise, deep down in her core, she wanted him to fight for her. To reach out and take what he once thought of as his.

Taking her cup to the sink, she gazed out the window to the once prolific orchard, and the scattering of rotting apples preserved in the frosted ground. The goosebumps on her arms matched the flutter in her stomach as Liam stepped forward and placed his hands on either side of her, caging her in.

"You think I don't notice the way you look at me, Vanessa?" He whispered the words into her neck. She'd never heard her name sound so sensual, and she inhaled sharply. "That I can't see the interest in your expression?"

Shit. "I thought you just wanted us to be friends," she murmured.

"No, I want us to be more than *just* friends."

"So it's all about what you want? What about me?"

He brushed her earlobe with his lips. Her breasts tighten in response. "Try to deny it all you want, but I know you feel the same. I think we both know the score."

"Do we?" she whispered.

He gently kissed her nape, then blew a soft breath over the spot. "Haven't you ever wondered what it would be like? Wondered if we could connect ... after all this time?"

"I've never allowed myself that luxury."

"Liar. That *luxury* helped me get through some awfully lonely nights, and I'd imagine it helped you do the same."

A moment of hesitation followed before he slid his hands beneath the hem of her shirt, wrapping his arms around her waist. She shivered in response to the skin-on-skin contact, then closed her eyes for a second, allowing herself to sink back into him.

"Did you ever think of me," he continued, "on those nights when you were restless and alone?"

"Maybe," she murmured. "Years ago."

"And now?"

"Letting go of the past is part of being an adult, don't you think?"

"It can be, or rather, should be."

"But those emotions lurk in the background, don't they? Returning in times of loneliness."

"True, but they're easier to deal with when we're adults."

Liam held her gaze through the reflection in the window, and when she closed her eyes, she felt him lean in, his lips skimming down her neck and throat. He was right. She wanted this. But their back-story played in slow motion across her mind, and no matter how hard she tried, she couldn't push it away.

He'd left once before, and she knew he'd leave again. And just like ten years ago, she wouldn't say a word. He'd only come back to deal with unfinished business, he'd said so himself.

Yet, she still turned in his arms, longing to feel his kiss, and when his hands held her face, and his lips found hers, it was like returning to a place she'd always imagined home to be.

They paused for breath. He held her close with gentle dominance and cocked his face slightly to the right, to mirror her stance. His hands still held her—his thumbs resting lightly on both sides of her jaw and his fingers in her hair. Their second kiss was even longer and more passionate, and when it ended, it left her desperately wanting more.

The concept of the perfect kiss may have been foreign to her ten years before, but with age comes knowledge, and Vanessa knew what she liked. Liam checked every clichéd box from a daydream long ago, and even though she vowed to stay in control, her grip on reality slipped with each passing heartbeat.

AFTERNOON LIGHT

Leaning forward, Liam kissed her neck and watched, fascinated, as her chest heaved with each inhalation and her skin tightened with goosebumps. Around her neck, the tiny horseshoe still sat where he'd placed it years before, and on her wrist, the charm bracelet he'd given her—bare, apart from the heart joining the links—dangled over her hand.

"I've missed you. So, so much." His words were sincere, but that didn't make them less fluid. Fragile.

"I've missed you, too."

He pulled back and smiled. "And you're actually admitting it?"

"I'm not fifteen anymore, Liam."

"I've noticed." He reached for the top buttons of her shirt, undoing the first three. Her skin, once tanned from hours working outdoors, was now pale—as if never scorched by passion. "So ... may I have an hour of your time?"

"Just an hour?"

"For now."

He took her hand in his and led her down the hallway. The sound of his boots on the hardwood floor echoed around the walls with every step. His eyes searched hers as they entered the bedroom. "Are you sure you want this?"

"I'm sure." He waited for her to voice the rest of her reply, the conditions he knew would follow out of pride rather than emotion. "But, no strings. No expectations."

"You think we'll sleep together and then go our separate ways? Not a chance. Not in this lifetime."

"That's not your decision to make."

"I'm half of the equation," he said, his voice soft, his smile reassuring. She went to close the curtains, but he stopped her. "Leave them."

"What if someone comes?"

"I want to watch you. You're not expecting visitors, are you?"

"No, but—"

He took her hands, pulling her closer. "Hey. Relax."

Liam took his time, carefully reading her response as he gave her his full attention. He'd never fully appreciated how a woman in sexy lingerie could bring a man to his knees, but as he helped her undress down to a delicate pink bra and matching panties, he wanted to fall at her feet.

He struggled against his conflicting emotions—desire, lust, and regret—not really knowing what the hell he felt. But there was no mistaking his arousal as it fought against his jeans. He'd waited for this moment for years, imagined it many times, but now he was here, the reality far surpassed anything in his imagination. He'd never expected her to be so beautiful—or him so nervous. Vanessa shivered, but when he asked if she was cold, she shook her head.

He noticed the thick woolen socks slouched around her ankles and chuckled.

"What's so funny?"

"You. Dressed in satin and lace … and work socks. You're perfect."

She glanced at him through her thick lashes. "Shall I take them off … the socks I mean?"

"Not just yet. I'm sure they'll come off at some point."

Vanessa locked her gaze on his as he unbuckled his leather belt. She removed her bra before he had the chance to help her, and he smiled at her modesty as she lifted the throw from the end of the bed and held it against her half-naked body. Even as she dropped the bra to the floor, she didn't break eye contact.

"You're not nervous, are you?" he asked.

She sat on the bed, watching as he unbuttoned his shirt and shrugged it off. The sound of his zipper opening made her glance downward. Her eyes widened. "A bit. Are you?"

"Will you think less of me if I admit I am?"

"No, but I'm surprised."

He peeled off his jeans and sat beside her, then reached up and brushed unruly strands of hair from her face. He kissed her gently and she shivered again. Not really the response he'd expected. "Why's that?"

"You always seem so sure of yourself."

Liam kissed her again, dipping his tongue into her mouth, the tiny kiss more erotic than he'd ever imagined, then pulled back to look at her. "Look at you, exquisitely beautiful and bathed in afternoon light. You take my breath away."

"You have all the words, don't you?"

His smile was soft as he moved closer, his hand resting on her thigh. "Seduction is more than intention and touch, don't you agree?"

He gripped a tassel and slowly withdrew the throw until her chest was bare, then gently pushed her back on the bed. She closed her eyes and covered her breasts with her hands, leaving her fingers splayed slightly, so both nipples teased through the gaps.

"Shit," he whispered, as he cast the throw aside. "I could stare at you all day." He bent down and trailed his lips across her collarbone—and further down as he sucked her taut skin into his mouth. He'd imagined her naked that November, as she lay on his bed back at the homestead. Yet the woman before him was infused with such vivid color that his black-and-white imaginings no longer held any significance.

Liam loved how her body had matured. Her small but perfect breasts, the downy blonde hairs dusting her thighs, and the delicate bone structure of her face. His hands gripped her panties. "Lift up." He caught her gaze and smiled as she followed his command. "You okay?"

She nodded. He dropped the panties to the floor and removed his boxers. "But you're a little … hesitant?" he asked as he tugged her socks off.

"A bit. I feel kind of naked without the socks."

Her playfulness amused him, and he chuckled again. He caressed the soft inside skin of both thighs with gentle kisses as her hands clenched the sheet. Squeezing her eyes shut she reached for the throw. "You don't have to do that."

"Are you sure?" he asked, his voice soft and laced with affection. He continued to brush his lips across her skin as he moved closer to his intended target, spreading her legs a little wider with each kiss. The throw, now draped back over her breasts and stomach, couldn't conceal her reaction as he brushed his facial hair across her tender skin, and pressed his lips against her. "Tell me if you want me to stop."

He held her on the bed with one hand while gently caressing her with the other. At first, she voiced her hesitation with a few breathless words. But as he intensified his hold and murmured endearments across her skin, her tense expression relaxed into a soft smile, and that smile expressed more than any words ever could. Because Vanessa had never been one to smile. Her smile was only given to a select few. It conveyed abandonment and a release of self-control.

She reached down and stroked his hair, her fingers combing from front to back, then held him in place. Exactly where she wanted him. He'd never expected her to exert such control, and the gesture sent blood throbbing into his already rigid erection. He didn't know why, but he'd expected her to be timid, and her sudden assertiveness turned him on more than he'd ever imagined it could.

Sensing she was close to climax, he intensified his touch, giving her a promise of what would follow. He couldn't see her face but heard her gasps and gentle moans, felt her hands tug his hair and moved with her as her back lifted from the bed. As she finally let go, she whispered his name—once, twice.

He slid up the bed. "You okay? You feel amazing."

Vanessa nodded. He stood, lifting her up to face him. They kissed —eyes closed, hands clasped where they fell, her breasts pressed tight against his chest.

She knelt, inhaled, and moved forward.

He repeated her words. "Hey, you don't have to—"

"Let me try. Please."

Liam pulled her hair into a loose knot at her nape, and held it as he watched. She moved slowly and hesitantly as he gently nudged into her rhythm. As that rhythm increased, he closed his eyes, struggling for control. His knees weakened, and when she looked up at him through those way-too-long eyelashes, he could hardly hold back.

"Stop. I'm gonna ... Stop, Ness!"

He pulled her to standing, kissed her mouth—her neck and breasts, his hands cupping their firmness as he rolled his thumb over her taut nipples. Easing her back onto the bed, he lay gently on top of her, holding her face as they kissed. Softly. Slowly.

Leaning over the side of the bed, Liam fished for a condom in his jeans pocket, ripped it open and rolled it on. He held her gaze, her eyes wide and darker than he'd ever seen, then slowly pushed himself forward, connecting with her slick heat.

Vanessa squeezed her eyes shut as her fingers clenched his buttocks and her legs wound around his back, pulling him closer. He eased forward gently as she uttered small moans and soft words of encouragement. It took a few minutes to find their rhythm—not surprising for their first time—and while Liam tried to hold onto reality, the more he moved and caressed and flicked his tongue into her mouth, the more that reality slipped from his grasp. "You feel amazing," he whispered into her neck. "I knew it would be like this."

"Liam ..."

"What? Tell me!"

Increasing his pace, Liam pushed harder, amazed when she matched him without hesitation. His gaze locked with hers as he remembered that November dawn so long ago, and they kissed as though the years between one touch and another didn't matter.

He whispered her name, told her secrets, asked what she liked. And in between, his tongue licked the salt from her skin.

❄

Afterward, they lay on their backs, both gleaming with sweat and panting as their heart rates returned to normal. Liam reached over and linked his fingers with hers before turning to look at her. She continued to stare at the ceiling, suddenly feeling too shy to return his gaze. Overhead, the blades of a helicopter rotated loudly as it returned to base. Vanessa barely registered the sound, and had only vaguely been aware of the phone ringing ten minutes before. But the earlier creak of the bed stayed in her mind, and the recollection made her smile.

His fingers traced the outline of her lips, still swollen and sensitive from his attention, before he reached down and gently kissed her. "You're smiling."

"This bed needs a tune-up."

"I didn't think you'd noticed."

"How could I not?"

"Thank you," he said softly. "That was amazing. You're incredible. It's been a long time coming."

Vanessa held his gaze for a moment. Amazing just about covered it, although she could think of a few adjectives of her own. Her past sexual experiences had barely risen above the ordinary, but the way Liam used his lips, hands, and very talented tongue, was about as far from her previous encounters as one could get. The old Vanessa would have let resentment and guilt overwhelm her, but not now. He reached over her to grab his watch from the bedside table, brushing his light smattering of chest hairs over her breasts, as if theirs was an already comfortable relationship.

"I know this is going to sound insensitive, but I have to go soon," he said as he flopped back on the bed. "It's Sophie's birthday. A group of us are having dinner in Clifton Falls. Why don't you come?"

That hollow feeling spread in her chest as he reached for her hand and brought it to his lips. "I'm not really good company at the moment."

"I understand. I'm sorry, I got carried away and I didn't really think things through properly."

"No problem."

"I might have a shower if that's okay. You want to join me?"

"You go ahead. I'll have a bath later."

"Okay."

He left the room with a glide to his step. Relaxed and unhurried like there was no dinner in Clifton Falls, no acknowledgement of her grief, and no plane to catch in a few days. She could hear him humming in the shower, and a few minutes' later, the run of water as he cleaned his teeth. When he walked back into the bedroom, she expected him to be draped in a towel, but he hadn't bothered to cover up. She found that strange, as if standing naked before her was the most natural thing in the world. Would she ever be bold enough to do the same? Walk right past him to the bathroom without an ounce of modesty.

He grabbed his jeans and boxers off the floor and tugged them on, then looked down at her as he buttoned his shirt. "I might stay in town tonight but I'll see you tomorrow, okay?"

As Vanessa watched him fasten his belt, she wondered why she'd expected more. She'd told him no strings, but she didn't expect him to race out the door with hardly a backward glance. She hated that it bothered her—that she felt so needy—but couldn't help her prickly response. "No problem. We agreed, no strings."

His smile disappeared. He bent forward and traced his index finger across her cheek. "Did we?"

She sat up and leaned against the headboard, her naked body covered by the sheet. "Strings lead to complications, you know that."

"Strings can also make beautiful music."

"It's just ... I've got so much going on, I need time."

"You've had ten years."

"And I spent nine of those thinking I'd never see you again." Silence stretched before them as he put on his watch. "Why didn't you come back sooner?" The words left her mouth before she could rationalize her reason for asking them. She pulled the comforter around her shoulders, the air in the room suddenly cool.

He sat on the bed, his sincerity showing in his expression. "I did. You were with someone else."

"And before that?"

He held her hands and entwined his fingers with hers. "I was with someone else. A pretty girl with makeup and tortoiseshell clips in her hair."

"I thought that was your type."

"So did I for a while there, but we were too similar … and too different. In the end, the compromises got less and less, and we both stopped trying." Liam gave space for a reply, but she honestly didn't know what to say. Her relationship with Julian was similar, so she understood what he meant. "I don't want you to think I'm using you. That's not what this is all about."

"I know. But you're leaving in a couple of days so—"

"So it was just sex to you?"

"What does that even mean? Just sex? You can't possibly think I've been lying in bed with you for the last three nights oblivious to your arousal. Do you think because I'm a woman, I don't feel aroused as well?"

"That's not what I meant. It's just, I've been waiting days for you to open up, and now, after we've finally connected, you're pushing me away."

"I'm not the one with other plans."

"No, but I offered a solution. I'm happy to call and cancel."

"Please don't. Your friends are important."

Liam grabbed his jacket from the bedpost and picked up his keys from the nightstand, then leaned over and kissed her gently. Once on the lips, once on the forehead. "I'll call you tomorrow."

48

MOANA O'LEARY

Grief is a strange process. Depending on the expert, they say there are five to seven stages that one experiences after a loss. Vanessa had been through shock, denial, and anger. She'd even done her fair share of bargaining with her God, but the guilt she now felt wasn't so much to do with the loss of her mother, but instead, surrounding Liam. Now, lying in her cold bed, still awake well after midnight, she wondered why she'd pushed him away. After all, she'd wanted him as much as he'd wanted her, but now, her *no strings attached* bravado from earlier had all but disappeared in favor of self-reproach.

Vanessa had imagined their reunion many times over the years, but the reality of it was nothing like she'd envisaged. He'd held all the strings when they were younger, and she'd expected him to be that way still, but he'd softened, and the balance of power had equalized.

She reached for the photo of her mother from the nightstand, taken the day of Vanessa's eight birthday. She still remembered the feeling of pride when her mother—in a short, paisley patterned shift, bronze lipstick, and flicked up hairdo—walked into the room carrying a cake topped with flaming candles.

Snuggling down in the bed, she clutched the photo frame to her chest, her eyes warm with tears. What had she been thinking—making love to Liam in the very house where her mother had died only days before.

The next morning, she pottered around the cottage, boxing up some of her mother's belongings ready for the charity store, while she waited for Liam's call. Between tears and tissues, she'd stop and think about him. The way he made love with soft words and forceful hands. The salty taste of his skin and the scrape of his stubble between her legs. She'd imagined their first time would be intense and over in a flash of heated passion, but Liam took his time—his mouth inching across her skin like he'd memorized the way long ago. She'd rarely experienced that heady sense of surrender, and she longed to feel it again. To have him look at her with fascination and breathe her in like he couldn't get enough of her scent.

Lunch held no interest. After five minutes of pushing scrambled eggs around her plate with a fork, she made a hesitant decision to visit the man who was consuming her thoughts. The past few weeks had been stressful for her—surely he understood that.

She grabbed her keys and locked the door. As she reached her car, she heard the telephone in the hallway. She ran back, dropping the front door key in the process. By the time she reached the phone, it had stopped ringing.

All the way to the farm, the hand of regret held her in a tight grip as she recalled that first day—all those years ago—when she and her mother arrived at the O'Leary's. Memories tumbled over each other. Whisper, that feeling of panic as she was sent to her bedroom to fetch her schoolbook and crayons, the woman praying under the spreading elm in the front yard, *Moko* lady, Billy and Rose's accident, and the day she and Liam kissed in his bed. The recollections were as vivid as ever, and as much as she might appear well-adjusted to the outside world, the events of the past still molded her future.

"Here she is."

Vanessa placed her keys on the sideboard and kissed Mick on the cheek as they exchanged hellos. She moved around the familiar kitchen, pouring coffee into two mugs before joining Mick at the table, as she had done so many times before. The checked cloth was new, and the kitchen now smelled of the unfamiliar—freshly baked bread and sprigs of spring lavender. But otherwise, even the plant weeping its dull and dusty leaves over the mantle of the coal range was the same, along with the same sage green countertop, and the same kitchen dirt filling the cracks of the hardwood floors.

"Is Liam here?"

"He left from Clifton Falls late last night. He tried to call you."

"Oh, okay. I took the receiver off the hook before I went to sleep. Steve Brown has called a few times when he's wasted, and I don't want to talk to him."

"What's he been saying?"

"Nothing much. Just asking if I'm okay. Making out he gives a damn. But he's a creep." She frowned. "I thought Liam wasn't leaving until tomorrow."

Mick's fingers fiddled with the handle of his mug, but his gaze stayed firmly on hers. "He said to give you a message in case he didn't reach you. 'The shit's hit the volatile fan.'"

"I don't get it."

"Haven't you heard the news? Stock markets around the world are falling like mallards on the first day of duck shooting season. He's on his way to the States as we speak. I had to drive to town with his gear and passport last night while he arranged a charter flight to Auckland. I arrived at the aerodrome with only ten minutes to spare."

"Is it bad?"

"It's early Tuesday there now. They're calling the nineteenth, 'Black Monday.' The next twenty-four hours will tell. I invested in shares myself a few years back. My friends were joining share clubs and making thousands all over the place, so I thought I'd get in on the act. Didn't think to ask Liam's opinion."

"I'm sure it will be fine."

"Yeah, maybe. All that aside, I'm glad you called in. I have something to show you." Mick stood and removed an old envelope from the top drawer of the kitchen sideboard. "Here. I've been searching for this for months."

Vanessa turned the envelope over, opened the flap, and pulled out a four-by-six black-and-white photograph.

"Oh my God." She threw the picture down on the table between them, her face feeling as cold and pale as the field of the white snow in her dreams. "Where did you get this?"

"It's all right, lass." Mick's voice was soft, and in his eyes, Vanessa recognized a look of tenderness similar to Liam's. "You can touch it. She won't harm you." He picked up the photograph, studied it and smiled. "Look at her. She's beautiful, isn't she?" He pushed it toward her. "Is she the one? Your *moko* lady?"

Vanessa held the photo, taking in every detail of the woman looking back at her. "Yes. I'll never forget that face. But how did you know? About her, I mean."

"She's Liam's great-grandmother, Moana. Barely lived thirty-five years, the poor soul. Moana wasn't a full-blooded Māori, you can tell by her features and fair skin, but she still had the *moko*. If you look closely, you can see a resemblance to Liam, don't you think? He has the nose and eyes of his European side, but the skin color, lips, and dark hair of his Māori ancestry."

Holding the photo with unsteady hands, Vanessa studied Moana's features before turning it over to read the photographer's handwritten inscription. "Moana O'Leary. *Te wahine ki te moko*, (woman with *moko*)." When she flipped it over, Liam's features looked back at her from the face of his great-grandmother.

According to Mick, Moana had lived a life shrouded in myth and legend. In the photo, thick black hair fell to her waist in waves. She wore European dress—a dark blouse collared in white lace held together with a disk-like pin, and around her waist—holding a full tartan skirt in place—sat a belt with a large shiny buckle. A wedding band graced her ring finger with pride, and long greenstone drop earrings adorned her ears. But her face told the most significant tale. Moana O'Leary's chin was indeed decorated with a beautiful *moko* tattoo.

"The night you were suspended from school," Mick said, his expression thoughtful, "I bailed Liam up. I needed to know the truth … if he'd ever touched or taken advantage of you. Of course, he pleaded innocence. But he explained why you slept in his room, telling me about the woman you saw, the one with the tattoo on her chin, the *moko*, and how afraid you were of her. I gave him the benefit of the doubt that time, only to find you in bed together before you'd even turned sixteen. I wanted to beat the shit out of him that day.

"I've searched high and low for this photograph for years," Mick continued, "and then, a few days after your mother passed away, I found it by accident, sitting under some old papers in my writing desk. I'd looked there ten times before without seeing it. I didn't give it much thought when you were younger, but it's played on my mind a lot lately, and I wanted to share Moana with you."

"So why do you think she visited me?"

"Who knows, lass? Maybe to protect you and guide you through troubled times. I know you found living here difficult, away from the dad you loved and with your mother's drinking."

"I did. Still, I have plenty to be grateful for."

Mick nodded in agreement. "According to my mother, Moana had a special gift. She was kind and loving and full of wise words for those who sought her guidance. She and my grandfather crossed cultural taboos of the time to be together. They married the day Moana turned sixteen, and she died on my mother's fourteenth birthday."

Placing the photograph back in the envelope, Vanessa pushed it across the table, creating a distance between herself and something she'd never understood.

"There's something you need to know." Vanessa waited for Mick to give her the nod to continue. "Liam never took advantage of me. I know I was only fifteen, but I had feelings for him, feelings I struggled to control."

"I understand. But Liam should have known better. You'd lived under my roof since you were a little girl. I know we aren't related, not by blood anyway, but all the same, I felt it was up to me to protect you.

You know what the valley's grapevine can be like. Rumors and unfair judgments are hard to shake in a small town, especially for women."

"So I found out."

Mick paused for a long moment before he continued. "So what happens next?"

Uncertainty flowed over her as she considered his question. It had been a long time since she'd shared her feelings with him, or with anyone, and she'd been trying not to think too far ahead. "I honestly don't know. But I've found a job."

"Really, where?"

"In the maternity annex at Clifton Falls General. It's only a twelve-month contract at this stage, but Amber, my friend from school, works there, so at least I'll know someone."

"And Liam? What if he wants to be part of your life now?"

"Then he'll have to get his butt back here and prove it. Otherwise, I guess he'll fall in love, get married, and give you lots of grandbabies."

Mick smiled, his eyes warm with amusement. "Maybe he's already fallen in love."

Vanessa chuckled. "You're a funny guy." She stood and picked up her backpack from the floor. "Right. I'd better go spend some time with Whisper before he thinks I've abandoned him."

"You and that darn horse. You're like strange soul mates."

Vanessa gave Mick a quick hug. "You're just full of spirituality today, aren't you, Mick?"

"What I read in my spare time might surprise you. I don't only read the *Reader's Digest*."

Several lonely days later, a knock at the front door by the milk truck driver, brought with it a large bunch of pink roses surrounded by sprigs of baby's breath. Her hands shook as she opened the card. A sketch of a small blackboard in a frame graced the front, complete with an eraser and chalk, and inside, two words posed a question:

Clean slate?

49

SHADOWS OF DOUBT

Spring had slipped into early summer by the time Liam returned six weeks later. The weekend was mild but windy, and as he rode Gracie to the trig station at the highest point of the farm, he thought about how maturity can slow you down. Not only in the physical sense, but also by giving you the patience to work through a process—time to evaluate. He'd been back in the country for less than twenty-four hours, burned out and disillusioned after working long days and longer weeks. During his absence, he'd spoken to Vanessa only a handful of times. He often wondered where she was on those late nights when her phone went unanswered, and as much as he didn't want to think about who she might be with, he couldn't quite catch the thought as it sped across his mind.

Still, it wasn't his business who she spent time with, so he kept their conversations light and, because of his workload, shorter than he wanted. He'd hoped she might have written, but there was no letter waiting for him on the mantelpiece when he arrived back at the farm. He'd called her as soon as he landed, but according to her housemate, she was on night duty, meaning nights of work and days of sleep.

Keen for a pint of the local artisan beer and the company of friendly locals, Liam left for the pub straight after dinner. As he walked through the door, everything about it looked the same as it had years before. It even smelled the same, and apart from a few Saturday night regulars, the place was almost deserted.

"Well, will you look who the cat's dragged in from the mud."

Liam hailed the bartender with a lift of his chin, eager to move away from Steve Brown as soon as possible. He hadn't made eye contact but could tell from his tone that the guy hadn't changed one bit.

"So you've finally come back to face the music, then?" Steve said.

"And what music would that be?"

Steve ignored Liam's response. "Mind you, you've paved the way for the rest of us."

"What the hell are you on about?"

"Your little sister. Vanessa."

Liam looked straight ahead and took a swig of his beer as soon as the bartender placed it in front of him. "Vanessa is not my sister."

"So you don't mind that I've been keeping her company, then?"

"As if."

"Didn't she tell you? We got to know each other *real* well over those last few months while she was tending poor old Ruth. In fact, we got to know each other as soon as you left town. She'd ride up to meet me when I worked on your daddy's farm. We'd share a drink, talk about life. Sometimes we'd even skinny-dip in the creek by the hay barn. Very nice. Eager for sixteen, she was. Still is."

"Piss off. You reek of bullshit." Liam didn't need to look at Steve to see the smirk on his face, he heard it in his tone.

"Well, I suggest you take another sniff because I'm not the only one. She spreads herself around the valley like warm honey on hot buttered toast. I must say, you taught her how to ride well."

Everyone looked their way as Liam slammed his glass down on the bar. "Screw you." He grabbed Steve's arm, twisted it behind his back, and pushed him against the counter. "Don't you ever talk about her like that again. Understand?"

"Hey, you two," the bartender yelled. "Break it up. Liam, get the hell out of here until you've calmed down."

As Liam let go, Steve fell to the floor with all the dramatics of a Hollywood stunt double.

"Don't worry," Liam said, "I'm going."

Liam drove down Tuckers Road toward the river mouth. Parking in his usual spot, he slapped his hand on the steering wheel as Steve's words echoed in his head. He was almost certain Steve was lying, but then he remembered what Mick had said about Vanessa being popular with the lads, and how sensual she'd been that afternoon at the cottage. Yet, she'd also been shy and nervous initially, covering herself with the throw until her reserve loosened as they kissed and touched.

As storm clouds rolled in from the horizon, Liam strolled along the beach, picking up pieces of driftwood as he went, and hurling them into the ocean with an exaggerated heave. He'd never thought of himself as the jealous type, but the more Steve's words echoed in his thoughts, the more seeds of doubt were planted. Maybe their afternoon together meant nothing. Maybe it was just sex for her. She was right. He didn't know her, not as an adult, anyway. He kept telling himself it was none of his business who she spent time with, but now, he was going to make it his business.

Six days passed before Liam asked Mick for Vanessa's new address. He'd needed some time, both to assimilate the bullshit Steve had dumped at his feet, and to readjust his body clock. He'd tried phoning her that morning, but like many of his calls from New York, it went unanswered.

It was a Friday evening, and cars lined Crosby Street, so he parked on a side road and walked the rest of the way. He knocked several times before anyone heard him over the ruckus inside. A girl with tousled hair, rows of rosary beads around her neck, and dressed in a cropped tee and purple leggings, answered the door.

"Just come in. It's a party. You don't have to knock."

"Thanks, but I'm looking for Vanessa Blinkly. I may have the wrong house."

"Right house. Wrong day. She's not here."

"Any idea where she is?"

The Madonna look-alike called down the hallway, struggling to be heard over the insistent beat of 'Radio Ga Ga.' "Hey, Davey?"

"Yo?" someone, presumably Davey, yelled back.

"Do you know where Vanessa is?"

"In Wellington, with the boyfriend. She'll be home Tuesday."

The girl turned back to Liam and looked at him through lowered lashes as she twirled a lock of hair around her finger. "Why don't you come in anyway? Looks like you need a bit of fun."

"Thanks, but I think I'll pass."

"So, what's your name?"

"Never mind. It's not important."

SLAP, SLAP.

Vanessa and Amber stood in the locker room, discussing their days off. Amber strolled to the tiny window overlooking the street below as she buttoned her shirt and tucked it into her jeans.

"Looks like it'll be a beautiful day tomorrow." Amber looked back over her shoulder at Vanessa. "Any plans?"

"I'm spending the weekend at William's. I want to visit Mum, take her some daffodils. Also, I have a job on and I can't wait to see Whisper."

"Any telegrams or carrier pigeons from Liam lately? When's he back?"

Vanessa grinned. "Not this week, and I have no idea. Anyway, we have this whole love-hate thing going on. Maybe I'm not as enlightened as I thought."

"I reckon enlightenment flies out the window when you're dealing with men."

"Yes, maybe you're right." Vanessa grabbed her bag from her locker. She wondered why she hadn't heard from Liam, but put on a brave face. "I might walk home. I could do with some fresh air."

"Okay. Have a great weekend, and don't get too moody when you visit the farm. He'll be back soon enough."

In the hour it took Vanessa to drive from Crosby Street to the Rata River Valley, she thought about Liam constantly. And as much as she tried to nudge those thoughts sideways, they always moved back to center.

All the way there, Radio Falls 88FM spouted a steady stream of classic rock and endless catchy jingles, which, despite her disinterest, annoyingly stuck in her head. So when 'Tiny Dancer' came on, she turned up the volume and sang along with Elton as a much-needed distraction. Stopping at the cemetery for a while, she lay daffodils on her mother's grave and talked to Ruth about her life, then drove to the O'Leary's under the threat of tears.

Vanessa noticed Liam's old pickup parked outside the front door as soon as she hit the top of the driveway. Mud clung to the tires, and freshly split firewood lay in the tray, ready to be stacked into the wood-shed. Of course, it didn't mean Liam was back. Mick sometimes used Liam's vehicle, depending on what he was doing. She relaxed as she parked by the back door, her normal point of entry.

She knocked on the door, not her usual approach, but today some-thing felt different. Her sleep had been restless and full of dreams of fields and snow, so she was a little uneasy. As she waited on the porch, she noticed a pair of stylish men's boots and some bright pink Nikes, which made her do a double take. She went to knock again just as the door swung open.

"Vanessa."

Liam leaned on the doorjamb, offering no invitation to enter, his shirt undone, and his feet clad only in socks. Vanessa glanced at his bare chest, a chest she'd once clung to for comfort, a chest she'd occa-sionally wet with tears and one she had now kissed tenderly. Dark navy jeans hugged his hips, and a clipped goatee beard—a style of beard she loathed—covered his normally smooth-shaven face. The thing was, he wore it well. She swallowed hard, and even though she knew better, Vanessa could have sworn her heart skipped a beat.

"What can I do for you?"

Slap. His tone was cold and impersonal. "Oh ... um ... I didn't realize you were back."

"Yeah. I've been back almost two weeks now."

Slap. "Oh. Okay. Is Mick home?"

"He's away with Molly for the weekend."

His gaze never left hers, but there was no warmth, no intimacy, and no familiarity in his expression. She cleared her throat, suddenly needing a drink of water. "I ... um ... thought I might go for a ride if that's okay."

"Sure. You don't have to ask my permission."

"I thought Mick would be here. Sorry, I should have phoned first."

"Liam?" A tall redhead with big hair, a tiny denim skirt, and long drop earrings appeared behind him, calling his name as if she owned it. "Are you ready?" She looked Vanessa up and down. "Oh, sorry, I didn't realize we had company."

"Cassie, meet Vanessa Blinkly." Liam's tone was still abrupt, as if the effort of the introduction annoyed him. "Vanessa is an old friend of Anna's brother."

Slap. Slap.

"Who? William? I met him the other day," she said in a broad American accent. "What a sweetie pie he is. Pleased to meet you, Vanessa." She offered her hand. "Cassie Bell from California. Have you come to borrow a cup of sugar? That's what you country guys do, right? Borrow cups of sugar?"

Vanessa pulled her lips in tight, kneading them together as Cassie flashed a perfect, white-toothed smile encased in a pair of overly glossy lips. Her hands slid into the back pockets of her jeans as she looked toward Whisper's field. "I came to see Mick, and to take one of the horses for a ride."

Cassie snaked her way around Liam, who was still standing guard at the door. "We're off to the market. Let me sneak in here and grab my shoes." She picked up the Nikes, the type of Nikes Vanessa loved. The type she'd seen in magazines, but that weren't available in New Zealand.

"Sorry, obviously today's not a good time," Vanessa said to Liam. "I'll just go say hello and ride him another day."

"It's not a problem," Liam replied. "He needs a good ride. Might calm him down. He's been pretty flighty lately."

The innuendo wasn't lost on her. Maybe that's all she'd meant to him that late afternoon at the cottage. A means to a calming end. "Okay, thanks." She turned to leave.

"And, Vanessa?"

She noted he hadn't smiled once and his tone had remained emotionless—as cold as a crisp morning frost, without the blue sky. He waited for her to meet his gaze and then paused before adding a little punch to his message.

"Next time—call, okay?"

Slap. Slap. Slap. "Of course."

As she made her way to see Whisper, Vanessa's throat burned and she struggled to blink away the wet heat behind her eyes. She looked away as Liam's pickup, with Cassie Bell from California riding shotgun, unsettled the dust of the driveway as they left for the market. Whisper stood perfectly still, watching her every move.

"I can't stay. I'm sorry, boy." She licked her lips and sniffed back the tears. "I love you, Whisper. I'll love you to the sky and back forever."

Whisper stepped back and took off around the perimeter of his field. She climbed the post and rail fence and watched him. He needed grooming. *Screw it and screw Liam.* Vanessa jumped down from the rail. Liam O'Leary and Cassie Bell, with the gorgeous pink Nikes and the big auburn hair, could go take a running leap. She'd go back to work, save hard, travel the world and fall 'so in love'—maybe with a hot Latino who 'couldn't keep his hands off her.' Someone who worshiped the ground she walked on, as Liam once had for Christie.

"Whisper, here boy. Here, my darling." Whisper came to her call. "Good boy. Let's go for a ride, then I'll give you a decent groom. You'd like that, wouldn't you?"

When Vanessa led Whisper back several hours later, she noticed Liam's pickup was once again parked at the front door. The mud had been cleaned from the tires, and the firewood neatly stacked into the woodshed, every log flush with the other, just the way he liked it. Neat. Orderly. So goddamn straight.

For him, it was like any other day—stack the wood, wash the truck, and shop at the market with Miss California on his arm for the whole damn world to see.

The slate remained covered in chalk dust.

FAITH DESTROYED

Cassie pulled up a chair next to Liam while they waited for Hamish to buy their drinks from the bar. "You need to talk to her," she said.

Liam had come to the same conclusion while he stacked firewood that afternoon, but he still let his ego answer. "Who?"

"The cup of sugar girl. She's the one messing with your head, isn't she? How did you feel when you saw her this morning?"

"Like crap."

"It won't get any easier until you deal with it. I don't understand you men. Why let things slide when one conversation could clear up whatever's bugging you?"

"Because, I'm pissed off and tired and burned out. I'm having to rethink my whole career, and frankly, I don't know what the hell to say to her."

"Start with 'Hi.' The rest will follow."

"Is that what you and Hamish do, Cass? Talk everything through until the problem gets lost in the layers of 'what's next?'"

Cassie laughed. "Pretty much. Well, I do all the talking, he just listens, then says, 'you're right, sweetie.' It drives me nuts, but I still love him, and his Scottish ass, to pieces."

Liam huffed a chuckle.

"She looked so sad this morning," Cassie continued. "Like a little fawn caught in the headlights. I felt sorry for her. You didn't exactly lay out the welcome mat, standing there acting all macho with your arms folded over your chest."

"There's nothing *little fawn* about her, believe me. And she's already in a relationship, so what's there to say."

"Well, don't look now, but your gorgeous *ex*-crush just walked through the door."

"Shit. Is she with anyone?"

"William and a couple of other guys. And she looks like she's had a trip to the salon this afternoon."

Liam turned to see Vanessa making herself comfortable at a table as William Cook hovered over her like some overzealous bodyguard. She laughed and chatted as if she didn't have a care in the world, but all Liam noticed was the haircut. Her long blonde locks, the locks he'd loved, had been cut into a short, blunt bob. It made her look like a teenager channeling the lead singer of Blondie, and Liam had always had a thing for Debbie Harry. *Damn.*

A short time later, Steve Brown walked in with a group of his biker mates. Liam watched as he sauntered in on bandy legs as if he owned the show. Steve winked at Vanessa when she glanced his way, and when she entered the hallway to the restroom a few minutes later, he followed. If anyone else noticed, they didn't seem to care, not even William. Liam returned to his conversation, reminding himself that who Vanessa spent time with wasn't his business.

She returned to the bar in under five minutes, her face flushed, and whispered something to William. He looked at Steve's friends, shook his head, then walked with her through to the garden bar.

Liam ordered another beer. He'd had three already, which was usually his limit, but the idea of getting wasted suddenly seemed appealing. Five empty beer glasses later, his angry alter ego made an appearance. He stood and stalked across the room.

"Where's Vanessa?" he asked William.

"In the beer garden. Why?"

"Not your business, mate."

Liam pushed his way through the door to outside. The space reeked of decay and hosed-down concrete. He noticed her sitting in the corner by a row of half-dead pot plants and expected to see Steve with her, but she was talking to a woman, who left as he approached.

She glanced up.

"Can we have a word?" He pulled out a chair and straddled it. "What have you done to your hair?"

"What have you done to your face?"

"You don't like beards?"

"Sure, but a goatee isn't a beard, is it? It's more of an indecision."

His face twisted in a smirk. "Bit like your fancy new haircut. Halfway between here, there, and nowhere."

Her fingers raked through her shorter locks as if she hadn't remembered having it cut. "So, what can I do for you?"

Liam decided to beat around the bush for a while. "Dad said he showed you a photo of Moana."

"He did." Vanessa fiddled with the buttons of her coat, her fingers reddened by the cold. Pulling the lapels tighter, she slipped her hands into the pockets. "It turned up a few days after Mum passed away."

Liam frowned, then scooted the chair closer and turned his whole body toward her. "My great-grandmother looks like the woman with the *moko*, doesn't she?"

"The spitting image." She studied him for a moment. "You still don't believe me?"

He shrugged. Her 'gift'—a term he used loosely and one he still struggled with—was an important part of Vanessa's identity, but Liam had never completely understood it. "You must admit, it's pretty far-fetched."

The rise and fall of Vanessa's breath filled the space between them. He shifted uncomfortably in his seat as he struggled with the link between the ghost of Vanessa's childhood and his great-grandmother.

"Not to me."

They sat for some time while Liam gathered his thoughts into words. "I think you got the wrong impression this morning. I don't mind you visiting the farm, but I'd prefer you call first, so we don't have to run into each other."

"What happened to the clean slate?"

"You tell me."

"Meaning?"

Liam told himself to shut the hell up, but Steve's arrival, Vanessa's flushed face when she returned from the restroom, and William's over-attentiveness all slammed into his alcohol-addled mind. And when everything mixed together in his thoughts, out jumped the jealous asshole, ready to wreak havoc. "I guess I owe you an apology," he said, his tone laced with sarcasm.

She took the bait. "For?"

"I didn't realize you were still in a relationship when we were together at the cottage."

"I'm not in a relationship. Who told you that?"

Liam shrugged and took a long draft of his beer. "Does it matter?"

"That's you all over, isn't it? Jump to conclusions, then take off to the other side of the world so you don't have to deal with anything."

"It wasn't like that, and you know it." Liam glanced up as a group of older women walked through the beer garden and into the bar. He knew he should walk away, but he couldn't resist one last dig. "Since when did you become such a bitch?"

"Since this morning, when you showed me what a bastard you were by introducing me as an old friend of William's."

"You didn't seem to think I was such a bastard when we were at the cottage."

"Yes, my mistake. I'm not always a good judge of character." She stood, pushed her chair into the table with force and stormed off.

"So I've heard," he mumbled.

WHISPER'S CALL

Vanessa was in the break room when the receptionist called her to the phone. Maybe it was Liam. She didn't know why he'd suddenly cut her off like she was a regretful one-night stand. The more she thought about it, the more his stance confused her. She wondered if his girlfriend knew they had slept together. Not that it mattered now; she'd learned her lesson. It seemed he didn't mean anything he'd said that afternoon at the cottage. *I've missed you. So, so much.*

She picked up the receiver. "Is that you, Vanessa?" Mick's voice sounded frail over the line, and a feeling of panic rose in her chest. He never called her at the hospital. "Sorry to phone you at work. Is it okay to talk?"

"Is everything all right?"

Mick hesitated for a few seconds—long enough to worry Vanessa even more—and his heavy sigh told her everything wasn't. "No, lass. It's Whisper. He got out onto the main road and into the path of a stock truck."

"Is he hurt?"

"The vet came about an hour ago. We had to put him down. He said we had no choice."

"What? No!"

"I'm so sorry. I know how much you loved him."

Vanessa slid down the wall, the receiver still to her ear as sobs overwhelmed her.

"Vanessa? Are you still there, lass?"

"Yes." She could barely form her words, barely see in front of her. "I'm here."

"We were wondering if you wanted to come up. Liam's dug a trench with the Caterpillar. We're burying him by the oak tree across from his field."

"Liam's still there?"

"We're doing it tomorrow. Can you be here by four?"

"I'm on a day shift tomorrow." She searched in her pocket for a tissue. Everyone around her seemed to be moving in slow motion as her heartbeat raced and her hand gripped the receiver. "Sorry ... of course I'll be there. I'll swap shifts. What did the vet say? Why couldn't he have saved him?"

"It was too late, lass."

"No, Mick, don't say that. Surely something could have been done. How did he end up on the road?"

"It looks like someone left the gates open."

"What? But who'd do that?"

"We're not sure, but we'll find out."

Vanessa hadn't driven to work that morning, catching a ride with Amber instead. When Matron let her leave an hour early, she walked straight past the bus stop and carried on down the hill on foot. She followed the port road and plodded along the coastal boardwalk to Clifton Falls South.

Everywhere she looked, children played ball and rode bikes, and washing was collected from clotheslines, as if it was just another day. She wondered who else had lost a loved one that day. How many pets had been put down, and how many human souls had gone to join her mother in whatever spiritual realm souls went to rest.

There had been no warning this time. No dreams of snow or the fields of home. No word from Whisper that their last time, when she almost didn't ride him because of her anger at Liam, would be their final moments together. And on her walk home, the image of Liam carrying Whisper from the road to the oak tree in the bucket of the front-end loader never left her mind.

Now her last connection to the valley, and the animal soul she'd loved more than any other, had gone in an instant. Whisper had always been a loner, so she understood why he'd gone the way he had. He hadn't known any better. He'd been given the opportunity, and it had been his final ride to freedom.

It was just after four when Vanessa arrived in the Rata River Valley the following day. Her cassette player had kept her company all the way, and when 'Wildfire' came on after several songs from Fleetwood Mac and U2, she cried, singing the words through a throat congested with tears.

She parked on the road verge where the northbound bus stopped each afternoon just after two—opposite the spot where she had waited many times. She grabbed her jacket from the back seat and walked across the fields to the oak tree. Holding a small bunch of carrots tied together with kitchen twine in one hand and her car keys clenched in the other, she peered into the gaping hole where Whisper lay. A faded green canvas covered his back, flank, and croup, and dried blood matted his tail, but his forehead, crest, and muzzle still looked perfect. She almost expected him to come up to greet her, and she wept uncontrollably as the reality and shock set in.

She heard the men, quickly followed by Molly, as they hurried down the driveway. Liam caught her gaze, his expression conveying concern and understanding, that same compassion he'd shown when her mother died. Even so, he said nothing, didn't come to her, or even speak her name.

It was just as well. She couldn't handle his concern right now. Instead, it was Mick and Molly who stood by her side. Mick who wrapped his arm around her until their breaths resonated in rhythm as the older man's eyes glistened with unshed tears.

Vanessa flinched as the Caterpillar rumbled into life, and as Liam scooped the first bucket of dirt from the pile to the right of the trench and let it fall, her eyes stung, and a hard lump threatened her throat. She felt the carrots slip through her hands, watched them land to the side of Whisper's muzzle. She sensed Molly to her right, and Mick, holding her hand, as he stood to her left.

The loads kept coming. *Scoop, thud. Scoop, thud.* Yet, when the last bucket of earth fell, she wondered how it was over so soon. How could her magnificent friend be there one minute and buried in the ground the next?

"Why don't you stay for dinner?" Molly said. "I have a lasagna in the oven."

Reaching into her pocket for another tissue, Vanessa blew her nose, then lifted her sunglasses and wiped her eyes. In some ways, she wanted to stay—to be part of their family, but she and Liam needed to talk, and now wasn't the time. "Thank you. But I'd better get back."

Mick draped his arm around her shoulder and gave her a tight squeeze. "I don't like the thought of you driving that road when you're upset."

"I'll be fine. I know it like the back of my hand."

She looked across the field to the highway, then back to Liam on the Cat. "Did anyone see what happened?"

"Not heard anything yet. We've put the word out."

She stared into space, running her sight along the sun-washed hill line to the west. "It was that bastard Steve Brown. I ran into him a couple of weeks ago. He followed me into the restroom at the pub and tried to grope me, so I slapped him—hard. He's responsible for this. I just know it."

"I thought so too," Mick said. "But according to his missus, he was in Clifton Falls all day. Anyway, I'll pass that on to the police."

"Was there any sign he'd been forced out of the gate?"

Mick shot Molly a concerned look. "Don't worry about that now. Let's see what the police say."

"Mick, please. I'm not a kid. I need to know." She looked at Molly for support.

"Tell her," Molly said softly.

Mick inhaled a shaky breath. He glanced at his son still on the Cat as Liam smoothed the soil over the gravesite. "I'm sorry, lass. He'd been pretty badly beaten on the croup and quarters. It's probably the only way they got him out onto the road."

"No! How could someone do that to him? This is all my fault. I should have taken him to Dad's like you suggested."

"Don't blame yourself, lass. I know it won't bring Whisper back, but we'll get to the bottom of it."

"Thanks, Mick." She choked back a sob. "I'll see you soon. Please, call me if you hear anything."

As she walked down the driveway to her car, she sensed Liam watching her from where he stood by the trench. He called her name as he sprinted over the grass and hurdled a fence to reach her. "Vanessa."

She kept walking.

"Vanessa. Wait."

She had almost made it to the highway when he reached out and grabbed her arm, bringing her to an abrupt halt.

"Stay the night. You're upset. You shouldn't be driving on your own." He seemed genuinely concerned, and it tripped her up a little. She turned her face toward the road as she grappled with the thought of her old room—the stained pillow, the lumpy kapok mattress with the blue and white striped ticking, and the torn curtain held together with a rusty safety pin. Somehow this seemed like an appropriate analogy—it felt like a rusty safety pin was barely holding her tattered life together at that moment.

"Someone beat him, Liam. Was it bad?"

She could tell Liam was carefully considering his reply. He still had that look of concern on his face. He glanced away, back to Whisper's grave. "Bad enough. I'm so sorry, Ness."

"What did he do to deserve this? It's all my fault," she said with a sniff. "I know I didn't open the gate and didn't beat him or force him onto the road. But I still feel responsible."

"What do you mean?"

Vanessa stood with her hands in her jean's pockets and scuffed her boots over the loose stones on the roadside. "It's getting late. I have to go."

Liam's hand reached to cup her face. She flinched. "If you won't stay, let me drive you. Dad can pick me up tomorrow."

Their eyes met for a moment. He still had that stupid goatee, but she'd never seen him look so striking, so sincere. She pulled away. She didn't want to give him the satisfaction of knowing how his presence affected her, especially not today. "Thanks for burying him instead of sending him to the knacker's yard. I appreciate it."

Liam smiled. "We'd never do that. We all know how much he meant to you."

She looked up at him, but couldn't speak. She swallowed hard, then breathed a deep sigh as she glanced down at her wrist to check her watch.

"Hey." He put his arms around her and caught her tears as they fell, the pressure of his head leaning on hers bordering on painful. "Don't go home."

With both arms folded across her breasts to keep her chest from connecting with his, she stayed in his embrace for a moment before her conscience screamed *betrayal*. She pulled back from the burn of his touch. "I can't stay here."

"Why not?"

"I don't know. Too many painful memories I guess."

He let her go—almost. His arm stayed loosely tethered around her waist. She avoided eye contact as the realization that she would never see Whisper again formed a tight ball in her gut.

She checked her watch yet again. "I have to go."

"Look, stay for dinner. Dad loves seeing you. I'll take you home later. Molly and Dad are going to Clifton Falls tomorrow. They can drop your car off."

Vanessa's gaze fell on the homestead, then returned to the road. Would she ever stand in this spot again—at the mailbox marked M & C O'Leary—now that her mother and Whisper were gone? As much as she'd hated the house when she was a girl, the thought she might not, saddened her.

"Please stay," Liam continued. "We'll share stories. You might find it helps you come to terms with it. If you don't want me to drive you home later, I'll follow you down."

"Last time I was here, it seemed you never wanted to see me again. Now you want to escort me down the highway because you're worried about my safety. Well, don't concern yourself. If I need help, I'll ask my phantom boyfriend."

"You haven't changed, have you? Still too proud for your own good."

She shook her head. "You think you know me so well, but you have no idea."

Vanessa turned on her heel and hurried to her car. She struggled to unlock the door, then sat with her forehead resting on the steering wheel, trying to calm her breathing and slow her heart rate. Her hands shook as she started the engine, and when she made a U-turn onto the main highway, the sudden blast of a car horn told her she'd had a close call.

The traffic was heavy that afternoon, and exhaust fumes from the stock truck in front filled her car, stinging her already raw nostrils. Her toes curled in her boots until cramp traveled up her legs and she had to pull over. She sat with her head in her hands, her fingertips pushing the skin of her forehead into her hairline. And as 'Wildfire' played through the stereo, more tears came in ragged gasps—wet and raw.

53

PETRIE BAY

Liam hardly slept that night. Living with his father and Molly was an intrusion into their world, and he was impatient to build his own place. But that wasn't the only reason for his restlessness, his heavy-handed treatment of Vanessa also played a large part.

It was just on noon the following day when he arrived at the bakery in the village where Ava Rigby once worked. As he walked in the door, William Cook was on his way out. The men didn't know each other well, but now, Liam saw the chance meeting as an opportunity to discuss Vanessa and offer William an apology for his recent behavior.

"Do you mind if we have a quick word?" Liam asked, following William outside.

William pulled his aviators out of his shirt pocket and put them on. The guy had a presence that some might call arrogant, and from what Liam knew of him, he didn't take, or dish, any shit. "If it's about Vanessa, I'm not the one you should talk to."

"Look, I'm sorry about the other night at the pub, but to tell you the truth, I'm worried about her."

"Don't you think it's a little late for the 'concerned brother' act? What's it been—eight, ten years? Vanessa's a big girl now. She can take care of herself."

William went to walk away without giving Liam a chance to reply, then stopped and turned back to face him. "Vanessa's jumped through hoops stuck in boiling crap to get where she is today. Don't come back here acting like some arrogant bastard and think you're gonna stir shit. She deserves better than that."

"By better, you mean you, I suppose."

William huffed. "Get your head out of your ass. Vanessa and I are friends, and whether you're around or not, that's never going to change. You used to be a decent guy, so one piece of advice for old times' sake. Don't let your ego off its leash until you know all the facts. She's had enough hurt in her life."

Instead of snapping an angry response, Liam bit his tongue. The guy was right, and the last thing he wanted was to get William's back up. As he'd pointed out, he was part of Vanessa's life, whether Liam liked it or not.

Three days had passed. Days of internal debate that eventually led Liam to the first rational decision he'd made since his run-in with Steve at the pub.

He traveled south along the coast road past Petrie Bay. As he drove, he berated himself for his stubbornness. He knew Steve was dishing bullshit—had even accused him of it—but for a while, he'd allowed jealousy to overshadow rational thought. That was until Mick reminded him that pride came before a fall and had called him an idiot when he'd failed to persuade Vanessa to stay for dinner after the burial. The term "phantom boyfriend" arose in his mind. Perhaps she wasn't back with the doctor after all.

In the daylight, Crosby Street looked much like any other road in this part of town, with compact wooden houses, built by the government in the fifties, sitting smack bang in the middle of each quarter-acre lot. As he pulled into the curb, he noticed no lights on in the house. He should have called first, but it was too late now. He made his way through the gate to the front door.

There was no doorbell, so he knocked with three short, hard raps and stepped back to survey the scene. All along the street, the front yards were either bare or full of unruly shrubs and overgrown grass. It seemed half the neighborhood had an old car parked out front, held together by moss and rust.

"Yep?" The owner of the voice was a short, stocky guy with a neck so thick he had to be a bodybuilder. The door remained half closed.

"Is Vanessa here?"

He looked Liam up and down. "Who's asking?"

"Liam. I'm a friend of hers."

The door opened fully. "Come in. I'll call her."

Liam followed him down the hall and into a small living room bursting with musical instruments, stereo gear, and mismatched furniture. On the walls, posters of Pink Floyd and Metallica covered the faded wallpaper, and a large corkboard overflowed with snapshots of Vanessa and guys he assumed were her housemates.

"She's in the shower. I'm Davey." He didn't offer Liam his hand.

"Liam O'Leary. I called in the other night. The night of the party."

"I remember. The weekend she was down in Wellington. Take a seat."

"Thanks." He sat in a worn armchair.

"Liam?" Davey's eyes narrowed. "The two of you grew up together. You guys are like brother and sister, right?"

It seemed nothing much had changed in ten years. Every man and his dog thought Liam and Vanessa were as close to siblings as they could get, and it was getting old. "Vanessa's mother was our housekeeper." He paused for a beat. "But there's nothing brotherly about my relationship with Vanessa."

Davey nodded. Liam noticed his look of suspicion.

"Shame about the horse," Davey said.

"It is. So how many of you live here?"

"Just the four of us. All guys, apart from Vanessa. But she's not here much. Just when she's on night shifts, and a few days during the week if she's too tired to drive to her dad's."

Both men stood as Vanessa entered the room. She stopped abruptly.

"Liam, what are you doing here?"

"You left your jacket the other day. I was passing, and I thought I'd drop it off."

"Right. I'll go jump in the shower," Davey said to Vanessa. "I'm leaving for the party in fifteen if you've changed your mind."

"No, I'm good," she replied. "Enjoy yourself and say hi to the guys for me."

Vanessa waited for Davey to leave the room before she said anything more. "Thanks for dropping off the jacket, but there was no need. Mick said he'd bring it down."

"I was in town anyway."

She nodded. Liam noticed her teeth chewing the inside of her cheek. She was nervous. "Okay, well, I'll see you out."

"We need to talk," he said. "Come for a drive?"

"I have a party to go to."

He shot her his best *bullshit* look. "Half an hour max, promise, then I'll drop you back." The way she crossed her arms over her chest reminded Liam of the first time he'd caught her riding Whisper. She'd always displayed a fierce determination when she was young. It seemed nothing had changed.

"I'm listening."

"Not here. I'm leaving the country in a few days. I don't want to go with this misunderstanding between us."

"There's no misunderstanding on my part. The words 'call first' made it perfectly clear."

He held her gaze. "Please. Half an hour."

Vanessa shivered a little, reached for her jacket draped across the back of the chair, and tugged it on. "Fine. Half an hour."

As she led the way down the steps and onto the street, she stopped. "Where are you parked?"

He stepped forward and opened the door of his brand new, double cab pickup. "Right here."

"You've bought a new truck?"

When he looked her way, he noticed the hint of a smile. "Thought it was about time."

5 4

NO COMPROMISE

Liam drove north past the airport and followed the highway before taking a right turn onto a narrow gravel road leading to the shoreline of the Pacific coast. The air held the cold, but the days were drawing out, and it was still light.

Apart from a few seagulls and a lone fisherman strolling along the shore with his rod, the beach was deserted. Out toward the port, a catamaran motored along the channel leading to the marina, its white and blue sails flapping in the breeze as two men dropped them to the deck.

He cut the engine and reached over to grab a blanket from the back seat, handed it to her, then locked the doors. Liam noticed her frown. "I've just spent two years living in New York, it makes you security conscious," he explained. Vanessa shifted in her seat and he did the same.

"So. What did you want to talk about?"

Liam cleared his throat and stared at the ocean—his gaze focused not on the waves crashing along the shoreline, but further out, to the horizon, where thoughts of life drift. "Us. And don't say, 'there is no us,' because we both know that's not true."

As Liam waited for her reply, he watched her delicate fingers fiddle with the tassels of the blanket, as if she found them fascinating—a process for collecting her thoughts perhaps. Or maybe, gathering her strength to tell him to piss off.

"What do you want, Liam? To pick up from where we left off at the cottage? What about Cassie from California? Your girlfriend who offered me a cup of sugar from the kitchen I'd spent years slogging my guts out in."

"Cassie is not my girlfriend. She's engaged to one of my closest friends, who happened to be too hungover to get out of bed that morning."

"Well, it's none of my business."

"So why bring it up?"

"Isn't that the reason we're here? To clear up any confusion?"

Liam went to speak, paused, then started again. "A few days after I arrived home last time, I ran into Steve Brown. As usual, we got up each other's noses. He told me he'd been hooking up with you since you were sixteen." The words sprung from a thought he'd never meant to verbalize. Once said, they could never be taken back. He kept going, his jealousy clouding his good judgment as he ignored William's earlier advice, unclipped his ego's leash, and let it bare its teeth. "What did he call you? That's right ... eager."

She shook her head. It was her turn to stare out over the ocean. "Is that what you honestly think? That I've been sleeping with Steve Brown?"

"No, of course not, but—"

"Screw you, Liam. After you left for Edinburgh, Steve told everyone, including my mother, that you and I had slept together. Suddenly, I was the most popular girl in the valley. An easy lay. I couldn't even buy a loaf of bread without some guy leering at me.

"But let's get one thing straight," she continued, "I have never, ever, had sex with Steve Brown, consensual or otherwise. Oh, he tried, even got my mother on his side."

"Shit. So why didn't you tell someone?"

"Yeah right. Vanessa, the weird kid with the wild imagination and an alcoholic mother. Who else would I tell if Mum didn't believe me? People love a good scandal, Liam. It makes them feel better about their own less-than-perfect lives. But I've left that world behind. So don't come back here and judge me with your double standards. I don't deserve it."

"I'm sorry. I didn't mean to judge you, but I guess that's how it came out. I'm just struggling to get past my jealousy." A short pause followed. "I know life hasn't always been easy for you."

Vanessa took a deep breath. "Most of us have a sad story, but I'm an adult now, and I've worked hard to edit out the parts that don't belong. Steve is part of my history, but I don't have to invite guys like him into my future."

"I'm not only referring to Steve. Your mother had a lot to answer for."

"Maybe. And okay, she wasn't the kind of mother I wanted—needed—her to be, but I loved her anyway. I longed for her to stop being a drunk and be there for me like other mothers. She couldn't do that, but because of our bond, she stays in my heart."

"I get that, I really do."

"Do you?"

"Of course I do. The bond between parent and child is often complicated and complex, even without problems like alcoholism." Liam's words were sincere. Over the years, he'd seen glimpses of the type of parent Ruth once was, and as time passed, could have been. They both said nothing for a moment before Liam asked, "And me? Am I someone from your past not worthy of an invite into your future?"

"You are one of the few people who has ever touched me with tenderness. And I still want that. Every time I look at you, I remember when I felt safe, loved, desired. And the night before we had sex at the cottage—when we lay together in bed without touching, I wanted you more than I'd ever wanted anything in my life. Wanted to know if I ..." She hesitated, and her breath caught as she struggled to focus beyond the windscreen. "If I could feel something. Anything."

"You mean sexually?" Liam reached for her hand and held it. "What about the doctor? Weren't you together for two years? Aren't you back together?"

"He treated me like a china doll. A doll he pulled down from the shelf and played with once a week." She shook her head, and spoke the next words so quietly, Liam hardly caught them. "Once a week. One position. One nil. Every single time."

"Are you saying he never made you come, never took care of—"

"I know he loves me, wants me," she interrupted, "but there's no passion. No passion at all. I can't relax with him. Can't let go."

"But surely you've had satisfying sex with other men?"

She sighed. "And another thing. Julian and I aren't together. We haven't been together for months. I only went to Wellington to collect some of my things."

"So why did Davey call him your boyfriend when I came to see you that weekend?"

"Davey has his own agenda."

"You mean, you? Is that why you live in that rough neighborhood? Because of Davey? I thought you'd be more ambitious."

Liam winced at his own words. Every time he opened his mouth, his foot inched in a little further. He held his breath, waiting to see what she would hurl back.

"Maybe I'm not some swanky financial trader traveling the world, but that doesn't mean I'm not ambitious. I used to think the sun shone out of your ass. Those first two years after you left, I ached for your return. But you made your choice, and now what? You come crashing back into my life like a jealous asshole with a bad case of entitlement arrogance, and you expect me to lie down and take it because you sent me a card scribbled with a cryptic message every January eighth." She gasped for breath.

"Vanessa—"

"I want to go home. You seem to think I sleep with every random guy I come across, but even if I did, I don't have to defend myself to you."

Liam had known when they left Crosby Street earlier that there would be no compromise tonight. Vanessa hadn't had time to readjust her thoughts, or indeed, her pride. But she had a point. He had judged her, but he still needed to defend his actions. "That's not what I said."

"What the hell, Liam? The implication was loud and goddamn clear." Vanessa pressed her index fingers into the inner corners of her eyes as she struggled to control her emotions. "You know what? Maybe it's best if I tell you how many men I have slept with."

"I don't want to know."

"Liar. You do want to know, and there's no chance you'll ever believe me until you do. It's three. I've only slept with three. My first time was a drunken one-night stand with William when I was seventeen, and I cried in his arms afterward because I missed you. I'm sure you can work out numbers two and three. And you can believe Steve as much as you like, but it doesn't make it the truth. Thanks to him, people talked about me as if I were the town bike, but I never deserved that title. I gained it by malicious default."

He stretched his arm along the seat and moved closer, rubbing his fingers over her nape. "I'm so sorry."

"Don't be." She held up her hands in an exaggerated stop gesture. "Just don't." She unlocked the door and ran across the sand toward the water. Her boots and clothes trailed along the beach behind her as she yanked them off.

"Vanessa!" He ran after her. "Vanessa, what the hell?" His mind flashed back to the panic he'd felt the time she'd dived into the ocean to cleanse her soul and soothe her pain. But this time, he had caused her misery and hurt.

By the time he reached her, she was already thigh deep in the surf, naked apart from her panties. His leather boots filled with water as he lunged forward and grabbed her around the waist. They fell backward, both becoming submerged as an ebbing swell dragged them further out. He stood, lost his footing again, pulling her down with him. She fought him with all her strength—like a drowning victim who's realized peace waits on the other side of the next swell if they could just let go and surrender.

Liam came up spluttering, the salt water burning his nostrils and the weight of his boots and jeans sapping his strength as he dragged her to shore and dumped her on the dark sand.

"What the hell did you think you were doing?" he yelled between panted breaths. "Trying to drown yourself?" He collapsed next to her and lay on his back, his chest heaving.

"I wasn't trying to do anything," Vanessa yelled back. "And I don't need you saving me. I don't need you at all." She tried to scramble away, but he gripped her ankle, sliding her back along the sand until her naked breasts pressed into his chest and their lips were inches apart.

"Well, that's too bad. Because I need you, so you'd better get used to it. And I'm sorry you didn't get the cards, and that I never called, but I'm not going to apologize for how I feel."

He stood and tossed her over his shoulder. Every expletive known to man emerged from her mouth as he held on tight and carried her back to the truck. He dropped her at the passenger door before retrieving her clothes from the beach.

She stood shivering, her arms crossed over her naked breasts. "Give me my things."

He held them out. "Here."

She shrugged on the jacket without breaking eye contact, then opened the door and tossed the rest of her clothes and boots onto the back seat.

"You're not riding home dressed in nothing but a jacket and wet panties."

"Fine, I'll walk then," she said and stormed off toward the main road.

Liam watched her leave, then reached into the back seat for a pair of old jeans and a t-shirt. He peeled off his wet clothes and changed. His boots were ruined.

She'd walked all of thirty yards when he pulled up beside her. He reached over to open the passenger door. "Get in the goddamn truck. You'll cut your feet to pieces."

She climbed in and slammed the door. He looked at her and felt a sharp twinge of regret. This evening had played out differently in his mind, and now, she probably disliked him even more than she had before.

5 5

OUT OF THE BLUE

On the way back from the beach, Vanessa wrestled with her emotions as she tried her hardest to block out his words: *I need you … get used to it.*

Now, to add salt to the wound, Liam had brought her back to his upmarket apartment on the waterfront, which no doubt cost more a week than she earned in a whole month of night duty at the hospital. She opened the passenger door, grabbed her things from the floor and took off down the driveway, still dressed in her wet panties and jacket. Amber lights shone from above, cutting through the light fog that covered the hillside as it drifted off the ocean below. As she walked, the vapor of her breath dissipated into the night air. It reminded her of Whisper and the many frosty days they'd spent together, and a lump formed in her throat.

She heard Liam's footsteps before he spoke. "Where are you going?"

She kept walking.

"Vanessa, stop. You're not walking home." He reached out and grabbed her arm. She stood limply, not looking at him, her only thoughts those of self-preservation. "Please, I don't want you to leave like this. Come on."

He guided her back to the apartment, her jacket clutched across her chest, and her feet bare. He kept her close as he unlocked the front door and led her inside.

Through the window, Vanessa could see a cruise ship—lit up like a Christmas tree—floating in the bay. And reflected in the glass, Liam hovered like a ghost from her past as he bent down to remove his wet boots. She turned and stared. The muscles of his chest and shoulders bulged with strength, a strength she'd once thought could keep her safe, and she struggled to shake the memory of his touch.

He stepped forward. "Let's get you into a hot shower."

Vanessa resisted his attempt to help her out of her jacket, crossing her arms over her chest again. He handed her a thick robe as they moved into the bathroom. She hesitated, all the fight from earlier gone. "Leave and shut the door," she murmured.

"Okay. I'll shower in the other bathroom." His expression was tender and caring. "Drop your clothes in the hallway. I'll put them in the machine."

"I'm not staying."

"Look, I'm sorry. You're right. I've acted like a jealous bastard, and I had no right. But don't go home."

"It doesn't matter," she said, her voice flat and cold—devoid of any emotion. "I've been judged and misunderstood all my life. I wouldn't want you to break the pattern."

"Don't let your fear of being hurt ruin this. You believe in that whole soulmate connection thing. What if I'm yours and you're mine?"

She looked at him with sadness, went to speak, then stopped and shook her head. She didn't know what to say.

"I'll be next door if you need anything." Liam left, closing the door behind him. She looked at her reflection in the mirror and almost didn't recognize the sad face staring back.

While she showered, Vanessa told herself she didn't need him—or want him—and vowed to resist any attempt he made to change her mind. But what about fate and that soulmate connection? Were she and Liam destined to be together? After all, Julian couldn't hold a candle to Liam when it came to passion. There hadn't been many men she'd been attracted to, but she found herself wondering if sexual attraction was the point of difference between one decent man and another. Julian was dependable and caring and altogether kind, but she likened their physical relationship to flat seltzer water—still refreshing but without the sparkle. Her joining with Liam was more like releasing the cork on a bottle of champagne, then getting drunk on the nectar, until you thought of nothing but pleasure.

Liam glanced up when she walked into the room. She noticed that he'd shaved off the goatee and looked all the better for it. More like the old Liam. *Her* Liam. He reached out to her, but she sat in the chair, ignoring his offered lifeline.

"Stay here tonight."

Vanessa shook her head.

"Please? I promise—no bullshit. Just us."

"It's not good for us to spend time together."

"Why?"

"Because I want to forget."

"But what about the things you want to remember?"

She hated how he understood her, almost as if he sat in her mind on top of her thoughts. "It hurts."

"I know." Liam leaned forward and rested his head in his hands. He looked up. "You said it's over, but are you still in love with him—the doctor?"

She moved to the sink and poured a glass of water. She took a gulp, and then another. "Julian's not the sort of guy that makes your heart flutter. He's not the romantic type. But he's a good, reliable man. He doesn't expect me to change sheets or be barefoot and pregnant. In fact, he hates the thought of bringing children into a world fraught with problems."

"And is that what *you* want? To never have kids? Don't trade that chance for a guy who's boring as shit in bed."

She managed a small smile as she returned to the chair. "I never actually said Julian was boring in bed."

"The implication was there."

"Yes, I guess it was. I shouldn't have said what I did. It was disrespectful." Vanessa didn't know why she'd made that implication. She'd never discussed the intimate details of her and Julian's relationship with anyone before, not even Amber. "But I wouldn't be here if Julian and I were still lovers."

He offered a hand and a smile. "Come here."

"No, I have to go. I'll call a taxi. It'll save you getting dressed."

Liam moved forward and crouched in front of her. His robe fell open over his thighs, showcasing the shape of his tight quads and the black hair against olive skin. He reached for her hands. "Please stay."

She shook her head, then spoke softly. "I've had to learn how to protect myself over the past few years. It's what gets me through. I've also learned that anger and reaction get you nowhere. I grew up with a ton of negative emotions I've worked hard to contain, but when we get together, things get messy. It's like those uncomfortable family occasions, where people who are generally nice, bicker with their parents or siblings. I don't expect you to understand."

"But I do."

"So let me go. I don't want anger and resentment eating me up inside."

"I understand. We shouldn't have slept together so soon after your mother's death. You needed support from me, not sex. And I'm so sorry. I don't mean to mess with your head. But I want to make myself clear—I'm not giving up that easily. I want to pursue this ... *us*."

"Why, when you don't even live here?"

"Because, even after all this time, I can't stop thinking about you ... can't let you go. But if you want me to step back, I will. When you're ready, let me know." He stood and watched her for a moment, as if he couldn't bear for her to leave and was willing her to change her mind. "I'll just get dressed, then I'll take you home."

"Please, you don't have to."

"I want to. I'll get you some dry clothes."

"I'm fine like this."

Vanessa sat in the passenger seat, her damp, sandy jeans uncomfortably tight around her butt and the smooth satin lining of her jacket rubbing against her aroused braless breasts. Liam had dressed in jeans, a cream cable sweater, and navy pea coat for the drive to Crosby Street, and as usual, her body reacted to the sight. Small details about him fascinated her. His stylish watch and yet another pair of boots, the neatly mani-cured nails, and the way he rocked his cologne—as though it had been made just for him. Yet she couldn't escape the feeling that being with Liam meant her world would soon be thrown uncomfortably off course.

Neither of them spoke on the ten-minute drive, and by the time he pulled into the driveway, she was already second-guessing her decision to come home. If she had stayed, they could be curled up in bed by now, wrapped around each other—just like old times.

He turned to look at her, his hand reaching out to brush a wayward strand of hair from her face. Vanessa sat still, uncomfortable in her damp clothes, her senses heightened by his presence. She'd never considered herself overtly sexual, but when he was close, the primal pull toward him shocked her.

She stayed in her seat, wanting to say 'thanks for the ride' as she reached for the door handle, but she didn't. They sat in silence for a few moments, both lost in their thoughts.

"What was it like for you, that first day at the farm?" Liam asked finally. "It must have been quite a shock."

"That's a random question."

"One I've always wanted to ask."

She'd never discussed her past with anyone, not even William, and Vanessa took a while to find the words. "Frightening—and disappoint-ing, I guess. It had snowed the night before we left, and when I woke that morning, our farm stretched white before me. I ran across the garden to the front field so I could make snow angels. Dad was calling me so we wouldn't miss the bus. I remember my hands and feet were like ice, and they ached all the way from home to the valley. It seems like my feet have been cold ever since.

"I didn't know why we had to leave Dad. When I saw the home-

297

stead, I couldn't believe Mum would bring me to such a place. Of course I know now. She had an affair with the guy next door, and with no money, she had nowhere else to go."

"Shit, really. I never knew that. So when did you first start having that dream? The snow one."

"As soon as I moved into my own room. I woke with a start that night. I'd dreamed of snow and angels made of ice dancing before me. I was scared and cold, so I tiptoed down the hall to Mum. Her door was locked. She was in there with Jake. I could hear him talking."

"Jake seemed like a good guy when he first arrived. I knew he and your mother had a fling, but didn't realize it started so early."

"I watched him that very first night. He kept staring at Mum and I couldn't work out why. I was too young to understand what was going on." Vanessa smiled sadly as she recalled how her mother had looked that day—full of energy and enthusiasm. "Anyway, next came my apparitions. *Moko* lady, and the woman praying under the elm."

"The weird thing is, Mum prayed under that tree every fine day of her life."

Vanessa looked at him in disbelief. "You think it was her … your mother?"

"It couldn't have been, could it? My mother's dead. But she matched the description."

"Wow. That's crazy. She didn't have colors around her. The woman, I mean."

"Colors? You mean an aura?"

"I would sometimes see auras when I was younger. Mum told me I was making it up, so I never talked of it. But seeing people bathed in color is an interesting experience. That's how I knew you were a kind soul and not just—"

"An arrogant asshole."

She chuckled, and the sound and feeling helped her relax. "Yes."

They sat in silence as a noisy car traveled down the street. Vanessa reached for her bag from the floor. It was time to go.

"Ask me something," he said. "Something you've always wanted to ask?"

She thought for a moment, his question searching through her mind. "How did your mother's death affect you?"

Liam hesitated. He leaned back on the head rest and closed his eyes, then spoke. "Badly. I was a mess for a while. Angry. Physically, I lost a lot of weight. Emotionally, I lost her loving arms ... her guidance. Dad and I clashed a lot when I was younger. I rebelled and Mum played the role of diplomat. She was always there for me, no matter what.

"Once I came to terms with her death—as much as anyone can when they lose a parent—I realized how fleeting life can be. It's a cliché, I know, but I've thought about the fragility of our existence a lot lately, particularly after the stock market crash. Before it happened, I bounced along on the top of the high like everyone else, buying into deals made on sand and ice." He laughed. "Shit, listen to me. I sound like a born again evangelist."

"Or, like you're ready for a change."

"Yeah, I think I am. I'm happy to be home, away from all that pressure. But I have to go back in a few days. Just for a while."

"Do you think you could live in New Zealand again?"

"Sure." He leaned forward and kissed her tenderly, his hand resting lightly on her knee. "If I had the right incentive."

She took a shallow breath. The flick of his tongue against her lips made her heart race, but still, the barrier remained. "I can't be that incentive."

He kissed her again. "Why the hell not when you kiss me like that?" he said smiling.

She smiled back. "Because we live in different worlds. My life is simple and your life is complicated."

"Well, maybe it's time for me to simplify it."

POINTLESS THOUGHTS

Vanessa pulled the curtain aside and peeked out to the street. Liam hadn't moved, and through the truck's windscreen, she could see him leaning back against the headrest. She longed to go to him but feared she'd start a chain reaction neither of them could contain.

She went out to the deck for a while, still in the same jacket and damp jeans, and looked up to the sky, running her sight along the hill line to the north. The moon sat above it like a puffball someone had kicked off the autumn grass, and as she studied its muted light, she found herself second-guessing her decision again—wondering if she should run out to the street and jump in his truck. But the next time she looked, the moon had fallen behind the clouds, and she heard Liam drive away.

Earlier, she'd wanted to ask him about the missing card, the one from 1983, but that would have meant stirring the mud, and there had been enough mud stirred that evening.

"Hey." Davey sat next to her. The deck was long and wide, but he moved in close, his shoulder touching hers. "What are you doing out here in the dark?"

Leaning back on her elbows, she turned her face toward the sky again, more to break his physical contact than anything else. "Counting stars and shuffling thoughts."

"Thoughts of Liam? Are you guys together?"

Vanessa hesitated. *Kind of. It's complicated.* She didn't have the energy to explain the intricate details of her relationship with Liam, so instead she simply said, "No."

"That's good. He seems like an arrogant prick."

Davey was right. Liam could be a proud and arrogant man. But during the time she'd sat alone with her thoughts and the stars, she had only recalled his softer side; his fierce loyalty to family and friends, and the way he'd taken care of her in his own way in her early years at the O'Leary's.

Davey turned, and his hand reached out to brush a strand of hair away from her face, as Liam always did. But Liam's touch differed from Davey's. Liam's was affectionate and tender—Davey's seemed opportunistic. "Come to my bed."

A deep sigh was sufficient response, but she followed it with words. "We've been over this before."

"Is it the housemate thing? Because if it is, I can move out."

"It's not that. I'm fond of you as a friend but ..."

"Friends become lovers all the time."

"I guess they do, but ..."

"But not us?"

That night, Vanessa once again dreamed of fields covered with white snow. Whisper appeared, his rolling eyes fearful and wide, then collapsed, his blood seeping out onto the snow-covered ground. She woke, panting and sweating, a scream trapped in her throat, and when she realized where she was, began to sob loudly.

Davey barged into her room and gathered her in his arms, soothing her with gentle words of reassurance. He always spoke his mind with her, but she knew, unless invited, he would never cross that physical line.

When Vanessa woke again around five, Davey was asleep beside her, his breathing soft and rhythmic, his face pressed close to her neck. She slipped out from under the covers, shivering as she left the warmth of her friend. Once in the kitchen, she lit the small chip heater, prepared herself a bowl of cornflakes, then sat at the table staring at the cereal in front of her. She convinced herself that the dream meant nothing, but that conviction didn't bring with it a sense of comfort. The field of the white snow had always been an omen of grief or sadness—an alarm of sorts—so why would last night's dream be any different?

She waited until eight to call her father. Once she knew all was well in the Blinkly household, she called Mick. Liam answered the phone on the third ring. They exchanged hellos, but his tone was neutral and gave nothing away.

"Is your dad home?" she asked.

"He's in the shower. Do you want me to give him a message?"

"No, it's okay. Is everyone all right?"

"Yes. Why?"

"It's just … Never mind, I'll talk to Mick another time. I didn't realize you'd be there."

"Yeah, I came up first thing. Dad and I are meeting with the accountant soon. Why don't you drive up and join us for lunch?"

She hesitated. Her shift didn't start until three forty-five. If she left the farm at two, she'd have plenty of time to get back. Maybe not the energy though. "Thanks, but I have work later. I'm not off again for another four days. I'll come up and see Mick then."

"Okay. But have dinner with me when I get back?"

"I'll see."

In the three days since her dream, Vanessa had begun to relax. The world still turned. Her dad, Karen, and the boys were all well and accounted for, and the guys in the house still teased her mercilessly, with Davey their ringleader. When she'd rung Mick the day before, he seemed fine, and he'd told her that Liam had arrived safely in New

York.

That night as she lay in bed, she couldn't stop thinking about Whisper's accident. There was no doubt in her mind that Steve was responsible for it, no matter what his trumped up alibi might be. Every so often Vanessa would catch herself plotting revenge. Davey kept a baseball bat under his bed, and she'd imagine herself taking that bat to Steve's restored Mustang convertible—his pride and joy—that he'd been working on for years. She'd even considered confronting him in the pub. Make sure his friends knew what a horse murderer looked like. Then she'd remind herself of the golden rule—do unto others, etcetera. And as much as she wanted to take that eye for an eye, she had to trust that karma would one day catch up with Steve Brown.

However, on the fourth day after the dream, she arrived home from work to find Mick waiting for her on the doorstep. He stood as she walked up the path, and the shape of his smile told her something was up.

"Hi. What brings you to Crosby Street?"

"I have some news."

She unlocked the front door. Her gut flipped as she recalled the dream. "Mick, you're scaring me. Is Liam okay?"

"As far as I know, but I could do with a cup of sweet tea." He followed her down the hallway and into the kitchen.

"Is this about Whisper?"

"It sounds like you were right, lass. Stuart Young's daughter from next door was riding to the trig station with a friend to watch the sunrise the day it happened. She reckons she saw Steve Brown, or someone that looked a lot like him, take to Whisper, forcing him out onto the road."

"So why did it take her so long to say something?" Vanessa poured boiling water into a teapot.

"Because she was frightened. Steve tried to pick her up one day on her way home from school. She's only seventeen and was scared stiff of him after that. Her mother knew, but Stuart's always been a hothead, so they kept it to themselves. But Steve was in an accident last night. Left the pub around eleven, tanked up to the eyeballs, and decided to drive home in that old Mustang. It seems about a hundred yards from the intersection, he took a bend way too fast and slammed into a power pole."

Vanessa recalled her premonition of Steve's fiery end and was almost afraid to ask the next question. "Is he all right?"

"No, lass. The silly bastard got himself killed. His car burst into flames on impact, shot the power pole to smithereens, downed the lines and plunged the whole valley into darkness. The power only came back on a couple of hours ago."

"What? I can't believe it." Vanessa handed Mick a cup of tea before reaching for her own. She sat at the table, took a sip and let the warmth sooth her. "You know he told Liam and everyone else that I'd slept with him. The lying bastard."

"I know. He was a good worker, but when I heard the lies he'd spread about you, we had words, and I never employed him again. But it was Jake who started the rumor in the first place. Said he'd seen you sneaking into Liam's room all hours of the night."

She thought for a moment. "I never did like Jake."

"Me neither. Slimy bastard. Some say there's good in everyone, but some fellas are mean bastards from the day they set foot on this earth until the day they die. They don't progress and don't learn from their mistakes, or their father's before them. They live their whole lives stuck in ignorance and fear."

"You're right about that."

"One other thing." Mick hesitated as if trying to form his words. "Liam said you phoned the other day and you sounded worried. You had a sign, didn't you?"

"Yes, I had a dream, a few nights ago. I worried myself sick for the first couple of days, and the day I relaxed about it, this happens."

"Whisper's revenge."

"You think?"

"No doubt at all, lass."

PROMISES KEPT

"Come and check out this guy leaning on his pickup." Amber moved to the side of the window, out of view of the target. "He's gorgeous, with a capital G."

Vanessa laughed, tiny dimples appearing on both cheeks. "You think every guy is gorgeous. Poor Reece."

"Reece has nothing to worry about. But if I were single, this guy could put his mug on my coffee table any day, not to mention his boots under my bed. Come look."

"No, I'm busy." Vanessa wasn't interested in some guy leaning on the side of his truck. She'd promised herself an hour at the new gym on King Street and was in a hurry to change out of her uniform. But then, Vanessa had been making that promise to herself for the past three weeks.

"Still, he most likely farts in his sleep and scratches his balls while he watches TV."

Moving toward the window, Vanessa buttoned her jacket, then looked out onto the street below. "Shit. It's Liam. I didn't realize he was back."

"You mean *your* Liam?" Amber said with an innocent grin.

"He is not *my Liam*, and you knew exactly who he was." Vanessa reached into her bag for her lip gloss.

"So what's with the lippy?" Amber's face warmed with an understanding smile. "Come on. I'll come down with you. You can reintroduce me to your ghost from the past."

They walked across the hospital grounds and along the path toward Liam. Until a few moments ago, Vanessa had been looking forward to a long weekend. She'd worked seven days straight and had four days off before a stint on night duty. But now, her best-laid plans were clouded in uncertainty. Outside, the afternoon wind picked up the cool air and Vanessa shivered.

Liam stood relaxed, with ankles crossed, and arms folded. As she approached, he caught her gaze and took several confident steps toward her.

"Liam, what a surprise." Vanessa's voice took on a high pitch of its own accord, and she swallowed hard. "Are you visiting a patient?"

He frowned as if an explanation wasn't necessary. "No." He said nothing more, but bent down and kissed her on both cheeks, his hands reaching for hers. All around them, vehicles came and went, husbands carried bags for their wives, and small children strolled after their fathers, en route to visit a new baby brother or sister. Vanessa was aware of these things, but paid little attention to them as Liam's thumbs rubbed across her knuckles.

Amber cleared her throat.

"Oh, I'm sorry." Vanessa pulled her hands from Liam's, joining them tightly in front of her. "Do you remember Amber, from Immaculate Heart? We work together in the neonatal unit now."

Amber shook Liam's outstretched hand. "Nice to see you again, Liam."

"Likewise." Liam's gaze returned to Vanessa.

"Well, I'd better go," Amber said. "You two will have lots to catch up on, I'm sure."

Neither of them responded.

"I'll see you next week. Enjoy your long weekend." Amber repeated her retreat.

"Um, sorry. Yes, bye."

"Does that mean you've got time off?" Liam asked as they watched Amber walk away.

"I'm not on again until Wednesday." Vanessa caught his cologne on the light breeze and felt her insides warm a fraction more.

"What are your plans? Are you free for dinner?"

"I promised a friend I'd go look at a horse after work. And, I planned to be at the gym right now, but that can wait."

"Can I come? To look at the horse I mean."

"If you want, but you'll be bored stiff." She rummaged through her bag for her car keys. "Damn. I just remembered I don't have my car. Amber and I carpool when we're on the same shift. The parking around the hospital is terrible."

"Hop in. I'll give you a lift."

She slid into the passenger seat. "I guess you heard about Steve Brown?"

"I did. Can't say I'm sorry." He shot her a sideways glance. "You had one of your premonitions, didn't you? That's why you phoned Dad before I left."

"Yes, kind of."

Liam said nothing more as he pulled out into the late afternoon traffic and drove several blocks toward the center of town. She suspected he'd picked up on her discomfort and wondered if he was feeling uncomfortable too.

He drummed his fingers on the steering wheel as they waited for the lights to turn green. "Are you still living on Crosby Street?"

"Yes, but I spend most of my days off at Dad's. They live twenty minutes out of town now. Dad sold the farm a few years back, when he received an offer too good to refuse. They moved here and bought twenty acres so the boys didn't have to go to boarding school. Dad grows garlic and experiments with hydroponics, and his work with horses keeps him busy. He's as happy as a pig in muck."

"Good for him. Not many people can say they love what they do."

"I thought you said you were away for three months. What's it been, seven weeks?"

Liam glanced her way. The warmth of his smile wrapped around her like a much-loved sweater on a wet Sunday afternoon. "I had something important to come back for."

While Vanessa worked with the horse, Liam leaned on the rail of the enclosure, watching her intently. The way she and the trainers greeted each other—with hugs and smiles and handshakes—her deep concentration as she murmured, swung the rope, and moved gracefully around the ring; and her bond with the haughty mare, all fascinated him. He'd always thought her rapport with Whisper was a one-off, but seeing her now, he realized what a gift she had, and a well-respected one at that.

Cassie had once said that she hadn't fallen in love with Hamish on their first date, or after their first kiss, or even when they first made love. Instead, she'd fallen in love with him at his first photography exhibition, and again when he cooked her a beautiful meal in a tiny cabin in the woods, and yet again when he hugged his mother in front of his friends.

She fell in love with him when he was genuinely himself—when he fascinated her.

As Liam watched Vanessa, he understood what Cassie meant. He was in love with Vanessa because, in spite of her sometimes prickly personality, everything she did, and everything she stood for, fascinated him.

Back at Crosby Street, as they sat chatting in his truck, Liam asked her questions about her work at the stables, and Vanessa eagerly replied. When he repeated his dinner invitation, she accepted with grace, and when he suggested she bring a toothbrush just in case, she left the truck and returned a few minutes later with a small bag and a smile.

HONEST TRUTH

Back at the apartment overlooking Carter Bay, Liam cooked a simple meal of pasta with a green salad on the side. There were no flowers on the table, no fine wine or white linen napkins, but that didn't matter. All that mattered was being together. He was certain they had a future, but Vanessa's heels were dug deep in parts of her past, and he also knew if he pushed her too hard, that rebellious streak that served as protection would cause her to back away.

Liam wanted to ask if there would ever be a chance of a relationship, but that question stayed firmly in the back of his mind. She needed time to get used to the idea first. Try it on for size and become comfortable with the fit and the feel.

They sat on the sofa to eat dessert—a caramelized apple cake he'd bought at the bakery—and ate without conversation, a movie playing in the background purely as a distraction.

"Are you okay?" he asked finally.

Their eyes met as she fiddled with the bracelet on her left wrist. "Yes, why?"

"You seem lost in your thoughts."

She moved to the small kitchen and placed her plate in the sink with the rest of the dishes. Liam followed her. She turned and held his gaze. "What are we doing here, Liam?"

"Well, I thought we were reconnecting."

"But, I don't want to start something that has to end in a few days when you get back on that plane."

"I agree."

"So why am I here?" she repeated.

"You of all people should know that. You're a … what do you call yourself?"

"An intuitive."

"So don't you have insights into your own life?"

"It doesn't work that way. My own life is clouded in confusion. It always has been. That's why I like a routine—it helps me stay focused and sane."

"And being here with me is upsetting your routine?"

She shook her head. "I don't know."

"Why can't we just go with the flow for a while? Why do we always have to swim against the current?"

She didn't miss a beat. "Because the flow can lead you to a vast ocean where you could easily lose yourself."

"Sometimes we need to lose ourselves to find what we're looking for."

"And you think I'm looking for you?"

Liam moved closer, resting one hand on either side of her. "Hope, more than think."

He kissed her, the sweet taste of apple fresh on his tongue, and the smell of gardenia oil—her scent of choice—teasing his nostrils. He rested his forehead on hers and wrapped his arms around the small of her back. "You're such a beautiful kisser. When I kiss you, it feels like coming home."

"And is that where you want to be?" she whispered. "Home?"

"It's the *only* place I want to be."

She moved away from him and looked out the window to the bay. "I need some air."

He decided to change tack. They'd been back and forth enough for one day. "There's a hot tub on the roof. You keen to try it out?"

She turned to look at him. "I don't have a suit with me."

"No one will see us. It's the off season."

"I'm not getting into a public hot tub naked."

He grinned. "I'll grab the towels and a t-shirt."

They stayed in the hot tub until their fingers wrinkled and the moon sat directly above them in the sky. Liam kept the mood light, even with her firm breasts on full display under the wet t-shirt. With the heat of the water and a sky full of stars, he'd watched Vanessa relax. They chatted freely, and as they did, she smiled and laughed in a way he'd never seen her do before. He wanted to reach out, hold her in his arms and kiss her, but they stayed on opposite sides of the tub, together but apart.

Back downstairs, Liam felt strangely alone when he heard the click of the en suite door. He showered in the other bathroom, and by the time he'd finished, Vanessa was already in bed, dressed in another of his t-shirts. He wondered if she realized how turned on that made him feel. Her, half-dressed in his clothes, with one shoulder bare as the fabric slipped down her arm. He sat on the side of the bed and watched her. This time, Vanessa asked if *he* was okay.

"More than okay." He slipped into bed. "Do we have a chance here, Ness?"

"Honest truth?"

He repeated the words she'd said to him years before. "Is there any other kind, of truth I mean?"

She smiled at the recollection, as he knew she would. Vanessa had a memory like an elephant. "I struggle with that emptiness one feels when the person you love most in life isn't there to take your hand when you need them. I don't want to feel that with you." The words floated on a breath as she looked at him with those perfectly pale brown eyes.

"What, that I'm the person you love most in life?"

Her hand cupped his face. It was the first time she'd instigated intimacy since his return. "I don't want to miss you all over again. I've done that once in my life already."

"Separation is part of being together, but I don't want that either." Liam pulled her closer. "But you're going to have to miss me for just a little while longer."

"But if nothing happens—"

"Not an option." His voice was low and thick with emotion. "And do you know why?"

"Why?"

"Because *you* are the person I love most in the world. The one I want to come home to, who makes me want to be a better man. But there's no pressure, Ness. If you need time, I'll wait. For as long as it takes."

Liam felt her chest rise and fall, and she said nothing for several seconds. "I don't want to get hurt again," she whispered.

"I know. It may hurt a little when we're apart, but we'll work through it, and I promise it won't be for long."

She didn't say she loved him back, but that didn't matter. He would wait.

Woken predawn by a siren, Liam reached out to touch Vanessa as she lay beside him. He moved closer, snuggled into her back and inhaled. They were going to be okay; he felt it in his soul. He knew he had to work on his 'entitled, arrogant ass,' but was prepared to take up the challenge.

She pulled away from his hold. "What time is it?"

"Just after five."

"Don't they know we're sleeping here?"

He chuckled. "I didn't know you were grumpy in the mornings."

"Am not. And it's not morning, it's the middle of the night." She threw back the covers with a flourish and stormed out of bed to the bathroom. When she returned, he could smell mint on her breath.

She snuggled into his chest and lay her leg over his. He pushed his leg between hers in response. She said nothing for a time, but just when he thought she'd gone back to sleep, he felt her hand move across his abs as her fingers traced circles on his skin. His whole body tightened, as if he was on high alert.

"Do you like making 'good morning' love?" she whispered.

He laughed. "Only if it's with you."

"How do you know? We've never had morning sex."

"No, but I've imagined it often enough."

"And was it good?"

He lifted her, holding her around the waist. "Come here and straddle me, and I'll show you just how good it was."

Liam couldn't believe it when she did as instructed. The warmth of her thighs intensified as she sat on his abs and rested her hands on his shoulders. She leaned forward and kissed him lightly on the lips. "Good morning," she said smiling.

"Good morning, yourself. I've missed you."

"I've been here all night."

"I mean over the past years … months, weeks. I thought about you so many times, especially when I first arrived in Scotland. I wanted to call you, just to hear your voice."

Delicate hands twined around the back of his neck. He grabbed the hem of her t-shirt, tugged it over her head and pulled her close, so her breasts rubbed against his naked chest.

"And while you were thinking of me, I was thinking of you." Her hands moved down his torso and back up again. "But the timing was wrong. As you said, I was too young, too emotionally immature."

He felt the bob of his Adam's apple against his throat when he swallowed. His breath quickened as she kissed the side of his neck. "And is the timing still wrong?" he asked.

"Not this time." She moved in a gentle rhythm. With her back held straight, her hips rose and fell softly on his. And with each downward movement, her butt brushed against his erection through the stiff cotton sheet. She paused for a moment, rotating her hips over his torso in lap dance fashion, and grinned.

"Lift up," he said.

She lifted onto her knees as he tugged the sheet free. When she lowered herself again, the touch of skin on skin was almost too much for him to bear as she rocked back and forth.

"What happened to your panties?"

"I must have dropped them on the bathroom floor."

"Shit!" He gritted his teeth and threw back his head. "I'm not doing too good here."

"You feel fine to me." She closed her eyes and arched backward. "So incredibly fine."

Liam's hands cupped her breasts. A "fuck" escaped his clenched teeth as her nipples hardened under his touch, and the scent of her drifted between them. "Tell me something?"

"Yes." She smiled and waited. "What was the question?"

"Um … When we had sex … at the cottage, did you enjoy it?"

She leaned back again, displaying her perfect breasts—peaked and ready. "Yes, very much. Did you?"

He reached for a condom from a box on the nightstand and handed it to her. "More than I ever thought possible."

"I'd wondered if it would be … a little uncomfortable." She looked down as she rolled on the condom, her cheeky smile matching his. "And …"

"Awkward?" He inhaled sharply and closed his eyes for no more than a moment.

"Yes. Awkward."

"And do you like that?" he asked. "A little discomfort?"

"I never thought I would, but …"

He pushed forward, his hands firmly on her hips as he gently controlled her rhythm. She gasped a whispered, "Liam," and buried her head in his neck.

"Vanessa," he whispered back. "Look at me."

When she did, he smiled, shining his love at her as he had done all those years before. She moved slowly, a sensual dance, hips rotating slightly. Each time he thrust up into her downward movement and filled her to the hilt, that touch of discomfort, followed by intense pleasure, reflected in her expression.

"Oh God, it feels so good. I've never been on top before, never been in control."

"What? Never?"

She pressed her forefinger to his lips. "Shh. No more questions."

"I don't think you'll be in control for much longer."

"No?"

"Hell, no."

He had planned to keep the pace slow. To watch the sweat build on her brow, the pucker of her nipples as he sucked and kissed her breasts, and to listen carefully to the measure of her words as they washed over his skin. He wanted to take her as gently as the light of dawn. But now, as she held his gaze and lost herself in the moment, he couldn't hold back.

"I can't hold on, Liam," she panted as her skin slapped against his and tiny droplets of sweat dripped down her cleavage. "Come with me."

"Always."

As Vanessa slept, Liam crept from the bed to make coffee, then sat at the table, staring out over the bay in silent contemplation, the morning newspaper spread out before him. For the first time in weeks, he allowed himself to view their burgeoning relationship in a more positive light. He turned as she entered the room, the sight of her in nothing but his t-shirt and a pair of too-big socks hijacking his resolve to let their re-kindled relationship develop slowly. *No pressure.*

"Good morning," he said with a smile. "My socks suit you."

She looked down at her feet. "Thanks, they're so warm." She stretched her arms over her head and rolled her shoulders back. He couldn't take his eyes off her or keep the grin from his lips. "What time is it?" she asked.

"Just after eight."

"I slept so well." She looked over his shoulder at the headlines. "It must have been the hot tub soak we had before bed."

Liam reached out and held her around her waist. She hadn't showered and he could smell the scent of their love on her skin. "Really? So me cuddling you most of the night, then a happy 'good morning' doesn't get a mention in the credits?"

"I'm reserving my judgment."

"What made you change your mind?"

She stepped away. "What do you mean?"

"About us. It's like you suddenly flicked a switch. One minute I'm an arrogant bastard or whatever it was you called me—"

"Jealous asshole with a bad case of entitlement arrogance," she said with a wry grin.

"Yeah that's it, and then the next minute you're all sexy and smiling and just too goddam gorgeous."

"I remembered something Mick said."

"Really? My dad?"

"He once said we have to make our own chances in life. I thought about it last night while we were in the hot tub. When I looked at you, naked and handsome and just too goddamn gorgeous as well, I realized your dad was right. Sometimes we have to reach out and take what we want."

Liam laughed. "So you're just after me for my body?"

Vanessa didn't answer at first, as she filled a mug with coffee and inhaled the aroma. She turned and leaned on the counter, and took a small sip. "Well, do you blame me? Your body *is* pretty damn amazing."

"As is yours. Perfectly perfect." He grinned as she lifted the hem of the t-shirt, showing a creamy length of thigh. "You know you're a brat, right?"

"So you've always said."

He moved to the kitchen and refilled his mug. "I have a proposition for you."

"Why am I not surprised?"

"Not *that* kind of proposition." His eyes danced with amusement as he studied her through the steam wafting from his cup. "Aww, you disappointed, Ness? You want me again already?"

She smiled in response to his question. "What's your proposition then?"

"I want you to look at a house with me later. I'm meeting the agent there at one."

"And what if I have other plans?"

He laughed at the look on her face. "Cancel them."

The bristle stiffened, and she straightened her back. "Excuse me?"

"Surely I'm more important?"

Her unexpected smile took him by surprise. She hated being teased when she was younger, but then, so many things about her had changed.

"Always the optimist."

He reached into the fridge for eggs and milk, and a carton of orange juice, which he poured into two glasses.

"How do you take your pancakes?"

"I thought you knew everything about me?"

"Give me a break. I'm not a mind reader."

"Lemon juice and sugar, thank you."

59

IN VIEW OF CARTER BAY

Liam watched as Vanessa studied the large Californian bungalow with a critical eye. The bones of the house seemed solid, but he'd shuddered at the decor the first time the agent showed him through. He hoped Vanessa would see through the cosmetic limitations and let her imagination fly free.

The living room stood lifeless and devoid of furniture, apart from an old sofa and a rectangular copper coffee table inlaid with a globe of the world. On the walls, orange and brown patterned wallpaper screamed the seventies, as did the navy-blue carpet tiles covering the floor.

"It's … interesting."

"Interesting is one way to describe it," Liam said with a grin. "But it has good bones, don't you think?"

"It seems solid. And the view is amazing. Nice neighborhood, too." She turned to look at him. "Have you put in an offer?"

"Not yet. I was wondering if you want in on the deal."

"What, we buy it together?"

"It makes sense. You told Dad you were saving for a place. It needs work, but most of it's cosmetic."

Turning toward the bay window, Liam looked out across the street to the curve of Carter Bay, sparkling navy blue in all its glory. He opened the latch, longing to hear the rush of the ocean, but the busy sounds of a city morning—cars, sirens, chatty students hurrying by—overshadowed those of nature.

"But who would live in it?" she asked.

"Us."

"What about your job in New York?"

"My contract finishes in six weeks. I've decided to take a twelve-month sabbatical. Dad needs a hand with the farm. The bank's breathing down his neck. Unfortunately, he invested most of Mum's insurance money in shares. I advised him to sell up eight months before the crash, not because of any insider knowledge, but so he could reduce his debt level. But he didn't. And the rest is history. Now he's bleeding in debt."

"I had no idea."

"We're in discussions with a guy who wants to build a luxury lodge on that block below the east hay barn. If I can persuade Dad to accept the offer, we'll sell off that block and the one next to it. We have the consent—all we need is Dad's scribble on the dotted line."

"Sounds like a win win for everyone."

"Yes. It will certainly help. So, getting back to this house. What do you think?"

"How much?"

He handed her the realtor's flyer. He wasn't sure if she'd have the money but wanted to give her the opportunity to consider the deal. "The deposit is twenty percent of asking. So half each, or whatever you can afford. One of my friends is a builder. He'll handle the project management."

"What about the interior decorating?"

He walked forward and wrapped his arms around her waist, his lips close to her ear. "Tone-on-tone texture, off-white walls, colorful art, comfortable bed. What do you think?"

"And who chooses the art?"

"We both do. In fact, I'm happy for you to decide on the interior, but I'll help by nodding my head in approval," he said as he walked to the window and pulled the latch shut against the cold air. "What about the energy? Does it flow?"

She looked around, then walked to the hallway. Liam followed two steps behind, watching her inspect each room.

"It feels fine. Do you know the history?"

"The same couple lived here all their lives but recently moved into a retirement complex. So, are you keen?"

"I don't know. Buying a house together is a big step. What if we don't get on?"

"What if we do? And if you're worried about the money, we can sort something out."

"I can pay my half outright. My company has funds to invest. Also, Dad had a savings scheme for me that matured last year. He didn't trust Mum with the money when I was younger, so I have that invested."

"You have your own company?"

"Don't you?"

Her comment amused him. It seemed William was right—Liam needed to get his head out of his stereotypical ass. Vanessa had a company, a career, and a passion; one that not only opened her heart, but obviously afforded financial security as well. Just because she hadn't traveled or studied abroad, didn't mean she wasn't a successful, well-rounded person. Liam nodded and smiled. "I do. Sorry, I—"

"Was jumping to conclusions."

6 0

TINY GIFTS

"Nurse Blinkly?" Vanessa looked up from the desk into the stern face of the ward matron. She reminded her of Sister Mary Monica from school days, and Vanessa had always been wary of her.

"Yes, Matron."

"A young man is waiting for you in reception. I don't approve of my staff having visitors while on duty. Make it quick."

As she hurried along the corridor, Vanessa wondered who it could be and smiled at Matron's sternness. It couldn't be Liam. He'd left just over five weeks ago and had said he'd be at least two months. As those weeks passed, she found herself counting down the days. While her life was generally busy, the evenings after day shift were the hardest. They'd had many long phone conversations between New York and Clifton Falls since he'd left, which only made her miss him more.

So when she arrived at reception, Vanessa was shocked to see Liam looking out the window to the park across the road. He turned, a slow smile lifting the corners of his mouth as he looked her up and down. She wanted to run to him. To jump into his arms and wrap her legs around his waist as they kissed, then let him carry her out the door. Instead, she hesitated, her lips trembling when she finally stepped forward.

He reached for her hands. "Hey."

She pulled them free as one of the doctors walked past. "You're back early."

"I am. Is that okay?"

She was so excited she couldn't speak, so nodded instead. They say that clothes don't make the man, but wow. Just—wow. Tight-fitting blue jeans, black boots with a Cuban heel, and a white t-shirt were all pulled together with a charcoal jacket. Added to that, a clipped beard and his face lightly kissed by the sun, and all she could do was clench her legs together.

He leaned in for a hug. "Damn," he whispered. "Look at you. What is it about a nurse's uniform on the woman you love?"

Vanessa cast Liam a warning glance. It was hardly the time or place for sexual fantasies. "I thought you were away for another two weeks at least."

"The job wrapped up sooner than expected. I thought I'd surprise you."

"Have you been to see the house?"

"No, I wanted you to show me."

She checked her watch. "I still have an hour to go on my shift."

"Okay. I need a haircut. I'll meet you at home in an hour. Oh, and, Nurse Blinkly?" Liam grinned. "Are you feeling all right? You look a little flushed."

She fanned her face with her hands. "It's warm in here, don't you think?"

He nodded slowly. "Very. It's good to see you again."

She smiled. "You too."

On the drive to their new home, the anticipation that they may be soon making love sent butterflies into her stomach. When she pulled into their driveway ten minutes later, Liam still hadn't arrived. Vanessa wound down her window and stayed in her car to wait. She shut her eyes, trying to capture the sight of him in her mind as he stood in reception, and wondered why she felt so nervous—almost shy. *Absence makes the heart grow shyer.*

He pulled up behind her and jumped from his truck with a huge bunch of white roses and green snapdragons in one hand, and a bottle of champagne in the other. He came to the driver's door, and opened it for her. "Are you coming, or are you just going to take your sweet time and make me wait?"

"I'm coming."

They stopped on the threshold as she waited for him to unlock the door with her key. He still hadn't kissed her. "These are for you." He handed her the flowers, then turned to open the door and stepped inside.

Vanessa inhaled the scent of the roses. "Thank you. They're beautiful."

"Oh, and I almost forgot. I meant to ask you something earlier."

"What's that?"

He leaned forward, so close his breath tickled her neck. "Well, it's just, this." His hands gently cupped the back of her head. He increased the pressure of the hold and brushed his lips lightly over hers. His kiss was gentle—almost chaste—his tongue barely caressing the tip of hers as she held the flowers upside down at her side.

Finally. She looked at him and answered his grin with a hint of a smile, but inside she felt as though the world had stopped turning, just for a moment. "You wanted to ask me something?"

"I just did. It's called non-verbal communication."

"Do you need to ask me anything else?"

He laughed. "I would love to." He kissed her again, firmer this time, as he gently cupped her face and pulled her closer.

"Gosh, that's a lot of questions."

"But damn, you certainly give the right answers." He stood and adjusted his jeans as she looked on in amusement, then threw his keys onto the entry table, the one she'd decorated with a brushed nickel lamp and a recycled wooden bowl. She picked up the keys and placed them neatly in the bowl. He looked back at her and smiled, then entered the open plan living area, setting the champagne on the kitchen counter.

He circled the room, taking everything in, before heading for the bedrooms. They kissed in every room, each kiss more passionate than the one before.

"You've done an amazing job," he said.

"Thank you. I'm glad you like it."

"I do, I like it a lot."

Back in the living room, they stood no more than a foot apart. He reached for her hands, his handsome face smiling down at her. "I'm so pleased to be home, Ness," he whispered. "These past weeks have been some of the loneliest in my life."

They came together and held each other for a long time. She could feel the energy between them—the warmth of his touch—and hear the beat of his heart. But rather than relax, emotion welled in her throat, quickly followed by warm tears. "I'm pleased you're home, too."

"Hey, don't cry. This is supposed to be a happy occasion."

"I'm sorry. I can't help it. The cleaners just finished two days ago. I've moved all my things in, but I still couldn't bear to sleep in our new bed without you."

"I'm glad you waited." He squeezed her a little tighter then pulled away. "I need to get something out of the truck. I'll be right back."

Vanessa left the room to freshen up, and when she returned, a deep round fishbowl filled with small gifts sat on the coffee table—each one wrapped in varying shades of blue paper, from baby blue to dark navy, and all tied with white ribbon. They sat in front of it, both on the sofa.

"Who are the gifts for?"

"My girlfriend."

She grinned. "Cute. And it's not even her birthday."

"No, but I didn't have a chance to deliver them at the time." He reached into the bowl and rummaged around, picking one and giving it a shake. He cocked an eyebrow. "If she plays her cards right, I might let her open 1978 later."

"What do you mean, 1978?"

His hands encircled her waist. "Each year, on January the eighth, I bought you a little gift. No matter where I was, or who I was with, I never forgot." He kissed her neck, then moved his lips across to the base of her throat.

"Really? Every year?" She lifted her chin to allow him better access, her hand moving to his thigh. She squeezed it tightly.

He pulled back and chuckled. "Nurse Blinkly, so enthusiastic. Just for that, if you're good, I'll give you 1979 as well. Come on." He stood and pulled her down the hall, the champagne and flowers forgotten on the kitchen counter. "I need you to help me with something."

"What kind of something?"

"Washing my hair. The barber got a bit carried away with that molding crap."

His intentions floated from his smile, and her eyes widened. "But I like it."

"Yeah, but I'm feeling a little dirty."

She had only ever made love in the bright daylight once before, that afternoon at the cottage, and felt self-conscious under Liam's gaze. Once undressed, he guided her into the shower cubicle. He pressed against her, already half erect, and firmly took hold of her upper arms. She turned and stood with her back to him, bracing against the wall as he rubbed a soapy sponge over her back and buttocks.

"I've been thinking," he said.

Vanessa struggled to grasp how he could think at all at that moment.

"When's your contract with the hospital up?"

"Early next year."

He reached around and cupped her breasts, squeezing them gently, then lightly flicking his thumbs over the hardened pearls of her nipples. "Are you keen for an adventure?"

She inhaled sharply and leaned back against him as she watched his hand move down over her hip before slipping between her legs, then slowly sliding back up her body. He repeated the tease several times, his need pressing against the cleft of her buttocks. "What kind of adventure?"

Scorching lips and an eager tongue sucked the skin of her nape, and he squeezed her breasts again, the pressure more intense this time. "Come with me to England next year."

"You really want me to come?"

Soapy fingers slithered over her skin until he found his target. He chuckled into her neck. "Definitely. From now on, we do things together."

Vanessa glanced at the ribbons of light casting shadows across the ceiling and briefly wondered if the blind, three-quarters closed to the world, was giving them enough privacy. The thought vanished in a flash, and she closed her eyes, pushing back against him in a steady rhythm. "For how long?" The words were a whisper as she stretched her arms up and returned her forehead to the shower wall. She never missed a beat, belly and butt clenching in unison.

"Just two years. I have a contract I'm considering." He groaned then turned her to face him, kissing her deeply as his fingers curled inside her. "Fuck! So beautiful."

"Okay … um … England? Oh … Holy shit. Liam."

"Is that a yes?"

"Yes! Yes!"

Later that evening, as they ate pizza out of the cardboard box and sipped champagne, Liam sat the fishbowl on the table and handed her the first gift.

"Do you remember the card from the year you turned sixteen?" he asked.

"Of course I do, it was the paper plane." Vanessa looked up as she recalled his words. "'I left you on a paper plane, creased and crumpled. There's no way back. The wind isn't blowing south.'"

Liam shook his head as he smiled. "And you wonder why I'm in love with you. Open it."

He watched her undo the ribbon, her eyes wide and her whole face bright with a smile. He'd often wondered if he would ever regain Vanessa's love and trust after the way he'd treated her—when his jealousy over Steve Brown's lies had him acting like an asshole. Yet here they were, together in their home; a home he'd wanted her to decorate so she could make it her space, one he would gladly share. He felt as though he had finally reached that moment—the one when all doubts and fears subside, allowing you to relax in the knowledge that the person you love more than anything, or anyone, loves you in return.

"A paper airplane. It's gorgeous! Thank you."

"I found it in a jewelry store in Edinburgh just after I arrived."

"Wait. The cards, the gifts. Each card represents a different charm —for my bracelet."

"Ah, there's that intuition of yours again. Now I suppose I'll have to let you open them all."

"Can I? Really?"

"I'll make you a deal. If you can tell me what I wrote on each card, I'll let you open the corresponding gift."

Vanessa went through each year, reciting the inscriptions word for word. As she opened each tiny box, Liam fixed the charm to her bracelet, then watched as she opened the next. By the time she reached the lighthouse, happy tears had streaked mascara down her face, and he sensed, without a shadow of a doubt, they would be okay.

She lifted her wrist and ran her fingertips over each charm. "This is the most wonderful gift I've ever had in my life, except for my horse-shoe necklace, and the Michael Murphy LP. Thank you." She reached over and kissed him. "I love you, Liam O'Leary. To the sky and back."

"I love you too, Ness. The pleasure was all mine."

61

ONE WISH

1988

Vanessa didn't know what to expect when Liam suggested an evening picnic several weeks later. He said to pack the essentials for an overnight trip, but wouldn't elaborate further.

It was late afternoon when they followed the coast road—or the scenic route as the locals called it—to the Rata River Valley. She expected to drive all the way to the farm, but Liam changed course about ten minutes from the general store. He pulled over beside a plantation of white pines and cut the engine. Fifteen feet below was a small inlet, bordered by a rocky outcrop that protected the cove from the elements and slowed the rush of the tide.

As soon as Liam stopped the truck, Vanessa opened the door and jumped out. She inhaled deeply. "Pine oil, sea, and sand. My favorite scents in the whole wide world."

Liam opened the back seat and pulled out a picnic basket, rug, and two folding chairs. "What do you think?"

"It's gorgeous. I love its energy."

"I know what you mean. Kind of feels like home, doesn't it?"

She smiled. To her, Liam felt like home every time they were together—every look, every kiss, every touch. Theirs had become a relationship where silence meant as much as words, and for what felt like the first time in her life, she could relax, safe in the security and warmth of their love.

"We can't make a fire, but I have plenty of food."

"Yum. Any dessert?"

"Depends if you're a good girl."

She cocked a brow. "I can be a *very* good girl if I put my mind to it."

"Don't I know it." He shook the rug and let it float to the ground, then grabbed the cooler from the truck. "Shall we eat first?"

She sat and made herself comfortable. "Before what?"

"Before you shower me with love and attention."

"Well, as it was only this morning when I last showered you with love and attention, I vote we eat. Although if we're going swimming, maybe we should do that first."

Liam removed his sunglasses. His gaze never left hers while he unbuttoned his shirt. Her eyebrows knitted together as she watched him. "You're up to something."

"Yes, I'm up for a skinny-dip with my girlfriend."

"We can't swim naked. What if we get caught?"

"Who's going to catch us? The bogeyman?" He scrambled across the rug, pressing her backward and tugging at her t-shirt as he brushed a soft kiss over the base of her throat. "You need to get naked, Nurse Blinkly. No one will catch us, I promise. Anyway, I brought something for you." He pulled her old sarong out of his backpack. "Here."

"You can't be serious. Where on earth did you find that?"

"I've had it for ages."

"But I looked everywhere for that sarong."

"Really." He flashed her a flirty smile. "You left it in my truck when we went to the beach that night. So, let me relieve you of your clothes, then wrap you in this excuse for a piece of cotton, and you can wade into the ocean, with your arms outstretched, so the fabric clings to your every curve."

"Hold on. Is this some fantasy reenactment of that night at the beach?"

"Maybe. I was so deeply infatuated with you by that night, my palms would sweat whenever I saw you, and guilt would squirm in my gut when we were alone together."

"So it wasn't all in my head?"

"Definitely not those last few days, but I thought I was protecting you by telling you it was."

"But you still kissed me."

"It was as if I didn't have a choice. I felt bad about it for ages afterward. I'm so sorry."

"Our first kiss was a good kiss."

"It was a *great* kiss. At the time, it was the best kiss I'd ever had, and they just keep getting better."

"For me too." Vanessa sat cross-legged on the rug. He watched as she removed her bra and covered herself with the sarong—flimsy from time, salt water, and sand. She stood and removed her jeans as he lay propped up on one elbow and watched her. "Are you coming?"

Liam threw back his head and laughed. "Drop the sarong, kiss me, and we'll see what happens."

"Stop it. I meant coming for a swim."

He jumped up, tugging off his jeans and boxers. "Come on. I'll race you."

Vanessa reached the water first. She'd always been able to outrace Liam, even as a child. The surf rolled onto the shore with a steady hush rather than the usual rumble. She stood in the water, arms outstretched as the fabric of the sarong billowed above her like a kite about to take flight. He came up behind her and kissed the contour of her neck as his arms encircled her waist.

"You are so incredibly beautiful."

She turned in his arms and kissed him. "Take me under."

"Pinch your nose." He lifted her up. "Ready?"

"Always."

By the time they strolled back up the beach, the sun sat low above the hill line to the west, and the wind had eased. The muggy air had intensified in response, but it wasn't unpleasant. They devoured the food, feeding each other grapes, olives, and bread and cheese as they talked.

"You've changed a lot over the last few months."

"Have I?" Vanessa said. "In what way?"

"You've relaxed." He smiled. "And I've never seen you laugh so much. I love that. You hardly ever laughed when we were younger."

"Laughter is one of life's great joys."

"As is sex."

She motioned to the towel wrapped around his waist and chuckled. "You seem to be feeling a little joyful right now."

"What do you expect? When I see you in the water, naked except for that sarong, I lose my self-control."

"I love seeing you naked, too."

"What?" He whipped the towel from around his waist. "Why didn't you say so sooner?"

"Because, there's a time and place."

He lay on his back, his hands clasped behind his head, and looked skyward. "Did you ever wonder what happened to the card from 1983?"

"I assumed there wasn't one."

"Well, perhaps you assumed wrong." Reaching for his backpack, Liam pulled out a white envelope and the smallest blue package of all. He turned the gift over in his hands, then smiled, cocking a brow.

"Are you serious?" she asked.

"There's quite a story to this one."

"I'm not surprised." Vanessa sat cross-legged and wriggled her bottom into the rug to get comfortable. "Tell me this story."

"Well, I'd gone to London with a few mates the Friday before your birthday. We went to a pub that night with some Australian girls, and as soon as the clock struck midnight, they lined up shots in celebration of the girl I'd left behind. I've never been so drunk in my life. I ended up in the middle of a fight I had nothing to do with and almost got myself arrested." Liam laughed at the recollection.

"Later that same day, I bought a card from a newsagent, then walked all over the place looking for a jewelry store, but everything was closed. I finally found an open-air market where a guy was selling trinkets off a large sheet of red velvet. As luck would have it, he was a silversmith by trade and had some really good stuff. Anyway, being Saturday, the Post Office was shut, so I couldn't post the card. I meant to post it on the Monday, but by then I'd had a hundred second thoughts, not about what I'd written, but about your reaction. I still feel kind of nervous about it, even now."

"How come?"

"You'll see." Liam handed her the card and gift, hesitating as she reached for it. The night had closed in, so he sat the lantern on top of the cooler.

She smoothed her fingertips over the upper right corner. "Loving the hand-drawn postmark."

"Couldn't break with tradition."

"It looks like it's been for a swim."

"You could say that. Just as well I used waterproof ink and a thick envelope."

"You're making me nervous." She chewed at the inside of her cheek. "Shall I open it?"

"Open the gift first."

As Vanessa gently removed the ribbon securing the tiny package, she didn't know what to expect. She opened the tissue paper, feeling excited as she touched the charm. "A wishbone." She leaned forward and kissed him. "I love it—it's adorable. Did you make a wish when you bought it?"

"I did, but remember, I was hungover and missing you like crazy, so my wish was rather bold. Impulsive even. And maybe, a little ambitious."

She frowned. "And you carried this card with you all those years? Are you sure you want me to open it?"

He nodded. "It's time."

Vanessa turned the envelope over and ran her fingers under the back flap, tearing the now-fragile paper. On the front of the card was a wishbone, drawn with Liam's usual precision and attention to minute detail—a replica of the wishbone in the tiny box sitting on the picnic rug. She opened the card, the words obscured by the shade of the lantern until she flattened it with the fingers of both hands. Her top teeth found her bottom lip before she pressed both lips together. Her gaze focused on the four word inscription. She inhaled deeply, then swallowed, her expression one of disbelief.

With shaking fingers, she traced the words. She went to speak, then stopped to gather a frown. "You wrote this? The year I turned twenty-one?"

"I did."

She kept shaking her head, not with determination, but rather with some suspicion and doubt.

"Shall I read it?" He didn't need the card to say the words. "One wish—marry me?"

Vanessa paused and took a deep breath. "Are you asking …?" She fell silent and looked at him in astonishment.

"The card says it all."

"And you wrote this in 1983?"

He nodded slowly. "We've established that fact already."

"You wanted to marry me then?"

He reached over, took her face in his hands and forced her to make eye contact, then kissed her tenderly. "And every year since. Shit," he said. "I'm so nervous, I forgot the most important part." He knelt on one knee, taking both of her hands in his, the smile on his face shadowed by the lantern light. "Vanessa Marie Blinkly, will you marry me?"

Vanessa sat for a moment and studied him. He didn't often show his emotions, even to her. Liam was a strong, in-charge type of guy, who took care of everything and never seemed to question why he should. But now, her sophisticated in-control man was all flustered as he proposed to her. "Is the wishbone in place of a ring?"

He rubbed his index finger over his sensual lips before answering, his expression one of amusement. "No. Of course not, but I wanted you to help me choose it."

"Well, I'm not sure if I can say yes until you have the ring."

"And here I was, thinking you'd changed. You're still a brat and always have been. Come here and do as you're told." He reached out, rolled her onto her back, and straddled her. "Say you'll marry me."

"Stop it," she said, laughing. "I'll pee myself."

"Say it." They wrestled together until he had her pinned to the blanket, kissing her until she was breathless. "So, Vanessa Marie Blinkly, did you mean it when you said you loved me?"

"Yes."

"And your answer to my question—is it a yes, or a yes?"

"It's a yes."

"I knew you wouldn't say no." They kissed, and as he pulled back, she heard him sigh with relief. "And in the meantime, I have something other than a ring to mark the occasion." He jumped up, jogged over to the pines and pulled a tiny sapling from the soil. He rested it on the palm of his hand and offered it to her.

"A baby Christmas tree? But what if it dies before we get it home?"

"It is home."

"What do you mean?"

"This land, it's ours. I bought it two years ago. It's just under six hundred acres. When we come back from the UK, we could build an indoor equestrian center. Then you can talk to as many horses as you want."

"Are you serious?"

"I'm always serious about business." He sat behind her, then pulled her back against his chest and held her around her waist. "And I want to build our dream home."

"Where?"

"Over there." He pointed north. "With a view of the Pacific and the forest."

"What about our house in town?"

"We'll keep it for a base. What do you think?"

"I'm so excited."

"Me too." He kissed the back of her neck as his hands cupped her breasts. "I think it's time to go to bed."

"What here?"

He chuckled and jumped to his feet, unhooked the bungee cord and pulled the canvas cover off the tray of his pickup. A mattress, pillows, and double sleeping bag lay there. "I want to sleep on our land, make 'goodnight' love under the stars, and breathe in the salt air all night long while I show you how much I love you. And, if the occasion arises, you can scream my name as loud as you like. Right, I'll turn down the bed while you use the bathroom."

"Bathroom?"

He reached into the back seat, pulled out a backpack and tossed it to her. "Here." He laughed at her expression. "Everything you need is on the other side of that tree. Take the lantern though."

They snuggled in their makeshift bed as the pines stilled and the ocean rolled on, regardless. Between kisses, they watched the first quarter moon, muted in the night sky, slowly make its way west with the rotation of the earth. "You happy?"

"Very," she replied. "This has been the best night of my life."

"Mine too. And I want us to agree on something. We may have two houses in the future, but I never want to spend another night apart. The commute is less than forty-five minutes, and if you need to stay in town for work, I'll drive into town."

"And if you need to stay in the valley, I'll drive to the valley."

"See, we have it sorted already. Who said you weren't a team player?"

"I've always been a team player when it's just you and me on the team."

He showed his amusement. "Is that right?"

"Did you ever think we'd end up together?"

"I hoped we would. I got a bit lost there for a while, hence the turtle card message. But when your mother died, I decided I couldn't just let life carry me along anymore. I knew I had to come back and at least try."

"But what if I'd been in a stable relationship?"

He turned to look at her, flashing a cheeky grin. "Stability is a crock of shit. Nothing in life is stable. It's taken me a long time to figure that out. Sure, our lives may run smoothly for months, or even years, but something will always come along to upset the apple cart. We have to learn how to maneuver our way through those times and hold on to what matters."

"Are you saying that if I'd still been in a relationship, you would have upset my apple cart?"

He chuckled. "You'll never know."

"It seems slow and steady did win the race after all." She grinned at his cheeky expression. "You're such a cocky bastard."

"You may be right about that." He leaned over and kissed her. "I never told you the story of Whisper."

"Is there a story?"

"Of course. Everything has a story." He grinned. "My uncle from Northland gave him to Mum two years before she died. They had an immediate connection, but the bastard didn't make it easy for her in the beginning, that's for sure."

"Hey, don't call him that."

"Sorry. Anyway, apparently Whisper was such a randy young colt, he'd jump over fences to get to the fillies. Naturally, they had to geld him. But before they did, he'd already sired two fillies and a colt."

"What? So Whisper has offspring?"

"Not only that, they breed them. If you're keen, we can take a look sometime."

Vanessa wasn't sure how she felt about this. It would be like getting another puppy straight after your first dog dies. "Whisper was my animal soul mate. I don't think I could ever replace him."

"I understand. Still, it's something to think about. You don't have to decide right now. Who knows, you might change your mind in a few years. And you know what else?" She waited for him to continue. "You're the only person who rode Whisper after Mum passed. He wouldn't let anyone else near him."

"Really. That's kind of special. I'd like to visit him tomorrow, and Mum."

"Good idea. We'll visit my Mum as well."

Vanessa threw her arms around his neck. "I love you, so much."

"I love you, too." Liam rolled onto his side, his hand sliding under her t-shirt. "Take this off. I want to feel all of you."

She slipped the t-shirt over her head and lay back, a soft smile on her lips as she presented herself to him—taut skin glowing in the soft light of the moon.

"You are truly breathtaking." He bent down, and flicked his tongue over her closest breast as his hand splayed out over her stomach. His fingers slipped over her skin to find lace and curls and warmth. Liam pulled her closer. One foot hooked around her leg as his hand inched downward.

"How do you do that?" she asked.

"What?" He tugged at her panties. "Lift up."

"Turn me on so easily, with just one kiss, one touch?"

"Is it a problem?"

"No. But ..."

"I'm your fiancé now. Turning you on is part of the job description. Just trust me and let go. I won't let you fall."

62

EPILOGUE

2004

The drive from Clifton Falls to home took just over forty-five minutes. In the first fifteen of those minutes, Vanessa had pulled over twice— once to make a call, and again when she reached Petrie Bay, restless to sooth her feet with the salt of the sea.

She left the car and strolled down the beach, dangling her sandals in her hand as she paddled through the shallows. The day was cold for summer. Grey clouds rumbled across the horizon and it reminded her of the many times, both happy and sad, she'd walked along this shore over the last twenty years. Now, she was here once again, alone, trying to make sense of the turn her life had taken.

She wondered how she would tell the kids. Luka had just turned sixteen and was impressionable, but always fun and full of cheek. And Dannielle? How would she respond to the news? Thirteen and over-flowing with attitude, her reaction would go one of two ways.

Sitting on a damp driftwood log, she'd cried for a bit—not a loud ugly cry, but more a trickle of tears that could be blamed on the bite of the wind if anyone noticed them. But there was no one to notice. The beach was almost deserted, the waves angry and full. She recalled the last day she and Liam had spent time here. It seemed like only weeks ago, that picnic, but when she thought back, it had been almost a year.

Her phone rang in her hand. It would be Liam, but she didn't want to talk to him right at that moment, so ignored the call. He'd insisted she carry a cell phone, when really, she couldn't think of anything worse. His argument was full of the usual 'what if' scenarios. *What if* he wanted to get hold of her? *What if* the kids needed her? *What if …*

Her text alert chimed. She glanced at the screen.

Where are you?

Her hands went to the keypad—an automatic response—and one she would normally make without thinking. *I'm at the supermarket … the hospital … almost home.* But today, she didn't want anyone to know where she was. Because today, she was at a place she'd never imagined being.

It was just after six when she arrived home. She'd stopped at the cemetery for a little while, laying fresh flowers on her mother's grave as she did from time to time. He'd phoned her twice more, sent another text, but when she walked through the kitchen door, no one was around. She loved this house, always had, with its view over the Pacific and a landscape full of native shrubs and trees. It had taken ten months to build, but it had been worth every hour of that time.

They'd stayed in the UK longer than expected, and had returned to New Zealand with two English-born kids and a dream. The equestrian center had been running for over four years, and as Vanessa unpacked the groceries, she wondered how she would manage it now.

"Mum, where have you been?" Luka said as he barged in through the back door. "Dad's over at the stables. He has something to show you."

"Can it wait until after dinner?"

"No. Come now." He looked her up and down. "Are you okay? You look terrible."

"Yes, fine. Just a little tired."

Liam breathed the sigh of relief when he noticed Vanessa and Luka walking toward the stables. Her insistent drive and determination worried him, especially lately. She'd been tired and withdrawn, and they hadn't made love in weeks. Like most couples, they'd been through their ups and downs over the years, but he'd never seen her so preoccupied.

They'd married in an intimate ceremony in the English city of Bath, just one month after finding out Vanessa was pregnant with Luka. They didn't invite guests or tell anyone until after the event, and Liam sometimes wondered if Vanessa ever missed not having a fairy-tale wedding, even though she insisted a white dress and flowers affair wasn't for her. She hated being the center of attention when she was younger, and he respected that.

In all the time they'd been together, he never doubted her love for him, even when that bristle brush came out and gave him a good scrubbing. But now, was she having second thoughts? Friends of theirs had split recently, and Liam couldn't imagine what it would be like to be in that position—to walk into an empty house and spend your evenings alone.

He went to greet her. They'd always kissed each other hello and goodbye, but today she stood back. He reached for her hand. "Hi. Are you okay? You didn't answer my calls."

"Sorry, I was out of range, and then almost home." She looked around the stalls. "Where's Carolina?"

"Come see." Liam guided her to the last stall at the back where a newborn foal was instinctively seeking out his mother's udder under Danni's watchful gaze.

"Isn't he beautiful?" Danni said, smiling at Vanessa.

She stepped into the stall, her hand reaching out to sooth Carolina's mane. "Oh my goodness. It's a he, and he's here already? Is he okay?"

"He's been here for almost two hours," Liam said softly. "His heart rate's good, and he's an inquisitive little thing. I don't think there'll be any problems. What are you going to call him?"

"Night Thunder." She burst into tears. "Look at his coat, it's as black as a moonless night."

Liam reached over and pulled her into his arms as Luka and Danni looked on. "Hey, don't cry. He's as strong as an ox."

"I know, but it's … he's just like Whisper, don't you think?"

Liam and Luka both chuckled. "It's a bit hard to tell yet," Liam said. "But it's great you've finally bred a colt."

"I have. I've bred a colt. A tiny Whisper."

"Yes, well, let's hope his temperament's better."

Later, they strolled back to the house to the sound of Danni's insistent chatter. Apparently, Luka was in love with an older girl from school, and while he protested at his sister spilling his secrets, he didn't deny it. It made Liam smile. Luka was always a cocky little shit, and the thought of him going steady with an older girl didn't surprise him.

After dinner, while the kids readied themselves for bed in their wing of the house, Vanessa ran a bath, shutting the en-suite door behind her. Liam stayed awake, reading until she'd finished her soak. He watched her brush her hair—long, slow strokes—and when she sat on the bed and said they needed to talk, he felt a weight heavy in his chest.

"What's going on?"

"You know how I haven't had a period in ages?" He nodded. They'd discussed it before—something called early menopause, but she hadn't mentioned it lately. "Well … I went to the doctor today." She stopped and took a deep breath.

His heart rate increased as he waited for her to continue. "Are you okay?"

"Depends on the definition. But yes, I'm fine."

He reached for her hand and squeezed gently. "So why have you been so tired and distant? Have I done something to upset you?"

She looked at him and frowned. "I'm twelve weeks pregnant."

"No, you're not. No way!"

"The doctor did the scan this afternoon." She lifted her novel off the nightstand and reached for the photograph underneath. "Here."

Liam studied the black and white ultrasound print in his hands. "Where is it?"

"The two little beans."

"Two?" He shook his head, his eyes wide as he stared at her, then back at the picture. "Twins? We're having twins? I thought you were sick ... or tired of me. I never thought for a moment you'd be pregnant."

"Don't be ridiculous. I never get tired of you, you know that. But there will be trouble soon enough if you don't get the snip, Liam. I'm forty-two and pregnant ... with twins. What are the kids going to say?"

Pulling back the covers in a flourish, Liam jumped out of bed. "Let's go tell them. This is the best news I've had in weeks."

She grabbed him by the arm. "Get back into bed right now. We're not telling the children tonight. I need time to prepare."

"Yeah, I guess you're right. Shall I phone Dad and Molly?"

"What's wrong with you? Just settle down. It's early days yet."

"I'm excited. I've always wanted more kids."

Vanessa turned out the light and slipped into bed. She moved to his side, and he looked at her and smiled. He'd always thought he was a lucky man, and as the years passed, he loved her more and more. They lay snuggled together, the night sky casting a moody light over their room through the open curtains. "Did you know Luka had a girl-friend?" he asked.

"I had my suspicions. My babies are growing up."

"Yep, but don't worry, we've got two more coming next year."

Vanessa looked at him and frowned. "Is that meant to be a joke, Liam O'Leary? Because if it is, it's not funny."

A wide grin lit up his face. "Who would have thought I'd be a father again at forty-eight?" He pulled her closer and kissed her gently. "You feeling okay about it?"

"I went to Petrie Bay today, to have a cry as I strolled along the shore. It's not something I imagined doing at my age, having more children. But I'm not unhappy about it. It's just an emotional time. Now I know why I've been so tired."

He turned to look at her. Her beautiful expressive face never seemed to age, and after all these years, she still fascinated him. He loved the way she cultivated her business persona while nurturing her spiritual side and motherhood as if the three meshed together like a well-oiled cog in her wheel of life. "You're a wonderful mother and I'll be with you every step of the way. So will Luka and Danni."

"You realize they're going to be super embarrassed when they find out, especially Danni."

"They just might surprise you."

"I think I've had enough surprises today to last me a lifetime."

He pulled the comforter around them. "We better get some sleep. I need to be up early to check on Night Thunder."

She shot him a sideways glance, her eyes full of mischief as she scraped her top teeth over her bottom lip. "I'm suddenly not tired, are you?"

He sucked in a breath and laughed. "Not one bit."

The End

Many thanks for taking the time to read *Field of the White Snow*. If you're not ready to leave Clifton Falls and the Rata River Valley just yet, you can read more about Vanessa's friend, William Cook, in *The Watershed,* the companion novel to *Field of the White Snow.*

But first, ask yourself this question. Can love span more than one lifetime?

Set in New Zealand and spanning four decades and three genera-tions of women, *The Watershed* is a tale of love lost and forever searched for. If you like your romance served with a touch of family saga, a hint of the paranormal, a dash of sensuality, and a moody male who will make your heart skip a beat, *The Watershed* won't disappoint.

Buy Now @ Amazon stores worldwide.

GLOSSARY OF MĀORI WORDS

Haka: a traditional war cry, war dance, or challenge performed by a group.
Mana: a person's honor, influence, prestige, or power.
Moko: A tattoo, often on the chin.
Wahine: A woman or wife.

THANK YOU

As you may have guessed, I'm a Kiwi, so I often write about Kiwi characters living in Kiwi locations. And down here in New Zealand, some things are a little back to front and upside down compared to where you may live.

The school year goes from February to December, we have a summer Christmas, not a winter one, autumn starts in April and spring in September. We also drive on the left side of the road, and the legal drinking age is eighteen.

Also, Kiwi authors love reviews, so if you enjoyed *Field of the White Snow,* please consider leaving a short review/star rating on Amazon and/or Goodreads. Your reviews matter, and I appreciate your time.

Cheers, (Kiwi speak for *best, kind regards, sincerely, have a great day, etc.)*

Frances.

ALSO BY FRANCES COWIE

The Watershed

Can love last more than one lifetime?

Set in New Zealand and spanning four decades and three generations of women, *The Watershed* is a tale of love lost and forever searched for.

Buy Now @ Amazon.com

The List Maker

Sometimes steamy, often funny, and with tension that leaps off the page, *The List Maker* is a standalone contemporary romance where the worlds of business and art collide.

Book One in the Imagined Kiss series.

An Artist - A Dreamer - An Imagined Kiss.

Buy Now @ Amazon.com

How About Thursday

"What makes you think I'd be interested?"

"What makes you pretend you're not?"

If you enjoy edgy chemistry between two passionate characters, download *How About Thursday* today!

Book Two in the Imagined Kiss series.

A CEO - A Temp - An Imagined Kiss

Buy Now @ Amazon.com

Lime Tree Hill

He needs a wife. She needs a safe haven.

What could possibly go right?

Sun, sand, and a sexy organic farmer.

Book One in the standalone Reluctant Kiss Series.

Buy Now @ Amazon.com

Reluctant Chemistry

"I wish we could live like there's no tomorrow

and love like there is."

The beach, the breeze, and a hot chopper guy.

Book Two in the standalone Reluctant Kiss Series.

Buy Now @ Amazon.com

ACKNOWLEDGMENTS

I attended a Korean calligraphy demonstration some time ago. On the wall of the library where the event was being held, a poster caught my eye. The characters, black ink on white card, drew me in for a closer look. I asked my sister-in-law to translate. She said, "The words say, *field of the white snow*."

I thought that was such a beautiful phrase and while I never intended to write a companion novel to *The Watershed* at the time, it wasn't long before Vanessa Marie Blinkly, the misunderstood friend of Billy Cook, whispered in my imaginative ear with her story of insight and trials.

Big thanks go to my usual supporters and team of beta readers, Jane, Laura, Kate, Marjorie, Samantha, Louise, Abby Lee, Sharlene, Betty, and Kate G S.

Also, I'm truly grateful to my editors, Timothy Burton for the very helpful developmental edit, the wonderful Liz Dempsey from The Error Eliminator, and once again, Steven Novak for the cover design. Any mistakes in the finished product are mine.

To those of you who buy my books, accept complimentary copies with grace, and connect with me via the net, thank you for taking time out of your busy lives to read my work. If you feel *Field of the White*

Snow is worthy, please consider leaving a short review on your retailer's website. Reviews not only help new readers find my work, but good or bad, your suggestions make me a better writer. If you want to keep in touch, you can do so by liking my Facebook page.

And last but not least, a special *hola* to Manuela, my first South American reader. I hope you like Vanessa's story. Liam traveled to Argentina because of you.

And in the words of Billy Cook from *The Watershed*:

Fantasy keeps us from falling into the depths
of an ordinary life.

Frances.

ABOUT THE AUTHOR

Frances Cowie's journey to writing romantic fiction began after waking one morning with the story of an old pump house, and three characters, Rose, William, and Jessa, floating around in her head. That story, *The Watershed,* was her first novel.

Frances resides with her husband in one of the most beautiful areas in New Zealand and has two adult children. She loves coconut chocolate, cupcakes, and strolling around her large garden. For more information, including sneak peeks of upcoming projects, visit Frances online:

www.francescowie.com